Selena Buttle-Jones, golden hair flying, tried to stop the mob.

"No," she cried out. "She wouldn't. I know her. She wouldn't. Not without reason."

"She robbed him and killed him," somebody in the mob shouted out.

"Why are we standing here talking?" the ugly man named Pike asked.

"Let's go."

The men shouting and cursing, surged up the street. Selena ran behind them clutching at their sleeves, pleading with them, but they shook her off refusing to look at her.

When they neared the top of the hill where King Sutton's two tents were pitched, three men appeared at the crest—Sutton flanked by his two blacks, Joshua and Jed.

"No farther," Sutton shouted.

"We don't want you," Pike called to him. "We want the Mex girl."

"Listen to me," Sutton called. "Let me tell you what happened." His voice was drowned out as the men swarmed up the hill. Sutton and his blacks fought valiantly but were overwhelmed. Selena found herself hurled to the ground. She pushed herself up and ran forward screaming at them to stop. Men scrambled into the first tent, smashing the canvas to the ground and scattering Sutton's provisions. Selena didn't see Esperanza. Had she escaped after all?

With Pike in the lead, the men ran to the second tent. Pike threw aside the flap and suddenly stopped. After a long moment, he turned away in shock . . .

THE
FORTY-
NINERS

John Toombs

A Dell/Bryans Book

Published by
Dell Publishing Co., Inc.
1 Dag Hammarskjold Plaza
New York, New York 10017

Dell ® TM 681510, Dell Publishing Co., Inc.

ISBN: 0-440-02535-4

Printed in the United States of America

First printing—September 1979

The Forty-Niners

BOOK ONE
SAN FRANCISCO, 1848

1

It began, for some, during a poker game on the second floor of Bidwell's Saloon on Montgomory Street.

W.W. Rhynne, his face expressionless, had finished glancing from the two kings in his hand to the stacked pile of coins in the pot on the green baize table. W.W. had played a patient game, betting on his good hands, folding quietly on the bad. Now he'd bluffed for the first time, risking his entire stake, and he'd been called.

"Let's see the color of your cards," McDowell demanded.

Rhynne shrugged. He figured McDowell for three of a kind.

"What's that?" Garrison, on Rhynne's left, looked up, startled.

What it was was a shout from the street below, and it was quite loud.

"It's Sam Brannan," a man at the window reported shrugging. "Appears he's back from Sutter's Fort."

A burly man threw open the saloon door and came running upstairs. His black hair was tangled, his clothes disheveled.

"Gold!" Sam Brannan shouted. "Gold! Gold from the American River!" Waving a whisky bottle above his head he pushed his way back through the small, curious crowd that had followed him up. A few seconds later Rhynne heard his booming voice downstairs again. "Gold! Gold from the American River!"

All the poker players rushed down after Brannan, leaving their drinks unfinished, their cards scattered on the tables.

All, that is, except Rhynne. For perhaps five minutes W.W. sat quietly smoking his cigarillo. Then, unblinking, he scooped the silver coins from the table and dropped them into his money belt. One by one he turned over McDowell's cards. Three tens.

He stood up then, smoothing the short cloak he favored over the money belt, nodding to himself as though in confirmation. All you needed was patience. Patience and a little luck.

Lady Pamela Buttle-Jones, her daughter Selena on the wagon seat beside her, drove down dusty Market Street toward the cluster of canvas-and-wood structures of San Francisco. She wiped her eyes with a handkerchief. Was it worth the effort?

she asked herself. Should we have given up the place in Monterey? Yet the money was almost gone and she was worried about Selena.

"We should have stayed another week in Santa Clara," Selena said, a bit petulantly. "You aren't well enough to travel."

"When I die, I promise you it will not be of the intermittent fever. Did you want to linger at Santa Clara because of my health or was Don Diego the actual reason?"

Her daughter stared down at her hands, saying nothing.

Pamela took a deep breath and gazed around them. "Isn't it beautiful, Selena? Look at the ships in the bay, the blue water, the green hills beyond. They're almost as green as the hills of England. But here the sky's so azure, so enormous."

Selena looked at her mother. "I feel there's something wrong. Something odd—don't you sense it?"

"The people," Pamela said slowly. "Where is everybody? Eleven in the morning and the streets are deserted."

They both turned toward the water. "The bay's so quiet, no lighters coming from the ships," Selena said. "And the ships themselves, there's no one on the decks."

Pamela gasped. "Could it be the cholera? Could we be entering a city of the dead?"

"We'd smell the cholera." Selena's nose crinkled. "Remember the terrible odor when the men died on the overland trail?"

"Well, at least there's one survivor," Pamela said dryly. She pointed to a bewhiskered man sitting on a bench in front of a general store with a brandy bottle in his lap. As they approached in their wagon, the man carefully set the bottle on the ground beside him, grasped a cane, and hobbled into the street. They saw then that he had a wooden right leg.

"Mary, Joseph, and Jesus," he said, staring up at the women. "Have I died and gone to heaven? There could never be two such angels in San Francisco."

Selena blushed, but Pamela only shook her head impatiently. "Where is everyone?" she asked him.

"Gone to the diggings, the diggings on the American River. John Marshall's found gold at Sutter's Mill and now they've all packed up and bolted. There's maybe a score of us left here in town. I'd be up on the river myself but for this." He tapped his pegleg with the end of his cane. "A wound I suffered chasing Santa Anna," he added.

"More likely you got drunk and shot yourself," Pamela told him.

The man squinted up at her. "I knew 'twas too good to be true," he said. " 'Tis hell I'm in after all." He hobbled back toward his bench.

"The Parker House," Pamela called after him. "Where do I find the Parker House?"

The one-legged man waved his hat in the direction of the bay. "On the plaza," he muttered, barely loud enough for them to hear.

He sat watching them until they turned onto Montgomery Street and disappeared from view. He shook his head. What were two such lovely colleens doing in this hell-hole? They wouldn't last a month, if that long. Yet the older one, she was sharp as a Bowie knife. How could she have known how he'd lost his leg?

Danny Kennedy rapped once on the door, waited, knocked twice, waited, knocked three times. The bolt slid back and the door of the small house in St. Louis opened a crack.

"Ah, Danny." His father, hidden in the shadows, opened the door just wide enough to let the younger man slip into the room. The shades were drawn; a single gas jet glowed yellow on the wall.

"Did you sign us on the wagon train?" Michael Kennedy asked.

"I did."

"And signed the names we agreed to?"

"That I did. Michael O'Lee and Daniel O'Lee."

"Good. In another week we'll be far from this city of tribulation." Michael poured an inch of whiskey into a drinking glass. "Danny?"

The boy shook his head.

" 'Tis the inspiration and the curse of the Irish," his father said, wiping his lips with the back of his sleeve. "Danny, read the letter again."

Danny went to the bed where he lifted the mattress and brought out three creased and tattered sheets of paper. He smoothed the letter on the table. "Shall I read from the beginning?"

"No, just the one part."

Danny nodded and began reading: "Men returning here from the mines report persons have collected as much as a pound of gold in a single day valued at over two hundred dollars. The gold is so plentiful it lies mingled with the sand in the beds of the rivers. During bright days it glitters so as almost to dazzle and blind the eyes."

Michael Kennedy, now Michael O'Lee, nodded to his son. "I can almost see it, Danny," he said, "a shining mountain of gold waiting for us. Waiting for us at the end of the rainbow in California."

Kingman Sutton spread the Augusta *Chronicle and Gazette* on the table beside the lamp. "Betsy," he said, "let me read you the correspondence from Washington."

Betsy Sutton turned from him with tears in her eyes.

"Here," King said, ignoring her tears for the common occurrence they were. "Listen to President Polk's report to the Congress:

"It was known that mines of the precious metals existed to a considerable extent in California at the time of its acquisition. Recent discoveries render it probable that these mines are more extensive and valuable than was anticipated. The accounts of the abundance of gold in that territory are of such an extraordinary character as would scarcely command belief were it not corroborated by the authentic reports of officers in the public service, who have visited the mineral district, and derived the facts which they detail from personal observation."

Betsy folded her hands on the table, laid her forehead on them, and sobbed.

King Sutton walked around the table to stand behind her, placing one hand on her shoulder. "Is there anything you want?" he asked. "Is there anything I can do?"

When she shook her head, King bent and kissed her auburn hair, then smoothed it with his fingers. When he felt the tug of her hair catching on the setting of his opal ring he carefully untwisted the strands before taking his hand away. Betsy didn't seem to notice.

For a long while he stared down at his wife, then at the wavering light of the lamp. The reflection of the flame in his eyes was the color of gold.

2

Selena twisted and turned on the narrow bed. She ran her hands over her nightgown along her thighs, upward over her hips to her waist, up to the swell of her breasts, then hugged herself.

What if the hands on her body were not her own but Don Diego's?

Selena shivered pleasurably, wide awake now. It was about midnight. She stared at the only light in the room, the dim rectangle of the room's single window. Outside a man shouted drunkenly on the street, his wild howl reminding her of the coyotes on the trail.

There were so many men here in San Francisco, so many kinds—dull and exciting, short and tall, fair and dark, coarse and genteel, and in every combination thereof. During the night, Selena had dreamed she sat on a throne, berobed and

17

crowned like young Queen Victoria, while men came to her, kneeling one by one at her feet, some requesting boons and largesse, others to be knighted.

Don Diego had been one of the men. In her dream, Selena had stood, raising a sword in both hands, and laid the blade on his shoulder. When he looked up at her with his piercing brown eyes, her hand on the sword trembled.

One man refused to kneel in her dream. He stood apart, in its shadows, watching her, and, though she saw his features only darkly, she knew he was smiling scornfully at her. Then, as more men came to pay her homage she became impatient, hastening the ceremony until at last there was no one left except the man watching from the shadows. Yet when she handed her sword to a courtier and approached the man, he was gone, leaving only the echo of his laugh and the impression of mocking blue eyes behind.

Selena frowned, striving to shut out the noises from the street. When they'd arrived in San Francisco the town had been almost deserted, the men at the gold fields. Day by day they had trickled back—some from the American River, others arriving from the south, from the capital at Monterey and from the City of the Angels. Now the town was livelier than ever. She wished the Parker House didn't have gambling rooms on the first floor. There was no quiet until long after midnight.

At last Selena slept again, a troubled sleep, for how long she did not know. She came awake with a start—someone was in the room. Her forehead was damp, the air close and oppressive. All around her the hotel slept. Her eyes searched the darkness. She saw nothing. Even the window was now dark.

Selena sat up, her legs against her chest, her hands gripping the nightgown below her knees. When a board creaked, her stomach tightened and a scream rose in her throat. But she held back the cry. Foolishness, her mother would tell her. You were the one who insisted on a room of your own, she would say.

A horse whinnied outside; a man shouted in the distance. Vaguely Selena remembered hearing, when she'd awakened this second time, the clip-clop of horses from the street. She relaxed. She *was* being foolish. What was the matter with her lately? So restless, so quick to lash out at others, particularly at her mother. Now she felt an undefined longing; tears came to her eyes.

A hand suddenly closed over her mouth, stifling her gasp.

A hand grasped her shoulder.

"Señorita Selena." She knew that voice. "It is Diego," he said even before she could think the name. "I have come for you."

A light flared. Selena, wide-eyed, saw Diego's dark face close to hers. Behind him were two other men. All three were dressed in black. A rolled kerchief was thrust between her lips, parting them, and she felt it being knotted at the back of her head. Then Diego was lifting her, carrying her to the door.

"Do not have fear," he whispered. "I will not harm you." He cradled her in his arms with one hand gripping her legs, the touch of his fingers seeming to sear the thin cloth of the nightgown.

One of the men brought her scarlet cloak from the wardrobe and Diego let her stand, wrapping the cape around her before taking her in his arms again.

"My mother," she tried desperately to say. But her words were muffled by the cloth in her mouth so that not even she could hear them.

"Vamos," Diego said to the others.

One of the men went ahead, signaling to them with a wave of his hand when he found the hallway deserted. Diego carried her down the stairs with the third man following. In the empty lobby a single oil-lit chandelier glowed overhead. The gambling rooms were dark and quiet. The Seth Thomas ticked loudly. Four-thirty, it was; Selena saw that now.

The three men crossed the lobby with their shadows rising and falling demon-like on the walls. In the street three horses waited quietly at the hitching rail, the light from the hotel glinting from their silver trappings.

Diego lifted Selena so that she sat side-saddle, then swung up behind her. With one arm circling her waist and the other on the reins, he turned to his companions. "Ay, amigos," he whispered. Urging their horses forward they crossed the square at a walk, starting a gallop only when on the hill leading from town. Then they sped up a trail silvered by a full moon haloed by fog.

At the top of the first rise Diego reined in and Selena found herself gazing back at the scattered lights of San Francisco. She did not know what to think or what to feel about her abduction; her mind was a jumble. A blast roared in her ear. She cringed against Diego. When she smelled the acrid odor of gunpowder she realized one of the men had fired his pistol in the air. Diego laughed, then turned his horse to the south.

As they rode, Selena became increasingly aware of Diego's body pressed to hers, his chest hard on her back, his leg hard on her buttock. He had wanted her, she thought, suddenly thrilled. Like a knight errant of old, he had carried her off, risking the wrath of the world, defying all for love.

As the motion of the horse lulled her, she imagined them coming to a sylvan meadow, the other two vaqueros riding on, leaving her alone with Diego. The two of them would stand on a rocky crag watching the sun rise over the Sierras, his arm about her waist, his lips teasing her hair as he confessed his love. She would enter the circle of his arms, her body straining to his, her lips yielding.

Diego. He was a man. He was confident. Not like those she'd known on the wagon-trail west, awkward, fumbling. . . .

She felt Diego's hand at the nape of her neck seeking the knot of the kerchief. The cloth loosened and fell from her mouth; she rubbed her sore lips.

"My mother," she rued. 'My mother will be furious."

Yet it was mock rue only. See now. Her mother, who always had men hovering around her, Barry Fitzpatrick on the trail and now that stuffy Robert Gowdy, wasn't the only one attractive woman men found desirable.

Diego laughed. "You are such a child. Do not fear. I will tell your mother."

Selena stiffened. A child! He thought of her as

a child! Wasn't she nineteen? When the time came she would show him she was a woman! When they reached—where?

"Where are we going?" she asked.

"To Rancho de la Torre. There, in two days time, we will be married."

"Married?"

"Of a certainty. You will become Señora Selena de la Torre."

Nonplused, she could think of nothing to say.

"We will have *una fiesta grande*," Diego was saying. He spoke grandly, emphasizing his Spanish words lovingly. "We will mount the best of the horses, each decorated with silver, your horse covered with a cloth sewn with silks of gold and with pieces of iron and copper so the horse makes a sound like many bells. The man who will be the godfather of our first child will ride to the chapel with you. The godmother rides with me. After the ceremony we, you and I, return together, as we ride now. At the rancho the vaqueros seize me to remove my spurs. I must redeem them with the gift of a bottle of aguardiente.

"We enter the casa; we kneel before my father to ask his blessing. When he gives it I raise my hand and the guitars play and the fandango begins."

"The fandango?"

"The dance. We dance and we drink and we sleep and we dance and we drink and we sleep again. We have contests, bull and bear baiting, drawing the cock. For two days, perhaps for three days, who can say? My Selena, you have never seen the like of such a fiesta."

Picturing herself whirled from man to man,

hearing their admiring shouts, seeing the eyes of the señoritas envying her as Diego claimed her and bore her off, Selena rested her head against his chest and blissfully slept.

The sun was rising red over the hills when Diego turned from the main trail. They followed a rutted road through woods and fields, coming at last to a sprawl of adobe buildings. Selena saw horses in a corral behind the ranch and cattle grazing in a field beyond the corral.

"We are here. Rancho de la Torre," Diego said with pride in his voice.

They dismounted amid barking dogs and cackling chickens. Several dark-eyed young girls came up solemnly to greet them. While one of the men unsaddled the horses, Diego led Selena past these señoritas, who were, she gathered, his sisters. He told her their names so rapidly she could remember only three, Maria and Esperanza and Teresa. When she caught Esperanza's eye the girl broke into quickly stifled giggles.

Diego bowed Selena through the door to a small bedroom. "I know you must be wearied," he said, nodding to the one large bed. "This is the room of my sister Esperanza." He smiled. "She will be your chaperone until the wedding tomorrow."

He might at least have asked her! When she began to protest, he took her in his arms.

"Ah, Selena," he said. He repeated her name, "Selena, Selena, Selena," punctuating each utterance of it with a kiss, first on her closed eyes, then the tip of her nose, finally her mouth.

She returned his kiss as his hands traveled from her back to the curve of her hips and up beneath the cloak to her breasts, the touch of his fingers cold through her nightgown. He held her breasts, cradling and caressing them until she moaned, clinging to him, his hands warming, his body hard against hers. Now, she thought. Now he will . . .

Diego stepped away, leaving her arms still extended toward him. Disappointed, still with a feeling of feverish longing, she dropped them to her sides. She had to take a deep breath to steady herself.

"We will go to the padre tomorrow morning," Diego said earnestly. "You're not of the Roman faith, are you?"

"We belong to the Church of England," Selena replied.

"Father Hidalgo will explain what you must do. Do not worry. The Mexican priests are more sympathetic to converts than the Spanish ones were."

He kissed her once more, tenderly on the forehead, then left. "Diego," she called after him, not wanting him to leave, wanting his arms about her, his lips on hers. But when she threw open the door he was gone.

She lay on the bed with the cloak over her, expecting to toss for hours. She fell asleep at once, however, not waking until early in the afternoon.

The rest of Selena's day passed in a blur of initial impressions of the rancho. She tried on dresses with the sisters helping, heard them laughing as they pinned here and tucked there. She had supper with women who ignored her, whispering among themselves as they ate—though she liked the food itself, which was spiced and tasty.

She met Diego's father, was awed by this tall, solemn-faced man who spoke so little English.

She met the rest of Diego's sisters—he had seven in all—and his one brother, a ten-year-old who looked very much like him. She learned from the boy that their mother had died of influenza when he was seven. Diego had made no mention of his mother during their few passionate meetings in Santa Clara a month before.

When at last she was alone in the bedroom she shared with Esperanza, a panic swept over Selena. What am I doing here? she asked herself. Am I actually going to marry this man tomorrow, this man I hardly know? Even though I'm not a frequent churchgoer, am I ready to give up my faith for him? Become a Roman Catholic? Will I have to live out my life here on this isolated ranch, seeing little of California and nothing of the rest of the world? If only, she thought desperately, I had someone to talk to! If only her mother were with her.

She turned, with that feeling of desperation, to Esperanza, who lay shyly on her own bed with the blankets pulled to her neck. She was so young, no more than fifteen, but she did at least speak English well. Perhaps talking to Diego's sister would help assuage her fears. And yet, Selena hardly knew where to begin.

"Esperanza," she tried, "your brother mentioned contests and dances at the wedding fiesta. The dancing I understood, I love to dance and sing, but the games are new to me. Bull and bear baiting, drawing the cock. What are they?"

"The men go to the woods," Esperanza said, "where they capture a bear and tie him to a tree. When he tires they cart him to the rancho and tie his leg with a long rope to the leg of the bull. Then the men goad them until they fight. Diego says you should always wager on the bear."

"And drawing the cock?"

"Oh, it's very exciting, Selena! Diego is always the best. The vaqueros bury a live cock in the ground up to its neck. Then one at a time they spur their horses toward it. When they near it they hold to their horse's mane with one hand and hang almost to the ground to grasp its head. If the vaquero can draw the cock from the ground that way, he wins a prize. And he keeps the cock as well."

Shuddering, Selena massaged her throat with her fingers. What strange customs! Could she ever become used to them? Her hands went from her throat to fleetingly touch her breasts. She remembered how she felt when Diego caressed them. What did strange customs matter? The ways of the English might seem strange to him.

"We are most pleased to have you for our new sister," Esperanza said shyly. "You are *muy bonita,* very pretty." She sat up in bed, her dark eyes animated now. "And now we will not have to leave the rancho and make our home in the great valley beyond Monterey."

Selena said curiously, "You were going to move to Monterey?"

"*Si,* to the house of our uncle, Señor Garner. He was an Americano who married the sister of our father."

"I've lived in Monterey. I would think you'd rather stay here. This land is so beautiful."

"We would stay if we could but we have many

leagues of land and many cattle and not enough men to do the work. We are a family of daughters, not sons. Diego, you see, is busy with his journeys to places like Monterey and San Francisco to sell hides and tallow to the ships. So he has no time to do the work that must be done here. I should not say this to you but it is the truth."

"I don't understand, Esperanza," Selena said uncertainly. "How will my marrying Diego change your plans to move to Monterey?"

"Ah, we know of your lands across the sea in England and of your wealth there. Your mother spoke of these things to Diego while she lay ill at the Mission of Santa Clara."

What could her mother have said? Selena wondered. She loved to reminisce about their onetime estate in England, but how was it that she chose Diego to tell her stories to? And did Diego actually think they still owned the estate? Believe they were still wealthy? Selena smiled to herself. Diego had a surprise in store! It served him right too— the way he'd assumed she would marry him without even asking!

"In years gone by," Esperanza went on, "the Indians worked the land. They have become untrustworthy, my father says, for they are always running away to the mountains of the Tulares."

"Perhaps he doesn't pay them enough," Selena suggested.

"Pay? I do not know pay."

"The money your father gives the Indians in return for their work."

"Oh, he doesn't give them money. If they have money they buy wine and drink and cannot work for many days. My father gives them food and a place to sleep and the padres teach them the ways of Christians. Yet they are ungrateful, most of them. In the spring when the rains stop they run away to the mountains, many times stealing our horses to eat on the way. If they can, they steal our cattle as well. I don't understand the ways of the Indians, I only know what they look like. Some of the young men are beautiful to the eye, so strong and lean and dark. The women are ugly. Don't you think so?"

Selena nodded. She too had found many of the Indians she'd seen attractive. Not the Indians of the towns—they were slack with large bellies and were often drunk. But on the plains and in the mountains the braves had been lithe and sinewy.

"When the Indians run away," Esperanza continued, "the vaqueros must ride to the great valley to the east and into the mountains beyond to bring them back. Or to bring others back in their stead. And when the vaqueros are gone the cattle roam wild because there are neither Indians nor vaqueros to tend them. Many times the women must do the work of the men as well as their own."

"And what is woman's work?"

"All that cannot be done from astride a horse," Esperanza said, shrugging with resignation. "Of course, when one is with child, the women do not work as hard."

Selena pondered this information. "You have such a large family. I have no brothers or sisters. I've always wondered if I'd like to have some."

"My mother bore nine girls and three boys. Seven of the girls lived and two of the boys. My mother, may her soul be with God, died two months after giving birth to Juanita, who was born dead."

"Twelve children. So many."

Esperanza raised her hands in another shrug. "Our women are strong and able to have many babies. Señora Estella Castro of Monterey bore twenty-six children, of whom twenty lived. Señora Maria de la Guerra bore twenty-four children. My uncle, Señor Garner of Monterey, who is a scholar, told Diego that women of California have a baby every fifteen months for twenty and more years. Diego said this is as it should be. But I think that it is not good to have so many babies. Often the babies of a woman's old age are weak and grow sick and die. I only wish to have twelve children, like my mother, nine girls and three boys."

Twelve children! Did Diego intend her to bear him twelve children? What *did* Diego expect? Involuntarily, Selena looked down at her slim body. She shuddered. No! She wanted no babies.

Selena took a deep breath. After a moment she blew out the lamp. "May all your wishes come true," she said.

Esperanza yawned. "Each night I pray to God they will," she said.

Selena lay in bed a long time listening to Esperanza's steady breathing. Then when the noises of the rancho had quieted and the night was still, she went to the window and looked out at the tendrils of fog reaching toward the ranch buildings from the fields and woods. Her body still tingled at the thought of Diego's kisses. She had thought no further than the pleasure. If they married, children would inevitably follow.

Suddenly she felt as if she were suffocating, as though the fog had encircled her with its cold dampness.

Quickly changing into the dress she had been given earlier in the day, she slipped from the door and made her way on bare feet to the stables. She took a bridle and saddle and carried them to the corral. There she saddled a horse and quietly led him away on foot until she'd walked through patches of fog, to a point at least a mile from the rancho. She hiked up her skirt, mounted and rode at a gallop toward the trail to San Francisco.

3

Selena tapped on the door. She waited, then tapped again. She heard muffled sounds from inside.

"Who is it?" Lady Pamela called.

"Selena."

The bolt slid back and the door opened. Her mother was in her blue dressing gown, holding a candle. With a cry of relief Selena threw herself into her arms, sobbing and laughing simultaneously.

"Selena, Selena, are you all right? Your hands are so cold."

Selena nodded. "I'm all right, mother," she said.

Pamela hugged her. She put the candle on the table and, after rebolting the door, opened the wardrobe. "Put this on," she said, coming back with one of her pink flannel nightgowns, "you're going to sleep here with me."

When Selena stepped from her dress, Pamela picked it up. "This skirt is so muddy," she said.

"I fell from the horse. I was riding along a trail to the south of here when the fog began pouring over the hills like a great wave. I ran into a branch of a tree and fell." She raised her nightgown to show her mother the bruise on her thigh.

"I'll get some arnica liniment."

Selena sat on the edge of the bed watching her mother rummage in the trunk. "Didn't Diego tell you? He said he would."

"Here, I'll rub this on." When her mother rubbed the lotion in with her palm, Selena winced. "Yes, he sent someone here with a letter. He said it was what you wanted, Selena. He said he'd come for me tomorrow—that's today now—and bring me to the wedding fiesta. The way you behaved with him in Santa Clara convinced me that it was what you wanted, Selena. Now tell me what happened."

Something in her mother's tone made Selena suspect she wasn't telling her the full truth. Pamela, though, kept her head bowed and Selena couldn't see into her eyes.

"Oh, mother," Selena said. "I didn't know what I wanted. I still don't know what I want. I thought I loved Diego. I felt so good when he kissed me." She saw Pamela stiffen and went on hurriedly. "When he kissed me, I did want to marry him, to be with him always, but do you know what he asked me to do?"

"Are you certain you want to tell me?"

"Oh yes. He said I had to become a Papist. I might have too, I think, for him. But do you know what else he wanted?"

"Selena, I haven't the slightest idea."

"He expected me to watch while they buried cocks in the ground and rode past and pulled their their heads off. Can you imagine? Ugh! Yet Diego is a wonderful horseman, the best I've ever seen, better than any of the men on the trail. Better even than Barry Fitzpatrick."

"Californios are known for their riding," Pamela said, trying to hide a smile over her daughter's expressed concern. "Now lie down, Selena, and let me cover you over."

"Leave the light on, mother."

Sliding into bed, Pamela put her arm around her. Selena, feeling warm and protected, like a child again, snuggled close.

"He called me a child," Selena said, "and I was so angry." She pulled up her legs and clasped her knees in her hands. "But he was right," she said brooding. "I must still be a child. When you're a woman you know what you want. I don't know what I want. I think I do and then I change my mind."

"Oh, Selena, even women don't always know what they want. Many go their entire lives without knowing."

Selena frowned, not completely believing her. "Imagine," she said, "he wanted me to have twelve children."

"Twelve!" Her mother stroked Selena's hair.

" 'A proper wife of a Spanish ranchero has twelve children, six boys and six girls.' When I heard that, I knew I couldn't marry Diego no matter how he made me feel. So I took one of his horses and rode home."

"You still have his horse?"

"I woke the boy at the livery stable and left the horse there."

"I'll see he's returned tomorrow."

"Diego will come for me, I know he will. He'll be simply furious when he finds me gone."

"He won't come here, Selena. His pride won't let him."

"I didn't care so much about changing my religion or seeing the bear fight the bull or watching him pull the heads off the cocks. I guess I wasn't telling the truth about that. I didn't care if he had lost all his money, either. It was the idea of those twelve babies. Having them. I couldn't, I just couldn't."

Pamela frowned. "Diego lost his money? I assumed the de la Torres were wealthy."

"They were once but Diego's sister Esperanza told me they had to sell the ranch and move to Monterey to live with their uncle. She said if Diego married me, though, they wouldn't have to leave because we had money and a great estate in England. Now what could have led them to believe that?"

"I'm sure I don't know," Pamela said absently. "If you think for one minute *I* misled him, you're mistaken." She settled back with her arm nestling Selena's head. "Now go to sleep," she said. "Everything will be all right in the morning."

* * *

Pamela rose early, dressing quietly so as not to rouse the sleeping Selena. Nevertheless she chose her costume with care. Black, of course. The traditional year of mourning for Lord Lester Buttle-Jones was up long ago but considering what Pamela had to do it was well to emphasize the fact she was a widow. Even if Robert Gowdy *had* been on the wagon train he couldn't actually know how she'd really felt about Lester's death in the avalanche.

The French silk, then, with its form-fitting bodice and full skirt thrust out by a small crinoline. Before Pamela drew the black veil over her face she hesitated. Perhaps just one spoonful of medicine? She reached into her bag, then shook her head. It would make her feel better, of course, but she needed every ounce of wit she possessed and the medicine had the tendency to relax her so there was the danger she might be caught off guard.

Afterwards, she promised herself. I'll wait until after my interview with Mr. Gowdy. Now that it was clear Diego de la Torre was penniless, she must set her other plan in motion.

"Never forget a back-up load," her father had reiterated when teaching her to shoot in those long-ago days in the English countryside. "A careful marksman remembers the need for a second shot." The Americans put it somewhat differently, borrowing a phrase from the red Indians—a second string for one's bow. But the idea was the same. Perhaps even Robin Hood had it.

Pamela shook her head. Her wits were wandering. She had no time to waste on vagaries.

Later that morning, she was shooting her arrow in Robert Gowdy's office.

"Impossible, Lady Pamela!" Gowdy leaned across his desk toward her. "What you suggest is absolute madness."

Pamela smiled. "Not 'lady.' Pamela will do. Do you remember Barry Fitzpatrick pointing out that the United States constitution forbids the use of titles? I thought him quite eloquent."

Gowdy scowled. "The constitution applies only to Americans. We're English, you and I. Or do you intend to become a citizen?"

"Certainly not. England's my home and always will be. When I have enough money to return, I shall. But I'll never go home with . . . how do the Americans say it?"

"With one's tail between one's legs, I suppose you mean."

"Most inelegant, yet highly accurate. I promise you I shan't go back to England with—well, in that condition."

"Lady Pamela, you're employing diversionary tactics again. Believe me, I'm fully aware of our common bond of country. But to give you five thousand dollars . . ."

"Not give. I asked you to advance me five thousand dollars, using my diamond earrings as collateral."

"And with that money," Gowdy went on, "you propose to travel to Sutter's Fort and on to the gold camps where you intend to establish a commercial enterprise of some sort."

"Not 'of some sort.' I'll sell flour, salt, pork, clothing, pistols, pickaxes, shovels, pans, and whatever else the miners need. Sam Brannan has more trade than he can take care of at Sutter's; I'll do even better at one of the mining sites. At Coloma or Ophir or Hangtown."

"There's a considerable difference between you and Sam Brannan."

"I admit he's had vastly more mercantile experience in California. *I* have determination."

"The difference I referred to is more fundamental. He's a man and you're a woman. And a lady, besides."

"I'm sure the miners would rather deal with a woman than a man."

Gowdy took a cigar from a humidor on his desk. "With your permission?"

Pamela nodded.

"To be blunt," he said, "they would rather deal with women, but not in the manner you suggest. And I'm afraid they have no conception of what a lady is. You don't realize what kind of men these are. They're the remnants of the regiment Stevenson recruited from the scum of New York City to fight the Mexicans. They're sharpers, gamblers, drunks, adventurers of every variety, Chinamen, Kanakas, Mexicans, Sydney Ducks."

"Sydney Ducks? And what are they?"

"Convicts shipped to Australia by our countrymen. California is a golden magnet drawing every unattached ne'er-do-well in the world."

"You're exaggerating, Mr. Gowdy."

He shook hs head. "Besides being in a place with twenty men for every woman, you'll have the elements to contend with. The snow in the mountains, the winter rains."

"These Sierra Nevadas can't compare to the desert we crossed," Pamela said. She raised the veil from her face and pinned it to her hat with a jet pin. "My face became so burned I looked like a red Indian. Look at me. Even now I've not regained a decent paleness."

"Lady Pamela, you're the loveliest woman I've ever seen. And the most obstinate."

"If you're unable to advance me the money, I shall understand," Pamela said, glancing about the office. "I assumed you had the means, but perhaps this position as ship's agent is not . . ." She paused.

"Damn it all, I have the money," Gowdy growled. "How you do obscure a point! Haven't you heard the tales of Mexican women captured by the Indians?"

"Are you referring to the Digger Indians?" She raised her eyebrows. "I wasn't aware their men were warriors."

"There are thousands of Indians in these mountains." He jabbed his cigar at her, sending unreadable smoke signals curling toward the ceiling. "And you can't trust one of them. They may prove to be even more dangerous than the Sioux or the Arapaho. On the way west we merely crossed Indian lands. Here in the California Territory they're being forced from their very homes. Even a savage fights for what he believes is his."

"Mr. Gowdy, you know better than to try to frighten me with stories of marauding Indians."

"I'm not attempting to frighten you, Lady Pamela. Only to warn you. To stop you from making a grievous mistake." He placed his cigar on a tray and leaned forward to put his hand over hers. "Because I have deep feeling for you, Lady Pamela. I realize you think of me as a tradesman, but say the word and I'll be your devoted servant for the rest of my life."

Pamela eased her hand from beneath his. "You forget I'm still in mourning," she said.

"For a scoundrel who didn't deserve you," Gowdy muttered. "And, damn it, it's been a time now."

"I'd rather we didn't discuss Lord Lester."

Gowdy inclined his head. "Of course. Not the thing to speak ill of the dead, true though it may be. But I am concerned about your future. If you were my wife, you'd have no need to ask for money. I have enough and more. And none of it tainted. I'll build you a house on one of the hills above Portsmouth Square. I'll buy you fine clothes and an elegant rig. Though there's no society as such in San Francisco, there will be." He paused, then added with quiet emphasis, "I could provide Selena with a proper upbringing."

"Do you mean I haven't?" Her words lashed out at him as she jumped to her feet.

"No, no, no," Gowdy protested, also rising. "You've moved mountains as it is. Certainly Lord Lester was no decent father for a young girl. I cast no blame; the poor child has suffered enough. But how can you expect to look after Selena and work to provide for her as well—you, a woman alone here?"

Pamela sighed. "You're right, of course. This isn't the best place for Selena. She doesn't belong in this raw, raucous town on the edge of nowhere. In London she would have been properly launched by now, even well married."

Pamela walked to the window and looked out at the forest of masts in the bay. From the street below came the jingle of bells on a mule team and the shouted Spanish curses of the muleteer.

"Someday," she said, "we'll board one of those ships and we'll sail for home, for England. Selena will once again ride like a lady, not like a barbarian. Selena will be courted as befits her heritage, not leered at by ruffians lolling in front of saloons and gambling halls."

She turned to face him and Gowdy shifted uneasily when he saw the fire in her eyes. "As God is my witness," she said, "I'll go back to England. Not as a pauper, as a lady."

He waited a long moment before answering. "The route to England doesn't go by way of Hangtown, Lady Pamela. Not for you. If you must go into commerce, stay here in San Francisco. Build your store on the land you already own near the Square."

"I never would have been able to buy that land without your help."

He waved her gratitude aside. "One day," he said, "this will be the greatest metropolis on the eastern shore of the Pacific."

"I don't have the time to wait."

"Not for five years? Ten or fifteen at the most?"

"I'm thirty-eight. When I lay ill with the fever at the mission at Santa Clara, I felt my mortality. Five more years?" She tightened her grip on her bag.

"Sit down, Lady Pamela. Please sit down."

"No, I choose to stand. Mr. Gowdy, I want you to consider me as you would any other petitioner. Now then. Will you advance me the five thousand dollars or not? Needless to say, the diamonds are worth far more."

"To hell with your diamonds. I may work for my living but I'm not a pawnbroker! I can't let you have the money. Your blood would be on my hands. God knows, Lady Pamela, I'd give you money for almost anything else. *Give* it to you."

"Tell me, then, who will lend me the money?"

"No one will. Merchants like Brannan might have the cash but they'd be fools to finance a competitor. Miners who've made their stake? No, the ones who haven't lost their gold dust to drink or gamblers are already bound for the States."

"What of the gamblers themselves?"

He scowled. "Men like W. W. Rhynne? You'd do better to try to shake hands with a grizzly than deal with his kind."

"You paint a bleak picture."

"I intend to. How else can I show you the truth? What you propose is a dangerous folly."

"Thank you." Pamela nodded at the papers on his desk. "I'm sure you have more urgent matters of business than mine. No, don't bother—I'll see myself out."

She reached the door before he could get there. As she started to close it after her, Pamela turned and smiled at him. "I really do understand, Robert," she said softly.

When she had gone, Robert Gowdy reseated himself, savoring the lingering scent of lilacs. After a time he relit his cigar. For him marriage to Pamela would in all probability be a disaster. She was as stubborn as only an English aristocrat could be. His people had been in trade for generations—not a title among them. And yet, if she would only smile at him once each day as she had just smiled at him, he'd run the risk twenty times over.

Avoiding the glances of passing men, Pamela carefully skirted mud puddles and made her way back to the Parker House. In the hotel, she found the manager perched on a high stool behind the front desk.

"Mr. Hotchkiss," she said, "could you tell me where I might locate a Mr. Rhynne?"

"W.W. Rhynne?" The manager's voice rose in surprise.

"I believe he's a gambler."

"Gambling is *one* of his ventures."

From the man's expression Pamela concluded the other ventures were even less respectable.

Hotchkiss glanced at the Seth Thomas on the wall. "This time of day you're most likely to find him at Bidwell's. He left here early this morning."

"You mean he lives at the Parker House?"

"Yes, ma'am, he's our guest when he's in town. He rents a room from us permanent like. He checked in last night."

Feeling suddenly lightheaded, Pamela grasped the edge of the desk to steady herself. She closed her eyes.

"Are you all right?" Hotchkiss asked.

Pamela took several deep breaths. "Yes, thank you. I'm merely tired." She walked slowly toward the stairs.

"About Mr. Rhynne," Hotchkiss began.

"Later," Pamela said, her lightheadedness increasing.

By holding the railing, she barely managed to climb the stairs. Her vision was blurring when she reached her room; she thought she would faint. Quickly, she unlocked the door and went inside to her dressing table. Through the thin wall she heard Selena singing to herself in the next room.

Opening a drawer, Pamela took out a bottle of amber liquid and poured a teaspoonful. She needed this medicine. When she swallowed it, a feeling of color came back to her cheeks. Since being ill with the fever she found that her strength ebbed rapidly and her natural optimism could turn to anxiety and depression without warning. At least Robert Gowdy hadn't noticed her malaise; at least neither he nor anyone else knew how desperately she relied on the bit of laudanum she took for it.

Gowdy was so different from Lord Lester, Feeling stronger, Pamela stared straight ahead and pictured her husband, recalling the early years, the good years before he was seized with his dream of being a king. The mad dream that destroyed him and almost killed Selena as well. She hadn't loved Lester for many years. Indeed, toward the end she had despised him. And yet she would never love another man as she had loved him at sixteen. The rapture of being young and in love could never be repeated. Not even Barry Fitzpatrick, the young guide who was her sometime lover on the wagon train west, had quite managed to do that for her.

And Robert Gowdy thought she might one day marry him. How absurd! She liked him; she knew she could trust him. As she had never trusted Lester. But she would never marry Robert. Indeed, she doubted if she cared to marry any man. Even for Selena's sake.

She closed her eyes and listened to Selena's voice:

> *"Oh, Susanna! Don't you cry for me*
> *I'm bound for California with my washbowl*
> *on my knee."*

Selena, her cross and her hope.

Her cross because Selena never thought beyond the moment. Despite her own hard experiences on the trail, Selena just hadn't grown up; she behaved as though she was younger than her nineteen years. By nineteen most girls were married. As Pamela had been. Actually by then she'd given birth to Selena. But her daughter never seemed to care about her tomorrows, never planned for the future any more than she seemed to remember the past. So Pamela had to do it for her.

Selena was her hope because, despite the fiasco with Don Diego, she still could marry well. Even in this desolate land. Because the girl was so beautiful no man could resist her. Golden hair, honeyed complexion, a lilting laugh, a perfectly proportioned figure. Her beauty was not only in her mother's eyes: everyone acknowledged it.

She was Pamela's cross, her hope and, Pamela told herself firmly, her joy as well. At least she was a joy when she wasn't acting the role of a young rebel. Directness, Pamela had discovered before, seldom succeeded with Selena, and had more than once been disastrous. She had changed somewhat for the better since her father's death but what Pamela liked to think of as woman-to-woman talk still seemed to bring forth perverse reactions from her. Thank God the girl had had the luck to find out about Diego before it was too late. For, in spite of all that had happened, Selena was surely lucky in escaping his clutches.

A movement caught Pamela's eye. Looking up into the mirror she saw a man watching her from her doorway. She spun around and stood up.

"Who are you?" she demanded.

He smiled. At least she thought that quirk of his lips must be a smile. About her own age, he was tall with black hair and a black moustache. He wore a short tan cloak with a vest of darker brown.

"W.W. Rhynne," he said, his eyes challenging hers. "At your service."

Rhynne? Of course, the gambler.

"They told me downstairs," he said, "that you were asking after me."

His eyes held hers and, unexpectedly, she found herself glancing away. She clenched her teeth to keep the color from rising to her face.

"A gentleman," she said, "doesn't enter a lady's room without her permission. Even in San Francisco."

W.W. Rhynne smiled, showing even and quite attractive glistening white teeth. "Some of our leading citizens would scoff if they heard me described as a gentleman. As for your being a lady, I accept your evaluation pending evidence to the contrary."

Pamela laughed, crossing her arms over her breasts and bowing slightly. "You have an unusual way with words, Mr. Rhynne," she said.

"Any facility I may have with the English language I owe to my mother."

"She was a schoolteacher?"

"My mother was a madam in a New Orleans bordello."

Pamela blinked, studying him closely to see if he was baiting her. His face gave her no clue.

"She read constantly in her leisure time," he said, "which, of course, was mostly in the mornings. She loved to read aloud, Shakespeare, Marlowe, Dickens, as well as Keats and the other romantic poets. Her favorite was William Wordsworth who, in fact, was the inspiration for my name."

"You're William Wordsworth Rhynne?"

"I have no middle name. I am Wordsworth Rhynne, though in these less than civilized regions I prefer being called W.W. W.W. Rhynne, your most humble servant." He sketched a bow.

This Rhynne was a humbug and a charlatan, she was sure. A master of glib phrases, a man not to be trusted. Why did she feel a stirring within her? A quickening of her heartbeat? How foolish.

"Where can we talk, Mr. Rhynne?" she asked. "I have a confidential matter to discuss."

"In my room? It's just along the hall. Number twenty-three."

"Certainly not. We may as well talk here, I suppose. Sit down, Mr. Rhynne. No, don't close the door."

He sat on a straight-backed chair with his tan wide-brimmed hat on his lap. For all his elegant words, she noticed, he hadn't waited for her to be seated first. She smiled to herself; she felt better, still lightheaded but now in an agreeable way. The medicine, as always, was taking more and more of a pronounced effect.

"I believe in being direct, Mr. Rhynne," she said. "I have a pair of diamond earrings which were appraised in England for the equivalent of ten thousand dollars. With the earrings as collateral, I propose to borrow five thousand dollars from you to open a store in the mining country."

His dark eyes held hers. "May I be equally direct? I have some questions."

She nodded.

"The extent of your experience in trade?"

"I have none."

"Do you have a partner? Your husband perhaps?"

"I'm a widow, Mr. Rhynne. My daughter Selena will assist me."

"Your daughter? And how old is she?"

"Nineteen."

He raised his eyebrows. "I would have said from the looks of you that she couldn't possibly be more than ten. No, wait, don't protest, false modesty isn't at all appealing. Is she the lovely golden-haired creature I glimpsed a few nights ago in Whittaker's?"

"We have had dinner there, yes."

"Your daughter is a phantom of delight."

"Wordsworth?"

"Wordsworth." He stood and paced to the door and back with his head down, his hands clasped behind him.

"I agree to advance you the five thousand dollars," he told her.

Startled, she said, "You agree?"

"If you meet certain conditions."

Pamela waited.

"First, you will pay interest at the usual rate."

"Which is?"

"Two percent per month. Second, in addition to selling provisions, our establishment will offer entertainment and games of chance."

"You mean it will be a music and gambling hall."

"Those are words commonly used to describe such places. I've just returned from the north. In the right location and with the proper management, we can clear two thousand a month."

"Two thousand! I hadn't expected so much. But I find gambling distasteful. I'll need time to consider, Mr. Rhynne. May I have a week?"

"Agreed." He stepped to her, bent down to grasp her shoulders and kissed her lips. Pamela gasped, her lips opening, and for an instant, no more, she responded to him. Then, turning her head away, she suddenly grew angry. Before she could strike out at him, he stepped back.

"If we become partners," he said, "consider that as payment in full of your first month's interest." He turned only to stop short.

In the open doorway, eyes wide and mouth agape, stood Selena.

4

Pamela and Selena climbed Telegraph Hill with the sky cloudless above them and the waters of the bay sparkling below. As if by unspoken agreement, neither mentioned Diego, though now and again Selena glanced covertly behind them. A day and a night had passed since Diego's horse had been returned by a man Robert Gowdy had hired; still, Selena expected to espy at any moment three horsemen in black.

"There's Mr. Rhynne," Pamela said as they neared the top. She gestured toward three men below them in frock coats and high plug hats. Rhynne kept looking from the pocket watch in his hand to the entrance of the bay.

Selena glanced at her mother.

"He's offered to advance me money to open a store in the mining camps," Pamela went on.

49

Selena nodded to herself, looking down at the tall man between his two companions. Was that the explanation for the scene she'd witnessed in her mother's room yesterday? An agreement sealed with a kiss? It was certainly unlike Pamela.

"It would be wonderful to get away from San Francisco," Selena said carefully. Actually her heart was leaping at the chance to go north, where there was gold and excitement. She added innocently, "Mr. Rhynne must be here to watch for the clipper too."

"Mr. Rhynne is a gambler," Pamela said. "I suspect he has his own private reason for waiting down there. As I told you, he'll help us in our store venture—but with conditions. We must also operate a gambling and music hall. And a saloon as well, I suppose."

"If we did, I could sing," Selena said eagerly. "That man who heard me sing in New York said I should be on the stage."

"You were a child then. I cannot have you exhibiting yourself in front of a group of drunken miners. Beyond the impropriety, it wouldn't be safe. There's no point in discussing it anyway because I've decided not to accept Mr. Rhynne's offer. I discovered after talking to him he's involved in another business besides gambling."

"Which is?"

"He provides entertainers for the miners."

"You mean singers and dancers?"

"No, I do not mean singers and dancers. You know who I mean. I mean women who cater to the baser instincts of lonely men. In our position, Selena, without prospects, we can't afford to be associated with a man of that kind."

"Who told you? Robert Gowdy? You know he'd say anything if he thought it would keep you in San Francisco."

"I'm sure Mr. Gowdy was telling the truth. You have no idea, Selena, what some men are like, how far they'll stoop to satisfy their lust for money and power. And if I have my way you never will know."

Selena knew Pamela was thinking of Lord Lester. He was my father, she wanted to say. I couldn't help loving him. But she said nothing, brushing away the thought as she brushed away all thoughts of that trek across the continent to California.

When they reached the top of the hill, they climbed onto a large flat rock to gaze out over the bay toward the Pacific Ocean. Overhead seagulls whirled and dipped. To their right was a hut with the windmill-like arms of the semaphore telegraph on top while below a ship was coming into the bay under full sail.

"It's not the *Flying Cloud*," Pamela said. "From her flag she must be a clipper on the China run."

Selena heard the disappointment in her mother's voice and thought guiltily that she herself didn't care whether or not there was news from "home." The *Flying Cloud* would have brought English mail, but to Selena, England was no longer home. California was.

When the ship passed the tip of an island in the bay one of the men with Rhynne threw his hat to the ground. "He's giving money to Mr. Rhynne," Selena said.

"I should have guessed they didn't climb halfway up the hill for the view. They had a wager on the time the ship would reach the island."

"Mother!" Selena clutched Pamela's arm. "Over there, riding up the hill. I knew he'd come."

A lone horseman, dressed in black and wearing the low flat-brimmed hat of the Californios, urged his mount to clamber over a steep rise, then galloped upward in a zigzag pattern. Sunlight flashed from the silver ornaments on the horse's trappings.

"It *is* Diego," Selena said. Her heart pounded. From fear? From longing? "What shall we do?" They were the only ones on the top of the hill and the semaphore hut was almost a quarter of a mile away.

"We'll go to meet him, of course," Pamela said.

Diego crested the hill and reined to a halt a hundred feet from them. Vaulting from his stallion with a single, fluid motion, he stood watching them. Despite his velvet suit with wide-bottomed slashed pants, he seemed, to Selena, somehow less imposing than he had at the rancho.

Diego approached them with a stiff-legged gait, as though once off his horse he had left his natural element behind. Pamela stopped, reaching out her arm to hold Selena back too. Selena had no intention of rushing forward, however. Though on first seeing Diego she thought she might throw herself into his arms, now that she faced him she saw him more as a threat, not so much to herself as to her mother.

Diego swept off his hat and bowed. Pamela nodded; Selena stared. Almost on tip-toe Diego walked toward them, like a wary puma stalking his prey, his eyes never leaving theirs. In his belt

Selena saw the butt of a pistol she had not noticed there the day before.

"You had no cause for fear," he said to Selena.

Pamela answered coolly for her daughter. "Selena changed her mind, Señor de la Torre. She does not wish to marry you. She will not marry you."

Diego glanced from Pamela to Selena and back again. "I talked with my sister, Esperanza. I love Esperanza with all my heart, yet her words, seeming as gentle as the breeze, often gather force and become as the whirlwind."

"Your sister didn't make my daughter change her mind. I didn't make her change her mind. Selena is old enough to make decisions. In our world, a woman of her age must decide for herself."

Her mother, Selena thought, was more than a match for Diego. She wouldn't have to say a word.

"You believe me to be . . ." Diego hesitated. "What is it the English say? A searcher for gold?"

"A prospector?"

"A man who marries for the dowry of his bride-to-be." His dark eyes flashed. "I am not. I renounce your money; I renounce your lands beyond the seas. I am Diego de la Torre. That is enough."

Pamela drew in her breath. "Don Diego," she said, "we have no lands, no money. Our fortune consists of one parcel of land forty-eight *varos* wide in San Francisco. We have nothing else. Nothing."

"At the Mission of Santa Clara you spoke of the green fields of your home in England where the lands of your husband who is now dead extended in all directions farther than the eye can see. You told me of your great house, your servants, your carriages, your many horses. You told me of all these things and more."

"You must have misunderstood me. My husband owned those lands I told you of but he lost them. They were sold to pay his debts. Sometimes having too much land is worse than owning none at all."

"You made me believe the lands were yours. You made me believe they became yours with the death of your husband. You made me believe your daughter Selena would receive a portion of the lands when she married."

His voice had become quieter, more deadly. Selena wished he would shout and wave his arms as the Americans did. That she could understand.

"When one person speaks Spanish as his native tongue," Pamela told him, "and the other is accustomed to English, there are bound to be misunderstandings. I thought *you* were the wealthy one with many leagues of grazing lands to the south." She smiled but Selena noticed a tic at the corner of her mother's mouth.

"So, señor," Pamela told him, trying for a light tone. "We were both mistaken."

Diego leaned forward until his face was inches from Pamela's. He sneered, "You laugh, you make sport. And you speak less than the truth. It is you who do not understand. I am in disgrace. Diego de la Torre is the butt of sly laughter in the cantinas, at the ranchos of my friends, in my own house. I cannot ride to a fiesta ever again. I can never marry, for who will have me? I have become like the mud on the ground, like the droppings of cattle. I am nothing."

"I'm sure—" Pamela began.

"I, Diego de la Torre of the de la Torres of Mazatlan, of the de la Torres admired throughout Castile, have been tricked by a woman. I have been held up to the scorn of the world by a woman. By you. My life is worth *nada* to me. *Nada.*" He flung his hat to the ground.

"Diego!" Selena, her heart thudding, pushed Pamela's arm aside and stepped past her. "This is not my mother's doing," she said.

"Selena."

Diego's voice was suddenly so soft, so tender, she felt an echo of the passion that had stirred in her such a short time before. "Selena." His hand came up in supplication and she remembered that same hand on her breast.

"Selena," said her mother quietly, with a quaver in her voice. Selena knew what she must do.

"Diego," she said, "listen to me. You did not ask for my hand in marriage. You never asked me. Never."

"I asked your mother." Diego seemed confused. "Your father is dead. I asked your mother who promised you to me."

Selena looked quickly behind her. Pamela's heightened color told her Diego spoke the truth.

"You never asked *me*," Selena insisted. "Perhaps in Spain or in Mexico a mother speaks for her daughter but not in my country. Not here in California. You must ask *me*."

"I will ask you then. Selena, will you ride with me for the rest of your days? Will you be my wife?"

Selena kept her eyes on him, resisting the urge to glance away. "No, Diego, I will not. I cannot. It is not what I wish."

Diego removed the pistol from his belt. Selena stepped back. Pamela gasped.

Diego flipped the pistol in the air, caught it by the barrel, and extended the gun to Selena. "Take this," he said.

Puzzled, she accepted the gun. Trimmed in silver, it had a shorter barrel than most of the pistols she had seen on the trail or in San Francisco.

"There is but one bullet in the chamber," Diego said. "It is for me. Shoot me, Selena, take my life. If you deny me your hand, my life is over; if you scorn me, I will become like a rider of mares. So you must kill me, Selena."

Selena tossed the gun to the ground. She had a sudden nervous compulsion to laugh, but when she looked at Diego's desperate face she almost reached out to comfort him. Yet she did not.

"Diego," she said. He looked at the ground at her feet. "Diego," she said again, "the horse I rode from the rancho has been returned to you. You will always be in my heart." Still he would not look at her. "I'm sorry," she said.

Selena turned to her mother, who stood staring down at the inbound clipper ship rounding the point at the entrance to the cove. "Pamela," she said, "it's time we went home." She took her mother's arm and together they walked past Diego to the path leading down the hill.

Diego watched them go. He was very tired. His rage was spent; a cold hatred had taken its place. He knelt to retrieve his pistol and thrust it under his belt. He picked his hat from the ground, brushed the brim with his sleeve, and placed it squarely on his head.

I will have her, this Selena, he promised himself. I will have her again and again until she begs for mercy and I will not give her mercy. I will send other men to her and I will watch when they are with her and I will laugh. She will become a *puta*, a whore, and worse, and I will watch and laugh.

The older one, the mother, I will kill. But not until she sees what I have made of her daughter.

As the two women descended the hill, Pamela walked slower and slower, often stumbling. Her eyes were moist and every so often she had to stop to dab at her nose with a handkerchief. To Selena, she looked ten years older than the thirty-eight she knew her to be.

"The fever," Pamela said when Selena asked if she was ill. "The aftereffects of the fever. The doctor said it sometimes takes months before you recover."

They came to Portsmouth Street, opposite the first wharf, where workmen were shoveling sand, rocks and dirt from a wagon into the water to reclaim the tidelands. From the town they heard the pounding of hammers and the rasping of saws.

"Pamela," Selena said, "you told me Mr. Rhynne offered to advance us five thousand dollars."

Pamela nodded.

"On the condition that we allow gambling."

Pamela nodded again.

"We'll see him later today and we'll tell him we

accept. We'll open a store and a gambling hall but we will not countenance . . ." Selena paused. "We will not tolerate harlots. We'll draw up an agreement to that effect."

Pamela took her daughter's hand and for a moment their eyes met. Pamela's fell away first. "Perhaps that's what we should do," she said slowly.

"Not perhaps. We will."

Pamela hesitated. At last her head dropped. "All right, we will," she said.

Selena walked on toward the hotel, her mother a step behind. I'm no longer following, Selena thought. She was frightened. Her mother was obviously wary of Rhynne, and so was she. Yet, anticipating her future in the brawling camps to the north, she did not slow her pace.

5

Arm in arm, Danny O'Lee and his father swung down the track from their lodgings at the foot of Telegraph Hill. The abandoned ships in the cove were dark but lamps were being lit in the canvas tents and wooden shanties on both side of the road as they walked.

The two men turned onto California Street, heading for the bayfront. Soon they were surrounded by its hubbub. Chinese wearing long queues pushed past them, mingling with Chilenos, Peruvians, Mexicans, an occasional Kanaka from the Sandwich Islands, Indians. They heard the twang of New England, the slow drawl of the South, the flat accents of the Midwest.

"Would you look at that?" Michael said to his son. They went over and joined the men in front of the Parker House. The men were watching two women, one on either arm of a frock-coated man, coming toward them from Whittaker's Restaurant. The older woman, dressed in black, was veiled, but the younger one wore green, a deep midsummer green. Golden curls fell from beneath her matching green hat to her shoulders. Her face glowed with animation as she talked to her escort.

"That's Rhynne, the gambler," someone next to Danny said. "Lucky devil."

Rhynne held the door to the hotel's private entrance and then followed the two women inside. The crowd of men lingered after the women were gone, shuffling their feet, then slowly dispersed.

"That lass was as lovely," Michael said, "as your sainted mother in the bloom of her youth."

Danny said nothing. When he had seen the golden-haired young woman something had leaped inside him. He closed his eyes trying to recall the exact tilt of her nose, the precise shade of her hair. She was the most beautiful girl he had ever seen.

"Come along, Danny, we can't be dawdling here all of this night. Ah, the colleen. It's out of your mind you are to be still thinking of her. For it's the gold in the ground we're after, not the gold in a lass's hair."

They stopped in front of a pitchman who stood behind a blue-painted board laid across two barrels.

"Ah, temptations on all sides of us," Michael said.

"Gentlemen," the pitchman cried. "I can tell by your looks you're sporting men willing to risk the coin of the realm or a pinch of dust to prove your eye is quicker than the hand. Look here." He lifted one of three large silver thimbles on the board to show them a shriveled pea.

"Now," he said, "keep your eye on the thimble with the pea." After shifting the thimbles hither and thither on the board, he raised his hands, palms out. "Now, who can tell me which thimble hides the pea?"

"Why," Danny whispered to his father, "it's clear it's under the middle one. This fool and his money will soon be parted."

A bearded miner put a pinch of gold dust in the pitchman's open pouch. "That one," he said, pointing to the middle thimble.

The pitchman raised the thimble; there was nothing underneath. "We'll try the others," he said, "to prove the game is on the up and up." He found the pea beneath the right-hand thimble.

"Sure, and it's one of the devil's own games," Michael said, frowning as they walked away.

In front of an auction house a plug hatted man had mounted the bottom rungs of a stepladder to harangue a semi-circle of men.

"Only a single dollar," he was saying as Danny and his father joined the throng. "One dollar for the opportunity of a lifetime. The chance to win a lot on Market Street certified to be eighteen *varos* wide and forty deep. Last month exactly the same size lot next door sold for one hundred and sixty dollars. Yesterday it brought five hundred. You heard me right, gentleman, five hundred American dollars. Next month they'll be selling for a thousand and more."

"And what may a *varo* be?" Michael wondered aloud.

"Three feet," someone in front of them said without turning around.

"The drawing's in one week's time," the man on the ladder was saying. "Only a week to wait before you make your fortune. No digging in water up to your knees, no cradling, no panning. Remember the words of the immortal bard, 'There comes a tide in the affairs of men which, taken at the flood, leads on to fame and fortune.' The tide's rising, gentlemen, the crest approaches. For one dollar, fame and fortune can be yours."

Danny and Michael moved off. From Bidwell's Saloon came laughter, the clink of glasses, voices raised in a wavering chorus of *Auld Lang Syne*.

"We'd best be off to bed soon," Danny said, "if we're to be up and away to the diggings in the morning."

"Listen a moment first. Do you hear the self-same heavenly music I hear?"

A man's voice was raised in song:

"The summer's gone and all the roses falling
It's you, it's you must go and I must bide."

The music wafted toward them from the open door of a narrow, dimly lit saloon beyond Bidwell's.

"We'll just go in and listen a wee bit," Michael decided. "We won't tarry long in this place. Danny, as I've oft told you, your mother sang that very song to you as a lullaby."

"It's I'll be there in sunshine or in shadow
Oh, Danny Boy, my Danny Boy, I love you so."

Still, you left her, Danny thought. Left me and Burke as well. Nothing his father put a hand to ever came quite right. And yet, though mother *had* been a saint, Danny had always loved his father best.

They wedged their way to the bar, Danny jostling the arm of the man to his left. The man, big and burly with a bushy black beard, looked down hard at him.

"Are you serving babes not yet weaned from their mother's milk?" he asked. The barman ignored him and set a bottle of whisky in front of Michael.

Danny sipped his drink. He had never learned to tolerate spirits. A drink, two at the most, and he fell asleep. His father, on the other hand, could drink for hours. In fact, he was already refilling his glass.

When the fiddler started *Old Dan Tucker* some of the men joined the chorus while others hunched silently over their drinks.

"We came by way of Panama," Danny's father was saying to two men on his far side. Danny envied his father's ease with lies when he needed them, also his capacity for hard drink and his nonchalance with women. He did not envy him his temper. It's what had gotten them into trouble in St. Louis. A man had been killed in a saloon brawl, and though Michael hadn't killed him, he'd been part of the fight. With the reputation of a brawler pursuing him, he'd thought the time opportune to leave for California and start life anew. He wasn't the only California-bound adventurer who had changed his name; many were doing so, for various reasons.

Michael was spinning a good yarn. "The black natives poled us up the Chagras while all the time we were battling the mosquitoes. We stayed at a hotel, a tent it was, and we had to wait for our coffee to be ground and I looked from the window and saw a girl chewing the beans and spitting them into the pot. Then it was by mule train we traveled to Panama City where we weren't allowed to shoot the vultures because the great birds cleaned the filth from the streets. When first we saw the sea I says, 'Begorra, 'tis the spitting image of the Atlantic.' And all the while I'd been expecting a different breed of ocean."

"You and the lad are just off the boat, I expect."

"This morning and none too soon, after waiting two weeks offshore for a breeze to blow us here. And that after sitting a month and more in Panama before we shoved our way aboard the *California*. And would you believe it? We crossed the Isthmus from west to east."

"You're ass backwards," the burly man next to Danny said.

"Pa, maybe you've said enough," Danny cautioned Michael.

"You tell him, Duke," another said to the burly man.

"As ass backwards as the day you were born," Duke went on. "If you're a-coming from the east coast to the west coast any jackass knows you travel east to west."

"Sure now, and I'm begging to differ," Michael said across Danny. "That steaming hell of a country is most peculiar, with more loops and bends than a shillelagh. So it was from west to east we went."

"And I say you're a liar."

Michael placed his whisky glass on the bar. Danny nudged him, saying in a low voice, "Leave it alone now, pa. No trouble, please."

Michael picked up his glass and saluted Duke. "I acknowledge the error of my thinking," he said. "Sure and I must have been standing on my head when we made the crossing to believe we went one way when in truth we went the other."

Duke grunted.

There was a murmur farther along the bar.

"One drink, no more," the barman was telling an Indian. "Niggers and Indians, one drink, then vamoose."

"Damn all these foreigners," Duke said. Several of his friends muttered agreement. He rapped his empty bottle on the counter until the barman exchanged it for a full one. "They come here and make off with all the gold that rightfully belongs to us Americans." A murmur of assent came from the men along the bar. "They come here with their fancy French sashaying and their strutting Spanish ways and try to take our women as well as our gold. It's not right."

"Seen the two women at the Parker House?" someone asked.

"I have. Two of the best-looking pieces I ever laid eyes on," Duke said.

Danny began to protest, then subsided.

"That filly," Duke went on, "I'd like to get my hand under her skirt for just two minutes. She'd soon lose her nose-in-the-air hoity-toity ways. I can tell a bawd when I set eyes on one."

"She's not a bawd," Danny said quietly. "Neither of them are. They're respectable ladies."

"Respectable and in league with Rhynne?" Several of the men joined in Duke's guffaw. "Rhynne, the premier whoremaster of San Francisco?"

Danny swung around to face Duke. "Take it back. Take back what you said about her."

Duke smirked, put down his glass, and drew himself up to his full height. He was six inches taller than Danny. "And look who's talking," he said. "A little black Irish mick. And what do you know of women, sonny? I'll wager you've never bedded a woman in your life. Not a woman of any sort, whore or otherwise."

Danny felt the color rise to his neck and face.

Duke put his head back and laughed. "You see, mates, I was right. Nineteen-years-old and never been kissed."

"I'm twenty-one," Danny muttered.

"Twenty-one!" Duke unfastened a pouch from his belt and dropped it on the bar. "Duke Olmsted is standing a round," he called out in a slurred voice. "To celebrate this here boy's twenty-first birthday, since, by God, it must have been yesterday or today, he's so green behind the ears."

The men at the bar roared their appreciation; those at the tables around the room got up and crowded over. Danny gritted his teeth and hunched over his drink. His father's hand touched his wrist. "It's not a man's size," Michael said gently, "nor the bombast in his voice that makes him a man. Nor is it the gratification of his lusts."

Danny tried to grin at his father. But he found

little value in Michael's words. It was Duke's words that rang in his head. How had the man known? he asked himself. How did they always guess? It was the shame of his life that he had never been with a woman, never kissed a girl with passion. Never.

"No," the bartender was telling the Indian, "not you. You had your drink. Vamoose."

Danny looked along the bar. The Indian's lank hair hung to his shoulders, on his head was a battered black hat, his face was brown and lined, his oversized nose was squashed almost flat. The Indian said nothing—Danny had not heard him speak at all—but held his glass out over the bar to be filled.

"You're drunk," the bartender told him.

Taking his last two coins from his pocket, Danny tossed them on the bar. "I'm buying him a drink," he said. The bartender looked from the coins to the Indian, all the while shaking his head.

Duke's hand grasped Danny's shoulder and spun him around. "He said no more drinks for the fucking Indian."

Danny took his almost full glass from the bar and threw the whisky into Duke's face.

Duke, surprised, released his hold and wiped his sleeve across his face. Danny stepped back. The crowd at the bar shrank from the two men, all except Michael and the Indian, who still held his glass extended over the bar.

"Get away," Danny said to his father. "I'm for it, pa. There's no need having all of them onto both of us."

His father nodded just as Duke swung a wheeling ham-handed punch. Danny ducked but caught the blow on his shoulder. He was flung against the bar and staggered back into the Indian. His shoulder stung as though he'd been hit by a club.

The Indian threw his glass over his shoulder, pushed Danny aside and weaved toward Duke. He tripped on a fallen chair, lurched to one side and fell face first to the floor. A miner prodded him with his boot. "Dead drunk," he said. Two men lifted the Indian from the floor and carried him out of the saloon.

Danny, forgotten, glanced at the open door. If he wanted to run, this was his chance. But he would not run. He would not run now if the whole world stood ranged against him.

The men returned from dragging the Indian into the street and clustered around the two men. Waiting. Expectant. Duke stared down at Danny.

"I don't want to fight no baby," he said.

He came toward Danny with his right hand extended. When he stopped a few feet away, Danny hawked up and spat in his open palm.

Duke stared in disbelief at the spittle, then roared and charged head down. Danny danced aside just in time, chopping at the back of Duke's neck with his fist, so that his bull-like charge ended in the arms of two of the spectators. While Danny clenched and unclenched his stinging hand, Duke turned, assumed the classic pugilist's stance and plodded towards him. Danny studied the burly man. Big, too big for him to lick. Yet Duke's belly lapped over his belt. And the man was unsteady from the drink.

As Duke brought his right arm back for another roundhouse clout, Danny jabbed his fist into his stomach and leaped away. Duke's mouth opened and closed but he made no sound. His arm still cocked, he stalked Danny around the circle of men. Once again, Danny jabbed his fist into his stomach, then, as Duke came on, darted away.

He might have continued his jabbing tactics had not his back struck the bar as he danced backwards. Go right or left? Duke swung before he could move either way. The blow caught Danny above the ear and seemed to explode in his head. The floor whirled up at him. His head thudded on a spittoon.

Dazed, Danny looked up to see Duke coming at him with a chair raised high. He scrambled back and away, beneath a table, and the chair splintered on its top. He grasped a table leg, pulled himself to the far side and came to his feet with the table between them.

Duke roared and hurled himself full-length across the table, his hands grasping for Danny's throat. Danny flung himself backwards. Duke rolled awkwardly from the table, regained his feet and came on, bear-like. Danny, sweat burning his eyes and his ears still ringing from the head blow, jabbed at the big man's stomach, once, twice, three times. Duke grunted with each blow, yet came on.

Danny jabbed again. Anticipating the blow this time, Duke caught his wrist and yanked him forward, twisting his arm. Danny howled in pain. Duke flung him to the floor, cocked a boot aimed at his head. Desperately, Danny squirmed away, then kicked upward with both feet. His lunging thrust caught Duke in the groin. The big man's foot shot forward, missed. Hands clutching his groin, he sank to his knees, a position from which he stared glassily, unable to move for the pain and nausea overcoming him.

"Enough is enough," the bartender said. He came around the bar carrying a black truncheon. "Take him away," he said to Duke's friends, "He's fouling my floor." As two men did this, the bartender turned more quietly to Danny. "It's best you be on your way." Then he told Michael, "If you were to ask my advice, I'd say take the lad and be gone from this town for the next month or two."

Michael nodded.

Danny and his father strode out to the muddy street. Around them the night was dark and chill, the fog high overhead. They paused in front of the saloon, savoring the clean night air while they got their bearings.

"This way," Michael said, pointing to the greater darkness of the hills behind the town. They set off arm in arm.

"The best brawl I've seen in all my days," Michael finally admitted, "that is, of those I've not been in on meself. You did yourself proud."

Now's the time, Danny thought. Now's the time to ask him why he left me and Burke when we were kids, not to come back for so many years. I didn't have the heart in St. Louis what with him in trouble and all. But now—now I've the right to ask.

Before the words could form on his tongue his father sighed, then cleared his throat and began to sing, his voice slow and sad, clear and full:

"The summer's gone and all the roses falling
It's you, it's you must go and I must bide."

The only warning was a footstep behind them.
Danny began to turn when a blow caught him on
the back of the head and he pitched forward to
his knees. He heard scuffling, oaths, started to rise
and was struck down again. Before his senses
clouded completely he heard his father's bellow:

"Ye sons o' bitches . . ."

Then no more.

When Danny opened his eyes the night was
quiet with the fog all around him. He pushed himself to his feet, and shook his head to clear it.
wincing with the pain. As he stood unsteadily, he
heard singing from afar.

He groped this way and that in the fog.

"Pa," he called. "Pa, where are you?"

He stumbled over something and knelt. His fingers found his father's cold damp face. Even
before Danny staggered back to the saloon and
returned with a lamp, he knew his father was
dead.

6

Kingman Sutton, bored by the drone of Wilkes Yancey's voice, fingered the fire opal he wore on his right hand. He glanced from Dr. Robinson's impassive face to the crackling log fire to the mirror above the mantel. Reflected in the mirror was Mary Yancey. Almost like a portrait, King mused. It was as if Wilkes had hung a portrait of his young wife where the gilt-edged mirror had always been.

Mary, regally tall and imperially aloof, her black hair in a chignon, her fitted bodice emphasizing her breasts, her mauve skirt sweeping the floor, looked every inch a Southern lady. In reality she was an Ohioan, Georgian only by way of her marriage to Wilkes the year before.

Mary's hand moved and King realized he had

been fancifying. Mary stood just outside the door to Wilkes' study. In the mirror, her hand came up across her breasts to her throat. She watched King, unaware that he in turn was watching her.

Mary's lips parted slightly. As they had parted the day before when, under the great live oak at the common corner of the Yancey and Sutton plantations, he had kissed her.

While Wilkes droned on, King recalled the tryst and what it had meant to him.

Her lips had responded before she drew back, bringing her hands up between them to hold him away. "King Sutton," she said, "you're taking advantage of a woman alone in a strange land."

He'd pulled her to him, ignoring her fluttering hands, his lips nipping at her neck, her ear, her lips. She relaxed, her body soft against his, her lips yielding to his kisses. Then she twisted free.

He advanced on her. "I've had enough of your teasing ways," he said.

"And you, Senator Sutton, with a sick wife at home."

He whirled and walked to his horse, unlooped the reins from a branch and swung into the saddle. She ran after him.

"Oh, King, King," she cried, holding to his booted leg. "I spoke without thinking. I know what it must be like for you. The horror you must suffer day after day." She pressed her cheek against his leg.

Still angry, he stared down at her lustrous black hair. Though outraged by her reference to Betsy, at the same time he seemed to stand outside himself observing the two of them beneath the oak, this beautiful girl clinging to the dashing older man with the flowing grey-streaked hair. And, as he watched, he'd planned the next move of his campaign.

It was time for one of "Sutton's Fancies." That's what they called them at the Georgia state capitol at Milledgeville. Not lies, certainly not lies, not even prevarications; no, "fancies." They were part and parcel of politics and, especially when they worked, were admired and quoted repeatedly by all.

"You'll only have a fortnight more to tempt and then deny me," he told her. Mary Yancey raised her green-gold eyes. How had a bore like Wilkes captured this prize on his visit to his Cincinnati kin? King could have understood her marrying any of the other four Yancey brothers, for they possessed a certain mad charm. But Wilkes? Wilkes was the runt of the litter.

"Only a fortnight? Why do you say that, King?"

"I've booked my passage on the *Eastern Star*. We sail from Charleston on the twenty-ninth, bound for California."

"California?" Her tone made the Territory seem as distant as Timbuktu. Considering the long voyage around South America, he thought, it was in fact much farther.

"I intend to seek gold to replenish the Sutton fortunes," he went on. That had a certain flair, he told himself. He'd discovered Mary liked the dramatic exaggeration, the romantic gesture.

"Oh, King, who will I have to talk to if you leave? The women scorn me for being a Yankee and the men, except for you, treat me as though I'd been carved from stone and mounted on a pedestal."

"The women envy you; the men are afraid of you."

"With you in California, I'll have no one."

"Have you forgotten Wilkes?"

"Oh, Wilkes. He's gone so often with his politicking to Charleston and Savannah and Milledgeville. And when he's home he's either balancing the accounts or writing his poetry."

The poetry, he'd forgotten that. Perhaps Wilkes had won her with a song. "A man for all seasons," he said.

From Mary's hints—and King, twice her age, needed only a few—he thought he could imagine Wilkes' lovemaking. King smiled. He'd often compared the preliminaries in bedding a woman to a duel, with the man and woman facing one another as antagonists. If lovemaking *were* a duel, he could picture Wilkes standing with his pistol pointed skyward. Long before the signal to fire was given, Wilkes' pistol would have discharged with a mighty pop.

"Why are you smiling?" Mary asked.

"Thinking of all the gold I'll find in California. Mountains of gold are waiting, they say, and rivers of gold where all you have to do is pick the nuggets from the water."

"California is so far from Athens."

"True, and the voyage around the Cape is fraught with danger. Danger from storms, from disease. Still we may put into port in Brazil or Chile where the señoritas are said to be lovely creatures."

"Don't tease me, King. You might never come back."

"I'll be gone two years at least."

"Two years! That's half a lifetime."

"You'll have forgotten me by then."

"Oh, King, you know I'll never forget you. Never."

Leaning down, he'd raised her face to his and was surprised to find tears on her cheeks. When he kissed her the taste of her mouth was the taste of salt. She opened her lips to him and her tongue met his before drawing away. He released her, his hand fondling her ear and trailing gently to caress the hair at the nape of her neck.

He clucked to his horse.

"King," she called after him. "King, will I see you again? Before you go?"

He'd spurred the horses, glancing back at Mary waving to him from beneath the oak. "Perhaps," he'd called, knowing his voice would be lost in the thudding of his horse's hooves.

Now, in Wilkes' study, King was considering his next move. Risk, he told himself. Risk was all. It must be an audacious gambit. Daring. At times, he thought he must want to be caught out. Punished. But that was foolish. Why would he? His mind had been in a jumble lately—there were too many complications in his life. So many that this California fantasy had a certain appeal. If he could make it real, it would give him what he wanted, freedom.

Mary's face in the mirror frowned. He saw the rise and fall of her breasts as she sighed and then her reflection was gone as she walked away toward the staircase. He pictured her entering her bedroom at the top of the stairs, imagined her sitting in front of a mirror to unpin her hair and let it cascade to her shoulders, standing while her maid unbuttoned her gown, the gown slipping from her white shoulders . . .

"The fate of this nation will be decided not by the mouthings of abolitionists or secessionists," Wilkes was intoning, "nor by the empty vaporings of politicians in Washington, nor by the industrial might of the North nor the undoubted power of King Cotton combined with the foreign powers who must align themselves with the South. No, our fate hinges on events in the West, in Texas and, more importantly, in California. Those will be the battlegrounds, peaceful battlegrounds one can only pray, where the destiny of the nation will be decided. There the decision will be made as to whether we can exist half-slave and half-free or whether the balance of power will tilt to the North so that we in the South must sever the bonds of a union we have prized for so long. Don't you agree?"

"Unhesitatingly," Dr. Robinson said.

King nodded. The fool. Peaceful battleground indeed. "What Webster or Clay or Calhoun would have taken two days to expound, you've reduced to two hours," he said. He stubbed out his cigar and stretched. "Your hospitality is unequaled," he told Wilkes, looking at the clock. "Only eleven, yet I must leave. My wife . . ."

"Of course," Wilkes said. "We understand."

"Tell Betsy I'll look in on her Monday next," Dr. Robinson said. "And make sure she takes the elixir I prescribed."

"I will, doctor." He bowed to Wilkes. "And my respects to your lovely and charming wife," he said.

"Thank you, Kingman. I expect Dr. Robinson

and I will amuse ourselves over the cribbage board before he leaves for town."

"Cribbage and Yancey brandy," Robinson said, "make an excellent combination."

King waved Wilkes back to his chair. "Don't bother," he said. "I know the way."

He closed the study door behind him. The house was quiet; no servants were about this time of night. As he made his way along the hall he glanced up the staircase curving into the darkness of the second story. Mary must be in her nightgown by now, probably in bed reading her latest romance. While she had disrobed he had been forced to listen to Wilkes' prattling. Damn Wilkes! he thought.

He removed his hat from the rack, hesitated, then replaced it on the peg. Outside, he walked quickly across the portico and down the steps to his horse. Once in the pine wood to the south of the Yancey place he dismounted and secured the reins to a tree.

King reentered the Yancey house as quietly as he could. One lamp still burned in the hall, his hat was on the peg where he had left it, the study was closed. He went to the study door and waited until he heard the drone of Wilkes' voice. Turning, he paused only an instant before climbing the stairs.

Now there was no going back.

The top of the stairs was in shadow so he could make out only the dark rectangles of the portraits on the walls and of the doors to the bedrooms. Wilkes' and Mary's room was just to the left across the hall.

He glanced over the railing and up and down the hallway. No one was about. Putting his ear to the bedroom door, he listened. There was no sound from inside. He grasped and turned the doorknob. The door eased open; the room beyond was dark. He slipped quickly inside and closed the door behind him.

There were four windows, two on each of the opposite sides of the spacious room, just as he remembered from the many times he had played here as a child. Pale moonlight shimmered on the long white curtains of the two eastern windows, giving the entire room an unearthly glow.

The bed was to his left, large and dark. King sat on the floor to remove his boots. In his stocking feet he silently approached the canopied bed, and lifted the white netting.

Mary lay on her back, breathing softly and deeply, one pale arm on top of the blankets, her shoulder bare. King let the netting drop and went to check one of the windows he had chosen as an exit. Yes, there it was. Holding the window curtain aside, he looked down at the roof of the portico he had often jumped onto as a boy, there to hang from the edge by his fingers, then drop into the flower bed beside the drive. He'd done it often thirty years before, and he could still do it today.

He took off the rest of his clothes and piled them by the window on top of his boots. Then he returned silently to the bed, opened the netting, drew down the covers and slid beneath the sheets. Mary stirred. King remained perfectly still, holding his breath while he relished the moment.

He slid across the bed until he was almost, though not quite, touching her. He felt Mary's warmth on his naked body. With his left hand he lifted a strand of her long hair and tucked it behind her ear.

"Wilkes?" Her voice was drowsy.

He leaned toward her and blew gently in her ear. She stirred again, shifting away.

"Wilkes? I'm asleep."

He waited until she quieted and then reached down between the sheets, found her thigh, and trailed his fingers up to the swell of her hips, to her narrow waist, and along her side to her bare shoulder.

"Not tonight, Wilkes. I'm so tired." Her voice, though, was firmer, more awake.

He nestled against her, fitting the length of his body to hers, feeling the excitement grow in him. With his mouth to her neck he flicked his tongue against her neck and along her cheek, seeking her lips.

"Wilkes. What are you doing?" She was wide awake now. He raised his hand from her waist, trying to imagine what Wilkes would do, found her nipple and twisted, hard.

"All right," she said. "I'm awake now, damn it. Just wait a minute." He felt the bedclothes move as her hands went beneath the covers to raise her nightgown above her hips. "I'm ready," she said. She lay on her back with her arms at her sides.

"Wilkes, what are you doing?" she asked uncertainly a moment later.

He had put his hand on her thigh, his fingers fluttering from one leg to the other and then dipping between where her flesh was dry and unyielding. His fingers splayed over her belly, feeling her uneasy tremor; he touched the hair below and found the division between her legs and, gently, caressed her with his fingers. Only after what seemed to him a long time did he feel moisture and hear her breathing quicken. Her body, as though of its own volition, began to writhe beside him.

He removed his hand and shifted away from her to the far side of the bed. "It's not Wilkes," he said. "It's King."

There was silence.

"King?" A whisper then. "King!" Almost a shout. She sat up.

"Quiet," he told her. "Don't wake the house. How would you explain me?"

"King." Her voice lowered quietly. "How did you get here?"

"The usual way. Up the stairs and through the door."

"Where's Wilkes?"

"Playing cribbage with Dr. Robinson. When the good doctor leaves Wilkes will light him to his carriage and I'll be able to see him from here."

"King, you have to go. This minute. What if Wilkes does find you here? He'll kill you."

"Wilkes?"

"If not Wilkes, then his brothers will. You know how they stick together."

"I had to come, Mary. I had to see you again before I left for California." He paused. "I love you, Mary."

"I don't believe you, King Sutton."

"Have I ever lied to you, Mary? You don't know the torture you've put me through these last months, seeing you, seeing your loveliness and not being able to reach out to you. Not being able to touch you or kiss you."

"King, you know how I feel. It's as though you're the only real person I know. You're the only one I can talk to, really talk to."

He sat up beside her and smoothed her hair with his hand, a strand catching in his ring. For a moment he hesitated.

"King," Mary said, "I go all weak inside when you touch me. Nobody's ever made me feel like that before."

He leaned to her, kissing her, and her lips parted. Their tongues met and she was in his arms, awkwardly, both sitting up on the bed, and he felt her bare shoulder under his hand. Then her head tilted back and she fell beside him, her back across the pillow. As he was pulling her nightgown up, it tangled under her arms. She reached down to help him. Still the gown wouldn't come off, so she pushed him away, raised her arms, and then he was able to remove it.

As she sat facing him, she seemed haloed by the moonlight coming through the curtains and the netting, her full breasts in shadow. He felt desire rise in him, demandingly, but he held his own urgent need back. He took her in his arms, guiding her down between the sheets with his mouth to hers, his tongue twining with hers, his body to hers—feeling the thrust of her breasts on his chest, her thighs on his legs. One of his hands explored between her legs, caressing her, and she quivered in his arms.

He kissed her neck, then lowered his head to the swell of her breast; his mouth closed over her nipple and he circled it with his tongue. She moaned. "Oh, King, oh, King," she said again and again. He slid his knee between her legs, parting them, and suddenly he was inside her, his mouth still at one breast, his hand kneading the other while her body strained to move with his.

She shuddered, a growing, all-encompassing spasm seeming to rise from her loins to shake her entire body. She shuddered again and again but still he held back, stretched taut yet waiting. Finally, after a prolonged, ecstatic gasp, she stilled and lay limp in his arms. He kissed her gently on the lips and eyes.

"Oh, King," she moaned. "I never knew it could be like that."

He turned her over. When she was on her stomach, he knelt, straddling her, his hands at her hips. "King?" He lifted her. "On my hands and knees, King?'

He spread her legs so his were between hers. His hands felt for her sex, caressing her as he entered her from behind, one hand on her sex, the other cupping her breast. She groaned, straining back against him.

"I can't again," she panted. "I can't, I . . . oh, King." She shuddered beneath him and he felt his response, let himself go at last and moved with her. Released. Fulfilled.

The netting was thrown aside and Wilkes stood staring down at them, a lamp in his hand. Behind him King had an impression of the dim figure of Dr. Robinson in the bedroom door.

King swung out of bed on the far side, went to the window, and began dressing. Wilkes stood immobile, gaping at him. The man seemed to be in total shock.

"Wilkes," King said, "you have the damnedest sense of timing of any man I know. If you were going to ask Dr. Robinson to spend the night, you should have told me."

He pulled the window open, stepped out onto the portico, dropped his boots over the side, lowered himself over the edge until he hung by his hands. He let go, landing with a thud on the hard earth. Brushing himself off he found his boots and walked across the lawn toward the woods. He did not look back.

When three of the Yancey brothers rode up to the Sutton place early the next morning, they found the overseer, Amos Beckworth, in charge and Betsy Sutton confined to her room. King had ridden off hours before. He had taken two slaves, the half-brothers Joshua and Jed. Where they had gone, Amos Beckworth had no idea.

When, ten days later, Dwight Yancey tracked King to the Charleston townhouse of a Sutton second cousin, he learned that King and his two slaves had been at sea for two days.

Bound for California.

BOOK TWO
HANGTOWN, 1849

7

When the Empire Hotel—W.W. Rhynne and P. Buttle-Jones, Proprietors—opened in Hang-town, California, in the spring of 1849, one of the greatest mass migrations since the Crusades was underway.

Over a year before, on January 24, 1848, James Marshall had made his daily inspection of the sawmill he was building for John Sutter on the south fork of the American River. He walked to the race, the channel carrying water to the mill wheel.

"I went down as usual," he told reporters later, "and after shutting off the water from the race I stepped into it, near the lower end, and there upon the rock about six inches beneath the water I discovered the gold. I pick up one or two pieces and examined them attentively. I then tried a piece between two rocks and found that it could be beaten into a different shape but not broken."

Sutter tried to keep the find secret until the mill was completed; he failed. As word of the discovery spread down the coast to San Francisco, to the capital at Monterey and to Los Angeles, it was greeted at first with skepticism, then mild interest, then with wild excitement.

Slips carried the first of the gold to ports on the Pacific. Mexicans by the thousands, many of them experienced miners, trekked north. Hawaiians and South Americans boarded ships bound for San Francisco. They became the Argonauts, named for the shipmates of the mythical Jason who sailed on the *Argo* in search of the Golden Fleece.

Word was slower reaching the United States. Not until President Polk's message to Congress in December did gold fever erupt with full force. But when it did, there was no surcease. Workmen quit their jobs, doctors closed their practices, and farmers put aside their plows in the rush to the West. Abrim with hope, yet fearful they might be too late, men set out on one of history's greatest adventures only vaguely aware of what lay ahead, ready to challenge this frontier, risking all for gold and the chance to begin their lives anew.

They listened to lectures with such titles as "The Geology, Mineralogy, Structure and Formation of the Rocks in which Precious Metals are Found." They read advertisements headlined "Ho for California." They studied the *Emigrants' Guide to California,* which told of riverbeds "paved with gold to the thickness of a hand." They formed companies to share costs—the Buckeye Rovers, the Hartford Union Mining and

Trading Company, and the like. And they over-equipped themselves with clothes and food, pistols and knives.

They traveled by sea, south to Cape Horn at the tip of South America, northwest on the Pacific to California—a journey of 13,000 nautical miles that might take a hundred days by clipper or as long as a year aboard a slower ship. They traveled by way of Panama, crossing the Isthmus in bungo canoes and on mules, only to wait months in Panama City for a ship north. They traveled by land from Arkansas and Missouri to Santa Fe, along the Gila River or through Mexico to Southern California. Or they followed the northern route from Independence—along the Platte, over the Rockies to the Humboldt, across the desert to the foothills of the Sierras and over those mountains to California.

In California, they panned for gold along many rivers—the American, the Yuba, the Feather, the Tuolumne and the Merced, and along all their forks and branches. They came in one popular phrase, to "see the elephant," which was to live life to the fullest, to seize the day, to break the mold of old routines.

Thousands upon thousands came, mostly men, a few women, a few children. There were farmers, gamblers, merchants, doctors, speculators, lawyers, con men, prostitutes. Most were young though a few were old—and forty-five was considered old. Many were well-educated, many naive, some were lucky, most were not.

They were the Forty-Niners.

* * *

The Empire Hotel, two stories of pine logs roofed with cedar shingles, was Hangtown's newest and largest building. It boasted a porch with a balcony on its top. It had six windows in the front alone, two of them paned with glass. The downstairs, other than a hallway designated the lobby, was one huge room housing the saloon and gambling hall; the hotel rooms were all on the second floor. Next to the saloon in an attached building was the store.

"The miners come in," Pamela said, her voice sharp with irritation, "they look at our merchandise, they handle it, but they don't buy it."

"They will," Rhynne told her. "They're testing the water before jumping in."

Pamela dabbed at her nose with her handkerchief. "You told me we'd clear two thousand dollars a month," she said. "We'll be lucky to clear two cents."

Rhynne gave her a calculating glance. "Have you been taking your medicine?"

Pamela looked toward the other end of the store, where Selena toyed with her hair in front of a mirror nailed to the wall. Lowering her voice, she said, "As a matter of fact, no. I've been out of it since two days ago."

Their eyes met. She tried to keep her gaze level under Rhynne's sardonic stare, but could not. How was she to go on? Her entire body ached. She had to force herself to eat food that nauseated her.

"Laudanum, isn't it?" Rhynne asked.

Pamela nodded, then sneezed.

"I'll see what I can do," he told her. Again she glanced toward Selena. Had she overheard?

"Pamela, be of good cheer," Rhynne said in a

louder voice. "The winter's over, spring's upon us. 'Whither is fled your visionary gleam? Where is it now, the glory and the dream?' "

"I think I'd appreciate more customers and less Wordsworth." Pamela tried to smile. "I don't know why I'm so melancholy of late. The rains, I suppose, and this never-ending muck."

"The rains are over, the mud . . . What's this, Pamela?" Rhynne, who had been testing the scales, held up one of the weights.

"The man who sold me the scales called it an 'Indian weight.' "

Rhynne opened the back door and hurled the weight up the rain-gullied hill behind the store. "I'll not abide it," he stormed. "Paying a man half what his gold's worth simply because he's an Indian."

Selena watched Rhynne return, slamming the door. She pulled her golden curls out over her shoulders, finally fastening a large blue bow in the back. All day she'd had a strange feeling that something was about to happen, yet nothing had and she was restless.

"Harry Varner uses Indian weights," she pointed out to Rhynne. "I've seen him." Varner ran Varner's Grocery, Hangtown's first and only other general store.

"Honest Harry Varner." Rhynne sniffed. "He's well-named."

"He frightens me, that Varner, as short as he is. He's always watching me with those rheumy eyes of his."

"If watching you were a crime, Selena, all men would have to be declared guilty."

"Men watch every woman in these god-awful mining camps," Pamela said.

Selena tossed her head. "Harry Varner," she said, "acts as though we're marauding Indians attacking his wagon train. Just because we opened this store."

"He probably sees us that way," Rhynne said.

There were shouts from outside and Rhynne went to the window as a man ran up to the doorway. "It's here," he cried. "It's here. Horobin's wagon is here."

"At last." Rhynne strode outside.

"Mother, do you need me?" Selena asked.

"Go ahead. I'll stay. If I wait long enough, I may sell something, even if it's only a pin."

Selena ran after Rhynne to where a wagon pulled by two mules had been backed against the front of the hotel. The two teamsters were attempting to wrestle down a bulky, blanket-wrapped object—a crate by its appearance—onto two planks laid from the rear of the wagon to the porch.

"Careful," Rhynne shouted. "It's the only one of its kind in all the diggings." The heavy object, some five feet long and four high, tilted dangerously, threatening to topple to the ground. Rhynne sloshed through the mud, put his shoulder to it, and together the three men slid it to the porch.

Rhynne stepped to the top of the porch steps and faced the gathering crowd. "Gentlemen," he called out, "you're just in time for the grand unveiling. Has anyone a knife?" A miner handed him his Bowie knife. Rhynne slashed the ropes and the blankets fell to the planking.

The crowd gaped.

"Never thought I'd see the likes in Hangtown."

"We're becoming right civilized."

"A piano!"

With one finger Rhynne picked out the opening notes of *On Top of Old Smoky*. "That, gentlemen, represents the alpha and omega of my musical repertoire," he said. "Can anyone here play? A piano without a piano player is like a woman without a man."

A miner, tall and thin and bearded like most of the others, was shoved toward the porch. Rhynne reached down and grasped his hand, propelling him up the steps. The man stood in front of the piano, tried a few chords, then struck up *Blue-Tail Fly*. Selena began to sing and one by one the men sang with her, "Jimmie crack corn an' I don't care. . . ."

Grinning, Rhynne turned to the two teamsters, saying, "Inside, inside," and they pushed the piano toward the door, the miner walking sideways beside it still playing it. When they'd shoved and pulled the instrument into the saloon, Rhynne shouted, "Drinks are on the house," which was all the men needed to hear. They trooped past the sign reading NO WEAPONS INSIDE, singing, "Jimmie crack corn an' I don't care, Ol' Massa's gone away. . . ."

Rhynne and Selena stood alone on the porch, listening to the boisterous laughter inside.

"You sing right well," he told her quietly.

"W.W., can I sing tonight? Now that the piano's here?"

"You can as far as I'm concerned."

"You mean Pamela? You know she'd say no."

"Aren't you of an age to make up your own

mind? I personally believe in the efficacy of presenting nay-sayers with a *fait accompli*. Once an egg's broken, like Humpty Dumpty it can't be put back together again."

"I'm afraid, W.W., of what Pamela would say. And what if the men don't like my voice? Though I suppose I should listen to you." She nodded toward the open window. "The piano arriving on the very day we open. You're a wizard."

"No, not a wizard. I'm lucky, have been ever since the day I left New Orleans. When a gambler's lucky he has to ride his luck until it turns and when it turns he has to quit. If you don't quit then, you're liable to go into a slide and before you realize it, you're through."

"And sometimes when a man thinks he's lucky he pushes that luck too far," a man's voice said.

They looked down and saw Harry Varner standing with his foot on the bottom step of the porch.

"Harry," Rhynne called out genially. "Drinks are on the house. We're celebrating the arrival of our new piano and the grand opening of the Empire."

"As you well know, I don't imbibe."

Standing below them, Harry Varner seemed even shorter than his five-feet-three. A moon-faced man with bloodshot eyes, he wore red suspenders and had the habit of hooking his thumbs beneath them, snapping one or the other as he talked.

"You should, Harry," Rhynne told him. "Might do you good. I hold whisky's a better tonic than Doc Braithewaite's blood-letting."

"Whisky's the devil's concoction." Unsmiling, Harry Varner stared straight at Rhynne.

I've never seen him smile, Selena thought. Not once.

"Care to look over our premises?" Rhynne asked.

"I've seen them."

"Like to try your hand at monte? Or perhaps faro's more your style."

"They're games of the devil."

"Then I'm afraid we don't have much to offer you."

Harry glanced at Selena before his eyes returned to Rhynne. "You're going to make a nice bundle with your drinks and your card games. Men's persuasions unfortunately being what they are."

"I expect to turn a fair profit. I deserve one. I've got a big investment in the Empire."

"I heard tell your store's not doing too well."

"It's only the first day, Harry. I'm a patient man."

"I concede patience is a virtue."

"As is charity. Faith, hope and charity, these three. And the greatest of them is charity. At times I think you could stand more charity, Harry."

Varner harrumphed. "Even the devil can quote scripture."

"And we all hope and pray it will help lead him to righteousness when he does."

"You don't really need the store, Rhynne. Soon you'll be looking around for more space for your hotel. You could easy tear out the wall and expand into where the store is now. You know and I know Hangtown's not big enough for two stores selling the selfsame provisions."

"And you were here first, eh, Harry? Sort of squatter's rights?"

"I was about to say something like that, yes. I *was* here first."

"Listen!" Rhynne swept his hand in a great arc encompassing the town around them. "Tell me what you hear."

"I hear Jessop's wagon hauling a load of logs. I hear chopping where they're building Felton's cabin down by the church. I hear shouts of drunken revelry from inside the place where you worship Mammon."

"You're wrong," Rhynne said softly. "This isn't my place of worship. When I want to be near my maker, I go among the young. They're still unspoiled. Or I go into the forest. 'Knowing that Nature never did betray the heart that loved her.' Harry, you're a sly devil yourself. I was about to reveal a truth to you and now see how you've derailed me."

"I don't think I ever heard a man talk more and say less than you do, Rhynne."

"What I was trying to point out was that there's building going on all around us. Hangtown's growing. There'll be room for both of us here, Harry, if you'll be patient."

Varner repeated slowly, "The town's not big enough for two stores."

"I can recommend a teamster with reasonable rates if you're planning to move on."

Harry kicked the porch step with his boot. "This

pine makes fine kindling. Once a fire gets started there's no stopping it. A fire could burn you out, Rhynne. I'd hate to wake in the night to the clanging of the bell and find the Empire aflame."

"Harry, if I didn't know you for a simple God-fearing man, I'd suspect you were trying to tell me something. That you were speaking in parables. Knowing you, though, I realize you're just chatting with me, passing the time of day."

"You can think what you like. Some folks think because I'm short they can take advantage. Run all over me. I'm telling you, Rhynne, they're mistaken."

"When I was a youngster in New Orleans," Rhynne said, "I traveled among men of evil and I learned evil ways, one of those ways being the knowledge of the game of skill and chance called poker. And as the fates would have it, I became adept at the game, or thought I had, and I gathered much money unto myself from the purses of my fellow men. I became, I'm afraid, puffed up and proud.

"I went to the Bayou Hotel where men even more evil than myself lived and played this game called poker in the back parlors. Being young I entered their smoke-infested gambling hells and challenged them at this pastime at which I had become skilled. Lo, in the space of two nights and one day, I was parted from my wealth, becoming in the process a much poorer and a much wiser man. And the lesson I learned was this: Don't bite off more than you can chew. And I pass the moral along to any who may have use of it. Don't bite off more than you can chew, Mr. Varner."

Varner snapped his suspenders. "It's been a rare pleasure talking to you, Rhynne," he said. "Miss." He nodded to Selena, who looked away.

"Likewise," Rhynne said.

They watched Varner talk off along the street in the direction of his grocery.

"Did he mean he'd actually try to burn down the Empire?" Selena asked. "Do you think he would?"

"Man is capable of infinite evil, Selena."

"Mr. Rhynne!" She tugged at his sleeve impatiently. He looked down at her with his dark eyes. "Not with me, Mr. Rhynne, don't play your games with me. Talk straight."

"Selena, you constantly surprise me. What a woman you'll be one day. I hope I'm around to see you then."

"I *am* a woman."

"No, you're on the brink of becoming one. To be a woman you must have loved and lost and learned to love again."

"Wordsworth?"

"No, W.W. Rhynne. To answer your question straight out, Selena, yes, Harry Varner's capable of burning down the Empire, or trying to at least. If he was pressed hard enough he'd be capable of burning this town down. He's a Sunday Christian. In return for his obeisance and his tithing, God is supposed to give Harry Varner a twenty-fold return. If Harry doesn't get it, he'll claim the dealer's stacked the deck. In this case, I'm the dealer."

Selena walked to the edge of the porch and looked up at the sun shining through wispy cloud remnants scattered across the great arch of the California sky.

"Oh, Rhynne," she said, "why must men be so petty and mean-spirited in such a glorious country? On such a glorious day?" She stood on tiptoe, her arms reaching upward as though to touch the sky.

He looked up and down the length of her body, half-smiled, then sighed and turned on his heel. "I'm needed inside," he said, leaving her abruptly.

Looking after him, Selena put her hands on her hips. They had told her in San Francisco that W.W. Rhynne was an evil man. Her mother had warned her time and again about him. But he didn't seem evil to her. Devious, perhaps, yet he worked hard, he was careful and patient. Quick to correct her though equally ready with a compliment. Certainly not evil. Selena frowned. She was a little, just a little, she told herself, disappointed.

8

Selena waited until her mother was asleep before she slipped from her bed to put on her new pale green gown. Although she couldn't see the dress in the darkness of the cabin, she knew the snug bodice flattered her. The neckline dipped in a bold V; she was saved from immodesty only by a lace chemisette covering her from breasts to throat.

If only she had a crinoline. Pamela had sent for one but it hadn't yet arrived and she hadn't found anything she could use in its stead. She didn't quite dare to borrow her mother's only remaining petticoat. The lack caused the green gown to outline her hips in a manner that made her feel both uneasy and daring.

She eased open the door—a piece of canvas stretched over a wooden frame—and went out into the cool night. The town lay silent around her except for distant shouts and singing from the Empire. When Pamela had insisted they have a cabin of their own, Selena had objected, wanting to live at the Empire as Rhynne did. Pamela had been firm and now, listening to the distant tumult, Selena admitted her mother had been right.

Holding her skirt off the ground, she started up the path beside the muddy road, the air around her sharp with the scent of sawn pine. The valley and nearby hills had been denuded of trees to build Hangtown.

Footsteps came toward her. Selena retreated into the shadow of a cabin as a man, muttering to himself in a gruff and slurred voice, lurched down the path. "Hangtown gals," he sang, "Hangtown gals," repeating the words over and over as though he didn't know the rest of the song or maybe was satisfied with just the first two words.

Selena drew back as he came near her hiding place. He stumbled, cursed, then went on without looking either right or left, intent only on finding his way home. As soon as he was gone Selena hurried on, the noise growing louder as she neared the Empire. The road swung to the left and she saw the hotel.

In the daytime, the Empire was a dowdy matron. Now, with two torches flaring outside the entrance and with the lower windows glowing a deep red, she was an enticing lady of the evening, luring men with the promise of forbidden delights.

While Selena watched from the road, the door opened and two men appeared. Abe Greene, Rhynne's barman, held a miner's arm twisted behind his back and was shoving him across the porch. When the miner tried to grab the rail, Abe hurled him down the steps to sprawl in the street. Then he shouted something Selena couldn't hear and went back inside. The man got up, brushed himself off, and wandered into the night.

Selena almost turned to flee back to the cabin. No, she told herself, she was no longer a child, no matter what Rhynne thought. Drawing a deep breath, she walked quickly past the store and around to the hotel's small back stoop. She opened the door and had to step back as she was assailed by the stench of smoke and stale liquor. She blinked and peered inside. Though the oil-lit chandeliers burned brightly over the gaming tables and the bar, the periphery of the room was shadowed, making it seem much larger and grander than she knew it was.

She was beginning to cringe from the curious eyes of the men when Abe Greene spotted her in the doorway. "Miss Selena," he said, coming toward her from behind the bar. "What are you doing here?"

"I'd like to see Mr. Rhynne, Abe. Please tell him."

Abe nodded, turning away, and Selena stepped outside and waited. In a few minutes Rhynne appeared in the doorway, hat on, wearing a red vest beneath his frock coat, a cigarillo in his hand.

"You asked after me, Miss Selena?" He was not surprised at seeing her; he looked almost as if he'd been expecting her.

"I've come to . . . to sing," she told him hesitatingly.

"Are you sure you want to?"

Just then voices were raised behind him. A man

cursed. Rhynne glanced over his shoulder but after a moment the voices subsided and he looked down at Selena again.

"Are you certain you wouldn't prefer to go home and be tucked safely in bed?" To Selena, the words sounded like a challenge.

"No," she said, angry now. "I'm here to sing. I can sing, you know."

"Not looking like that. Not here."

She glanced down to see if her dress, put on so hastily in the dark, was in disarray. "There's nothing wrong with the way I look," she told him.

"That lace what-do-you-call-it"—he flicked at the chemisette with his finger—"makes you look like a lady schoolmarm."

Her hand came up between her breasts. "I'd be practically unclothed without it," she said. She pictured herself without the chemisette, the deep V of her neckline revealing the paleness of her skin against the soft green of the dress. Did she dare?

Rhynne smiled at her as though he read her thoughts.

"Wait," she told him. She walked around the corner of the hotel and there slipped the arms of the dress from her shoulders and pulled the chemisette over her head. After rearranging the dress, she came back and folded and laid the lace on a table outside the door. She patted her hair smooth.

"All right?" she asked. Feeling his eyes on her breasts, she blushed but forced herself to stand without flinching.

Rhynne held out his hand. "Come with me," he said.

He led her across the room, past the bar and the card tables to the piano. The men stopped to stare after her. "Give me a flourish, if you please, Ned," Rhynne said to the piano player.

The room quieted except for two men quarreling at the bar and, when someone shouted at them, they too fell silent.

Selena wanted to turn and run. Trembling, she stood facing the roomful of men. There were so many of them, drunken, sober, leering. Their flushed faces, ranged around her, closing her in, seemed to threaten her. Her head swam. When she tried to breathe deeply she coughed from the smoke.

Look at one of them, she told herself firmly, just one. You don't have to sing to all of them, only to one.

There, that one.

He stared at her from the far end of the bar with adoration evident in his eyes. Wavy black hair, a boyish clean-shaven face. He was young, probably her own age. He was not actually good-looking, yet there was something about him that attracted her, an innocence, a vulnerability that made her want to please him. If only he wouldn't stare so! His eyes. Were they green? They must be green.

If no one else liked her singing, she decided, he would. She would sing to him and for him.

"Do you know *The Girl I Left Behind Me?*" Ned asked. Selena nodded.

Rhynne threw up his hand. "Gentlemen," he shouted. "I give you—Selena."

The pianist began to play and, standing stiffly

beside him, she sang to the black-haired, green-eyed young man:

> *"I heard of California gold,*
> *I thought I'd go and try it;*
> *And foolishly I left my home,*
> *I surely can't deny it."*

The black-haired youth frowned. Didn't he like her voice? Didn't he like *her?* She faltered but went on. He wasn't watching her anymore, had turned to the blond-bearded man beside him. What was he doing now? He'd seized the blond man by the throat; they were flailing at each other.

Abe tried to pull them apart. The boy swung at Abe. Men pushed forward, shouting and craning their necks, trying to see what was going on. Ned played louder, Selena stopped singing, tears in her eyes. She saw Rhynne dart across the room toward the bar.

Rhynne stepped between the two fighting men, grasping each by the arm and hustling them out the front door past the gun table. "Now then," he said once they were on the porch. "What's this all about?"

They both tried to speak at once.

"One at a time. You first." Rhynne nodded to the youth. "I've never seen you around these parts before. What's your name, son?"

"Danny O'Lee," the boy said staunchly. "This bastard here insulted her, he insulted the lass. Selena."

"The mick's a liar. I was paying her a compliment, governor, when all of a sudden this one's at my throat."

"You're English Bob, aren't you?" Rhynne asked.

"All the chaps call me that."

"Now listen to me," Rhynne said. "I'm not about to let myself get the reputation for running a rowdy establishment. You can have a good time at the Empire, yes. A bit of noise is all right, but brawling, no. Men don't buy spirits or play faro when they're fighting. I'll decide the merits of this quarrel or else both of you are through here. Banished for good. Do you agree?"

"That's all right with me, mate," English Bob said.

Danny nodded.

"You first, O'Lee. Tell me what happened."

"Like I said, I was standing at the bar listening to the young lady sing, thinking she's singing to me, she is, when this bloody Englishman says, 'I'd give two hundred dollars to get between the sheets with that wench.' So I says to him, 'Take that back,' and he says to me, 'Take what back?' and I says, 'What you just said,' and he says, 'Fuck you.' So I made a grab for him and that's all there is to it."

"English Bob?"

"I thought we'd be hearing a bit of the blarney from this lad but that's the size of it. I was complimenting the young lady on her charm like the lad here says and for no reason at all he was at my throat."

"Danny," Rhynne said, "English Bob was paying Selena a compliment. After his own fashion. You owe him an apology."

"You'll see me in hell first."

"Enough." Rhynne's voice became steel. "You gave me your word, son. You'll apologize."

Danny met Rhynne's eyes and then his glance fell away. "Sorry," he said to English Bob.

"That's all right, bucko. No hard feelings." They shook hands and started for the door.

"Just a minute," Rhynne said, as English Bob went back inside. "Listen to me. It's not so much a man's words that count, it's the meaning behind them. Learn the difference. I've been called a son of a bitch by a man who wanted me to know he considered me his boon companion, and I've been called a son of a bitch by a bastard who meant I was a son of a bitch. To his way of thinking, English Bob couldn't have paid Selena a greater compliment than saying he'd pay two hundred dollars for her."

Rhynne, who had been reaching for the door latch, suddenly stopped and stared straight ahead.

"Are you all right?" Danny asked.

"All right?" Rhynne smiled. "I've never been better. I just caught sight of an idea that glittered like gold. I fear that when money is mentioned, I lose interest in most other matters. Ah, the music's started again. Inside with you, Danny O'Lee."

Rhynne put his hand on Danny's shoulder and together they reentered the Empire. The men, crowding around the piano, had their backs to them. Rhynne raised his eyebrows when he saw Selena perched on top of the piano with her skirts drawn up to reveal her crossed ankles.

"Another chorus," English Bob called and Selena sang:

"Hangtown gals are plump and rosy
Hair in ringlets, mighty cozy,
Painted cheeks and jossy bonnets—
Touch 'em and they'll sting like hornets!"

The men joined in and when the song was over they waved their hats and cheered.

Something struck Selena's shoulder. "What are they throwing?" she asked Ned.

"Gold. They're throwing nuggets. Pick them up."

Selena looked down at the nuggets scattered on the floor.

"No," she said, "no, I won't. Abe will. Abe can pick them up and give them to me later. I won't be seen on my hands and knees scrabbling for money."

The piano player shrugged. "They want more," he said. "Which tune will it be?"

"It won't be any tune." Rhynne stood beside them. "Leave them unsatisfied," he said. "Leave them wanting more."

Rhynne raised his arms toward her and Selena, smiling and waving at the clamoring men, slid from the piano. She took his arm and the miners cleared a path for them to the door. She walked close beside Rhynne, her heart thudding, repeating over and over to herself, they like me, they like me.

Selena woke much later with a clanging in her ears. She sat up, her head awhirl from the singing and the cheers of the men, reliving the elation she had felt as she looked down into the admiring faces from her perch on the piano.

That clanging. The fire bell! She threw off the blankets and ran to the window. Drew aside the red calico curtain. The sky glowed orange. Fire!

With a sinking feeling she recalled Varner's threats to burn the Empire.

"Mother, mother," she cried, shaking Pamela. Her mother groaned in her sleep. She shook her until Pamela sat up.

"Get up, get up," Selena said. "The Empire's on fire!"

Selena threw a robe over her nightgown, pulled a shawl around her shoulders. Behind her Pamela was sleepily getting out of bed. Selena ran out into the night and up the path leading to the hotel. Shouting men ran past her. She heard the crackle of flames.

When she reached the top of the first rise she realized something was wrong, not the way she thought it would be. The flames came not from ahead but from off to her right. Not the Empire! She ran on. No, not the Empire—the hotel stood dark against the sky.

Breathing a sigh of relief, she slowed, following the men hurrying along the street. Flames shot skyward from a building ahead of her. The church? The stable? Not the church, for there was the cross at the peak of the roof. Not the stable either; the stable was farther on.

"It's Varner's," a voice next to her shouted.

She left the road and climbed to the top of a rise from which she could look down at the burning building. It *was* Varner's. The log grocery was engulfed in flames. Men had formed two long lines on the street and were passing buckets from hand to hand, throwing the water on the nearby cabins and the church. It was too late to save Varner's.

Selena noticed a figure in the shadows near her. A familiar figure. Rhynne. She walked to him, seeing his eyes flick toward her then return to the blaze. The firelight gave his face an unearthly appearance.

"Rhynne?" she said tentatively.

"Did I congratulate you on your triumph tonight?" he asked, still not looking at her.

"No," she said in a hushed voice.

"You deserve to be congratulated. We both do." For the first time he looked down at her. "You'd think," he mused, "worried as Varner was about fire, he'd have taken greater precautions."

She felt a shiver of fear.

Rhynne leaned down and kissed her on the mouth. His lips were cold on hers, without passion. She shrank away, then turned and ran. When she paused, out of breath, to look back, Rhynne was again staring down at the flames. She couldn't be sure but she thought she saw him smile.

9

Pamela made her morning toilette with no special quietness but Selana didn't rouse. When she was ready to leave for the store, Pamela shook her daughter awake.

"Get up and bar the door after me, Selana," she said. "After all the commotion last night I wouldn't feel safe otherwise."

As Pamela walked up the path toward the Empire, she noticed the stench of burned timber was still in the air. But the sun was out and a multitude of golden butterflies fluttered in the clearing, birds chirped and called, and bushes near the trail had blossomed out in showy pink. She must ask Reverend Colton what they were.

She realized she'd put the burning of Varner's store out of her thoughts. W.W. was her partner; she refused to think ill of him. Pamela sighed, knowing she had ignored many things in the last few years that she would never have countenanced back home in England. But survival came first! Not only hers. Selena's as well.

Three blue-shirted miners approached, gallantly stepping off the wooden planks into the mud as they neared her.

"Morning ma'am," they said almost in unison.

"Good morning," she answered.

In front of the Empire a small group of men were gathered in a loose circle, all talking loudly.

"I say we ought to run 'em out of Hangtown. Bastard foreigners."

"Yeah, but did they have it in for Vanner any more than some others I could name?"

"You a greaser lover, Lou? You like them stinking Spanish Chilenos?"

"Hell, Harry cheated all of us when he could, you know that. And you better think twice afore you call me names, Pike. Just 'cause I got a Kanaka for a partner you ain't got no right to . . .."

"Nothing wrong with Kui. Hell, we all like him. It's them others."

"Good morning, gentlemen," Pamela said, coming up to them. "It's good to see the sunshine, isn't it?"

They greeted her, standing silent while she unlocked the door to the store. But before she'd closed herself inside, they'd started up again.

Pamela's first customer was a Digger Indian clad in a dirty white sheet he'd draped about himself after the fashion of a Roman toga. She couldn't help but smile at the Indian's incongruous appearance as she weighed his gold. He stared at her from unreadable dark eyes. What did he think about all the people who'd suddenly appeared in his territory? He showed no emotion, but what smoldered underneath? Surely resentment at the very least.

A leather thong was tied across his forehead and knotted at the back, the thong decorated with red and blue beads. She wondered if the beads had any significance. More than likely not—some sharp Yankee trader had probably given them to him in exchange for gold.

Shortly after the Indian had carried off his provisions, Rhynne came in.

"I see you're doing business early," he said.

"I suspect we both know the reason why."

He shrugged. "At least that brave got an honest measure."

"But did Harry?"

"Vengeance is mine, sayeth the Lord."

Pamela raised her eyebrows. "As long as God didn't have help. I heard some of the miners outside blaming the Chilenos. They spoke of running them out of town."

"The boys do get carried away. Sometimes I think the old Spanish proverb says it about right: Children speak in Italian, ladies in French, God in Spanish and the devil in English."

"Certainly I've heard many of the devil's words in English since I've come to California. However, I suspect that if my Spanish was better I'd hear the same words in that language. Men are men."

"I fear that's true. We stand abject before you."

"W.W., you've never stood abject before anyone in your life."

"I haven't met many ladies," Rhynne said. "However, what I came over to tell you was that the boys will be having a wake for old Matt Murphy tonight and I suggest that Selena stay at home with you."

"Matt? He's the one who fell into the mining pit?"

"Coyote holes they call them in these parts. Matt was too clever for his own good. This hole was filled with water and Matt was paid to pump it out. Not having a pump, he killed a dog and threw the body into the hole."

"What on earth for?"

"He left dog's blood around the hole, so as far as we can figure out he intended to report the blood. 'A man's been murdered and drowned,' he'd say and when we all pumped the hole dry we'd find the dog and Matt would have earned his fee. Unfortunately for Matt, he'd had a few drops to drink and threw himself into the hole along with the dog."

"But why should you tell me to keep Selena home? She's always home at night."

"Because when men settle in around a twenty-gallon keg of brandy with quart dippers for glasses, they aren't likely to be responsible for their actions. And since the wake isn't being held at the Empire, I'll have no control over them."

"You haven't answered my question."

"Selena sang at the Empire last night, Pamela. She was, to put it mildly, a sensation. The men loved her, didn't want her to stop."

Pamela's hand rose to her mouth.

"Oh, come, Pamela, you must have known she'd defy you sooner or later. What's wrong with her performing there? I'm on hand as well as Abe and Ned. Besides, the miners themselves wouldn't harm a hair of her head. They look at her and dream, yes, but if one of them tried to hurt her the others would kill him then and there."

"It's demeaning. I won't have them gawking at her."

"Then what *is* Selena to do? Have you thought of that, Pamela?"

"She'll assist me in the store."

"But the store is yours. Ours. What does Selena have? She's not a child; she's a beautiful young woman. Every man who sees her desires her, to put it bluntly. How long will it be before she finds one who interests her? Do you want that to happen? In Hangtown?"

"Of course not. There's no one even remotely suitable for Selena here."

"That's my point exactly. Let her be the toast of the Empire, give her something of her own, some acclaim, and she won't need a man. She won't need one man when she's adored by hundreds."

"I don't like it."

"You'd do well to accept it, though. But I don't want her out tonight. Keep her home with you."

Selena came out into the sunlit afternoon, shutting the cabin door behind her. She yawned and stretched, then laughed as a chipmunk flicked his tail at her and fled from sight. She was in no hurry to go to the store since she'd yet to tell her mother about last night. Not the fact that she intended to continue singing at the Empire. She hugged herself recalling the excited praise of the miners. Even Mr. Rhynne said she'd done well.

Her arms dropped and she frowned. Had Rhynne set the fire at Varner's?

The sound of voices caught her attention. She climbed onto a knoll in back of the cabin and looked toward town. A procession was headed her way, twenty or more miners, some of whom seemed to be carrying a box or crate of some kind. As they came closer she saw it was a rude, unpainted coffin. There was no pall or bier, only ropes passed under the pine box. She shuddered; she hated to be reminded of death.

The first of the men looked up and saw her.

"Howdy, Miss Selena," he said. "You sure were a treat to hear last night."

"Thank you." She nodded to the coffin. "Whose funeral is it?"

"Matt Murphy. But we don't aim to bury him yet. Got to have the wake first down to his cabin. Can't put an Irishman in the ground without the wake."

He waved and went on. Most of the others raised their hats to her as they passed.

She scrambled down from the hill and wandered to the creek below, avoiding the holes where men had dug for gold. She amused herself for a time waving branches at the grizzly cubs Tiny Johnson was trying to tame. He'd killed their mother and kept the cubs tied to a pine by the stream, hoping to raise them and make his fortune exhibiting them in the East.

Ah well, it was no more ridiculous than many other dreams. The little bears were ungainly but still young enough to be cute as they swatted and chomped at the branch she teased them with.

The admiration of the miners made her feel a

little like she had when Diego held her in his arms. Would she ever have a man to love and marry? Certainly Pamela expected her to marry well and she had no objection to that. But right now she wanted . . . she wanted love. Love and being held and caressed. She wanted someone to love her to desperation.

Still—who? Not one of the miners! Her nose crinkled. Although that black-haired young man last night *had* been appealing. At least before he'd acted like such a rowdy, nearly ruining her performance.

"Selena!"

She looked up to see her mother standing on the path above the creek.

"Come to the cabin at once," Pamela told her.

As Selena tossed the branch away and started up the bank, the sun disappeared behind a cloud. I *will* go on singing at the Empire, she told herself. I know mother isn't well, that she has to take medicine, but I must have a life of my own.

When they were inside the cabin, Pamela faced her. "You deliberately deceived me. I won't have such behavior!"

"Oh, mother, I'm not a child. I had every intention of talking the matter over with you today. But don't tell me you won't have it, because I'm going to sing at the Empire anyway."

"I object to the secrecy and deception more than the singing. Can't I trust you, Selena?"

"Not if you always oppose me."

"Well, you shan't sing tonight. Mr. Rhynne tells me it won't be safe for us to be out after dark. It seems there's a wake for . . ."

"I'm aware of Matt Murphy's wake. Why

should that affect my singing at the Empire? You've talked to Mr. Rhynne, haven't you? You've convinced him I shouldn't sing again." Selena began to cry.

"That isn't the way it was at all, Selena. Calm down and listen to me."

Selena turned away from her mother and covered her ears with her hands. "I won't. Don't talk to me any more. I refuse to listen." She threw herself on her bed and sobbed.

That night, Selena raised her head from her pillow and listened. Pamela was asleep. Usually she slept heavily, but Selena double-checked her mother's breathing, which was deep and regular. She eased herself from her bed then and stood upright in the dark cabin. She'd fallen asleep for a while herself—what time could it be? Not too late to slip away to the Empire at any rate. W.W. couldn't refuse to let her sing once she'd begun. She'd simply walk up to Ned and say, *"The Minstrel Boy,* please"—that was always a good song to bring a tear to the eye—and the miners wouldn't let anyone stop her.

She put on the pale green gown again, leaving off the chemisette, put her white shawl around her shoulders and quietly let herself out of the cabin.

Danny O'Lee put the dipper back on the plank table and stood up. If he stayed longer he'd have to fill it again and already his head spun with the brandy he'd downed. Would he ever learn to hold his drink?

He'd come to help speed old Matt on to the next

world, though what that world might be like he didn't know, for all the priests said. He'd had his drink for Matt and sung a song and it was better to go now. He'd scarcely known the man, but any son of the old sod deserved a decent send-off.

"You're not leaving so soon?"

Danny turned to English Bob with a grin.

"Sure, mate. You wouldn't deny a man has to relieve himself?"

English Bob grinned back and waved his hand. "Be my guest, Danny me boy. Never let it be said an Englishman kept an Irish lad from his appointed duties."

Out in the darkness with the chill damp wind in his face, Danny's head cleared. He looked back at the light spilling from the open door of Matt's cabin and heard the shouts and laughter. He was tempted to go back. Instead he sat on a pine stump. Bob was likely to need a bit of help getting home tonight and better he should stay sober and see to him than have the Englishman die in a coyote hole like poor Matt.

Off in the pines an owl hooted. From the creek came the shrill jabber of frogs. The night held the threat of rain but it was unmistakenly spring, the time a lad should have a lass to lie with. And when would that happen up in these mountains where women were scarcer than gold? Especially when the woman he coveted was the most beautiful colleen ever born? And he with barely enough money to feed his belly each day?

A man stumbled out of Matt's cabin, then another and another. Danny recognized the voice of a newcomer to Hangtown, a man named Pike he didn't much cotton to.

"I say we go and get the stinking bastards, put 'em to the whip and make 'em confess what they done."

More men spilled from the open door. There was a drunken chorus of agreement.

"Run every foreigner out of town."

"Hanging's too good for 'em."

"Ain't they got a woman or two up there?" Danny recognized English Bob's voice. "We could have some fun, damned if we couldn't."

"On to Spanish Ravine!" someone shouted.

Danny rose from the stump. No more use trying to talk sense to drunkards than to tell the creek to flow backwards. He'd best go up to the ravine and warn the Chilenos.

Not that they'd listen to him either. A great bloody brawl it shaped up to be, but at least their women could get away. And perhaps on the way back he could dissuade English Bob, though short of bashing him on the head it wasn't likely.

Danny set off on a trot.

He ran down the path toward town. The half-moon slid from behind a cloud and he saw his way clearly in the silver light. He also saw the back of a skirted figure ahead of him and his breath caught in his throat. Whoever she was, no woman would be safe from that mob behind her. He increased his pace.

Selena heard running footsteps and turned just as the man came close enough to grasp her arm. She screamed.

"Shut up, you fool!" Danny gasped, out of breath. "Wherever you live, get home quick!" Then, recognizing her, he instantly let go and stepped back. "Miss Selena! For God's sake, get back to your cabin."

"Who are you? You have no right to order me about."

"My name's Danny O'Lee and I've no time to argue." Already he could hear the shouts of the men.

He pulled at Selena's arm. "Hurry."

She pulled as urgently in the other direction. "I'm going to the Empire to sing and neither you nor anyone else can stop me. Take your hands off my arm this instant."

"You can't go there tonight. There may be a riot." He tried to pick her up and she struck at him, writhing away. In exasperation he shook her so hard her teeth clicked together.

"Which is your cabin?" he demanded.

"Let me go!"

"If you don't tell me I'll have to drag you off into the woods to keep you safe. I'm warning you."

"You can't make me . . ."

He grabbed her around the waist and hoisted her over his shoulder, one hand holding her knee, one her wrist. She was momentarily quiet with shock and outrage as he stumbled back along the trail in the pitch dark, the moon once again hidden. When he rounded a turn, the torches coming toward them were plain to see. Snatches of bawdy songs swept along to them on the breeze.

"You see," he panted. "They're drunk and up to no good, and you can get plenty hurt."

"It's the next cabin," Selena whispered.

At last he was there. Unceremoniously he

dumped her to the ground, yanked open the door and shoved her inside. "Stay there," he ordered.

"I'll get even with you, Danny O'Lee," she said, angered by his brashness. "I'll get even with you if it's the last thing I do."

He shut the door. What a spirited lass! But he was afraid she still hadn't realized her danger or that what he'd done had been for the best. Why, he couldn't bear to think of Selena touched by any man in that mob. And worse than touched, the way they were tonight. Had she no sense?

Danny waited for the drunken men by the cabin, taking no chances. Rain began to fall, and by the time the first few reached him, the rain had increased. It threatened to become a gully-washer.

Danny stepped out from beside the cabin. "Sure and it's back to that keg of brandy I'm heading," he shouted in his best brogue. "Who's for having another drink to keep out the cold and damp? Bob, me bucko, are you with me?"

"Danny, is it you?" English Bob called.

Danny wiped the rain from his face and made his way to Bob. The men had stopped and were milling about uncertainly. "Come along, mate," he said. "On to the brandy and I'll drink you under the table."

"It'll take more than one Irish bastard to do that," Bob warned.

Danny took Bob's arm and turned toward Matt's cabin.

"Hell, I could use another dipperful meself," someone said hesitantly.

"I'm for going back," another voice put in. "We barely broached that damn keg."

"Old Matt's snug and warm in the coffin, which is more than I am," another muttered. "I had my fill of rain this past winter."

Danny took a deep breath and started off, English Bob beside him. Behind him the men fell into a straggled line. Like as not now he'd have to drink till he passed out but it would be worth it. He'd saved Selena. And the bloody Chilenos, too, come to think of it.

He looked up, letting the rain strike him full in the face. With a little help from heaven, of course.

10

Pamela climbed the stairs to the hotel's second floor and tapped on Rhynne's door.

"Come in," he called.

By the time she opened the door W.W. had pushed his chair away from his desk. In his left hand he held a short-barreled pistol she recognized as a derringer. When he saw her he tucked the gun inside his coat and rose with a sweeping bow.

"Were you expecting Harry Varner?" she asked, nodding to the bulge made by the derringer.

"I prefer not to take chances. Honest Harry made some rather wild accusations after the fire."

"Reverend Colton told me Mr. Varner had disappeared. He seemed to think the man went back to San Francisco.

"Another story," Rhynne said, "has him holed up in a mountain cabin panning for gold."

For a moment she considered asking Rhynne outright if he, in fact, had burned Varner's store. She remembered her father's words: "Pam, when a crime's been committed, ask yourself one question. Who benefits most? Nine times out of ten you've named the guilty party."

"It's clear that we were the chief beneficiaries of the fire," she said carefully. "Now that we have the only store, we have almost more business than we can accommodate."

Rhynne gestured toward the papers on his desk. "You're quite correct. According to the figures from both the store and the hotel, my original estimate of our profits will prove modest."

"There's so much business I need another clerk."

"You have Selena."

"W.W., that's the main reason I came up here this morning. I see less and less of Selena. She sleeps late after singing at the hotel, then, when she finally gets out of bed, she's either taking piano lessons from Ned or else practicing her new songs. She's hardly any help to me in the store at all."

"She's happy, Pamela. Have you noticed the way her face glows?"

Pamela put her hand on the desk and leaned toward him. "How long will that last? She's satisfied now, singing in this out-of-the-way corner of the world, but will that be good enough for her tomorrow? And what will she have when all this is over? Nothing."

"Do you remember what it was like to be Selena's age? Leave her alone, Pamela. Let your daughter go. You have to let her make her own mistakes, make her own life for herself. 'Bliss was it in that dawn to be alive, but to be young was very heaven!' "

"Stop it!" Pamela's voice roise. "You're the one who's responsible, W.W. You and you alone. You give her whatever she wants. You encourage her to defy me, her own mother. You don't know what Selena's capable of. I'll have no more of it."

"What are you afraid of, Pamela? That your daughter will surpass you? That she'll manage to wring more from life than you have? You're a lovely woman but you're in danger of becoming a dried-up shrew. A bitch."

"How dare you talk to me like that? You, a common gambler, a—a whoremaster!"

Rhynne picked the quill from his desk and hurled the pen against the far wall. It fell onto the blanket covering his narrow cot.

"Pamela," he said, his voice deathly quiet. "I was getting ready to write to a friend in Frisco. I don't believe I've ever told you about him. His name's Charlie Sung and he's beholden to me. I was writing for you, Pamela. You can't have much laudanum left by now. You don't, do you?"

She lowered her head. "Enough for three days, four at the most."

"Charlie Sung, of course, is a celestial. He has ways of satisfying the most unlikely requests, ways not available to the rest of us."

"If you knew the torment I suffer. How ill I am without the medicine."

"Do you know what Doc Braithewaite calls

laudanum? G.O.M.—God's Own Medicine. Do you know what I call it, Pamela? I call it opium, for that's what it is."

"I don't care what Samuel Braithewaite calls it and I don't care what you call it!" Pamela turned her face from him and lowered her voice. "I need the medicine."

"Then remember this. I'm the only one in Hangtown who can get it for you. Braithewaite's in short supply; I asked him. The shipments from the east coast aren't adequate. The price in Frisco is astronomical."

Rhynne put his hand on her shoulder. "Forgive me for causing you distress, Pamela. We're partners but you're more to me than that. I have a deep affection for you." His fingers traced small circles on her upper arm. "Look at me, Pamela. Don't hide your face, look at me."

Reluctantly she looked up, not wanting him to see her crying. He took her in his arms and she rested her head on his shoulder.

"It's all right, Pamela," he soothed her. "Even the strongest women cry." His palm rubbed her back as she sobbed against him and despite herself, she felt a stirring, a need. A need so long denied.

She stepped away, drying her eyes with her handkerchief. "I'll be late opening the store if I don't go," she said.

She saw him glance down at his pocket watch on the desk. The store wasn't supposed to open for another half hour, but he said nothing. Pamela stopped at the door, hesitating before she spoke.

"You will write to your friend? To Charlie Sung?"

"Of course I will."

She closed he door. Hating him. Hating herself. Hating her need for him.

When Pamela found the lobby of the hotel deserted, she placed her carrying bag on the counter and listened for the sound of footsteps. Hearing none, she took out the laudanum bottle and a whisky glass, filled the glass half full and drank it. She stood, breathing hard, waiting for the exhilaration she knew would come.

By the time she walked into the street she felt better. So much better that she was able to smile almost gaily at the young man sitting on the log railing in front of the store.

"I'll be open in a minute," she told him, taking the key from her bag.

"To see such a pretty face, I'd gladly wait the rest of the day," he said.

"Enough of your blarney." She preceded him into the store and sat on the stool behind her desk.

"And how in the name of all the saints does everyone know I'm Irish?" said Danny O'Lee.

Pamela looked at his face and smiled. He couldn't be anything but Irish. She remembered him now. Danny O'Lee. "A wild Irish boy," Selena had called him. "I sang for him, for him alone, and what did he do? Started a great brawl. And there's more besides, but never mind that. I never want to set eyes on him again. Do you know, Mr. Rhynne suspects O'Lee isn't even his real name? Who knows what crimes he might have committed back in the States?"

Pamela smiled, trying to imagine the misdeeds this devil-may-care lad could be guilty of. Nothing more serious than breaking a few colleens' hearts, she was sure.

"And have you the luck of the Irish?" she asked him.

Shoving aside a stack of tinned beef, Danny sat on a counter facing her. "That I do not. For three weeks I've been at the diggings here and around Coloma and all I have to show for it is eighteen dollars and fifty cents. I could earn as much in a day by pounding nails into boards in town."

"The luck I referred to was with the lasses."

"If lasses were gold, I wouldn't have even the eighteen dollars and fifty cents. I'd have nothing.' Color rose to his neck and face.

Pamela didn't know what to say. "Well, you're a fine-looking lad," she told him comfortingly. But this only seemed to increase his confusion, so she opened her ledger and wrote the day's date at the top of a new page.

"I thought you might be able to help me," he said at last. She stopped writing to look up at him.

"And how might I do that?"

"Let me tell you how it's been with me these last weeks. I staked a claim and I panned for gold and there was nothing in the stream so I moved on and still there was nothing. So the next week I joined up with English Bob, he being a friend of mine, and we built a cradle. Took us all of one day it did. Then we took turns with one of us shoveling the sand and gravel into the cradle while the other poured in the water and rocked it. I'm not complaining, but it was a hard week's work. Point is, between us we made thirty-seven dollars what with gold at fourteen dollars to the ounce,

and half of that was Bob's. We split up then, Bob
and me, and I went down the south fork of the
river looking for where the diggings might be
good. Yet whenever I asked, 'Any luck, mate?'
the men shook their heads, not wanting to tell
me, and they chased me off if I waited to watch.
So I figured I had to use my head better if I
wanted to find gold. So that's why I'm here. To
ask for your help."

Pamela, though charmed by his youthful earn-
estness, was puzzled. "And how might I help
you?" she asked, smiling.

"As you know," Danny went on, "some sand
bars—they're called placers—are rich with gold
while others lie barren. And the men mining the
rich placers won't let on they're doing that out of
fear thousands more will flock to the site."

"Yes, I've heard that."

Danny reached into his shirt pocket, took out
a much folded paper and spread it on the desk.

"This is a map of the diggings," he said. He
tapped his finger on her open ledger. "And in
here are the accounts of most of the miners . . ."

"And," she interrupted, "my records of who
pays in gold and who asks for credit."

"Right. If I knew who paid in gold I could find
out where their mines are. Then I could go to the
rich diggings to make my claim, not to the poor
ones."

Pamela placed the ledger on top of the map.
Should I help him? she asked herself. She
shrugged. What would be the harm? She began
leafing back through the pages. "Danny O'Lee,"
she told him, "you were right to use your brain
and not your brawn. Here I've been keeping these

accounts all these weeks and an idea like yours never occurred to me."

"You'll be helping me then?"

She nodded.

"Miss Pamela," he began. He leaned over as though to kiss her on the cheek, then drew back, his face reddening, "I just want to say that you are a very grand lady."

On a night two weeks later Pamela was in her cabin writing by candlelight.

"My dear Mr. Gowdy," she wrote, "I believe that I closed my last letter by informing you that I was safely ensconced under the magnificent roof of my own cabin in the quaintly-named settlement of Hangtown. The central attraction of the cabin, which is shared by Selena and myself, is a fireplace built of stones and mud, the chimney finished off with alternate layers of rough sticks and this same rude mortar . . ."

There was a rapping. Pamela put down her pen and crossed to the door.

"Who is it?' she asked.

"Danny O'Lee, ma'am."

She unlatched and opened the door. Danny stood smiling at her, his hat in one hand, his other hand behind him.

Pamela's eyes softened. "I'd ask you inside," she said, "but I'm alone."

"I wasn't expecting to visit long in any case. I'm fresh in town and heading for the Empire where I'll seek lodgings and then celebrate my good fortune."

"Your plan worked then. Oh, Danny, I'm so glad."

"In ten days time"—he lowered his voice to a whisper—"I've taken two thousand dollars and more of the dust from a placer on the creek not far from here. And there's more to be had in the same spot."

"You do have the luck of the Irish after all."

"Thanks be to my secret partner." He grinned at her. "So I brought you a gift from the diggings."

"Danny, I didn't expect anything for helping. I don't want anything."

"A gift to match the gold of your hair," he added, smiling broadly. From behind his back he brought forth a bouquet of yellow flowers.

"Oh, Danny." She took the flowers in her arms. "They're so lovely. They're like daisies, yet not exactly like any I've ever seen."

"I don't know their proper name myself."

"But what do the miners call them?"

Danny said gravely, "With sorrow I have to tell you they're known in the diggings as Mule Ears."

Pamela laughed. "Oh, Danny O'Lee, I love them, Mule Ears or not."

After Danny left, Pamela put the flowers in a vase and returned to her letter. She found she had to force herself to go on, sighing with relief when she came to the last few sentences. "By messenger," she wrote, "I am sending a portion of the profits from our venture here in the mountains. I will be deeply indebted to you, even more than I already am, if you will buy land for me in the town as close to Portsmouth Square as possible. Use your best judgment. I do not wish to specu-

late or to have you trade in my behalf; my desire
is to add to my landholdings as I did years ago
in England, the country which will someday, God
willing, once more be the home of . . .

"Pamela Buttle-Jones."

Putting one of the flowers in the buttonhole of
her brown taffeta dress, Pamela went to stand in
the doorway of the cabin. The night was warm,
the stars bright and close overhead, the moon a
thin sliver above the hill to the west. The bitter-
sweet scents of spring were all around her, in the
pines, the burgeoning earth, the lilac fragrance
she herself wore.

She crossed her arms under her breasts, drawing in a breath and letting it out with a tremulous
sigh. A yearning filled her, vague and undirected,
yet strong and persistent. She remembered running through fields of flowers when she was a girl
with the wind in her hair while in the sky above
a great red kite dipped and soared.

And she remembered Danny's smile—so like
Barry Fitzpatrick's. Would she ever see Barry
again? Pamela shook her head and went back
across the cabin to remove her bag from its peg
on the wall. Pausing to take some of her medicine, she walked slowly up the path toward the
hotel. I should check our supplies, she told herself. Tom Horobin was due in a few days and
he'd expect her to have their order ready. She
heard the night sounds of the distant woods but
as she walked they were replaced by the hubbub
coming from the Empire.

She hesitated at the foot of the porch steps,
finally deciding to call on Selena to see if she
wanted to add anything to their order. She crossed

the darkened hallway of the hotel and eased open
the door to the gambling saloon until she was
able to see through the crack without being seen
herself.

Selena sat on a high stool on the stage Rhynne
had built for her, her feet on a rung, her hands
clasping her scarlet skirts to her knees, her face
aglow as she sang. The men joined in on the
chorus, clapping, calling out for more. Pamela
studied the faces in the crowd, looking at each
in turn, then shook her head and frowned.

When the song ended, Selena stepped down
from the stage, pushing aside the hands of the
men. She stopped beside a gaming table, standing with hands on hips, talking to a man Pamela
couldn't see.

"And what was your name before that?" Pamela heard her daughter ask. And then Selena was
back on the stage, whispering to Ned. As she
started singing she pointed to the man at the
table and he stood up, trying to retreat but
hemmed in by the crowd. Pamela saw it was
Danny O'Lee.

Selena sang:

> *"Oh what was your name in the States?*
> *Was it Thompson or Johnson or Bates?*
> *Did you murder your wife,*
> *And fly for your life?*
> *Say, what was your name in the States?*

Danny O'Lee broke from the crowd, the laughs
and hoots of the men following him from the
room. Pamela eased the door closed and walked
out onto the porch. There was no one about.

Going down the steps, she looked along the street. No one. She walked past the store and, off to her right, saw a figure outlined in the darkness.

"Danny?" she called softly.

"Miss Pamela?" His voice schoed his surprise. "Ah, you see the luck of the Irish isn't as good as you thought," he said.

"Take my hand, Danny," she told him. His palm was warm in hers and she led him back to the Empire, across the porch, through the hallway and up the stairs.

"Which room is yours?" she asked.

"The last."

She led him there, standing aside while he unlocked the door. Once inside, she slid home the bolt. "Wait," she said, her fingertips touching his chest. She went to the bed, and, as quickly as she could, removed her clothes. Naked, she slid between the rough blankets.

"Come here to me, Danny O'Lee," she said. When he was beside the bed she reached out for his hand. "Take off your clothes, Danny," she said.

"Miss Pamela," he began, "never in my life . . ."

"Hush," she said. "Not a word."

Then he was in the bed beside her. She felt him trembling so she took his head in her arms, nestling him against her, letting him lie next to her for a long time until his trembling quieted. When she felt him stir, seeking her, she guided his head down to her breasts, trembling herself when his lips closed on her nipple. Her hand slid down his body and found his sex.

Afterwards, she lay holding him in her arms. She was fulfillled, fearful and happy, ashamed yet defiant. Joyful.

"Danny O'Lee," she said, "when I was a young woman in England I once saw a great star trailing a train of fire. For days on end it was there in the sky and then Halley's Comet was gone. It won't return in my lifetime, perhaps not in yours. Some things come only once, Danny. Do you understand?"

She felt his head nod against her bare breast.

Outside in the hall, W.W. Rhynne turned and went quietly to his room. His face was as expressionless as ever, but his eyes glinted like the eyes of a man who has just filled an inside straight.

11

"Can I help you, Mr. Rhynne?" Putting down his hammer, John Griswold looked up from the bed of a wagon.

"I need some lumber. About forty board feet should do it."

"Think I've got what you need," Griswold said, climbing down from the wagon. "Have to be pine, if that's all right with you."

Rhynne shrugged.

Griswold pulled the corner of a tarpaulin from a pile of lumber stacked next to the shed he used as his carpentry shop. He stacked four boards at Rhynne's feet.

"Could you deliver them to Abe at the Empire?" Rhynne asked.

"Guess I could. It's a dollar-twenty a foot."

Rhynne raised his eyebrows. "Heard you charged Callahan a dollar."

"That was two weeks ago. Prices go up every day. But seeing how it's you, Mr. Rhynne, I'll make it a dollar."

"Abe will pay you."

"Planning on building some shelving for the hotel?" Griswold asked.

"No, thought I'd put together a bookcase."

Griswold nodded. "Need nails?"

"I have plenty left from when the Empire was built. Reminds me, though, I do have need for some hinges. Four of them."

"Can't help you there. You'll have to use canvas strips. There's nary a hinge to be had in Hangtown."

"On second thought," Rhynne said, "maybe I won't need the hinges after all. Tell Abe I said to serve you one on the house when you deliver the lumber."

"That I will."

John Griswold watched Rhynne leave the yard whistling *What Was Your Name in the States?* I should have asked for a dollar to start off with, Griswold thought. He was charging one-twenty now, that was true enough. Rhynne, though, was a man to stay on the right side of. Lumber to build himself a bookcase. A bookcase with hinges? Now that was a queer notion. What would a man want with a hinged bookcase?

When Rhynne got back to the Empire, he found Tom Horobin waiting for him on the porch. Inside the hotel he heard Selena practicing on the piano.

"You asked me to stop by before I left for

Sutter's," Horobin said after shifting his cud of tobacco to his right cheek.

"That I did. Care for a drink, Tom?"

Horobin shook his head. "Four years back I broke a leg hauling supplies down into a defile while I was tight as a drumhead. I'll do my drinking after I get to Sutter's tomorrow."

"I've a special order for you, Tom. That's the reason I asked you to stop by. Don't know where you'll be able to get it filled, though."

"San Francisco?"

"Perhaps. Then again, you may have to send to Monterey. Or inquire at the ranchos down that way."

Horobin spat tobacco juice over the porch rail. "You're rousing my curiosity, W.W.," he said. "What is this special order?"

"A bed."

"A bed, is it? Well, now, a bed shouldn't be too hard to come by. Have you thought of having Griswold build you one?"

"I need a special bed. A one-of-a-kind bed."

"All Griswold's beds are one-of-a-kind. Everything Griswold makes is. I don't think he ever followed a pattern in his life."

"Anybody with a few dollars can have Griswold make him a bed if he's got the time to wait."

"John never was one for hurrying. What sort of bed did you have in mind, W.W.?" Horobin raised himself up to sit on the porch rail.

"I want the grandest bed ever seen in Hangtown, the biggest and most elaborate bed you can find in all the West. I want a bed with high posts and a canopy, a bed wtih a carved headboard and a carved footboard, a bed fit for a king, yet with room enough for the king and the queen and three or four others besides. I don't want a bed you can flop into. I want one that you have to climb up onto a step-stool to get at. I want a bed so magnificent that after this California gold rush is forgotten, W.W. Rhynne and his bed will be remembered."

"W.W.," Horobin said admiringly, "now that is what I'd call a *real* bed."

"It's what I mean to have."

"A bed like that would cost as much as a man earns in three or four months."

"I know, Tom. Just find the bed for me. I trust you to drive a hard bargain. I'll pay you what the bed costs and ten percent for your trouble. Plus your regular cartage fee to haul it here to the Empire."

Tom Horobin hunched himself from the rail. "Anything else, W.W.? I've already got Miss Pamela's order for the store and Abe's for the saloon. Anything else special for you?"

"Only the bed. The next time you come up Hangtown way, I'll expect you to bring it."

"I'll have your bed, never fear. You'll notice I'm not asking what you want the bed for. I know you'll tell me when the times comes. Is this something between the two of us and the gatepost?"

"No, it's not. On the contrary, you might mention the bed around town, what kind I want and all. In fact, I'd appreciate it if you would."

"I take your meaning. The word will be all over Hangtown by nightfall." Horobin turned. Staring along the street, he said, "Now if that doesn't beat all."

There were four persons in the procession coming toward the Empire, three men and a woman. A man on horseback led the way, a man of perhaps forty, dressed elegantly in black with flowing black hair tinged with grey. The horse sidestepped as the rider reined him toward the hotel.

"Mighty fine looking animal," Horobin said to Rhynne.

Rhynne nodded, looking past the rider to the two men who followed him. Both sat stolidly astride mules, an older man and a younger, the older with a grey moustache and a short grey beard, the younger clean-shaven, muscular, and huge. Rhynne stared at his hands; he had never seen such hands. They were twice the size of an ordinary man's. Both of the men were black.

Behind them were two heavily laden pack mules and behind the pack mules was the woman. As they came closer, Rhynne realized she was very young, certainly less than eighteen, dark-skinned, Spanish most likely, with a black shawl hiding her hair and covering her upper body. She too rode astride a mule, her long brown skirts torn and soiled.

The horseman looked about him with frank curiosity, taking in the rough log structures, the men in the streets and those lolling in doorways; the two blacks stared straight ahead, yet Rhynne sensed they missed nothing. The girl, though, stared down at her hands clenched on the reins, almost as though she was in a stupor. Rhynne was about to look away when he noticed she was a pretty girl with high cheekbones and delicate dark features. If she smiled, he thought, she would be beautiful.

The horseman stopped at the foot of the steps.

"I'm Kingman Sutton of Georgia," he drawled, "by way of Cape Horn and San Francisco. Could either of you gentlemen tell me where we might set up camp? I'd prefer a location convenient to the diggings."

"You could go on another half mile," Rhynne told him, "then take the right fork and climb to the pines at the crest of the hill. Good a spot as any."

"I'd be careful if I was you, mister," Horobin warned. "Some folks hereabouts don't take kindly to bringing slaves into the diggings."

"Some folks should pay heed to their own affairs and not meddle in matters that don't concern them."

"No harm intended. I was only passing along some friendly advice."

"I heard the same kind of talk in San Francisco. They're hypocrites, the lot of them. Ready to shoot an Indian for sport, they are. What do they say? The only good Indian is a dead Indian. And then they turn around and threaten the protectors of a race less fortunate than our own. I don't give a damn what hypocrites think."

Rhynne glanced at the two blacks behind Sutton, noting they bore a family resemblance to one another. They stared back at him, expressionless.

"And what can you tell us of the state of affairs in San Francisco, sir?" he asked quietly.

"They're damnable. The city's fair on its way to becoming the hell-hole of the Pacific. No decent lodgings to be found, rats and fleas everywhere. So many rats, in fact, they're selling cats for ten dollars each to hunt them. All the prices are outrageous. I paid a dollar for an egg; a five-cent loaf of bread sells for seventy-five. The food, what there is of it, is abominable. They're beaching the abandoned ships and using them for sleeping quarters. Men live in shacks and tents, they sleep in the open or on bales of hides waiting shipment east."

"They call that section of the town 'Hide Park,' I believe," Rhynne said.

"It's a town no longer. These days San Francisco styles itself a city. Not a city of houses that would smack of sense, though. No. They're building bordellos and gambling saloons instead. Not that they don't have their place, sir," he said with a nod to Rhynne. "Yet a man doesn't want to spend the whole of his life drinking, gambling and whoring."

"I can't quarrel with that," Rhynne said. "If only we could become children again we could avoid the problem. That's impossible, I know. 'Nothing can bring back the hour of splendor in the grass, of glory in the flower.'"

"I doubt if we'll ever see grass or flowers growing in San Francisco again," Sutton said. "Not only do more ships arrive daily to be abandoned by their crews, now one hears reports of a great overland migration this year. Wagon trains from all parts of the East are gathering in Missouri waiting for the grass on the plains to sprout high enough to feed their livestock on the way across."

"Gold fever can be an extremely contagious disease, Mr. Sutton."

"And deadly as well. If it weren't for certain unfortunate circumstances . . ." He stopped, looking past Rhynne and Horobin. Rhynne glanced over his shoulder to see Selena standing in the doorway dressed in her green gown. Her loosened hair fell over her shoulders in a golden cascade; her blue eyes sparkled.

Sutton dismounted and sprang up the steps, hat in hand. At the top he paused to sweep his hat across his body and bowed with a flourish. "Colonel Kingman Sutton at your service, ma'am," he said to Selena.

Rhynne looked closely at Selena as she smiled up at Sutton. Somehow she seemed different this morning. She had never looked lovelier, yet the change he had noted wasn't only in her appearance. Her whole manner was subtly enlivened. She looked radiant. Could it be because of Sutton? he wondered.

"You have the advantage," Sutton was saying to her. "I don't believe I know your name."

"Selena. Selena Buttle-Jones."

"I've traveled fifteen thousand miles from the state of Georgia. Until this moment I'd wondered whether the journey had been in vain."

A month ago, Rhynne knew, Selena would have blushed and been afraid to breach propriety by speaking to a strange man. Not now. Though she inclined her head, her eyes continued to look up into Sutton's.

"You should always wear green," Sutton told her. "The colors of springtime suit you."

The two of them acted as though they were alone, Rhynne thought, as though no one else were near. As though no one else mattered. His eyes narrowed. Would Sutton threaten the plan he had in mind?

"Mister—perhaps I should say Colonel—Sutton has brought an imposing crew with him to help search for gold," Rhynne said to Selena.

She blinked, looking at Rhynne as though she hadn't heard him. "A crew?" she asked.

"There," Rhynne said impatiently, nodding to the street. For the first time Selena looked at the two blacks and the Spanish girl. She drew in her breath and walked past Sutton to the porch rail to stare at the girl on the mule. The girl raised her black shawl to cover the lower part of her face.

Holding her skirts in one hand, Selena ran down the steps and past the pack mules. She stood in the road and kept staring up at the girl. Sutton followed her from the porch, stopping a few feet behind her.

"I know you," Selena said to the girl.

The girl turned her head away.

"You're Esperanza. Esperanza de la Torre."

The girl said nothing.

"Last year," Selena went on, "your brother Diego brought me to your rancho. We talked. You told me you wanted twelve children, three boys and nine girls."

When the girl remained mute, Selena swung around to Sutton. "How does she come to be here with you?" she demanded.

Sutton shrugged. "I found her wandering about Sacramento like a stray cat. I fed her and she followed me. She never speaks so I don't know how she came to be there. Followed some miner to the diggings only to have him die or else desert her. At least that's what I suspect."

"Is she . . . ?" Selena eyed him quizzically.

"Not what you might think. She cooks for us. Nothing more. Why, she's only a child."

"If she is Esperanza, she's sixteen."

"That old? I would have said fourteen at the most."

Selena turned to the girl. "Esperanza," she said, "I'll come to see you. If you need me, if you ever need me, you are to come here to the hotel."

For the first time the girl's dark eyes looked up, sliding across Selena's face and away.

"I don't think she understands English," Sutton said.

"She does. She understands. She's been hurt, can't you see that? Terribly hurt. Don't ever do anything to harm her. Will you promise me that?"

"I'd promise you anything in the world, Miss Selena," Sutton said.

"This is important. Don't flirt with me. Answer me."

"I promise, Selena."

She nodded once, then ran to the porch, up the steps and through the open door into the hotel.

Sutton swung into the saddle.

"I'll wager we'll see more of you," Rhynne said.

"With your instincts, you'd make a passable gambler," Sutton told him. He stood in the stirrups and, like a troop commander signaling an attack, waved his entourage forward.

After Sutton was gone and Horobin had hitched his wagon and driven west toward Sacramento, Rhynne returned to his room. He studied the row of books on the shelf above his cot, finally taking down two copies of Wordsworth's *Lyrical Ballads*. He leafed through one of the slim volumes, pausing time and again to read a well-remembered passage, now smiling to himself, now shaking his head in wonder.

Then he took the books and ripped off the covers. Starting from the front, he peeled the pages free one by one until they lay in two piles on the desk.

He opened the desk drawer and rummaged inside until he found a pair of scissors. With them he cut each page of one of the books across the middle. Using the pen on the desk he numbered each of these half-pages, once on the lefthand margin and again, with the same number, on the right, beginning with "1" and stopping only after he reached "100."

Again he took the scissors and cut the half-pages, this time down the center, keeping the two stacks separate. He repeated the process for the second book except he didn't number the pages. He put each of the four stacks of several pages in its own envelope, numbering them 1, 2, 3, and 4, sealed the envelopes and placed them at the rear of his desk drawer.

Rhynne descended the stairs, went outside, and into the store. Pamela was using her counter scales to weigh gold dust for two miners. When she saw Rhynne, she nodded to him, and after the miners left she hurried across the room to where he waited.

"When, W.W.?" she asked. "When?"

"Perhaps tomorrow."

"Don't you know for sure? I can't wait much longer."

"Come to my room tomorrow night at ten."

"To your room? You know I can't do that. I won't."

"Do you want the laudanum?"

"You know I do."

"Tomorrow night, Pamela," he said, turning on his heel.

"Rhynne," she called after him.

He didn't answer.

The next morning Rhynne forced himself to get out of bed at six. After shaving and putting on his oldest trousers, he left the hotel through the back door and headed for the storage shed a hundred feet away.

He closed the shed door behind him. The windowless building was dark and musty, forcing him to light a lamp. The four boards from Griswold's leaned against the wall where Abe had put them. Rhynne laid one of the boards across two sawhorses, sawing it into foot-and-a-half lengths. By the time he had cut up all four boards, he had to pause to wipe his face with a handkerchief.

He stood up, stretching, then began nailing the boards together. Before nailing the final two, he notched them. When he finished he examined his work: a box a foot-and-a-half to a side, completely enclosed and nailed shut. On one side of the box the two notches met to form a slot three inches long and a half-inch wide. Rhynne nodded to himself. His work was crude but he was satisfied.

He built a second box, identical in every way to the first. Placing the two side by side on a workbench, he studied them. Again he nodded.

With a shovel, he struck the side of one of the boxes, leaving an ugly indentation. With the same shovel he struck the other box in the same spot. Again he examined the result. Although the scars on the wood weren't precisely the same, they were close enough.

No one was about when he carried the first box into the saloon and placed it on the counter behind the bar. He returned for the second box and took it to his room where he shoved it far beneath his cot.

Once he made his donation to the Reverend Colton's church, Rhynne told himself, he could begin.

12

"He was like someone out of the Bible," Selena told her mother. "Like Moses leading the Israelites into the Promised Land."

"A Moses on horseback? Leading two slaves and a Mexican girl?"

"It was the way he looked. The flowing hair touched with grey. His face was stern yet underneath he's a kind and gentle man. I could tell. And he's suffered a great loss in his life. A tragedy of some kind. How else would he get those lines in his face?"

"I think aging might have something to do with it."

"He wasn't *that* old. You didn't see him, did you?"

"No. *I* was working in the store at the time."

"I'm going to help you clerk all the rest of the

day," Selena said. The two women were walking beside the road leading from their cabin, where they had just eaten their noon meal, to the Empire.

"You're positive this girl with him was Esperanza? You couldn't be mistaken?"

"It was Esperanza de la Torre. Even though I only met her once, I'll never forget her. She was so alive, so positive about what she would do when she grew up and married. She's changed." Selena put her hand to her breast. "There's been some terrible tragedy in her life too, something so shocking it's made her into a different person."

"Selena, you're being melodramatic. The fact is that Mexican women age young."

"She's only sixteen, mother."

"I wonder where her brother is."

"Diego's probably in Sonora by now. You sound as though you're afraid of him."

"I don't trust him. And he does have reason to hate us. He thinks I misled him, you'll remember. And he knows you rejected him."

"You don't trust Diego. You don't trust Rhynne. Whom do you trust?"

"Robert Gowdy, for one."

"Though you don't really like him. As a man. Is there any man you do like? Besides that brash Irish boy who brought you the flowers?"

"You mean Danny O'Lee."

"Or whatever his name is."

"Selena, you were cruel to him. I was ashamed of you for the way you treated him."

"Oh, mother, I was ashamed of myself for singing that song. Afterward, not at the time, because I was getting even with him. Still I shouldn't have done it that way. You don't realize how I feel when I'm on that stage. When I'm singing, I feel I can do no wrong. That whatever whim I have is right merely because it's mine."

Pamela sighed. "I don't understand you any more, Selena."

"But later, after I made sport of Danny O'Lee, I felt sorry for him. I wanted to comfort him. Like a mother would, I suppose. Don't you ever feel that way about Danny? He *is* the right age to be your son."

Pamela stopped and looked at Selena.

"Did I say something wrong, mother?"

"No, of course not. When you're thirty-eight as I am, you won't want to be reminded of your age either. As for Danny O'Lee, yes, I suspect I do feel like mothering him at times. He's a likable lad. You should apologize to him, Selena."

"Perhaps I will. Someday." They walked for a time in silence. "Are you feeling better, mother?" Selena asked. "At times I believe you are and then I wonder."

"I have a great deal on my mind. Money for one thing, paying back our loan from Mr. Rhynne. Some other troubles with Mr. Rhynne for another. And my sickness."

"If anybody has something on their mind, it's W.W. I've never seen him as distracted as he's been this last week. I'm positive he's plotting a coup of some kind."

"Mr. Rhynne is always planning a coup. Just like a man—he's never satisfied. Give him a shilling, he'll want a pound; give him a pound, he wants two." She paused. "Did he burn Varner's, Selena?"

"I— I don't know. I think he did. I'm not sure."

"From the way you acted after the fire, I was convinced you knew he did."

They saw a burly black-bearded man running toward the Empire from the opposite direction. He leaped up the steps, threw open the door and disappeared inside.

"Could someone have struck it rich?" Selena asked.

"Look, he's coming out again. Who is he?"

"Pike, he calls himself. He's new in town. I've only seen him once or twice. He's a braggart."

Four other men followed Pike from the gambling saloon. They hurried off up the street.

"Let's ask Abe what the commotion's about," Selena said. The two women went into the hotel lobby and Selena opened the door to the saloon. She was surprised to find Abe alone.

"Ah, Miss Selena," he said, coming to the door. "And Miss Pamela."

"What's happening, Abe?" Selena asked him.

"What is it always?" Abe ran his hand over his balding head as though pushing back imaginary hair. "A brawl of some sort. That fellow Pike says English Bob got a knife between the ribs."

"Oh," Selena gasped. "Not English Bob. He's always such a gentleman."

"Most men around here like Bob," Abe said. "Still and all, I don't know about the gentleman part. He did have a go-round with that young Danny O'Lee, you'll remember. And there's been other times when he's been known to gouge and knee with the best of them, or so I'm told."

"You don't think Danny O'Lee . . . ?" Pamela began. She put her hand to her mouth. "They've done some panning for gold together," she said. "It wasn't Danny O'Lee with the knife, was it?"

Abe shrugged. "Pike didn't say. Didn't know, I gather. The way he told the story, he was on his way to his tent, Pike was, and English Bob comes staggering toward him all doubled over, his bloody hands to his stomach. When Pike tries to help him, English Bob falls to the ground saying, 'I'm a goner,' or words like that."

"I haven't seen Danny O'Lee these last few days," Selena said. "He's probably at the diggings. And I doubt he even has a knife."

"Where's Mr. Rhynne?" Pamela asked Abe.

"Said something about paying his respects to the Reverend Colton when he left here half an hour ago. If I was you, ma'am, and I know Mr. Rhynne would say the same, I'd stay far clear of trouble of this sort. You know how it is with no law in the territory. What can you expect in a country where a great man like John Charles Fremont is court-martialed out of the Army? The men here see theirselves as judge, jury and hangman all rolled into one."

"Let us know the minute you hear what happened to English Bob," Pamela told him.

"That I will." Abe started to shut the door, then hesitated. "Do either of you ladies know why Mr. Rhynne put this slotted box behind the bar? I asked him this morning and he just smiled."

"Box?" Pamela and Selena both asked at once. They went to the door and stared at the pine box, shaking their heads.

"Just curious," Abe said, going back behind the bar.

"I'm sure Danny O'Lee wouldn't do such a

thing," Pamela said as they walked to the store. "Though he's got a temper I can't imagine him with a knife."

"Do you want me to go to the church and look for W.W.?" Selena asked.

Pamela considered. "I think not," she said finally. "This will all turn out to have nothing to do with us."

"I can't imagine," Selena said, "what W.W. wants with Reverend Colton."

"And what, Mr. Rhynne, do you want with me?" Reverend Colton asked. They were seated in the minister's small office at the rear of the church.

"I want your help, Reverend."

Colton steepled his hands. "A strange request. Considering." His speech had a Scottish burr.

"The older I become, the more I realize what I've missed in life."

"It's never too late to find God, Mr. Rhynne."

"It may be for me. For others, I hope it's not."

Reverend Colton said nothing.

"I squandered my youth," Rhynne said, "in the pursuit of pleasure. If only I hadn't been born into a life of poverty."

"A man can rise above his circumstances."

"A strong man like yourself can. I'm not strong, never have been, either in body or in spirit. Temptation finds me an easy prey today as it did when I was a lad living in a house of ill repute."

"You grew up in a bordello?"

"In New Orleans. My mother was the madam."

"You said you were raised in poverty. I've heard women of that sort described in many different ways, but never before have I heard them labeled as being poor."

"It was a spiritual poverty I referred to. My mother read to me from the English poets, never from the Bible. Only later did I realize that some of our greatest poetry is in the Good Book."

"For myself, I like to believe it also contains some of mankind's greatest truths."

"My point exactly. When I was a child, these truths were denied me."

"And the child is father of the man."

"You know Wordsworth, Reverend Colton."

"A line or two." He stood up and nodded toward a shelf on the wall behind him. "I think I have the largest library in Hangtown," he said. "All thirty volumes. Forgive my boasting. Pride is one of my sins."

Rhynne looked over the Reverend's shoulder. "And only a few of your books concern theology."

"Worldliness is another of my sins. And as a somewhat worldly man, I have to admit I suspect the purity of your motives in coming to see me today."

Rhynne reached into his pocket, took out a deerskin pouch, and dropped it on the minister's desk.

"My intentions are as pure as the gold in that poke," he said.

The Reverend Colton weighed the pouch in his hand.

"About five hundred dollars worth of gold dust," Rhynne told him.

Colton placed the pouch on the desk between them.

"It's yours," Rhynne said. "My gift to the church. Let's say it's a guilt offering."

"In both meanings of the word? Gilt and guilt?"

Rhynne smiled. "In both meanings."

Colton dangled the pouch by its leather thongs. "No strings attached, Mr. Rhynne?"

"None at all."

Colton opened a drawer of his desk and dropped the gold inside. "You're most generous," he said. "The only gift I'd prize more would be the return of the prodigal son, yourself in this case, to the ways of God. If that were to occur, I'd personally kill the fatted calf."

"That's one of the parables I've never understood. All the attention is lavished on the prodigal while the dutiful son is ignored. Human nature, yes. But good theology?"

"Mr. Rhynne, I've never completely understood that story myself. Perhaps something was lost in the translation from the Greek."

"I've enjoyed your frankness, Reverend." Rhynne held out his hand. "I only regret we haven't talked before this." They shook hands.

At the door, Rhynne turned, reaching into his vest pocket. "I quite forgot," he said. He opened a volume on the Reverend Colton's desk and inserted a slip of paper. "The Empire is conducting a lottery," Rhynne said. "As a man of the world, I thought you might like to have the first ticket. There's no obligation, of course."

Colton took the paper from the book and examined it. "You've given me number one," he said. "This ticket appears to be cut from a volume of poetry."

"Wordsworth's *Lyrical Ballads*. A great favorite of mine. Since we have no printing press in Hangtown, I had to sacrifice it."

"And the prize?"

"I've not quite decided. I'm considering awarding the winner a week's free lodging in the Empire's best room furnished with a new bed I've ordered from Horobin. It's all rather nebulous at this point."

"I could never accept such a prize. My parishioners would think I'd allied myself with the devil."

"I understand. If you should win, and the chances are ninety-nine to one you won't, a gift of cash to your church would be forthcoming."

"I don't see how I could refuse that."

Rhynne nodded. "Good day to you, sir. Between now and when we meet again, I suggest we both reread the parable of the prodigal son."

"I'll pray for you, Mr. Rhynne," Colton said.

After Rhynne closed the door, Reverend Colton looked from the door to the slip of paper he still held in his hand. He shook his head in puzzlement, then reached for his Bible.

"I'll go next door and find out if Abe has heard anything more about English Bob," Selena said.

"You may as well," Pamela told her. "We certainly aren't busy. Where is everyone today?"

In the gambling saloon, Selena found Abe behind the bar polishing glasses.

"No," he said in answer to her question. "I haven't heard a word. No one's been in since you saw that bunch of them leave. No one at all."

Selena nodded and went outside to the porch.

When, looking to her left, she saw a group of men approaching the hotel, she ran down the steps into the street. As the men went past, she saw that four of them were carrying English Bob on a canvas stretched between two poles. Although Bob's eyes were closed, she thought she saw the rise and fall of his chest.

"Here's the doc now," one of the men said.

Dr. Braithewaite, followed by a miner, walked quickly toward them.

"Put him down, put him down," Braithewaite ordered. "Over there out of the sun."

They laid English Bob in the shade of a cabin across from the hotel. The men, hushed, crowded around. Selena stood on tiptoe trying to see over their shoulders.

"What happened to him?" Braithewaite asked as he knelt beside the wounded man.

They all spoke at once.

"Knifed."

"Up to McCowan's Hill."

"The new man. The one with two slaves."

"At his place."

"The Mex girl did it," Pike said. "English Bob told me. She stabbed him."

Braithewaite stood up. "He's hurt bad," he said. "All I can do is bandage him up and pray. And give him morphine for the pain."

"Will he make it?"

Braithewaite raised his palms. "It's in God's hands," he said.

A murmur ran through the crowd.

"The Mex gal," Pike said. "She's the one what did it."

"Let's get her. Bring her back. Hold court."

"All legal-like. We'll try her and hang her."

"A woman? We can't hang a woman."

"We'll give her a trial. That's what the trial's for, to see if we hang her or send her back where she come from."

"Damn greasers. Stealing our gold."

"Them and their knives. Guns ain't good enough for them."

"A rope's good enough. As long as they're dangling at the end of it."

"Don't be hasty," Braithewaite said. "You don't rightly know what happened."

"He's right," Selena said. "It could have been his fault."

"She knifed him. English Bob said so."

"She must have had a reason," Braithewaite said. "Bob might have tried to force her."

"English Bob's not that kind. A regular gent he is."

"She's a Mexican. You know what they're like, doc, enticing men into their tents to rob them."

"Then knifing them."

"No!" Selena cried out. "She wouldn't. I know her. She wouldn't. Not without a reason."

"She robbed him and killed him."

"Why are we standing here talking?" Pike asked.

"Let's go!"

The men, shouting and cursing, surged up the street. Selena ran behind them, clutching at their sleeves, pleading with them. They shook her off, refusing to look at her. They cheered and pointed upward as they passed under the oak that had given the town its name, the oak where three men were hanged for robbing a storekeeper.

The mob bore right at the fork, silent now, intent, grim, determined. More men joined them, the mob growing. Selena gasped for breath as she tried to keep up. They halted at the foot of the hill, looking up the steep slope dotted with stumps and slashed by gullies left by the winter's rains.

At the top of the hill Selena saw two tents in front of a stand of pines. When she saw that the tents seemed deserted, she sighed with relief. They had fled, she told herself. Esperanza was safe.

The men, thirty or more by now, began climbing the hill. Selena followed. When they neared the top, three men appeared at the crest—Sutton flanked by his two blacks, Joshua and Jed. The men lower on the hill hesitated, then came on, scrabbling upward. Sutton watched until they were no more than twenty feet from him, then raised his hand.

"No farther," he shouted.

"We don't want you," Pike called to him. "We want the girl. The Mex girl."

"You shan't have her."

Pike turned to the mob. "Are we gonna let him and his two niggers stop us?" he asked.

"No!" they shouted.

"Then let's go get 'em!"

"Listen to me," Sutton called. "Let me tell you what happened." His voice was drowned out as the men surged up the hill. The young black, the one called Jed, seized the first man to reach the top, raised him over his head, holding him there for a moment, then hurled him at the others. Three men went down but the others scrambled past, sweeping Sutton and the older slave before them. They surrounded the young black, ten or more circling him warily. Jed waited, ready, the men still circling, afraid to close on him.

As Sutton lay struggling on the ground, Selena tried to force her way to him. An arm seized her from behind, thrusting her away, and she fell. She pushed herself up and ran forward, screaming at them to stop. Men swarmed into the first tent, smashing the canvas to the ground and scattering Sutton's provisions. Selena didn't see Esperanza. Had she escaped after all?

With Pike in the lead, the men ran to the second tent. Pike threw aside the flap and suddenly stopped. After a moment, he turned away. The others crowded past him, looked into the tent and then they, too, turned away. Selena pushed by them and drew back the flap.

Esperanza lay on her side on the ground inside the tent. At first Selena thought she was asleep, hoped she was asleep, but knew she wasn't. Esperanza's hands were still on the knife and Selena saw blood pooling on the ground from the wound in her stomach. Crying out wordlessly, Selena knelt beside her, cradling Esperanza's head in her arms. The girl's lifeless eyes stared past her.

13

"Is she dead?" Sutton asked. He knelt beside Selena who still held Esperanza in her arms.

"Yes." Selena felt numb. Stunned.

"I'll have Jed and Joshua dig a grave."

"Is there a priest? A Catholic priest?"

"I'm sure there isn't." King Sutton put his hand on Selena's shoulder, then got up and went out of the tent.

Selena laid Esperanza on the ground and made the sign of the cross over her before covering her with the black shawl. When she left the tent she saw Sutton some distance away leading the two blacks, both with shovels on their shoulders, toward a knoll. The other tent was a shambles; the men from town were nowhere to be seen.

Selena turned away and walked into the pines. Without purpose, without direction, she stumbled ahead beneath the giant trees, the pine needles slick under her feet, the forest around her dim in the hush of late afternoon. She heard the faint gurgle of water, made her way toward the sound and after a short time came to the top of a steep bank. Looking down, she saw a glen through the trees where water spilled over a series of falls to form a pool directly below her. Beside the pool dirt and sand had been piled, the tailings where miners had once panned for gold.

She climbed down the bank along a zig-zagging track to the stream. She knelt on a flat boulder to splash water onto her face, the chill shocking her back to awareness. Still kneeling, she scooped water into her palms. As she drank, she became aware of the reflection in the pool of the boulders on the opposite bank, the spires of the pines, and the white clouds drifting serenely across the azure sky.

Esperanza was dead. A sob wrenched Selena and she cried, the reality of the young girl's death overwhelming her. Never again would Esperanza gaze into still waters, never again walk beneath the vault of the sky. Selena lowered her head into her hands.

When at last she quieted and looked up, she shivered. The sun was now behind the hills; the glen lay in deepening shadows. A movement in the water caught her eye. Glancing down, she saw the reflection of her own face and, next to hers, a second face. She gasped and spun around. King Sutton stood behind her.

"I didn't mean to startle you," he said, taking a step back.

She stood up and flew at him, pounding his chest with her fists. He raised his hands to defend himself, finally grasping her by the wrists to hold her away.

"Damn you," she cried. "Why didn't you help her? Why didn't you take her away?"

He released one of her hands and she swung, striking his shoulder. Reaching out, he slapped her face hard, sending her head jerking to one side. For a moment she stared at him, her eyes wide, and then she covered her face with her hands.

"We'd just returned from scouting the diggings," he said. "The three of us, Jed and Joshua and myself. I heard the girl moaning so I looked into her tent to see what was wrong. She said a man she didn't know had attacked her and she fought him, hurt him with a knife, and she was afraid. It was the first time the poor child ever spoke to me. By that time I could hear the mob coming up the hill.

"I told her to run and hide in the woods, we'd delay them, and I left her there and we made our stand at the top of the hill. You saw what happened."

"Why didn't you shoot them? You have guns. I saw them when you rode into town."

"Because there were thirty of them and only three of us. I don't mind long odds but I'm no fool. They had guns too. If I started shooting there'd be four dead now, maybe more, instead of only one."

Selena rubbed her stinging cheek. "It's not your fault," she said. She was terribly tired. "I know you did what you could."

"I tried."

"It's not your fault," she said again. "It's mine. I killed Esperanza."

"You? You don't know what you're saying."

"I thought I was in love with Diego. Diego's her brother. I was going to marry him. He might have kept the ranch. Esperanza might still be there living with us. She'd be married by now with a baby on the way. I killed her."

"Selena, you're talking nonsense. I don't know what happened between you and this Diego or between you and Esperanza, but I know you didn't kill." He spoke slowly, as to a child. "You are not responsible for her death. They killed her, those madmen. They didn't listen to me, didn't want to listen."

"If I hadn't . . ." Selena began.

King took her by the shoulders and shook her. "Stop it. With that reasoning we could blame ourselves for all the troubles of the world. Listen to me. Last year I was deer hunting. I stopped to talk to Tuttle, a friend of mine, and five minutes later he was dead, struck down by a stray bullet. If I hadn't talked to him, would he be alive today? Did I kill him? Answer me, did I?"

Selena shook her head.

"Of course I didn't. We have to do the best we can. What happens, happens."

She sighed, shivering.

"You're cold," he said, putting his arms around her, holding her to him.

Selena pushed him away and walked to the water's edge, where she looked down into the pool. When she heard King Sutton behind her, sensed him inches away, she looked for his reflection in the water. Not seeing it, she turned. He seemed to loom over her. Backing away, she almost fell into the water. He reached down and lifted her into his arms.

She felt the beating of her heart, the quickening of her breath. "What are you doing?" she whispered.

He didn't answer. He carried up the long zee of the path, holding her close against his body, his warmth strangely comforting to her. When they came to the top of the hill he carried her through the pines, the sun slanting between the trees. He laid her on the sunlit grass in a glade and knelt alongside her.

"Esperanza is dead," she said softly.

"Esperanza's dead, yet we're alive." He brushed a lock of golden hair from her forehead. "We're alive. Say it, Selena."

"We're alive."

"Again. Louder. Say it again."

"We're alive."

"Again. Louder."

"We're alive," she screamed.

"Yes, yes." He pulled her to him, kissing her. Selena raked his face with her nails.

"I've hurt you," she said. Blood-red slashes streaked his cheek.

He shook his head.

"I don't want to hurt you." She held his head in her hands. "I never want to hurt you. I never want to hurt anyone."

With one hand he stroked the back of her head; with the other he held her breast, kissing her lips.

Selena moaned, lying back on the grass, King following with his lips to hers. She responded, kissing him, her body writhing against him.

"Oh!"

She cried out, holding him from her with her hand as a trembling grew in her, a mounting warmth, a strange awakening quivering, which shattered her and passed on, leaving her limp in his arms.

"King." She said his name for the first time.

His hands were on her calves, stroking her legs beneath her dress, caressing the softness of her thighs. Hard hands, a man's hands. She shifted away from him yet his hands followed, insistent, and again she felt the warmth rising within her. She clung to him, eyes closed, trembling against the maleness of his body.

She felt his hands desert her, heard him fumble with his clothes. She waited for him, wanting him, wanting to be held and caressed by those hands.

"Selena?" he asked.

"Yes, King. Yes, yes, yes."

The shock of him against her, in her, made her open her eyes. He kissed her eyelids, crooning to her, his words without meaning. And then he was saying her name over and over, "Selena, Selena, Selena," and the warmth mounted in her, became a storm, shaking her. She grasped his hair, pulling it, screaming at him to stop while her body urged him on as she rose and fell beneath him. He seemed to burst within her and she cried out and fell back.

He left her. Drew away to lay on his back beside her.

Selena opened her eyes, glancing across at him.

His eyes were closed; he was smiling. On his right hand a fire opal gleamed redly.

"King," she said. She felt empty. Incomplete. "King, why did you stop?"

He opened his eyes. Selena turned onto her side, clutching his shirtfront in her hand, shaking him. "King," she said, "answer me."

"Selena," he said. "I can't again."

She raised her hand, pounded at his chest, clawed at his face. He grasped her fist in his hand pressed her arm back until she was pinned to the ground. She squirmed, trying to free herself.

"King!" she cried.

He tore at her bodice, ripping the cloth asunder, exposing her breasts. She drew his head to her, to her breasts, felt his tongue on her nipple. Again the flame grew in her and she moaned, her fingers clutching his hair as her body shook uncontrollably beneath him.

When Pamela arrived at the Empire at ten o'clock that night she was surprised to find the gambling saloon dark. Upstairs she saw the glow of lights through the red calico curtains of three rooms—Rhynne's and two others.

She yawned. She hadn't been able to stop yawning all day. Even though she had slept for ten hours the night before, her sleep had been restless and troubled and she'd awakened unrefreshed. She knew the reason. She had been without laudanum for two days.

Yet she would never give herself to Rhynne.

Then why was she here? she asked herself. Why was she skulking in the darkness across from the

Empire? Was she afraid of Rhynne? No, it wasn't fear; the thought of Rhynne filled her with distaste, a repugnance even more distressful than the agonies brought on by the lack of laudanum. Yes, laudanum. She no longer referred to the opiate as medicine. It was laudanum.

I'll confront Rhynne, she decided. I'll demand he help me. He's not a cruel man. Devious, not cruel. I'll offer him money, give him a greater percentage of the profits from the Empire. She sensed that Rhynne didn't desire her as other men had in the past. Rather, she thought, he was taken with the idea of possessing her as he might desire a painting or a piece of sculpture.

She looked carefully up and down the road. Did she actually expect Diego to come riding into Hangtown bent on vengeance? Ever since she heard that Esperanza was dead she had wondered what Diego would do when he found out.

Seeing no one about, Pamela crossed the street and climbed the steps to the Empire, walking rapidly. If she didn't go quickly she knew she wouldn't go at all. No one was in the hotel lobby so she climbed the stairs. Rhynne's door, the first on the right, stood slightly open and, tapping once, she stepped inside.

Rhynne, who had been writing at his desk, stood and nodded to her. She sat primly on the edge of the only other chair.

"You're dressed in mourning," Rhynne said. "I haven't seen you wearing black since we left San Francisco."

Pamela said nothing, her eyes avoiding his yet still noting his red vest, the gold watch chain looped from vest to pocket, the fawn-colored trousers, the leather high-topped shoes.

Rhynne tapped his fingers on the desk. Why, he's ill-at-ease, Pamela thought, just like a schoolboy. The thought reminded her of Danny O'Lee and she felt herself reddening. Rhynne didn't appear to notice.

"I closed the Empire as soon as I heard about the young Mexican girl," he told her.

Rhynne, she thought, will I ever untangle your contradictions? She nodded, still saying nothing.

"Is Selena all right?" he wanted to know.

"She's staying the night with Clara Colton. It must have been terrible for Selena, knowing Esperanza as she did. Selena went to Sutton's camp, where those men were, and she saw the girl just after she'd killed herself. Then she wandered off into the brush. When she finally came home her clothes were dirty and torn."

"When you're older, as we are, Pamela, you become hardened to tragedy. More's the pity."

"By the time I talked to her, Selena seemed to have accepted Esperanza's death."

"Esperanza. Doesn't it mean hope in English? Yes, I'm sure it does."

"Selena was in such a strange mood, sobbing and laughing, pacing about the cabin. She didn't want to talk to me about Esperanza."

"English Bob, by the way, is better. Unless infection sets in, he'll live. *He's* not talking either. The waste, the terrible waste."

"W.W.," she said, "I've come for my laudanum."

He nodded. Kneeling, he pulled a black traveling bag from underneath his bed. The cot was gone, Pamela saw; this was a brass bed. Rhynne unsnapped the bag and removed a small medicine bottle, slipping it into his pocket as he stood up.

"I'll pay you for the laudanum," Pamela told him. "I'll pay you well." She drew a deep breath. "In gold and nothing else."

"So young Danny O'Lee is to have your favors and I'm not?"

"Danny O'Lee!" She felt suddenly lightheaded but when Rhynne stepped toward her she held up her hand. "You know?" she whispered.

"I know. No one else does."

"How dare you bring up Danny's name. You're certainly no gentleman, Mr. Rhynne."

"I think you told me that once before. In San Francisco. At the time I said I didn't pretend to be. I still don't."

"You also said you'd wait to see if I was a lady or not."

"Yes, and I've decided. You are." He took the medicine bottle from his pocket and handed it to her. "I'll do the best I can to get laudanum for you."

"I'll pay you." She took a small glass from her bag, poured in a bit of laudanum and drank it.

"That won't be necessary." He picked up his chair and turned it to face hers. Sitting down, he took her hands in his. "Pamela," he said, "with you, tonight, I'm as shy as a boy."

Though she looked down at his hands holding hers she did not pull away.

"When I found out about your need for laudanum," he said, "then later when I became aware of you and young O'Lee, I thought I'd force you to bed with me. I was a fool. That's not what I really wanted."

"And what is it you really want?"

"Someone to talk to."

"To talk to?" She smiled as he watched her warily. Then, putting her head back, she laughed until tears came to her eyes. She took her hands from his, found a handkerchief in her bag and dabbed at her face.

"I was afraid you might find me amusing," Rhynne said.

"Oh, W.W., I'm not laughing at you. I'm not, I'm not. I'm just so relieved."

"I'm not sure I like that sentiment any better."

She took his hands, holding one in each of hers, and squeezed them. "If you had forced me," she said, "I would have hated you. Eventually I might even have killed you. I detest the idea of being forced. It's not you, I don't detest you. It's having to do what I don't want to do. The violation. Do you understand?"

"I suppose I do."

"Do you know, W.W., I'm almost disappointed. Does that make sense?"

"Do you mean you want to . . . ?"

"No, no, I don't. Perhaps someday, if the time is right. Not now. Not tonight."

"I can wait, Pamela. In fact I'd rather wait. I'm a very patient man."

"And you only want to talk?"

"Is that so strange? Whom do I have to talk to? Reverend Colton? Abe? Ned? The miners in the bar? The gamblers? What do I really have in common with most of them? Besides, they're men and I'm not attracted to men. I much prefer women."

"W.W., I'll gladly talk to you whenever you wish. But why this intrigue?"

He shrugged. "I suppose I don't know any other way."

"Even ordering this new bed. I heard about that, you know."

"New bed? No, this isn't the new bed. I don't expect it to arrive for some weeks yet. This is from the room next door. I grew tired of the cot."

"And the new bed? Why do you need it?"

"Ah, it's a grand and glorious scheme, Pamela. I'm buying the most magnificent bed in California and installing it in our largest room. And there'll be a lottery and the winner will be rewarded with a night in the bed. I expect to sell one hundred tickets for a hundred dollars each."

"Who would pay a hundred dollars for a night at the Empire? No matter how grand the bed may be?"

Rhynne stood and walked to the window. "Well," he said, not looking at her, "I suppose I might as well tell you now as later. I've let the word get around that the bed will be occupied."

"Occupied?"

"By the most beautiful woman in the western hemisphere."

Pamela, puzzled, said, "I've heard Selena called that." She stood up sharply. "W.W.! You don't mean you're offering Selena as a prize. You wouldn't do that!"

He turned and put his hand on her arm. "Of

course I'm not. Her name's never been mentioned and never will be."

"And what happens when you hold your drawing and someone claims his prize? What will you do then?"

"That's the glory of the scheme." He reached under his bed and dragged out a rough pine box with a slot in the top.

"I thought that box was behind the bar downstairs," Pamela said, growing even more puzzled.

"This is a second box, identical to the first. In this one I've put one hundred lottery tickets. When the drawing is held, this will be the box we use. And every ticket will have the same number on it."

"And who is this lucky winner?"

"The Reverend James Colton. Who will promptly request a cash prize in lieu of the advertised award, the money going to his church."

"Rhynne, someday you're going to outwit yourself."

"Not with this lottery. We'll end up with nine thousand dollars to divide between the two of us."

"One hundred times one hundred comes to ten thousand."

"There are certain expenses. I made a donation today to the Reverend Colton's church. And there'll be the second one when he wins."

They heard hoofbeats approaching on the street outside. Pamela went to the window and peered between the curtain and the frame.

"Only some miners," she said after a moment.

"You seemed worried."

"I was and am. About Diego de la Torre."

"Wasn't that the Mexican girl's name?" he asked. "Who is this Diego?"

She told him of Selena's elopement, not concealing her part in it. "I misled Diego," she said.

"And you think he means to harm you or Selena?"

"He lost Selena. And now his sister's dead. I don't know what he might do. I'm afraid, W.W., I'm afraid."

14

The man who called himself Pike threw his pan to the ground. He had found nothing to repay him for his ten hours of panning, not a gold nugget, not a flake, not even a bit of dust. Another day wasted.

Bad luck had dogged Pike all his life.

Back home in Missouri he had tried farming and failed. He had clerked in a grain-and-feed emporium. He had not failed there. Six months after he was hired, the store failed. After his wife left him, he stole horses and made a tolerable living at it for a time, only to be caught red-handed. Faced with a hangman's noose, he escaped from the county jail and fled Pike County in '47.

The run of bad luck wasn't his fault. Was he to blame for two years of drought, for the hardscrabble Missouri soil, for all the damn foreigners?

The bad luck followed him west. Even before his wagon train reached the mountains he'd come down with the scurvy, his hands and feet swelling. Then he was caught borrowing a few cans of food to keep himself going, caught only because the swelling by that time was so bad he could hardly walk, much less run. That bastard of a wagonmaster had abandoned him at Fort Bridger.

California, so far, had been more of the same.

After finally making his way to Sutter's Fort, he suffered a fierce attack of diarrhea and didn't get to the diggings until October. The winter rains started the next week and so he had to wait till spring. In March he started panning, working fifty pans or more of dirt in a ten-hour day. He'd shoveled the dirt, sorted it, panned the best of the lot, his hands in the ice-cold water for ten minutes and more at a time as he whirled the gravel to wash away the lighter sand and separate the gold from the remaining heavy sand.

Pike wouldn't have minded the hard work, he was used to hard work, if he had found gold. He hadn't, only enough to keep him in salt pork, bread and dried beans. So he'd teamed up with another Pike County man, helping him work a cradle—a box on rockers—one of them shoveling dirt into the hopper while the other added water, all the while violently rocking the cradle. The gold, what there was of it, lodged behind the cleats along the cradle's bottom. They made a few dollars, no more, before Pike's partner drifted off after hearing news of a strike to the south.

Pike could always hire out, of course. He could make five or six dollars a day working for somebody else on a Long Tom, shoveling dirt into the coffin-shaped trough, washing it along the trough to a sieve, then into the riffle where the gold particles were caught by wooden bars.

He could have worked for others but he didn't. He knew better. Every time he hired himself out, whether in Missouri or at Sutter's, he had been cheated. He knew that employers, for whatever reason, saw him as an easy mark.

The grain-and-feed boss hadn't paid Pike the wage he'd been promised, blaming the lack of business. At Sutter's, they said he was too slow. Who in hell wouldn't be slow when they had diarrhea? The day after he was fired he saw a Mex doing his old job. Talk about adding insult to injury! Everybody knew how slow they were.

Bad luck piled on top of bad luck. Now, back on his own again, any change in his luck would have to be for the better.

Pike walked up the hill to the oak where he had made his camp. His morning's fire was a black circle on the ground. Beyond the dead fire his blankets were spread on pine boughs. Should I break camp, he asked himself, and move on? Or should I stay? He worried the question, turning it this way and that in his mind. He had just decided to give this claim another day and was heading for the woods in search of fuel for his fire when he heard the hoofbeats.

With one hand on the butt of the gun in his belt, Pike looked down along the creek. A hundred yards below him three horsemen, dressed in the black and silver of Californios, were dismounting to water their horses. Pike watched as one of the men pointed down the creek and another shook his head, gesturing on along the trail they had been following. The third man listened, looking from one of his companions to the other as though undecided.

Lost. The damn greasers were lost. You might know, Pike told himself, relaxing.

One of the horsemen, the undecided one, saw Pike. Saying something to the others, he left them and started to climb the hill on foot. Probably wanted to know the way to Coloma. All they had to do, Pike knew, was follow the creek downstream to the town.

Hands on hips, Pike waited for the Mexican, a thin, wiry man with a small black moustache, to reach him. When the Californio was still twenty feet away he removed his black hat and held it respectfully in front of him.

"Lost?" Pike asked.

"*Si*. We are strangers in search of Coloma."

Pike pointed across the creek into the hills, smiling to himself. They'd end up twenty miles out of their way, maybe even get lost in the mountains.

"Are you Señor Pike?" the Mexican asked.

"I'm Pike," he said, surprised.

The Mexican took a pistol from beneath his hat and shot Pike in the right shoulder. Pike spun back but did not fall.

"I am Diego de la Torre," the Mexican said.

Diego shot Pike again, in the left shoulder this time, the force of the bullet knocking him to the ground.

Pike grunted with pain, trying to reach the gun in his belt. Diego stepped on his hand with the heel of his boot, took the gun from Pike's belt and tossed it into the brush. He slid a knife from Pike's boot and hurled it away.

"I am the brother of Esperanza de la Torre," Diego said.

Pike stared at him through a haze of pain. Esperanza. He recognized the name. That was the greaser girl who had killed English Bob in Hangtown two weeks back. Her brother. This was her brother.

Diego thrust his pistol in his belt and removed a long knife from its sheath. Bending down he grasped the top of Pike's trousers and pulled them toward him, slitting them with his knife, the blade slicing through belt and fabric, the buttons ripping off. Pike reached for Diego, tried to reach for him. He couldn't move his arms.

Diego peeled Pike's trousers down to his knees, then gripped Pike's sex in one hand. Pike screamed. Diego held the point of his knife inches from Pike's eyes. When Pike tried to scramble away, Diego twisted his hand. Pain seared through Pike. All he could see was a jagged red mist. He screamed again. He couldn't move. The pain grew, became unbearable, then grew worse.

Pike screamed again. And then he fainted.

Fainting was the only good luck Pike was to have that day.

Danny O'Lee whistled as he rode his new two-hundred-dollar mule down the trail toward Hangtown. What a glorious day! Even with the morning sun still behind the Sierras, he knew the day would be clear and hot, yet not unbearably hot for already a breeze stirred at his back. A grand day for a man to go into town for provisions. And perhaps stop by the Empire for a bit of sport.

He started to sing:

> *"Did you ever hear tell of Sweet Betsy from Pike*
> *Who crossed the wide praries with her lover Ike?"*

Wouldn't anyone sing on such a day? Especially a man whose claim was even richer than he'd supposed at first, a man with a whole day ahead of him with nary a cloud in the sky, a man heading for town with a bit of gold dust in his poke, a song on his lips, and a beautiful colleen waiting at the end of his journey?

Today he would speak to Selena. No longer the inexperienced lad of a few weeks back, he would march up to her and ask her to walk out with him. What else could she say but yes on such a day as this?

Surely she no longer held a grudge for his high-handed doings on the night of Matt Murphy's wake. Already he could feel her tiny hand on his arm, see her blue eyes looking up at him, hear her lilting laugh as he told her the story of his luck at the diggings.

To think that Pamela was her mother. Why, Pamela must be old, possibly forty, the age of his own mother when she died. She didn't look that old. He would never forget Pamela; he'd always admire her. There's be a corner in his heart for her always. But she wasn't Selena. Golden-haired Selena!

He came down the hill into town, the tents and shacks on both sides of the road only outlines in the grey dawn. There were more of them then he remembered seeing when he'd left just two weeks before. Soon Hangtown would be the biggest city in California if not in all the West.

Only one blight marred Danny's happiness. He had not found Duke Olmsted, the man who'd murdered his father in cold blood. Wherever he had gone he'd asked after him. He'd not found a trace of the man. Duke seemed to have vanished from the face of the earth.

At the bottom of the hill, Danny turned into the town's deserted main street. Soon the mules, horses and men on foot would stir the dust into a haze and fill the air with their oaths and shouts, but now in the early morning the town lay unsullied before him, the only movement the smoke drifting from an occasional chimney.

"Whoa!" he called to his mule.

Something had caught his eye. There, on the great oak just ahead, the hanging oak. Danny dismounted and peered up. A body dangled from one of the lower limbs of the tree, twisting and turning in the wind.

He walked to the tree. The man's body was naked. Danny uttered an inarticulate cry of protest when he saw the slash of dried blood between the man's legs. His eyes went up to the rope around his neck, to his livid face, finally to his mouth. His mouth. What was in his mouth?

Danny gagged. He ran to the side of the road and vomited into the ditch.

* * *

That night Danny O'Lee stood at the Empire bar staring at the whisky in his glass, oblivious to the talk around him.

"Rhynne says he thinks it's this Diego Dellator, or whatever he calls himself."

"He's the brother to the girl that killed herself."

"Why Pike? What did Pike have to do with the girl?"

"He egged everyone on, didn't he?"

"Don't know. Wasn't there."

"From what I hear, seems no one was there."

"Why did the little Mex girl have to go and kill herself? We'd of had a trial and she'd of been let go. Nobody's about to hang a woman."

"Not with them in such short supply, they ain't."

"Maybe English Bob's lucky after all."

"You mean him dying the way he did?"

"Right. We thought he was a goner and then Doc Braithewaite said he'd get better if he didn't get infected and then the next thing we know he's dead."

"I'd of hated to be him if he hadn't died. With that Mex butcher after me."

"Stuffed Pike's parts in his mouth, they say."

"Here's the lad what found him. Danny, tell the gentleman."

Danny shook his head, still staring at the golden glow of his whisky. He raised the glass, sipped and grimaced.

"We ought to have law in Hangtown."

"Didn't some of the boys ride out looking for whoever did it?"

"That they did. They didn't find nothing 'cept

Pike's camp. A few hoofprints, Pike's gun and knife, nothing more."

"Whoever killed Pike, why he's a hundred miles from here by now."

"I wouldn't be too sure. He's crazy, isn't he? A man'd have to be crazy to do something like that. It's not natural. Like eating people. And if he is crazy, he'd do something crazy like staying around. Listening to folks talk about what he done. Watching."

"You mean he might be here? Now?" The miner looked around him. Though the room was full, the saloon was unusually quiet. "Where's Rhynne tonight?" the miner asked. "Why don't we have some music?"

"We want Selena," someone shouted.

"There's an army man over at Coloma," the man next to Danny said. "Maybe he could help track this Dellator. I saw him when I was there last week. A lieutenant. Has part interest in the Coloma store, they say."

"What's the army doing in these parts? Still looking for deserters?"

"More than that. The army has a survey party up in the Sierras. They're talking about building a rail line from the East."

"They'll never get over them mountains. I come over them myself and I know what I'm talking about. They'll have to bring her through all that desert down south if they can get her here at all."

"There's Rhynne. W.W., let's have us some music. The funeral's supposed to be tomorrow, not tonight."

Ned climbed onto the stage and took his place

at the piano. When he began to play the miners stomped their feet in time to the music. "Selena, Selena," they chanted. They clapped their hands and banged their glasses on the bar.

Rhynne jumped to the stage and raised his arms. "Gentlemen," he said, "I give you the Empire's own, the most beautiful girl in the whole of the western hemisphere, performing on our new stage."

As Rhynne walked around the room turning down the lamps, Ned played a fanfare. The men stared above the stage where, on a platform seemingly suspended in midair, Selena stood framed by lights.

Danny stared up at her too as the crowd hushed.

Selena remained perfectly still, as if performing in a living tableau. She was dressed in a formal gown of dark blue velvet, with frills of lace at her neck and wrists. Around her shoulders was a wispy silk scarf of lighter blue. When she smiled it was like a portrait coming to life.

She's changed, Danny thought.

It wasn't just that she stood high above the crowd, out of reach. Nor that she was dressed elegantly, almost primly, a lady from the toes of her strapped slippers to the tips of her white gloves. It was more than that. There was a difference in the way she held herself, in her poise, her seeming disdain for her surroundings. As though in the last few weeks she had become a woman.

Then she sang, sad sentimental ballads for the most part. The miners cried and cheered and cried some more. She sang *Home Sweet Home* and they sang along with her and Danny could feel the heartache in the room, the loneliness of men thousands of miles from the women they loved. Tears filled his own eyes even though he had no home to return to. He ordered another whisky and sipped it.

For the first time in months he thought of his little brother, Burke, waiting back in St. Louis. Like as not the lad believed himself deserted for good and all. Their father going, their mother dying, and now he, himself, had been away for over three years.

Danny wiped at his eyes. Best not to fret over the boy. Wasn't he living with kin, after all? He was called O'Lee now too. There were no more Kennedy's now, only O'Lees. Danny O'Lee and Burke O'Lee. Well, Uncle Hornung would keep Burke O'Lee safe and raise him decent.

Danny thought some more about his own name. He didn't feel like a "Danny" any more. He'd done fairly well for himself and he felt himself growing. He felt more like "Dan." Dan the man. Dan. He liked the shortened version of his name. All he had to do was call himself that and everybody else would too. Well, he would see. He would think about it. Meanwhile, he downed his drink.

He looked up. Now Selena was singing *Sweet Betsy From Pike:*

> *"Out on the prairie one bright starry night*
> *They broke out the whisky and Betsy got tight.*
> *She sang and she shouted and danced o'er the*
> *plain,*

*And showed her bare arse to the whole wagon
  train."*

As the miners howled their approval of the
rowdy refrain, calling for more, the lights on the
platform dimmed and Selena was gone.

"Selena," Danny cried, pushing his way past the
men crowded below and in front of the platform.
"Selena," he shouted, remembering his vow to
speak to her. He stumbled against someone, muttered apologies, at last found the stairs to the platform. Selena was nowhere to be seen.

"Where is she?" he asked Ned, his voice
slurred.

"Laddie, she's gone," Ned said.

"I want to talk to her."

Ned shook his head. "She keeps to herself
these days," he said.

Danny pushed his way back to the bar, ordered
another drink, and finished it in one swallow.

"You can have a roll in the hay with her for
a hundred dollars." The man next to Danny
jerked his thumb at the pine box behind the bar.
"If you're the lucky one."

"A hundred dollars?"

"It's a lottery. Ned there will sell you a ticket.
Don't know if there're any left or not."

"I'll buy a ticket. I'll buy five tickets." Danny
left the bar in search of Ned. He wasn't at the
piano. Danny felt confused. As tight as Betsy had
been in the song. He wanted to cry or sing, he
didn't rightly know which. He stumbled over to
the faro game.

The dealer looked knowingly at him from
across the table. "No luck with the women to-

night, bucko?" he asked. "Then you'll be lucky at cards."

"I've never played," Danny said.

"Had a man in here last night," the dealer said as he shuffled. "He'd never played before. Went away a three hundred dollar winner."

The man next to Danny took a cheroot from his mouth. "Bet any card to win or lose," he said. On the table Danny saw a box the size of a deck of cards along with a printed layout picturing one card of each rank.

Danny laid a five dollar gold piece on one of the pictured cards. "The lad bets the six," the man standing next to the dealer on the other side of the table said. The players were putting their money on other numbers. One placed his bet on the ace and put a penny on top of it.

"What's the penny for?" Danny asked.

"He's coppering his bet. Means he's betting the ace to lose."

"The lad cuts," the dealer said, slapping the cards on the table. Danny cut.

"Cut 'em deep, see 'em weep," one of the players said.

The dealer placed the cards face up in the box. "Bets down," the lookout man next to the dealer said. The dealer removed the first card from the box and placed it to one side. An eight.

"That's the soda," the cheroot smoker told Danny. "Doesn't count."

The next card was a four. The dealer laid the four beside the soda. "Four loses," he said. The card now on top of the deck was a six. "Six wins."

The lookout laid a five dollar gold piece on top of Danny's. "A winner," he called out. "Gentlemen, place your bets," he said in a bored voice. Danny saw the lookout carried a derringer in his shirt front.

"I'll let it all ride," Danny said, remembering hearing his father say those same words.

The dealer removed the six from the box and placed the card on the win pile. A two was the next card. "Two's a loser," the dealer said, "and" —he removed the two—"six wins again." The lookout paid Danny his ten dollars.

"If I was you," the man beside Danny said, "I'd move my bet to another card."

Danny shook his head. "Let it ride," he said. Two aces came up, win and lose. "A split," the dealer called out as the lookout took half of every bet on the ace.

"Rhynne's money," someone said.

After Danny won five more times he had six hundred and forty dollars in front of him. A crowd began to gather around the table, some men betting with him, some against.

"Seven straight wins on the six." The word passed from man to man.

"Eight straight wins on the six!"

Danny won again and still again. The dealer called for more money for the bank and suddenly Rhynne was behind the table, shuffling and dealing the cards himself. Danny won twice more. And still again. As each card was taken from the box, the crowd around the table cheered or groaned. There were thousands of dollars scattered over the playing surface.

Rhynne shuffled.

"I've never seen such a run of luck," he said to Danny. "Sure you want to go on?"

"Quit now," the man with the cheroot said. "Don't be a fool. Quit winners."

Danny stared down at the money. "Let it ride on the six," he said.

While Rhynne took out a handkerchief and mopped his forehead, Danny sipped at a whisky that had appeared beside him.

The cards were cut, the soda set to one side.

"The jack loses," Rhynne said. "The six wins." The men at the table cheered.

"Make your bets."

"I'll let it ride once more," Danny said. "One more win and I quit."

"You're faded," Rhynne told him, removing the winning six from the box. Another six, the six of diamonds, lay beneath it.

"The six loses," he said. "The ten wins. The lad loses."

Rhynne raked the money toward him. The men around the table clapped Danny on the back, shook their heads, drifted away. Danny walked stiffly and precisely to the bar. He found only one man there, his head resting on his hands.

Blearily the man looked up. "Been bucking the tiger?" he asked.

Danny knew he was asking whether he had been playing faro. "Yes," he said.

"How'd you do?"

"Lost five dollars," Danny said. The man once more settled his head on his folded hands.

Danny woke in his room at the Empire in the early hours of the morning. His head ached, his stomach churned, his tongue felt thick. He got up and groped his way outside to the privy. Then he walked to the well, raised the bucket and drank from the dipper. No more whisky for me, he told himself, it's the devil's own drink.

The night air felt clean and cold on his face as he walked down the hill away from the hotel. Selena. He'd promised himself he'd see Selena. What matter the hour? Was he a man or wasn't he?

Ahead of him he heard horses galloping away. Was it morning already, he thought blearily, seeing the sun through the trees. No, he realized, not the sun. Fire. He ran. A cabin on fire, the flames licking up the sides to the roof. He'd been to that cabin before. He'd pushed Selena in through that door.

It was Selena's cabin ablaze in the night.

15

Danny ran to the cabin. The door hung from one canvas hinge; smoke boiled from inside. Putting a handkerchief to his mouth, he plunged through the doorway.

And tripped, falling to his hands and knees. He groped behind him until he touched . . . what? A body. He found a man's arm, gripped him under the shoulders and dragged him outside. In the flickering light from the fire he recognized Rhynne, a red weal on his forehead. Rhynne groaned and sat up, his hand going to his head.

Danny swore, tugged Rhynne several yards further from the fire, then left him and ran back toward the cabin. In the distance the fire bell clanged and he heard men shouting. On hands and knees he crawled into the cabin. Though the air was clearer near the floor, his eyes stung; he could see nothing. Flames crackled in front of him and the heat seared his face.

His searching hands found a bed and on the bed a woman. Danny stood and lifted her into his arms, staggering toward the door, toward where he thought the door must be. The odor of lilacs mingled with the stench of the smoke. He saw the yellow tongues of flame first to his right, then to his left.

He stumbled against the wall, choking, tears filling his eyes. With one shoulder touching the wall he walked to his right. He almost fell through the doorway when he reached it, lurching out into the clear air. Hands held him, while others took his burden from him.

"Is it, is it Selena?" he gasped.

"It's Miss Pamela," someone told him. "She's alive."

Danny rubbed his eyes, looking behind him. The entire cabin was ablaze. Flames licked up the sides and leaped from the roof, and smoke was whirling off on the early morning breeze. Men began passing buckets from hand to hand, not to save the cabin, for it was too late for that, but to prevent the fire from spreading.

Danny ran to the cabin door. The heat struck his face like a blow. Covering his eyes with his arm, he crouched and was about to dash inside when hands grasped him. He shook them off. Someone caught him around the legs, hurling him to the ground.

"Selena," he cried out as he was pulled away.

"She's not in there."

Danny blinked and looked up dazedly.

Rhynne stood swaying in front of him, wincing

as he touched the bruise on his head with his fingers. "They have Selena," Rhynne said flatly.

"What happened?"

It was Ned the piano player who answered. "There were three of them. They burst into the cabin and overpowered me. I was there because the women were afraid. Because of what happened to Pike. One of the men held me while they bound Selena. Pamela was . . . asleep. They took Selena. I saw them. They must have knocked me out before they started the fire. I don't remember."

"Bring horses. We'll get them," Rhynne said.

Danny pushed himself to his feet. "I'm going," he said.

Diego led the way, his two companions just behind him. One, a woman dressed like a man, led Selena's horse. Selena was slung face down on the horse's back with her hands tied to her feet beneath the animal's belly.

A mile from Hangtown, Diego turned off the trail and led them into foothills. The dark of night slowly gave way to a grey dawn. Selena clenched her teeth to keep from moaning. The rope chafed her wrists and ankles, her arms and legs ached, her head pounded. Every jounce of the horse sent pain jolting through her body.

She opened her eyes to see the ground rushing by in a blur of dirt and rocks and horse's hooves. She couldn't tell where they were.

As they climbed into the hills they crossed deep dry gulches where, during the winter rains, streams had hurtled down into the valley. The ground became rockier, the going rougher and slower, and the horses were forced to pick their footing with care. Selena saw a scattering of boulders and shrubs on the slope behind them. Far below in the valley, a dwindling finger of smoke curled upward.

The trail turned abruptly back on itself in the first of a series of switchbacks. They finally crested a rise and came out on a rocky mesa. A strong breeze there pulled at Selena's hair and parted her dressing gown.

Diego held up his hand and they stopped. He dismounted, climbing to an outcrop of rock to gaze back along their trail. When he returned he spoke to his two companions in Spanish, calling one of them Ramon, then came to Selena, pulling a knife from his belt. She shut her eyes.

She felt Diego cut the ropes binding her hands and feet. He pulled her from the horse. When she tried to stand her numb feet betrayed her and she stumbled and fell to the ground. She struggled to her feet as Diego watched her with his hands on his hips. She had to brace herself against the horse to keep from falling again.

The woman dressed like a man came to stand at Diego's side. She was as slim as a boy, her face lean and taut and beautiful, her hair black as the night. Her brown eyes studied Selena and Selena thought she saw a flicker of emotion in the sudden downward curl of the woman's mouth. Pity? Disdain? She couldn't tell.

"Selena," Diego said, "this is Rosita. She is my wife."

Selma stared at the other woman. She was confused. His wife? Then why had Diego abducted her from the cabin? She had assumed, without really thinking, that he had carried her off as he had the year before in San Francisco. To marry her by force. Or . . .

"What do you want with me?" Selena asked.

"You deceived me," Diego told her. "I have vowed vengeance on you and on all Americanos. You have no honor. You are all animals and I must treat you as I would an animal. Americanos killed my sister, Esperanza. Whenever I find an Americano alone, I will kill him. I will kill him without question, without warning, without mercy."

"Diego," she said, "I didn't kill Esperanza. I loved her. Diego . . ."

"I am no longer Diego. He is dead these many months. In English Diego is called James. Jamie. J.M. It amused me to take J.M. as my initials. I am now Joaquin Murieta."

"Diego," she said, going to him. The name Joaquin Murieta, though the mere mention of it would soon bring more fear to the frontier than any other outlaw of the era, meant nothing to her. He was Diego.

"Joaquin."

"Joaquin." She put her hand on his arm. "I tried to save Esperanza. My heart ached for her."

For a moment his eyes seemed to soften and he looked at her almost with longing. Then he stepped away and spat at her feet.

"You'll be no better than a bandit," Selena said. "You'll be hunted down and killed."

"No," he said, his eyes glinting. "Not a bandito. Never. I'll be a hero to my people. I will take only from the rich and give only to the poor."

Before she could answer he turned from her and spoke harshly to Rosita. Taking the rope from the ground, Diego's wife tied Selena's hands behind her back, then thrust a cloth gag in her mouth and knotted the ends behind her head, making the corners of Selena's mouth sting.

Grasping the rope, Diego pushed her forward. Diego. She couldn't think of him as Joaquin. She would never think of him as Joaquin. Taking the reins of his black stallion, Diego signaled to Rosita and Ramon and the two mounted and rode on along the trail.

Selena's bare feet stung from the rocks underfoot as Diego shoved her in front of him. They went down a narrow track among scrub pines. After a few minutes Diego left her, tied his horse behind a clump of bushes and returned with a rifle. When he motioned Selena to the ground, she dropped to her knees and turned to look up at him. He put his hand at the nape of her neck and shoved her forward so she fell face down on the rocks. She gasped with pain. Twisting around, she saw Diego climb to a ledge where, stretched full-length on his stomach, he looked back the way they had come.

Only then did she hear the clatter of hooves far down the mountainside. Diego, tense and alert, waited with the rifle cradled in his arms. Selena saw a rock near her foot. Just beyond the rock the bank dropped steeply down into a jumble of stones, leaves and broken branches. She stretched her foot until her toe touched the rock.

The horsemen—surely, she thought, they were from Hangtown—came closer. Now she could hear the creak of leather, the occasional jingle of spurs, the sound of voices. They must be at the crest of the hill where Diego had halted to cut her free. She could no longer hear the horses. Were the men on foot now, searching for their trail?

Now! She shoved the rock as hard as she could and felt a surge of hope as she heard the rumble of a small landslide. Diego turned toward her, cursing under his breath. Selena listened, hoping to hear the approach of the men.

There were no shouts, no cries. Hadn't they heard the slide? Again hooves clattered over the rock shelf. The sounds receded, grew faint. They had not heard her. They were leaving, following the false trail of Rosita and the man called Ramon. Selena shrank within herself.

Diego waited. Dark clouds drifted overhead. A hawk circled. Still he waited. Finally he stood up and, leaving her on the ground, walked back the way they had come and stood there peering for a while.

"Your friends have gone," he told her when he returned. He gripped Selena under the arms and lifted her to her feet, shoving her against a boulder whose edge cut into her back. Without a word he brought his palm stingingly across her face, then hit her again with the back of his hand.

The blows spun Selena around. When, briefly, he unbound her hands she flew at him, trying to reach his eyes with her nails. He grasped her wrists, one in each hand, then took them both in one hand, bringing them down in front of her. He looped the rope around her wrists, the fibers biting into her skin as he tied her hands together.

Diego removed a long looped rope from his saddle, tied it to the rope on Selena's hands and then to the saddle itself. Then he mounted and set off along the narrow track, pulling Selena behind him. The gag in her mouth stifled her cries.

She was forced to follow his horse, her bare feet stinging. Diego stared ahead as though concerned only with keeping to the trail. When they crossed a meadow where the grass was cool and soft underfoot, Selena ran forward, clutching at his legs with her bound hands. He shoved her away and spurred his horse. She fell to the ground. As the horse dragged her, her dressing gown caught on a branch and ripped open.

Now Selena tried to stand so she could run to keep up with the trotting horse. But she could not get to her feet, so she let herself go limp, closing her eyes as the horse dragged her forward. Diego stopped. He dismounted, walked back to her and yanked her to her feet.

She opened tear-misted eyes to look up at him. Her wrists and shoulders throbbed with pain. She could no longer feel her feet. With his fingers Diego brushed her hair from her face. She thought she saw his eyes glaze over. Remembering? Then he was mounted again and she was stumbling along behind him.

After what seemed an eternity, he stopped. They were on a rise. When she looked into the valley below them she saw, on top of a knoll on the far side, a cabin with a thin trail of smoke rising from the chimney. The cabin's roof sagged. A trapper's cabin, she thought, built before the gold rush. Perched on top of the knoll, with the trees on all sides cut away to leave only protruding stumps, the cabin was situated like a small castle on the crest of protecting cliffs. Other than the smoke, there was no sign of life.

Diego put his fingers to his mouth and whistled a shrill bird-like call. There was no answer from the cabin. Diego whistled again. Now from the cabin came a coyote's howl. Diego grunted and moved on into the valley.

Selena staggered behind him. Her feet were raw and bleeding, and her wrists, shoulders, sides and breasts all ached. Her breath came in panting sobs. With her sight clouded by pain, she had to hold to the rope to guide herself.

Diego dismounted in front of the cabin, untied the long rope, but left her hands tied and the gag in her mouth. Selena blinked, trying to clear her vision as the cabin door opened. She saw a man with a rifle in one hand. At first she didn't recognize the short, heavily bearded man. His hair was unkempt, his red flannel shirt soiled.

And then she knew who he was. Harry Varner.

Diego nodded to Varner and, when the other man stepped aside, pulled Selena after him into the cabin. He led her to a bunk, turned her and pushed her down on her back. She could think of nothing except the pain radiating from her feet, up her legs and through her entire body.

She must have fainted. When she opened her eyes she saw Varner and Diego facing each across a table and eating. Intent on their food and drink, they were not speaking. When Diego finished he stood up and without a word left the cabin. A few minutes later Selena heard him ride away.

Varner walked to the bed and stared down at her.

"So this is the whore of Babylon," he said easily.

He began breathing hard. Thinking he was about to strike her, Selena shut her eyes and turned her head away. The next she knew his footsteps were receding and she heard the cabin door close. She opened her eyes. Varner was gone. The cabin, she saw, was small, half the size of the one in Hangtown. Her eyes widened. Pamela. Rhynne. Were they all right? Surely Diego had taken them from the cabin before he fired it. He must have, she reassured herself. But had he?

She saw Varner's gun leaning against the cabin wall just inside the door. She flexed her numb fingers. Yes, she could move them. Could she hold the gun with her wrists tied? Was the gun loaded? It must be. Could she pull the trigger? She thought she could.

Selena swung her legs from the bed, raising herself to a sitting position. She put her feet on the floor and screamed from the pain, though the sound was muffled by the gag. Tears flooded her eyes. She looked down at her swollen feet. They were smeared with blood, puffed and purplish.

She lay back on the bed. A moment later, Varner came into the cabin carrying a bucket of water. After a few minutes she heard the kettle steaming on the stove. What was he doing? She almost didn't care, so great was her agony.

Varner walked to the bed. He picked her up by the knees and swung her around so her feet were off the bed and she was sitting up again.

"Put your feet in," he told her.

She looked down to see a pan of steaming water on the floor next to the bed. She hesitated.

Varner grasped her ankle and put her foot in the water. Selena, moaning with pain, jerked it out. She tested the water, finally putting both feet in.

Varner knelt beside her. Using a wet cloth he gently washed the dirt and sand from the wounds on the soles of her feet. She sat on the edge of the bed taking deep breaths as the heat of the water soothed her.

"Just as Jesus allowed the sinful woman to anoint his feet," Varner said, "so I will anoint yours."

As Selena stared down at him he repeatedly dropped the cloth in the pan and washed her toes and her insteps. He raised her torn gown to wash her ankles. His words and tone frightened her more than if he had threatened her. His hands on her feet frightened her. Was he mad? Had the burning of his store deranged him?

She glanced frantically around the cabin, saw two calico-covered windows, the table, the black stove, the rifle leaning next to the door. Was this to be her prison—with Varner her jailer?

A call from outside startled them both. Selena held her breath; Varner stiffened and dropped the cloth into the pan of water.

The call came again: "Hooo-eeee."

Varner clumped to the door, picked up the rifle and went to the only window at the front of the cabin. He looked through a rent in the curtain.

"It's Jack Smith of Howard," he said more to himself than to Selena.

Selena, sitting on the bed with her feet still in the water, felt a stir of hope. Jack Smith of Howard. She knew him as a miner, an old-timer in the district. How could she forget that name?

He had come to Hangtown from San Francisco where, because of a confusing number of Jack Smiths, each had added his father's name to his own. This was Jack Smith, son of Howard.

Varner glanced at her. "If you try to warn him," he said, "I'll kill the both of you."

Varner opened the cabin door and stepped outside where Smith could see him yet where he could also watch Selena.

"What might you be wanting with me, Jack Smith of Howard?" he called.

The other man's voice came from a distance. Selena pictured him sitting astride his horse at the bottom of the knoll looking up at the cabin.

"Have you seen three men? Californios. They made off with the girl Selena this morning. The singer at the hotel."

"That I haven't," Varner said.

"Have you seen anyone?"

"Nary a soul. I've got the miseries, had 'em all week, and I've been at the cabin all morning. Anyone riding in these parts, I'd of heard 'em."

"If you see them or get word of them, see the news gets to Rhynne in Hangtown. The whole town's up in arms."

"That I will, Jack Smith."

If Smith left, Selena knew no one else was likely to ride to Varner's. Why would they suspect Varner? She would remain his prisoner. For how long? For what purpose? She must make her presence known.

Unable to stand, she swung herself around so that her feet were on the bed and her hands hung over the side. She reached for the pan. Her fingers gripped its edge, and she raised it until the water ran across the floor and into the cracks between the boards.

She looked up at Varner, who was still talking to Jack Smith of Howard. He wouldn't kill Smith and herself. He wouldn't dare. Selena swung her arms and sent the pan spinning across the room. It clattered against the far wall.

"What was that?" she heard Smith ask.

Varner looked behind him into the room. When he saw Selena sprawled half off the bed and the pan next to the wall, he smiled. Still smiling, he turned to Jack Smith. "Just my dog," he said. "Critter upset some pans."

She heard Jack Smith answer and then she heard him ride off.

Varner came back into the cabin. After he leaned his rifle against the wall he went to the stove. He picked up the kettle and carried it across the room, took the pan and refilled it.

Coming to the bed, he placed the pan on the floor. She cringed away. He lifted her bound arms and swung her around so her feet were over the edge of the bed. Kneeling beside her, he once again began tenderly to bathe her feet.

16

King Sutton kicked a stone and sent it skitter-
ing into a gully. They had lost the trail. Sutton
had sent four men, two on each side of the original track, to look for signs. So far three of the
four had reported back. They had found nothing.

The fourth man rode in from the south.

"No luck, colonel," he said to Sutton. They had
started calling him "colonel" when they elected
him their leader. As though the title gave them
more confidence in him.

Jed pointed toward three horsemen approaching up a long slope, a blue-coated army officer in
the lead. As the men drew near, Sutton saw that
the officer was a lieutenant. He was about thirty
with a short black beard and a campaign hat
shading his eyes.

When Sutton rode to meet him, the officer

reined in and the other two men stopped a short distance behind him.

"Lieutenant Sherman," the officer said, "at your service, sir. We rode out from Coloma to offer our help."

"We've lost their trail," Sutton admitted. "Followed the tracks of their horses up from Hangtown to a mesa a ways back, then lost them here on the rocks."

"I'll see what I can do," the lieutenant said. He rode to where the rest of Sutton's party waited. There were five of them, the slave Jed, Danny O'Lee, Doc Braithewaite and two others. Rhynne was back in Hangtown coordinating the search.

"I've done a bit of tracking in my time," Sherman said. "What do you know of these bandits? The reports reaching Coloma were sketchy."

Sutton repeated Rhynne's description of the early morning raid.

"I can tell you're a southerner, sir," Sherman said when Sutton had finished.

"I'm proud to say I hail from Georgia."

"A fine state, Georgia. I hope to have the opportunity to go there someday."

"You'll be made most welcome, lieutenant. I only trust you'll be able to come in time of peace, not war. I'd hate like hell to have to fight you."

The lieutenant nodded. "My sentiments exactly, sir."

They joined the others and Sutton led them back to the last trace they had found of the fleeing horsemen. Sherman dismounted, knelt beside the trail and studied the hoofprint while Sutton watched.

"I was taught the little I know of reading sign

by an Arapaho," Sherman told him. "I never completely mastered the art, but I can tell whether a horse is shod or barefoot, whether he ran or walked, and whether he's ridden or wandering loose. I try to recognize the difference in tracks. The worn heel of a boot, the size and cut of a moccasin, the curve to a horseshoe."

"What do you see here?"

"If I'm not mistaken the horse is a stallion or gelding from a rancho near Monterey, probably ridden by a woman who passed this way an hour ago."

Sherman stood and faced the men waiting on their horses. "By your leave, colonel," he said to Sutton. He had heard the men use the title and hadn't questioned it.

"Of course, lieutenant," Sutton said.

"Dismount and form a line," Sherman told them. "We'll spread out like a skirmish line and sweep to the east with no man more than twenty feet from his neighbor. Look for droppings, snapped twigs, disarranged branches, bent grass." He turned to Sutton. "You and I will hew to the middle," he said, "with the men on either side of us. If that meets with your approval, sir."

Sutton nodded.

As the men formed a ragged line, the lieutenant said to Sutton, "The Indian who taught me to read sign could tell from an indication as small as a single blade of grass the direction a man or animal was headed and the time, within an hour, when he had passed. I've heard of Indians studying the insect markings in a track to judge how old the track was. I've never credited that story myself."

He looked to right and left, then raised his arm and signaled the men forward. They tramped past the spot where Sutton had waited for his outriders, dipped into a ravine and up the far side, and crossed a series of rain-washed gullies.

As Sutton walked, his eyes to the ground, he rubbed his cheek where Selena's nails had raked his face, remembering the young girl's passion on the day Esperanza killed herself. Excitement rose in him. He desired Selena more than he had ever desired a woman before. He wanted to conquer her, to tame her, to make her his alone.

Hanging was too good for those three Mexicans. The bastards. If he had his way, and he meant to, he'd strip them to the waist and give them thirty-nine lashes each and when they thought their pain was ended he'd give them thirty-nine more. Only then would he hang them. Not with the quick clean jerk that breaks a man's neck. No, he'd haul them slowly off the ground and let them dangle until they strangled to death. Even that lingering death was too good for them.

On Sutton's right, Danny O'Lee plodded doggedly ahead, his lips moving slightly as he walked. He was praying. Asking God to save Selena, to let her be found unharmed. Danny had made a rich strike; in Hangtown they'd hailed him as a brave man after he saved Pamela and Rhynne from the burning cabin. Yet, without Selena, the money and the praise were as ashes in his mouth.

Should he offer to say the rosary twice over every night for as long as he lived if Selena was returned safely? Danny decided not to make the offer. "You don't make deals with the Almighty," his father had once told him.

Sherman held up his hand. The party halted, hands on guns, waiting while the lieutenant angled off to the right. He was back in a moment.

"Only some Digger squaws," he said. "No use questioning them, they'll tell us nothing."

As they went on, Sutton saw a number of Indian women in a nearby meadow. They had work baskets suspended from their backs, held on by thongs of leather across their foreheads.

"Gathering plant seeds," Sherman said. "They mix the seeds with pounded acorns and grasshoppers for bread."

Sutton grimaced but noted that the younger squaws were quite attractive with their firm bare breasts and slender legs.

"Ho, lieutenant. Look here." It was Doc Braithewaite.

"Stay where you are, all of you," the lieutenant shouted when two of the men started to veer on toward the doctor. "I'll take a look first."

Sherman knelt beside Braithewaite to study the horse droppings. Farther on he discovered a single hoofprint.

"The same shoe as before," he said to Braithewaite. He signaled the men in. "We're back on their trail," he told them.

They returned to their horses and, as they mounted, Sutton saw a rider coming from the direction of Hangtown.

"It's Jack Smith of Howard," Braithewaite said when the man drew nearer.

"Any luck?" Sutton asked Smith as the rider reined to a halt.

"None." Smith spoke more to the lieutenant than to Sutton. "I rode through the diggings to the east. They haven't seen hide nor hair of them. I even went by Varner's place. Nobody there 'cept him and his dog."

Sutton nodded. "We lost their trail but now we're onto it again," he said. "Thanks to Lieutenant . . ." He turned to the army officer. "What did you say your name was, sir?" he asked.

"Sherman. William Tecumseh Sherman."

Rosita and Ramon rode slowly up a creek into a ravine where crags rose on both sides of the trail and an occasional stunted pine grew among the rocks. They stopped near a freshet, watered their horses, then hobbled and muzzled them. Following Joaquin's orders, they had thrown off their pursuers on the mesa. Now they prepared to wait for his return, their flanks and rear protected by the high hills on both sides of their camp.

After they ate, Rosita splashed through the creek and began climbing the bank on the far side. Ramon took his rifle and zigzagged his way up the near slope. When he reached an uptilted shelf of rock he lay prone with his body concealed behind a jumble of boulders.

Below Ramon, the valley narrowed like a funnel as it entered the ravine. He was in a good spot. He looked along the sights of his rifle to the creekbed directly beneath him, then slowly swung the gun up past the scattered boulders in the ravine to a pine grove at its entrance. Far beyond the pines lay Hangtown.

He waited. He saw Rosita scanning the trail from her hiding place among the rocks fifty yards across from him. Suddenly she tensed. When he followed her gaze back along the trail he saw a wisp of dust in the distance. The dust grew to a cloud.

Not Joaquin then. From the size of the dust cloud he knew there must be at least eight riders. He smiled to himself. He and Rosita could hold this position against a hundred, at least till dark. And then they would slip away.

He watched the riders approach at a lope and, as they drew closer, recognized the blue U.S. army uniform of the lead horseman. Ramon felt his heart pound in his chest. His brother, Jorge, had been one of *los ninos* killed fighting the Americans at Chapultepec. Jorge had been sixteen.

How had their pursuers found them? Ramon wondered. He had clouded their trail well. He frowned. Joaquin, when he came, would be angry. Ramon shrugged. Time for that later.

The riders, centered in his sights, were too far away for him to risk a shot. He must wait till they reached the defile below him.

Ramon watched the horsemen follow the trail into the stand of pines. At first he could see the riders through the trees, for there was little undergrowth, but then the grove thickened until the men were hidden from his sight. Ramon judged their pace, fixing his eyes on the spot where he knew they must emerge. They'll come out when I count to three, he told himself.

Uno . . . dos . . . he held his count for an instant . . . *tres.* The horsemen did not appear. Ramon hunched his shoulders and shifted his legs, which were splayed on the rock. Still he saw no one. He glanced at Rosita on the other side of the creek before looking back to the pines. Squinting, he tried to penetrate the late afternoon darkness. He held his gaze. There. A man, only his face visible, standing beside one of the nearer pines.

Ramon lay still, his breathing quick and loud. From behind him the creek splashed downhill toward the trail. A hawk wheeled overhead. Ramon looked from the bird back to the shadows under the pines. The man was gone.

Ramon waited. He drew in a long breath as two men rode from under the trees, their horses at a walk. The Army officer was in the lead. He scanned Ramon's side of the slope, a rifle under his arm, the other horseman following twenty feet behind with his eyes on the opposite slope. The two of them came on past clumps of brush and into a jumble of boulders. They're in range, Ramon thought. Barely, but in range.

The lead rider stopped and raised his hand, his gaze fixed on Ramon's hiding place. Without warning Ramon's side cramped; though he felt a knot of pain he did not move. Slowly the cramp eased. The two men below him, their eyes still on the slope, appeared to talk. Ramon sighted on the officer, then raised his rifle to adjust for the distance. He felt the wind blowing steadily from behind him.

The officer pulled his horse around and headed for the shelter of the pines. Had they seen him? The man's companion swung about and followed. Both were going back.

Ramon fired. For Jorge, he told himself.

Sherman's horse lurched forward, throwing him against the saddlehorn. He grasped for the horn as the horse stumbled and fell sideways. Sherman leaped clear. He hit the ground rolling, coming to rest flat on his stomach. He reached for his rifle a few feet away. Dirt puffed next to him—he hadn't heard the shot. Crouched over, rifle in hand, he ran for a cluster of boulders just as another shot cracked from the hillside.

He sprawled behind the protecting rock. He glanced over his shoulder but couldn't see Sutton. His wounded horse whinnied, struggled to stand, but could not; its right rear leg had been shattered. A bullet ricocheted from the rock above Sherman's head.

A minute passed, two minutes, three. Sherman looked around the outcropping and saw a blur of movement on the hill. He sighted, pressed off a shot; the shot was answered at once from high on the ravine's near side. At least two of them then.

"Come back," Sutton called to him from the pines. "I'll cover you."

"Wait." Sherman aimed and fired. His horse stiffened, head dropping to the ground. One leg pawed the air, then fell back. For a moment Sherman stared at the dead horse. He sighed and looked away.

"Now," he called to Sutton.

At the first shot from the pines, Sherman thrust himself off the ground, running low and flat out. He stumbled in a gopher hole, almost fell, kept his feet, saw branches above him. He flung himself onto the pine needles beside Sutton, his chest heaving, the sharp odors of pine and gunsmoke mingling in his nostrils.

"There's two or three of them," Sutton said.

"One high on the right, another halfway up on the left. Might be a third. I can't be sure 'cause the one on the right's been moving around so much."

Sherman looked along the line of men positioned behind the screen of pines. "Anybody know this country?" he asked.

"I've done some prospecting hereabouts," Jack Smith of Howard said.

"How long a ride to get around these cliffs? So we can take them from the rear."

"Couple of hours anyway. You'd have to go back five miles or more and then swing to the east. It's even farther the other way."

"Then that's what we'll do," Sherman said. "Two men can loop around behind to come at them from the rear, two more can get above them on the north by climbing the slope, two on the south. The rest of us will stay here and keep them pinned down. We'll have to hurry. We've only a few hours till dark."

"They could be to hell and gone in two hours," Sutton said. "What's to stop them from riding right out of the upper end of that ravine?"

"Probably nothing," Sherman said. "That's the risk we'll be taking."

"Could we overtake them if they rode out?" Surprised, they turned to look at Danny O'Lee. "Could we?" Danny asked again.

"I'd put our chances at less than one in three," Sherman told him. "Considering the poor horses we've got. Of course, having to take the girl along should slow them."

"I say we don't wait," Sutton said. "I say we go in after them right now."

"I'm with the colonel," Danny said. Several of the other men nodded.

Sherman shook his had. "It's too dangerous. We'd be attacking what amounts to a fortified position."

"I'm going to get Selena out of there now," Sutton told him. "How many of your men are with me?"

"I am." Danny stepped to Sutton's side. One by one the others joined him.

"I can see I'm a minority of one," Sherman said. "We'll attack."

"Jed and I will go up the left slope," Sutton said.

"I'll take the right," Danny told him.

"I'll go with him." It was Jack Smith of Howard.

"I'll still send two riders around to invest their rear in case we get pinned down here." Sherman pointed to the two men who had accompanied him from Coloma. "Maguire? Biggs?" They nodded.

Sutton went to his horse and returned with a rifle. He handed it to Jed who stood weighing it in his hand before grinning at Sutton.

The two men set off through the trees. When Sutton reached the last of the pines he paused, looked at Jed. "I'll go first," he told him.

When he heard the first covering shot from the pines, Sutton dashed ahead, throwing himself behind the first of the boulders at the base of the hill. He looked back to see Jed sprint from cover. A single shot rang out from the crest of the opposite slope. Jed stumbled and fell full-length in the dirt.

A third rifleman. Sutton glimpsed him, a figure in black. He squeezed off a wild shot. Behind Sutton, Jed lay groaning. The black man raised himself to his hands and knees and began crawling toward him. Sutton put down his rifle and ran to him, grasped him under the shoulders and pulled him behind the shield of boulders. Ripping away Jed's shirt, he exposed a bullet wound in his upper right chest. Jed's breathing was ragged and shallow.

Sutton heard a scrambling and looked behind him to see Braithewaite running toward him. The doctor knelt at his side. "I'll see to him," he said.

Sutton turned, picked up his rifle, and sprinted up the slope to the next group of boulders. An occasional shot came from the pines behind him but there were none from above. He ran from boulder to boulder, heedless of the danger. Yet he drew no fire. Just below the spot where the gunman had waited when he and Sherman first approached the ravine, he sprawled on the ground, breathing hard. There were no sounds from either above or below.

Sutton eased himself out from behind the boulder. Deep in the ravine ahead of him he heard a horse whinny and then the thud of receding hoofbeats. He pushed himself to his feet and ran to the ledge from which the gunman had fired on them. No one was there. Sutton stood, half expecting to draw a shot. The ravine remained silent.

Sutton looked back to the pines and, after waving Sherman forward, ran ahead to the top of an outcropping of rock. He saw three horsemen galloping away with a fourth riderless horse behind them. Selena. Where was Selena? Sutton raised his rifle. Too late. They were around a bend in the ravine and out of sight before he could fire.

Sutton swore. He climbed down the hill, reaching the trail beside the creek just as Sherman and two others rode up. Danny O'Lee and Smith were already on their way down the other side of the ravine.

"There's three of them," Sutton said, "riding up out of the ravine."

"What about the girl?" Sherman asked.

"Selena wasn't with them."

"Could we be on the trail of the wrong men?"

"I don't know. They looked like the three Rhynne described. Californios. I can't be sure."

"They sure act guilty as hell," Jack Smith said.

"They might have killed Selena," one of the men said.

"Or left her somewhere." Sherman looked up the ravine. "The only way we'll find out is by going after them."

"Wait." They saw Doc Braithewaite climbing down the slope.

"How's Jed?" Sutton asked him.

"I bandaged his wound. If we get him back to town he might pull through. The bullet seems to have missed his lung."

"Thank God." Sherman started to turn away.

"Wait," Doc Braithewaite said again. "I left Jed because I just remembered something."

They all looked at him.

"Something about Harry Varner," Braithewaite said. "I remembered that Harry Varner hates dogs. Never could stand one anywhere near him."

17

Harry Varner took the Bowie knife from his boot and cut the gag from Selena's mouth and the ropes from her hands. He watched as she first massaged her wrists and then the corners of her mouth. Even with her feet swollen, her dressing robe and nightgown torn and soiled and her hair in disarray, she was beautiful. A handmaiden of Satan, he told himself, who uses her beauty to lead men into the fires of damnation.

He went to the stove, ladled stew onto a tin plate, then poured a cup of coffee. When he carried the meal to the bed, Selena looked up at him with misted blue eyes. Quickly handing her the plate and cup, he turned away. Weeping was one of their tricks. His wife, before she left him, had used all manner of stratagems in her attempts to lure him from the path of righteousness.

Varner took the pan from the floor beside the bed and threw the water on the ground outside. After wringing out the cloth he had used to cleanse Selena's feet, he laid it on the sloping wooden rack to dry. When he reentered the cabin he saw that Selena had put her plate and cup on the floor next to the bed and had drawn a blue blanket to her chin. She lay staring straight up at the ceiling.

"Be you wanting more to eat?" he asked.

"No." She spoke the word so low he could hardly hear her.

He stood looking down at her pale face haloed by her golden hair.

"I want you to take me home," she said, glancing at him for the first time.

"You're in no fit condition to travel."

"I can ride."

"I ain't got a horse. I had a mule that died on me a month ago. You'd have to walk and you can't."

"Send for someone in town to come for me. Send for . . ." She started to say Rhynne but thought better of it. "Send for my mother."

"I ain't had a horse since the fire," Varner said. "When I had to sell it to pay my debts." He closed his eyes and saw the flames licking along the sides of his store and erupting upwards into the night sky. His breathing quickened. "You and Rhynne," he said, "you fired my store."

"I had nothing to do with the fire."

"I saw you kissing him while you both watched my store burn. I saw you on the hill. The devil himself, Rhynne is, and you're his handmaiden.

The devil's mistress is what you are. You'll both burn in the everlasting fires of Hell."

"Mr. Varner," she said, "don't talk that way. You don't know what you're saying. Remember, you were the one who threatened to burn the Empire. Have you forgotten that? I'm telling the truth when I say I knew nothing of the fire at your store. Nothing."

Varner went on talking as though he hadn't heard her. "They tie witches to the stake," he said. "They tie them hand and foot and throw torches on the kindling. You can hear the flames spit and crackle; you can see the fire licking its way towards the evil women. When their gowns catch fire they scream for their protector but he never comes." His voice rose. "You can hear their screams and smell the burning of their flesh as their souls are doomed to everlasting damnation."

Selena turned her face to the wall.

Varner trembled. He swung about and walked to the door where he leaned his head on his forearm. He drew a deep shuddering breath as images circled in his mind. He felt his body being swept around and around as by a great whirlpool while he struggled to keep from being sucked into the depths.

As his head slowly cleared he opened his eyes to see the pine boards of the door. Exhausted, he slumped into a chair at the table and laid his head on his arms. How long he slept he didn't know but when at last his head jerked upright the cabin was much darker than he remembered.

Selena was asleep.

He walked across the room to stare down at

her fair skin and her blond hair tumbling loose over the blanket. He watched the rise and fall of her breasts beneath the blanket and, when she turned in her sleep, he saw her body outlined on the bed.

Gently he lifted the top of the blanket and drew it down until only her feet were covered. The side of her robe was torn from just beneath the shoulder to the knee. Through the rent he saw the bruised skin of her back, the curve of her hip, and the white of her upper leg. He shivered as he felt excitement grow in him, the desire so long denied. Selena twisted on the bed, moaning in her sleep. A moan of pain? he wondered. Or of remembered passion?

Quickly Varner covered her with the blanket. She was a temptress. He must put away all temptation, put Satan behind him. Going to the table he struck it with his fist, three, four, and five times until his hand throbbed with pain. Slowly the excitement waned, lessened without dying, receding to the edge of his consciousness.

Walking about the kitchen area of the cabin, Varner collected all the old tin cans he could find, then took a thick ball of twine from a shelf. His arms full, he went outside. Only when he was halfway to the bottom of the hill did he remember his rifle. Putting the cans and twine on the ground, he hurried back to the cabin. Selena still tossed in her sleep. Varner took the rifle from beside the door and retraced his steps.

On the low ground around the knoll, he tied the end of the twine to the bottom of a shrub, unwound the twine, cut it and tied the other end to a can which he had filled with pebbles, all the while keeping the cord as taut as he could. When he had encircled the knoll with trip-cords, he stepped outside the circle and walked some distance away. Then he turned and approached the cabin as a stranger might, noting the most visible parts of his warning system.

By the time he was finally satisfied, the sun was behind the hills and the cabin lay in shadow. Carrying his rifle, he climbed the hill and went inside. Selena's eyes were closed, her breathing regular.

Varner struck a lucifer to light a lantern. With rifle and lantern in one hand and the bucket in the other, he walked the half mile to the stream. He returned, taking care to avoid the trip-cord, and heated the water on the stove. When it steamed, he poured the water into a pan and carried it to the bed.

He shook Selena by the shoulder, watching as her eyes slowly opened. She was awake all along, he told himself. He nodded to the pan of water and, going across the cabin, put more wood on the fire. The lantern on the table threw his shadow onto the cabin walls. When he looked over his shoulder he saw Selena sitting on the edge of the bed with both feet in the water.

Varner went outside, returning with the cloth he had used to bathe her feet, and knelt beside the bed.

"Give it to me," Selena said, reaching for the cloth.

He shook his head. "It's my penance," he told her, dipping the cloth in the water and anointing her feet. He cleansed her ankles, stroked higher, pushing aside the thin cloth of her nightgown.

Selena drew her feet up onto the bed. When she leaned forward to cover them, the blanket fell away from the top of her body and Varner saw the white skin of her throat and the shadow between her breasts. She pulled the blanket up around her neck.

Varner reached down and took the blanket and yanked it from her hands. He threw it into a corner of the room. Selena screamed, her hands rushing to cover her breasts.

"The Lord has decreed," Varner said, "that harlots shall be stoned until they are dead!"

"I'm not a harlot!"

"Men pay a hundred dollars for the chance to satisfy their lusts on your wanton body. You're being sold by Rhynne to every man in the diggings willing to pay his price. Who will enjoy the charms of the beautiful Selena? Who will sate himself on the pleasure offered by her flesh? Who will look upon her dove-white breasts? Who will have carnal knowledge of her? And you're not a harlot? Not a whore?"

He gripped the top of her gown in both hands and tore both gown and robe, sundering them, leaving her half-naked. When she twisted away, he pinned her wrists above her head with his hands. She screamed from the pain of his fingers on her bruised skin. He stared at her writhing body, then threw himself on her, releasing her hands to roughly caress first her breasts and then her legs while she beat at his face with her fists, screaming at him to stop.

All at once his body went limp. Selena moaned, shifting away, extricating herself from beneath him. Pulling her robe together, she tried to cover her nakedness as she cringed away from him. Varner lay face down on the bed beside her with his shoulders heaving. She realized he was crying.

"Even now," he said, "my faith is no proof against the weakness of my flesh."

She looked down the length of his body and saw the hilt of a knife projecting from a sheath on the side of his boot. Sitting up, she leaned forward and took the hilt in her hand, then, watching Varner, eased the knife out of its sheath. Once freed, she held it in her hand, staring at the curved and deadly blade.

She held the knife so that it barely touched the side of Varner's flannel shirt. She closed her eyes, gathering courage to plunge the blade into him. No, she couldn't. Yet she had to. Varner was mad. There was no telling what he might do. She tensed and thrust the knife forward. The blade met nothing but air.

She opened her eyes to see Varner standing beside the bed watching her. "Give that to me," he demanded, holding out his hand.

Selena, crouching on the far side of the bed, shook her head. As Varner reached for the knife, she slashed wildly at his hand. He stepped back, watching her warily. She saw his eyes go from the knife to the floor and back to the knife. He smiled as he stooped beside the bed. Standing again, he swung the pan he had used to bathe her feet, hurling the water into Selena's face.

She gasped, blinking and spluttering as he clambered across the bed to grasp her wrist. He twisted her hand and the knife dropped onto the blanket between them. He released her, seized the knife and stood up. His eyes seemed unfocused as they stared at the foot-long blade.

Mumbling to himself, Varner snatched the roll of twine from the table and began cutting it into equal lengths. When he was done, he threw the knife to the floor, where it quivered point down in a pine board. He approached the bed with the lengths of twine in one hand.

Selena huddled against the wall at the head of the bed. When Varner reached for her, she screamed. He took her hands in his, trying to draw them together. She fought him, striking out at him with all her strength. Though he was short, her own height at the most, Varner's shoulders were broad and his arms heavily muscled. When he pressed his body on hers, she knew she was no match for him, yet she struggled on, stopping only when she lay exhausted beneath him.

He lashed her hands to the head of the bed, one on each side, and though she pulled and twisted she could not loosen the bonds. Kneeling beside her, he grasped one of her ankles while she kicked futilely at him. He tied her ankle to the foot of the bed, circled the other with cord and tied it to the other side so she lay spread-eagled on her back.

Varner then drew the tattered robe and gown apart so that she lay naked to the waist. She saw his mouth working as he looked down at her, saw his chest rising and falling in what were almost sobs. He stepped back to take the hilt of the knife in his hand, easing it back and forth until the point came free. He came toward her.

Selena screamed.

"When I have finished with you," he said in a

low voice, "you'll no longer be able to tempt men. I'll be free of your wiles. Men will gaze upon you only to turn away in revulsion."

She stared in horror at the knife blade glinting in the light from the lantern. Varner reached down. She closed her eyes, twisting from side to side. She felt a slicing pain above her right breast. When she opened her eyes she saw he had traced a circle in the skin around her breast, leaving a thin red line on her flesh.

"No, no, no," she moaned.

Smiling, he stooped to pick up the wet cloth from the floor. He pushed the cloth into her mouth and tied the ends behind her head.

The lantern on the table began to sputter. Varner went to the rear of the cabin and rummaged on his shelves for an oil can. When he had the wick burning high, he again went to the shelves, this time to get a handful of candles. He used the lantern to light one, then placed it in hot wax on the floor beside the head of the bed. He lit the other candles until seven flames burned in a semicircle around the bed, three on each side and one at the foot.

He knelt beside the bed, his lips moving silently. Selena realized he was praying.

She twisted her head from side to side, trying to speak, trying to plead with him, to invoke God's name. She choked on the water dripping into her throat from the cloth in her mouth, gagging as she struggled to breathe.

Varner rose to his feet. With the knife in one hand, he grasped her breast with the other. She gagged again, screamed, and fainted.

A clatter came from outside.

Varner stiffened. The sound was not repeated. He released Selena, went to the window at the front of the cabin and held the curtain aside. All he saw was the black of the night.

He walked around the bed, pinched out the candle flames, then turned the lantern low and set it on the floor. Taking his Hawken rifle, he slipped from the door to crouch in the shadows in front of the cabin, waiting for his eyes to grow accustomed to the dark. By the light of a quarter moon low in the west he saw the outlines of the hills and the pines. There was no hint of movement in the deeper darkness around the knoll.

Had he really heard the rattle of pebbles in one of the tin cans? He was no longer sure. Was the sound, if there had been one, an animal prowling in the night? How could he be sure? Going back inside the cabin he went to the window and rested the rifle on the sill. He sighted blindly at the trail leading to the cabin and fired.

There was no response. Drawing the rifle back, he placed the butt on the floor and reloaded. He was slow at it, being unaccustomed to the gun, and could load and fire less than once a minute. He shot into the night again and once more placed the butt on the floor to reload.

He listened. There was no answering shot. He must have been mistaken. There had been no clatter. Perhaps he had heard the cry of an animal. Should he, though, reconnoiter to be sure? Dare he leave the cabin? His only safety, he felt, was here.

Varner looked toward the outline of Selena's body on the bed. She was quiet, unmoving. He put his hand to the log wall, bracing himself as he felt a tingling rising to his head. The whirlpool sucked him deeper into blackness. He fought to free himself, afraid of what awaited him in the depths.

He shook his head to clear it. What was that? Had he heard a noise in front of the cabin? Just beyond the door? Like a whisper in the night, a whisper as soft as the breeze. Yes, it must have been the wind. Or a man? A man who stalked him, waiting to punish him for his transgressions?

Varner put his head beside the partly open door. He heard nothing. He eased the door shut and slid home the bar. Again he looked toward the bed. I should have guessed, he thought. She had summoned the devil. She had prayed to the evil one and brought him here.

He had heard her mumbling while he prepared to punish her for her sins. Now he knew what she had been saying. At times he had opened his Bible to Matthew and shuddered at the sound of the words on his own lips. Now he repeated them.

"Amen," he chanted, "Ever for glory the and power the and kingdom the is thine for. Evil from us deliver but temptation into not us lead."

The Lord's Prayer said backwards—an incantation to call forth the powers of evil. Selena had summoned the devil and the devil's minions. And he had heard them abroad in the night, circling the cabin, their wings beating the air above him. Yet he was safe here. He would fear no evil as long as he walked the path of righteousness.

He could destroy them by killing the harlot. With her death they would return to those nether regions from which she had called them. He felt for his knife. Not in his boot. Where was it? Had she somehow spirited the knife away? Or had he left it on the bed?

A thud shook the cabin. Varner looked around him in confusion. The thud came again, the bar across the door cracking as the door shuddered inward. Yet the bar held.

Varner raised his rifle, firing point-blank at the door as the pine boards were smashed inward. A log thrust through the opening into the cabin. The curtain was ripped from the front window. Men rushed into the room through both door and window. Varner retreated, stumbling backward as he tried to reload, only to have the gun twisted from his hands.

He picked up the lantern from the floor and swung it in an arc, releasing it, hurling it at them. The lantern crashed against the wall, the oil making a trail of fire to the floor. Varner backed toward the window at the rear of the cabin while men beat at the flames. He turned to see a face appear at the window behind him. He was trapped.

He ran to the table, unseen in the swirl of smoke. Taking the can of oil, he unscrewed the top and flung the oil onto the flames. Fire burst up around him. Men shouted. He saw Selena being carried from the cabin wrapped in a blanket. He saw men retreating before the flames. Varner stared at the wall of fire in front of him, then began backing away from the heat until he came to the log wall at the rear of the cabin. Fire hemmed him in; there was no escape.

His mind spun. The whirlpool sucked him into its vortex. His soul was twisting and turning. He no longer struggled. He let himself be pulled into the depths. And beyond. And then he saw his fate. The everlasting flames of Hell.

He had expected no better. He had hoped and prayed for something else, yet he had expected no more than this. He knew the evil that dwelt in his heart. Broad is the way that leadeth to destruction. The wicked shall be turned into Hell, into the fiery furnace, into the bottomless pit. Man's fate is to burn through all eternity.

He accepted his fate, facing the flames calmly. But then the fire enveloped his body, and he screamed.

18

"What in the name of hell do you mean?" King Sutton leaned across Rhynne's desk. "You could call off the lottery any goddamned time you wanted to."

Rhynne tapped the ashes from his cigarillo. They were in his office in the just-completed addition to the Empire. "Of course I could, colonel, if I wanted to return ten thousand dollars to miners scattered between here and Mariposa. What I meant to say was that I don't intend to cancel the lottery. It's scheduled for tomorrow and will be held tomorrow."

"You're making Miss Selena appear to be a . . . a . . ." He groped for the right word.

"I think 'pretty waitress girl' is the phrase they use in San Francisco."

"I'll say it plain out, Rhynne. You're making her seem a common whore."

"Selena's name has never been mentioned in connection with the lottery. Not by me."

"Then you're the only one who hasn't mentioned it. What do you think the man who wins the drawing tomorrow will expect? To go to bed with *you?*"

"Hardly. Yet what's expected and what actually occurs are often different things. If you understand my meaning." He put his cigarillo on a tray and stood up. "Come with me, colonel, and I'll show you one good reason I'm not about to call off the lottery."

The two men crossed the gambling saloon to the hotel. At the top of the stairs Rhynne unlocked and opened the first door on the right and stood aside.

"Look in here," he told Sutton.

"My God, I've never seen its like."

A majestic bed filled most of the room. Each corner of its purple velvet canopy was decorated with a high plume of rose-colored feathers. When Rhynne pulled a tasseled cord, velvet curtains parted to reveal a coverlet of white and gold, the colors matching the ornate white headboard topped by a golden crown.

"I'll concede this is a bed fit for a queen," Sutton said.

"Or a king. It's a Louis XIV. Not that he ever slept in it; I'm told these beds were more for show than for use. A man was known by the bed in his parlor in those days. Not much different from the way some Hangtown miners have their teeth pulled so they can replace them with gold ones."

"Sir," Sutton said, "this bed must have cost you a fortune."

"One thousand dollars. Tom Horobin found it in a San Francisco bordello, as a matter of fact. He was told they'd had it shipped in from Mexico."

"Thousand dollars or not, Miss Selena isn't about to bed down here with some sweating miner."

"Of course she isn't. Didn't she tell you?" Rhynne lowered his voice. "I fully expect the winner of the lottery to decline the prize."

"She mentioned something of the sort. Surprisingly enough, she seems quite unconcerned about the lottery. She must have a great deal of faith in you, Rhynne. Why she does I'll never fathom."

"Because I'm an honorable man after my own fashion."

"Be that as it may, I can't imagine any man in the gold country who wouldn't give half his claim for her, much less turn her away after winning her. I wouldn't."

"You have a ticket?"

"Number forty-three."

"I realize most men would, like yourself, welcome the chance to know Selena better. Yet I can imagine a man who wouldn't. Or, even if he did, couldn't. But the less said, the better. Don't you agree?"

"Rhynne, you are one smooth son of a btich."

"Which, I take it, is considered a compliment in the state of Georgia."

"Sometimes I wish I were back in Athens," Sutton said as they left the room. They went down the stairs to the porch. "Here I am with two slaves to work my claim and what do I have to show for it? I promised Jed and Joshua their freedom when we made our fortune in gold but we've mined barely enough to cover expenses. And then there's this O'Lee lad who's hardly weaned yet from his mother's milk who seems to have found Eldorado itself."

"Beginner's luck."

"I wish to God I had some."

"You have had. Jed's recovered, hasn't he?"

"That man's as strong as an ox. And Joshua's a good nurse. They're half-brothers, you know. Jed was working the Long Tom the week after Braithewaite took that bandit's bullet out of his chest."

"I hear Joaquin Murieta's been busy in the south. They say he robbed a gold shipment and killed the driver."

"I wish we'd get law and order in this benighted Territory. He'll not be caught until we do. When he is caught they should sever his head and charge admission to see it."

"A charming idea, colonel."

"Anyone who'd deliver Miss Selena over to that madman Varner deserves no less. She seems to have finally recovered, though."

"The young have short memories. Did she actually kiss that Lieutenant Sherman like they say?"

"On the cheek, Rhynne, on the cheek. I think the lieutenant was quite taken with her. He told her he's thinking of resigning his commission."

"Because of Selena?"

"No, no. He can't make ends meet on his army pay. The prices in the gold country are outrageous. I don't see how anyone can prosper."

"Mr. O'Lee appears able to."

"Damn O'Lee and his cherub's face. All the women want to mother him. They seem to think he's incapable of taking care of himself and here he is doing better than the rest of us put together."

Rhynne smiled, recalling Selena's overly casual questions about Danny O'Lee. Sutton had cause to be jealous.

"She's a beautiful woman," Rhynne said. "And very young and very much in love. With the idea of being in love, that is. No one man can hope to hold her for long. No man should try."

"You're right, of course. Absolutely, completely correct." King Sutton looked at a group of miners passing on the road. "She's a contagion worse than our lust for gold. She's like a fever. You think the fever will break and you wait and wait, yet it never does. And there's no known cure. You burn until you're consumed."

"Have you considered marrying the girl?"

Sutton gave Rhynne a strange look, seemed about to speak but instead shook his head, turned abruptly and walked away.

Rhynne stood staring after him. That man's luck has turned for the worse, he told himself, yet King Sutton was refusing to recognize the fact. He was like an ill-made candle that yields a magnificent light only to gutter after a few short hours.

Rhynne shrugged. He left the porch to stroll along the road, nodding right and left to the miners going by.

"Tomorrow's the big day?" one asked him.

"Three o'clock sharp."

"I'll be there. We'll all be there."

Rhynne stopped in front of a cabin where a

blue sign with red lettering had been nailed to the door: "Dr. Samuel Braithewaite, Surgery and Physic in all branches. Sets bones. Draws teeth painlessly. Bleeds. Advice gratis."

Rhynne knocked, opening the door when he heard Braithewaite's, "Come in."

"I need your help," Rhynne told him.

The doctor tilted his chair back. "As the sign says, my advice is gratis." Behind the doctor Rhynne saw a shelf displaying a microscope, stethoscope, a glittering array of other instruments, a mortar and pestle, and a great jar of leeches.

"It's not so much advice I need," Rhynne said. "It's more to do with the lottery at the Empire. The drawing's tomorrow afternoon at three."

"I've kept informed of your venture even though I didn't buy a ticket myself."

"Precisely why I'm here. I need an unimpeachable citizen of Hangtown, one who didn't enter the lottery, to draw the winning ticket."

"There's always Reverend Colton."

"I doubt if he's available."

"I'd have to take time from my practice," Braithewaite said.

"Yes, I thought of that, doctor. Would an honorarium be in order? I had in mind two bottles of my best forty-rod. For medicinal purposes. A donation to the advancement of the well-being of Hangtown."

"I think I can arrange my schedule so I'll be on hand to draw the winning number," Braithewaite said.

Rhynne held out his hand.

* * *

King Sutton waited until the Empire closed sometime after midnight before he made his way to the shed behind the hotel. When the last light winked out upstairs he crept across the yard to one of the windows at the rear of the gambling saloon.

He pushed up on the window. The sash, which he'd unlocked earlier in the evening when he stopped in the saloon for a drink, slid up easily. Sutton hoisted himself over the sill and into the room.

After closing the window behind him, he went to the shadowed recess behind the stairs leading to the platform. He sat on the floor, prepared for a long wait. The clock in the hotel lobby chimed twice. Otherwise, there was no sound in the building. Could he have misjudged Rhynne?

He heard footsteps near the bar, saw the outline of a man carrying what appeared to be a box. Sutton smiled. No, he hadn't misjudged his man. Wordsworth Rhynne, with his Louis XIV bed and his lottery, was undoubtedly a clever man.

King Sutton enjoyed outwitting clever men.

Selena and Pamela stood in an upstairs window of the Empire watching the crowd on the road outside. Rhynne had set up long plank tables and was serving venison, salmon, beef, beans, oyster soup, coffee, and, as long as they lasted, brandied peaches. He had closed the saloon until after the lottery.

"You look tired," Pamela said. "Are you sleeping any better?"

Selena sighed. "Oh, mother, I'm so tired it seems I'll never summon up the energy to laugh again. If only there was some magic potion to make me sleep without dreaming, I'd . . ."

"No!" Pamela's voice was sharp. "Best not to rely on pills and potions. You're young; this will pass."

Selena glanced at her, then turned her head away. "The dreams are different now. Not those nightmares I had just after Lieutenant Sherman and the others rescued me, when I'd wake up still smelling the awful burning stench . . ." Selena broke off and covered her eyes with her hand.

"You don't have to talk about it," Pamela said. "I understand."

"You used to tell me I always slept like a baby, no matter what. I never will again." Selena touched her left breast delicately. "Even though his knife barely cut through the skin and the scar is almost invisible, I feel it inside like it's cutting into my heart."

"Oh, Selena, my poor little girl."

"And last night I dreamed about a comet like the one you saw when you were young. The comet came to earth, plunging into the forest. I ran toward it in my bare feet over pine needles. The woods were on fire all around me. I ran and ran. Suddenly the fire was gone and I heard men's voices calling me. 'Selena, Selena.' I was afraid so I kept running and wherever I looked there were men watching be. They didn't do anything, just watched and called to me, but I could tell they were waiting until I fell to—to . . . I don't know what.

"Then somewhere in the woods I heard crying.

I wanted to run away yet I couldn't. I had to see who it was. I came to a glade in the forest and there, beside a stream, was a cradle and somehow I knew there was a baby inside crying for its mother. For me."

Pamela put her arm about her daughter's shoulders.

"It was my baby, mother. The one I had on the trail. The baby I've tried to forget. She needs me, mother. My baby needs me."

"Selena, it was only a dream."

Selena turned and put her arms around her mother, holding to her and sobbing. They embraced, both crying now, Pamela murmuring, "Oh, my baby, my baby."

At last Selena lifted her head. "There's more."

"To the dream?"

"That, too. In the dream I ran to the cradle and looked inside. It was empty. There was no baby after all. Where is she, mother? Where is my baby? Where is Lydia May?"

"Wherever she is, I'm sure she's all right. Her grandfather Tedder would see to that."

"She needs me, I know she does. And that's not all."

Pamela waited.

"I need *her*, mother," Selena said. "And it's too late. I need her and it's too late."

Danny O'Lee sat on the steps in front of the Empire watching the miners mill about in the road. Rhynne, Danny thought, seemed on edge. Testy. Was he worried about the drawing? Why should he be? He must have cleared a bundle. Including five hundred dollars from Danny O'Lee.

And King Sutton, strutting around like the cock-of-the-walk. Strange. Danny didn't know what to make of it. He had seen the way King looked at Selena and the way she looked at him, old as he was. What did he have to be so pleased about today? And here he was, coming toward the Empire.

"Ah, if it isn't that fine broth of a lad, Danny O'Lee." King Sutton extended his hand. Danny got up and reluctantly shook it. "The lad with the golden touch. The King Midas of Hangtown."

"You'll not hear me complain."

"And why should you, young O'Lee? A handsome broth of a boy such as yourself? I imagine any day now you'll hie yourself off to San Francisco to sample the forbidden fruit of the city."

"I was thinking of traveling there on the riverboat once the rains set in."

"Good, good. You've earned it. I hear Madam Reba has ten new girls direct from Paris at the Union. That's Paris, France. There's nothing to match a mademoiselle, they say, for a lad's first dip of his wick." He clapped Danny on the shoulder. "Tell Madam Reba that King Sutton sent you. She'll see you get nothing but the best."

Danny felt his face flame. He scowled. King Sutton smiled, gave him a mock salute, and strolled off. Damn him, Danny thought. Damn him, damn him, damn him.

W.W. Rhynne mounted the platform in the middle of the road. He raised both arms above his head.

"Gentlemen!" he called. "Gentlemen. Let me have your attention, please."

The crowd gathered around the platform.

"The time has arrived at last," Rhynne said, "to discover which of you men will savor the delights of the magnificent new bed which the Empire Hotel has imported from France, sparing no expense."

The men cheered.

"Soon we'll know the name of the lucky gentleman who will take his place in the personal bed of King Louis XIV, the Sun King of France."

"Never mind the king," someone shouted. "Where's the queen?" The men laughed appreciatively.

"Hurry up, Rhynne, let's get on with it," one called out.

"All in good time," Rhynne said. "I know that before we have today's grand finale, the drawing of the winning number, you'll all want to hear the oration prepared for this occasion by our candidate for the legislature, the Reverend James Colton."

The crowd groaned.

"Not seeing the Reverend in attendance, however," Rhynne went on, "we'll have to forego that pleasure." The men cheered. "And so, there's nothing for it but to conduct the drawing. Would some of you bring up that table?" Two miners carried a table to the platform.

"And to select the winning ticket we have a man honored in this community for his probity, a man for all seasons, a graduate of the prestigious Castleton Medical College of Vermont, Dr. Samuel Braithewaite."

Doc Braithewaite was pounded on the back as he made his way forward. He climbed onto the platform beside Rhynne.

"Doctor," Rhynne said, "there's one point we should clarify before we begin. Have you yourself entered this lottery?"

"No sir, I have not."

"And do you have any financial interest in it whatsoever?"

"You haven't forgotten that forty-rod, have you?"

There was a chorus of guffaws.

"Two bottles of the Empire Hotel's best whisky will go to our eminent physician and surgeon in appreciation of his many services."

"Cut out the palaver," Jack Smith of Howard called, "and let's have the drawing."

"My thoughts exactly," Rhynne said. "Abe!" he shouted to the bartender standing on the porch of the Empire. "Will you be so good as to unlock the hotel and bring us the box containing the tickets?"

Abe nodded and went into the hotel.

"After the drawing," Rhynne said, "all losing tickets will be redeemed at the bar for one drink of your choice. No man goes away dry."

Abe returned with the pine box, climbed onto the platform and set the box on the table.

"Here we are," Rhynne said. "The box you've all been eyeing these last few weeks. Now, Mr. Griswold, will you perform the opening honors?"

John Griswold inserted a metal flange in the notch at the top of the box and pried off one of the pine boards.

"Doctor, please mix the tickets thoroughly before you draw one."

Doc Braithewaite put his hand into the box, stirred the contents for a few moments, then held a ticket aloft.

"Will you read the number, sir?" Rhynne asked him.

"Forty-three," Braithewaite said.

Rhynne stared at him, open-mouthed. King Sutton, who had been lounging against a wagon at the rear of the crowd, raised his arm. Danny O'Lee pushed his way past the miners to the platform.

"I believe that's my number," Sutton said. "A king's bed for a King." The men parted to make way for him as he walked leisurely to the platform.

Rhynne snatched the winning ticket from Braithewaite's hand. A large "43" was printed on a quarter-page cut from the *Lyrical Ballads*.

"You seem a mite surprised, W.W.," Braithewaite said.

"More than a mite," Rhynne said.

"Here's the other half of the ticket," King Sutton said, holding it toward Rhynne.

Danny O'Lee leaped up the steps at the rear of the platform and drew a handful of tickets from the box. Each had a "43" printed on it. Abe tore the tickets from his hand, dropped them back into the box and, with the box in his arms, jumped from the platform and headed for the hotel.

Danny pushed his way forward. "You," he shouted down at King Sutton, who stood in front of the platform, "are a cheat."

"Be real careful what you say, lad," Sutton told him in a low voice.

Danny raised his arm and there was a hush.

"King Sutton's a liar and a cheat," he shouted.

"You're forcing my hand," Sutton said dangerously.

"A liar and a cheat in spades," Danny shouted.

"Then, sir, seeing that you persist, I must call you out."

"And just what do you mean by that?"

"I'm challenging you, O'Lee, to a duel. Will you meet me on the field of honor? Are you man enough?"

19

King Sutton arrived first at the meadow. Although they had tried to keep the time and place of the duel secret, he found more than a score of men waiting. Smiling, Sutton waved to them, then turned to his seconds, Doc Braithewaite and Jack Smith of Howard.

Pointing to a cottonwood tree a short distance away, he asked, "Would you say that's ten paces?"

"A bit more than ten," Smith said.

"Would you say the first limb is heart-high, doctor?"

"Heart-high or thereabouts."

Sutton raised his Paterson Colt, cocked the hammer, aimed and fired. Gunsmoke drifted across the meadow; a small hole had appeared in the tree trunk next to the limb. Sutton cocked and fired the pistol two more times. When he finally lowered the gun there were three holes in the trunk separated by not more than two inches.

"That's what I call real good shooting," Smith commented.

"I could always hold my own in Georgia."

"Perhaps the O'Lee lad will change his mind," Doc Braithewaite said, "when he sees those holes."

"That was my intent," King Sutton said. "I don't want to kill the boy unless he forces me to."

"They're here." All except Sutton turned.

Rhynne came first, an unlit cigar tilted in his mouth. Danny O'Lee came next, dressed in his mining clothes of red wool shirt and blue trousers. He looked neither right nor left as he walked down the hill toward the meadow. Ned followed him, holding a Paterson Colt away from his side as though he wanted as little to do with the gun as he possibly could.

The three men stopped at the edge of the meadow. Rhynne motioned Danny to wait, then walked across the grass to King Sutton.

"I heard shooting a few minutes ago," Rhynne said. "I was afraid we might be too late for the festivities."

"I was practicing, W.W.," Sutton told him, nodding to the bullet holes in the cottonwood.

"That's real fine shooting. Real fine. King, I'd like to talk to you in private," Rhynne said, nodding toward Braithewaite and Smith. Sutton's seconds walked a short distance away.

"This duel does you no credit." Rhynne paused. "It's murder; no more, no less."

"The duel's not of my making. I don't want to kill him, W.W. You know that."

"I don't know what you want. But kill the boy you will if you fight him."

"He called me a liar and a cheat in front of all of Hangtown."

"You did change the numbers on the tickets."

"Are *you* calling me a cheat?"

"Take it any way you like. You know I'm not afraid of you, Sutton. I'm dealing from the top of the deck—you marked those tickets so you'd win."

"After you'd marked them yourself. Every ticket in that box had a 'one' on it."

"So the Reverend Colton would win the lottery. To protect Selena. I gave the miners the time of their lives, I gave them weeks of hoping and wondering and savoring and dreaming. I gave them all that, not to mention a free drink. I protected Selena, and I was about to make a generous contribution to Colton's church."

Sutton stared steadily back. "By changing all your number 'one's' to my 'forty-threes,' one of those men you took a hundred dollars from, namely myself, attempted to have his hopes realized. Listen, Rhynne, it's not being found out that angered me, or the fact it was O'Lee. I have my honor to defend. I'd be branded a coward for the rest of my life if I hadn't called the boy for what he said."

"This isn't Georgia."

"Still I am a Georgian. And a southerner. Even if I wanted to back down, and I don't, I couldn't now. The only way out is for O'Lee to apologize."

"He's not about to."

"Then we settle the matter on the field of honor."

Rhynne shook his head and went back to Danny.

"Did you see that tree King Sutton used for target practice?" he asked him.

"That I did. And I see King all dressed up like an undertaker, too." Sutton was all in black— broad-brimmed hat, frock coat, and trousers.

"Have you ever fired a Paterson Colt in your life?"

"That I have not."

"Then why in the name of all that's holy did you agree to use them?"

"I've never fired anything else either. 'Cepting a pepperpot a few months back. All the barrels went off at once and that cured me of guns."

"How old are you, lad?"

"Twenty-one less a fraction."

"You've a long and happy life ahead of you. With the gold from your claim you can go off and live like a king. Marry a lovely colleen and raise a grand family. There's no end to the . . ."

"I told you before, W.W., I'm not about to apologize to that bastard. Talk till doomsday and I'll be no more likely to show the white feather than I am now."

Rhynne looked at him closely, noting the pale spots at the corners of his mouth and the heaviness of his eyes from lack of sleep.

"You're a brave one, lad," he said.

"I'm not. I'm afraid."

"I know you are. That's why I said you were brave."

Danny took a folded sheet of paper from his pocket and handed it to Rhynne.

"I've a young brother in St. Louis," he said.

"If anything happens to me I want him to have half of what's mine. Last night I sat down and wrote it all out on the paper in your hand."

"And the other half?"

"It's to go to Selena."

"Selena?" Rhynne frowned. "Are you certain that's what you want?"

"As sure as I'm standing here." Danny smiled thinly. "Mr. Rhynne, shouldn't we be getting on with the sport?"

Rhynne gripped his arm. "As you wish." He turned to Ned. "The pistol's loaded?"

"All five chambers."

"You fired the gun? You know how common misfires are."

"She's in perfect shape."

Rhynne led them across the meadow to where Sutton and his seconds were waiting.

"Do you wish to continue, Mr. Sutton?" he asked formally.

"I do."

"Do you wish to continue, Mr. O'Lee?"

"That I do."

"So be it. We've agreed that the weapons will be .36-caliber Paterson Colts. Is that correct?" Both duelists nodded. "You will stand back-to-back and at my signal you'll walk five paces and stop with your weapons pointed downward. I will then say, 'Fire, one, two, three, stop,' at one-second intervals. You may turn and shoot, one shot only, from the time I say, 'fire' until I say 'stop.' Is that understood?"

Again both men nodded.

"Ask the boy if he'll take back his words," Sutton said to Rhynne.

"Mr. O'Lee, will you apologize to Mr. Sutton for your remarks of yesterday?"

"I'll see him in Hell first."

"He refuses," Rhynne said. "So be it. Gentlemen, take your places."

Sutton and O'Lee faced each other and then both turned on their heels so that they were back-to-back with their Colts aimed at the ground. The men at the fringe of the meadow scrambled out of the line of fire.

"Cock your weapons," Rhynne said. The two hammers clicked back.

"Take five paces."

Both men walked five steps and stopped.

"Fire," Rhynne said.

Danny whirled about and raised his pistol. Sutton turned more slowly, raised his Colt and aimed. Danny fired first. Sutton didn't move.

"Missed him," Ned muttered.

When Rhynne's count reached three, King Sutton fired. The pistol flew from Danny's hand and he clutched his stomach. Rhynne ran to him.

"Get down," he said.

"I'm all right," Danny told him. "I'm all right."

"Get down, damn it. You're in shock. You can't feel the bullet yet."

Danny sat on the ground. Rhynne pushed him onto his back, opening his clothes to find the wound.

W.W. looked over his shoulder. "Doctor, you're needed," he called to Braithewaite. The doctor was already hurrying across the field, black bag in hand. Sutton stood where he was with his smoking gun in his hand.

Rhynne bared a bleeding gash on Danny's stomach. The doctor took forceps from his bag, inserted the ends into the wound and drew out a bloodied piece of metal. He wiped it on his sleeve. "It looks like part of the pistol's hammer," he said. He spread the wound with his fingers. "I think the bullet must have missed him completely."

Rhynne stood and quickly walked to King Sutton. "He's got an abdominal wound," he said. "Can't tell how serious. We'll have to take him to town. Are you satisfied now?"

"Will he apologize?"

"He's in no condition to be asked. For God's sake, are you bloodthirsty?"

"I'm satisfied."

"Good." Rhynne returned to Danny. "Sutton's satisfied," he said. "Doc, let's get your patient to Hangtown."

"Some of the boys brought a door along just in case. We'll put the lad on it and carry him back."

When Selena, on the porch of the Empire, saw the men straggle over the hill toward the hotel, she ran into the road to meet them. There. What was that? A man being carried on a door. Danny! His eyes were closed. Was he dead? Had King Sutton killed him?

She ran forward and turned to walk beside Danny. "Is he . . . is he badly hurt?" she managed to ask Doc Braithewaite.

"Should be right as rain in a few days. All he needs is rest and quiet."

Selena reached down and took Danny's hand. It was warm to her touch. Did he have a fever? Was his wound infected?

"Oh, Danny," she said, "you'll be all right. I'll take care of you until you are." She thought she saw him smile.

Selena spied Rhynne walking a short way behind her. Releasing Danny's hand, she waited until he reached her, then walked with him. "Take Danny to the hotel," she told him. "I'll look after him there."

"I intended to, Selena."

"Give him the Louis XIV bed. Bring up a cot and put it in the room. I'll nurse him. I won't leave him until he's well again."

"I'll do whatever you say, Selena." Rhynne smiled ruefully. "The winner of the lottery was supposed to have the use of that bed."

"King Sutton? Never! I'll not have it." She lowered her voice. "He didn't win fairly. You know he didn't. The bed's for Danny O'Lee, not for that would-be murderer."

"I'm confident Danny will recover."

"How can you be sure? Remember what happened to English Bob. Everyone said he was getting better and the next thing we knew he was dead."

"Doc Braithewaite's due to win one," Rhynne said.

"Look." Selena nodded behind them. "He's actually going to show his face here in town after what he did."

Rhynne looked over his shoulder to see King Sutton walking down the hill toward the hotel.

"He's no monster, Selena. He did what he thought was right. After all, Danny did insult him in public."

"I don't want to hear another word. You men all stick together, no matter what."

She ran back along the road and stood in front of King Sutton with her hands on her hips, blocking his way.

"You might have killed him," she said in a low, intense voice.

"Selena."

"Don't you dare try to sweet-talk me. You shot him. You rigged the lottery so you'd win and when he caught you out you as much as tried to murder him. You wanted to murder Danny O'Lee, a lad who never lifted a finger against you or anyone else in his entire life. And you tried to kill him in cold blood."

"Whoa, Selena. Wait and hear me out. It's not the way you seem to think."

"I don't want to listen to you. I never want to speak to you again as long as I live. Murderer!"

"Selena."

"Oh, and I thought I cared for you. Even after you took advantage of me. Oh!"

She whirled and ran from him toward the hotel, where she found that the men had already carried Danny inside. She flew up onto the porch and then up the stairs to the Louis XIV room. All she saw was Danny's pale face on the white pillow. She ran across the room and threw herself down beside the bed, taking his hand in hers. "Oh, Danny," she whispered, "you'll be all right, I know you will."

"He'll be just that, Miss Selena." She noticed Doc Braithewaite for the first time. "All he needs is rest. The young man's more tired than hurt. The wound's superficial."

"I'll take care of him, doctor. I'll nurse him. I nursed my mother when she had the fever last year."

"That'll be fine, Miss Selena. I've undressed him and bandaged the wound. He was lucky; it wasn't the bullet that hit him, merely a part of his own gun. The wound should be cleaned in about eight hours and bandaged anew. Other than that, all he needs is rest. If he should run a fever, and I don't expect one, let me know so I can leech him."

"I will, doctor."

After Braithewaite took his bag and left, Selena put the back of her hand to her own forehead and then to Danny's. If he was feverish, she thought, he was no more so than she.

"Selena?" Danny opened his eyes and looked up at her.

"Danny, you're going to be all right. The doctor said you would."

"Selena?"

"Do you want a drink of water, Danny? I'll go to the well and fetch you one if you do."

"Selena, do you know what came into my head when I was hit and thought I wasn't long for this world?"

"No, Danny. What?"

"I said to myself, Danny O'Lee, if you live, and it's like as not you won't with a bullet in you, you're to go to Selena, go to her first thing and say, 'Selena, I love you.' Selena, it's the truth. I do love you." He took her hand and pressed it to his lips.

"Oh, Danny." She sat on the bed. He pushed her hair back from her forehead, his fingers tender and gentle. Then she was kissing him, her lips wandering over his face until they found his lips.

Once they did, they stopped and held and held.

At the bar downstairs, King Sutton drank down his whisky and strode to the door while the men in the gambling saloon watched him in silence. No one had approached to shake his hand or to drink with him.

He paused on the porch, hands thrust in his pockets, listening to the talk that had swelled behind him as soon as he had left the bar. He frowned. First there had been the miners' resentment when he put Jed and Joshua to work panning for gold. Then the girl Esperanza had stabbed English Bob and committed suicide. And today the duel.

Yet what else could he have done?

Now his course was clear. He'd move on. Where? Did it matter? Perhaps to Coloma or to one of the southern mines. And leave Selena? He laughed drily to himself. Rhynne had been right when he said no man could hold her and no man should try.

Good luck to you, Danny O'Lee, he thought. You'll be needing all you can get.

"Mr. Sutton?"

He turned and for a moment thought Selena was walking along the porch toward him. No, of course it wasn't Selena, even though this woman's walk and coloring and voice all reminded him of her.

King Sutton raised his hat. "Ma'am?" he said.

"I'm Pamela Buttle-Jones."

"Ah, yes, of course. Miss Selena's mother."

"I thought you'd want to know that Danny O'Lee will be all right. Dr. Braithewaite found that the wound was superficial after all."

"I never meant to harm the lad, merely to shoot the pistol from his hand."

"You must be an excellent marksman, colonel."

"Some have told me so."

"My husband was forced to fight a duel years ago to defend his good name. Fortunately, neither man was hit and the duel ended in a public house over a bottle of brandy."

"I was the loser today," King Sutton said.

Pamela nodded. Was that why she had approached him? she wondered. Because she felt sorry for him? Was it her fate to lose her heart to the world's defeated? she asked herself.

"At least I was the loser until this moment," King Sutton said. "Selena told me she had a widowed mother. I never imagined she'd be so young, so beautiful, and such a lady."

"Mr. Sutton, I'm thirty-eight years old. Beauty fades along with youth, and there are no ladies, I'm afraid, in California. Otherwise, I thank you."

"A woman, like wine, improves with age. If I could take you home with me to Georgia you'd see that we southerners appreciate ladies. I'd be the envy of every man in the state."

"You're from Atlanta, Mr. Sutton?"

"No, I live near Athens. The Suttons have owned a cotton plantation there since before the Revolution."

"It's a pity we're not in Georgia. I'm sure I'd adore having you show it to me."

"We can imagine we are." He swept off his hat and bowed. "May I accompany you to your door, Lady Buttle-Jones?"

She smiled up at him and took his arm. "You may, sir," she said. And when he raised her hand to brush her fingers with his lips she did not object.

At the Empire, Rhynne locked the gold dust in his new strong box and made a final entry in his ledger. The lottery had turned out better than he had expected. Better than he had hoped, even. He looked at the figures in the book in front of him. Income, ninety-nine hundred dollars. Outgo, sixteen hundred and ten dollars. Profit, eighty-two hundred and ninety dollars.

By altering the tickets, King Sutton had saved him a five hundred dollar donation to Colton's church; Selena hadn't gone to bed with the winner after all; and Danny O'Lee had come out of the duel with a scratch and new-found respect.

Rhynne had only one regret. Of what possible use was a thousand dollar bed?

Upstairs on that bed, Danny O'Lee trailed his fingers along Selena's cheek to her throat, along the curve of her bare breast to the nipple, where he paused, down along her side to the curve of her hips, to her leg, between her legs and up along her thighs, parting them.

She shivered in anticipation.

"Danny," she whispered, "do you think you should? You're wounded; you might have a fever. Do you really think you should?"

"The first three times didn't seem to hurt me."

She smiled. "You're right. You know best, Danny. In fact, Dr. Braithewaite should be pleased. You seem to be getting better all the time."

BOOK THREE
SAN FRANCISCO, 1851

20

"Welcome to San Francisco, Captain Fitzpatrick," William Coleman said. After the two men shook hands, Coleman motioned the captain to a chair beside his desk.

While Coleman lit a cigar and Fitzpatrick rolled a cigarette, the two men studied one another. Coleman seemed as thin as his cigar and slight, almost effete. Dressed in grey with a pale blue cravat flounced at his neck, he was the epitome of the successful San Francisco businessman.

Barry Fitzpatrick was quite different. His buckskin clothes, sun-bronzed face, and lean hard body made one think of a mountain man or the leader of a wagon train or a seasoned veteran of the Mexican War.

He had, in fact, been all three.

273

"I think you probably know why the Committee hired you," Coleman said.

"I have an idea."

"You came well-recommended, captain. General Winfield Scott himself communicated with us praising your services to our country in the Mexico City campaign of '47. In fact, he said there were only two other men who fought in that war that he'd recommend as highly. He mentioned a Captain Robert E. Lee and a Lieutenant Ulysses Grant."

"Both are fine officers."

"And then after the War, I understand, you resigned your commission and served with the Texas Rangers. Again your commanding officer had nothing but praise for you. He mentioned a month-long pursuit of bandits along the Nueces in particular."

"Anyone would be proud to have served under Colonel Hays."

"You're not much of a talker, are you, captain?"

"I've noticed that people who talk a lot don't always do a lot."

"Well said. That's the very reason the Committee of Vigilance hired you. We want a doer, not a talker. This city's had its fill of talkers. And its fill of corrupt politicians and judges more interested in enriching themselves than in seeing justice done. This city's overrun with the worst sorts of knaves and cutthroats. We're awash with Sydney Ducks, con men, gamblers, arsonists, and prostitutes."

Coleman went to the window. "Come here,

captain," he said, "I'd like to show you something."

When Barry joined him the other man put one hand on his arm, pointing with the other to city block after city block where only chimneys stood amidst the charred rubble.

"When I rode in last night," Barry said, "I saw you'd had quite a fire."

"A quarter of the city destroyed. We've had fire after fire ever since the one on Christmas Eve of '49. Arson. They set fire to the city hoping to steal in the confusion. Or just for the merry hell of it. What's more, our streets aren't safe for decent folk. Robbery, assault, murder, you name it and San Francisco has it. In spades. And do you know how many murderers we've hanged here these last three years?"

Barry shook his head.

"Exactly none, captain. Nary a one. The sheriff's helpless; the police are in the pay of the criminals. They must be. Is that any way to run a city of 35,000 souls? I ask you, is it?"

"Not to my way of thinking."

"Nor to mine. And that's the reason for the Committee. I organized the Committee. Not formed it, the idea wasn't mine, the germ came from the vigilance societies in the mining camps where the whole town acts as jury. Here, though we're too large for that, the principle's the same."

"Just who's on this Committee?"

"You'll meet them. We're businessmen for the most part. For example, I'm a commission merchant and I buy and sell real estate. Most of our substantial citizens belong, those with a stake in the city's future. We're not interested in making a fast dollar and heading for greener pastures. We want to build a city where our wives and children can live without fear."

"I understand."

"We know monetary rewards aren't the solution. There's a bandit terrorizing the southern mines with a purse on his head. Five hundred dollars. A Joaquin Murieta. The reward seems to have encouraged him to commit new outrages, if anything."

"I've heard of Murieta."

"We're not lawmen, that's the rub. Most of the professional men are with us and the newspapers too. But when a crime's committed we're apt to run off wildly in all directions. That's where you come in, captain. You're to be our chief investigator and constabulary combined."

"I wouldn't do anything illegal, Mr. Coleman."

"We don't expect you to. Since when is apprehending criminals illegal? You'll turn them over to the Committee and we'll proceed from there."

"And when do I begin?"

"At once. The biggest flouter of law and order in the city right now is a gambler. The police won't touch him. Why should they? They're on his payroll. He's owned brothels in his time, has a gambling saloon in Hangtown, even ran a crooked lottery operation there a few years back. Now he's moved to San Francisco and opened a hotel gambling hall he calls the Golden Empire. His name's Wordsworth Rhynne."

"What hard evidence do you have against him?"

"None, I'm afraid. That's your job. Only last

week a man named Kingman Sutton complained to me about a scheme Rhynne enticed him into. Seems Rhynne issued stock in a mining company, then salted mines near Hangtown and suckered a lot of newcomers into buying. Sutton says he lost his shirt."

"Know anything about this Sutton?"

"He impresses me as a gentleman. Owns a cotton plantation in Georgia. He has a slave here in San Francisco with him, as a matter of fact."

"I'll talk to him. Is there anyone else involved with this Rhynne?"

"He had a partner in his Hangtown gambling hall. A woman, believe it or not. She's back in the city too. I believe her name is Pamela Butler Jones."

Captain Fitzpatrick jerked to attention. "Not Pamela Buttle-Jones? A woman in her late thirties? A beauty?"

"That sounds right. Do you know her?"

"I did years ago." Barry Fitzpatrick watched the smoke from his cigarette curl toward the ceiling. "She was in a wagon train I led west before the gold rush. An English gentlewoman. Only there was a lot more to her once you came to know her. And, as I said, a beauty."

William Coleman looked thoughtfully at Fitzpatrick, who had a deeply reflective look on his face. "To the best of my knowledge," he said, "she's not involved with Rhynne now. If this woman is a friend of yours, I suggest you see she has nothing to do with him in the future."

"I intend to."

"And as for Rhynne, you're to get rid of the son of a bitch any way you can. This is war, captain, just as the conflict with Mexico was war. It's the good people of this city warring on the criminals. No holds are barred; our only concern is to win. Do I make myself clear?"

"Perfectly."

"Good. When you have something to report, come here to my office or go to the Committee's rooms on Battery Street near Pine. The first report I expect from you is one telling me that Wordsworth Rhynne is no longer among us."

Captain Fitzpatrick rode out of Market Street, reined his horse to the right and climbed one of the higher hills overlooking the city and bay. The house, which he had no trouble finding—it was half a mile from any other—was unfinished, with only the frame rising skeleton-like against the sky. As Barry drew near he heard the pounding of hammers and the rasp of saws.

He dismounted and tied his horse to a post in front. He drew in his breath. She stood in one of the unfinished rooms on the first floor, her back to him, a furled yellow parasol in her hand. She was wearing a gown of golden brown and a large feathered hat. Her figure was just as youthful as he remembered, if not more so; her hair just as lovely as he remembered, perhaps lovelier.

Unexpectedly, he felt a tightening in his chest. After all these years, he thought.

Stepping lightly across the littered floor, he came up behind her and leaned down and kissed her on the neck. She started in surprise, spinning around to face him. He stared in amazement. It wasn't Pamela after all. This girl was much younger, couldn't be more than twenty. How could he have been mistaken?"

"Why, it's Barry Fitzpatrick," she said. "You haven't changed a whit."

And then he knew. "You must be Selena," he said.

She felt the color flood her face as she remembered all that had happened on the trail west. But she raised her eyes to his defiantly, determined not to let this meeting reduce her to the awkward girl he had once known.

"You're every bit as handsome as I remember," she said. She walked around him as though to examine him from every side. "We were just wild about you. All the young girls and most of the older women as well. Or don't you remember our wagon train?"

"How could I ever forget that hellish journey? Though I'd like to."

"Mr. Fitzpatrick, so would I." She looked into his bright blue eyes. "So would I."

"Then forgotten it is. We'll not mention the past again. Most people call me captain now, but it's still Barry to my friends."

"Oh, Barry." She stood on tiptoe and kissed his cheek. "Ah, you're turning red. Perhaps you've been away from women too long."

"I've been to Texas and Mexico. Oregon before that."

"And you've just arrived in San Francisco? You must find this the biggest, noisiest city in all the west. I went to a costume ball last night where I met a newspaperman from the East. Do you know what he said about San Francisco? Wait, let me be sure I have it right." She struck a pose.

"He said, 'I've seen purer liquors, better cigars, truer guns, larger Bowie knives and prettier courtesans here than in any other place I have ever visited. San Francisco can and does furnish the best bad things available in all of America.' And, Barry, I love it."

"You can't mean what you're saying."

"Oh, but I do. Everywhere else people work from dawn to dusk. All day long men sit in their stuffy offices making money while their wives are home cooking meals and scrubbing floors and washing clothes. Here in San Francisco everyone lives just to live."

"And to make money?"

"Why, good heavens, you have to have money to live." She danced away from him with her skirts swirling. "Do you like our new house, Barry?" she asked. "On a clear day you can see almost to Sacramento."

"It's a grand house."

"Sixteen rooms. It will seem huge after our one-room cabin in Hangtown. I can hardly wait till it's finished."

"Your mother must have done well."

"She did. When we returned to San Francisco she found her land more valuable than she ever dreamed possible. Men clamored to buy. They actually lined up in the sitting room of our house on Rincon Hill waiting to offer her money."

"I trust she's no longer involved with this Wordsworth Rhynne."

"With W.W.? Why do you say that?"

"I understand he's considered a rogue and a villain."

She laughed. "W.W. a villain? Oh, he'd love that word. I must tell him what you said." She tapped her parasol on the floor. "You look so somber, Captain Fitzpatrick." She stopped smiling and stared at him. "You are serious, aren't you?"

"Yes, I'm serious. I came here to caution your mother about associating with Rhynne."

"Well, you must stop being serious this very instant. I become impatient with serious men." She took his hand and pulled him after her across the room to the foot of the stairs. "You must see the upstairs, Barry. I have the most wonderful bedroom you've ever set eyes on."

He followed her, smiling and shaking his head. When Selena reached the top of the stairs, two workmen stood and doffed their caps.

"Horce, Manuel," Selena said, smiling dazzlingly at them. "The house looks just magnificent."

They mumbled their thanks. Barry didn't think the two men had even seen him, so taken were they with Selena.

"You've changed," he told her when he finally caught up to her in the upper hallway.

"Isn't that what growing up is for? To become different? Wouldn't life be boring if we were always the same, day after day?" Selena stepped over a two-by-four. "This is my room," she said. "I intend to put the bed over there. You don't know about my bed, do you? It's a Louis XIV, all curtains and cords and tassels."

Barry stopped in the doorway.

"Don't be shy," she told him. "Surely there's nothing improper about entering a lady's bed-

chamber when all of San Francisco can see us."
She swung her parasol toward the city below
them.

"I don't know that I'm shy," he told her, smiling. "It was something altogether different. As I
looked at you, I realized I'd never seen a lovelier
woman. Never."

"Why, good heavens, Captain Fitzpatrick. And
you a well-traveled man, too."

"Wait." He made no move to approach her.
"I had a feeling, a premonition if you will. A
warning. It told me to go back to my room at the
Oriental, pack up, and leave."

She poked the point of her parasol at a curled
shaving on the floor at her feet. "Why, captain,"
she said. "I think you're being most ungallant.
Threatening to run off no more than ten minutes
after meeting me again." She speared the shaving
and flicked it aside.

"Selena!"

She looked up. The shout had come from
below. Selena walked past Barry, smiling up at
him, and crossed the hall to one of the front
rooms. She waved down to someone Barry
couldn't see.

"It's Leland," she said when she came back.
"Leland's one of our leading merchants, you
know. I promised to go riding with him today.
And just when we were having such a fascinating
conversation."

He bowed. "Miss Selena."

When she was halfway down the stairs he
called after her. "You've forgotten your parasol."
He stood at the top of the steps holding it toward
her.

They heard footsteps below them. "Selena, where are you?" a man's voice asked.

When she realized Barry had no intention of coming to her, but was simply going to stand there smiling at her, Selena ran up the stairs, grasped the parasol and ran down again. "I'm here, Lee," she said gaily. She glanced up the stairwell. "I thought you'd never come. I've been so *bored* waiting."

Later that day, Captain Barry Fitzpatrick pushed his way to the bar of the Golden Empire, surprised at the spaciousness and ornate furnishings of the gambling hall. The light of many chandeliers glowed through the smoke-filled air; croupiers called monotonously from behind card tables; a dark-haired girl in a low-cut bodice spun a ball on a whirling roulette wheel, the ball circling and circling before clicking into the zero slot.

"Your pleasure, sir?" the barman asked.

"I'm looking for Wordsworth Rhynne."

"Mr. Rhynne? Just a second." He signaled to a big man lounging beneath a painting of a diaphanously draped woman testing the water of her bath. "Mr. McSweeney," the barman said, "this gentleman here's inquiring for Mr. Rhynne."

McSweeney towered over Barry. He seemed as large as a grizzly and moved as quickly. Barry had a fleeting memory of an English big game hunter he'd met in Oregon telling him, "Your bloody grizzly is more dangerous than the most ferocious tiger." Best not to underestimate McSweeney.

"I'm Captain Fitzpatrick," Barry said. "Tell Rhynne I'd like to have a word with him."

"It's *Mr.* Rhynne," McSweeney said.

Barry shrugged. "Tell Mr. Rhynne."

McSweeney walked away but when Barry started to follow him the big man stopped and turned, thrusting his finger to within an inch of Barry's chest.

"You'd best be waiting here, I think," he said.

Barry felt the excitement of the challenge course through him. McSweeney eyed him appraisingly but made no move to back down.

"Sir," McSweeney added. His tone took away all the respect the word might otherwise have held.

Barry turned and went back to the bar. He wasn't here to fight anyone. He was downing the last of his whisky when he sensed someone standing behind him. It was McSweeney.

"Mr. Rhynne says, 'Bring the gentleman up,' " he said. He scanned Barry's buckskins.

"I'm not armed," Barry told him.

McSweeney nodded and led him upstairs to a thickly carpeted hall lit by glowing lamps in sconces along the walls. He tapped on a door, opened it, and stepped to one side. Barry walked into the room.

Rhynne's office was spartan, the furnishings consisting of a pine desk, two chairs, a single potted fern near the window, bookshelves and a clock on the wall behind the desk. Only the dark leather bindings of the many books contradicted the room's frugal image.

"I'm Captain Fitzpatrick," Barry said.

"I've heard of you. Excuse me, captain." He looked at McSweeney who was waiting in the doorway. "Has there been any word?" he asked.

"There's been no change."

"Let me know the minute you hear." McSweeney nodded and shut the door.

"Ned Heineman, a friend of mine, was taken ill last night. He's the best piano player in all of San Francisco." Rhynne put both of his hands palm down on his desk. "Now, how can I help you, captain?"

"I've been hired by the Committee of Vigilance."

"So I've heard. I've been expecting you since word of your coming circulated. I wondered if you'd turn out to be Wordsworth's 'happy warrior.' "

Barry looked at him questioningly.

"The man 'that every man in arms would wish to be.' "

"Ah," Barry smiled. "You'll have to judge that for yourself, Mr. Rhynne. May I speak in confidence?"

"Of course."

"I have some advice for you. Leave San Francisco."

"I like you, captain. You come directly to the point."

"The Vigilance Committee will see to it that you leave, one way or the other. Why not steal a march on them by leaving on your own?"

"Would you, Captain Fitzpatrick, if you were in my position?"

"Probably not. Though I'd realize I might be making the biggest mistake of my life."

"My feelings exactly. Do you want to know why Coleman would like to see the last of me?"

Barry shrugged.

Rhynne smoothed his mustache. "He needs a piece of property I own to build an auction house on."

"I know nothing of that."

There was a knock. When Rhynne called, "Come in," McSweeney opened the door. He stood shaking his head. It was several seconds before Barry saw that the big man was crying.

"Out with it, Mac," Rhynne said.

"He's dead, Mr. Rhynne. Ned died a few minutes ago."

"Damn." Rhynne struck the desk with his fist. "Did they decide what it was?"

"Cholera."

The word hung in the room like an intimation of doom.

"Thank you, Mac," Rhynne said. "I'll see to the arrangements myself."

After McSweeney shut the door, Rhynne stood up and extended his hand. "Thank you for the warning, captain," he said. Barry hesitated a moment before shaking Rhynne's hand.

"Don't be oversure of yourself," Rhynne said. "Little is as simple as it seems." Barry said nothing.

Once the captain had left, Rhynne walked to the window and looked down into the Square. He stood to lose more than he cared to think about in Sutton's mining scheme. Captain Fitzpatrick posed a threat; he was a dangerous man. And now Ned was gone.

Wordsworth Rhynne wondered if his luck had begun to turn for the worse.

21

"Are you going out again?" Pamela asked.

Selena turned from the pier glass. "Lee's asked me to dine with him tonight. We were to have lunch but—well, I changed my mind." She didn't feel she wanted to talk about her encounter with Barry Fitzpatrick. Not yet.

"Who else will be with you?" Pamela's voice was sharp.

"Oh, mother, will you stop worrying about my reputation? You know Leland's already asked me to marry him. I'm the one who doesn't want to get married. All Lee talks about these days is building a railroad over the mountains. I don't find that especially romantic."

Selena eyed herself appraisingly in the glass.

"Well, at least you've given up the idea of

singing in public places. I never did approve of that."

"You were quite right, mother," Selena told her. She wondered what Pamela would think if she knew why she didn't want ever to sing publicly again—in the Golden Empire or any other fancy hotel in town. Selena rearranged a curl above her forehead and smiled secretly at her reflection.

She'd intended to keep up her singing when they'd returned from Hangtown. When W.W. had told her positively he wouldn't have her in the Golden Empire, she'd put on her very newest French brocade and bearded him in his office at the back of the hotel.

"Why is there any difference between singing in Hangtown and your new hotel here?" Selena had demanded. "They'd like me just as well in San Francisco."

"How well they'd like your singing has nothing to do with it." Rhynne sighed, looking at Selena's determined face. He'd put off talking to her, knowing she wouldn't accept what he had to say.

"At least you could let me try."

"Selena, I'm going to take you somewhere. But first you have to promise me you'll never tell your mother."

"Not tell Pamela? Where on earth are we going?"

"Promise me, Selena."

"But why?"

"Because I value your mother's friendship. I'd never do anything to hurt her and if she finds out where I've taken you she'll be very upset. Does that satisfy you?"

"You're in love with my mother, aren't you?" Selena asked shrewdly.

"My dear girl, I expected you to become wiser with age but there's such a thing as being too smart for your own good. Now, will you promise?"

"All right, W.W., I give you my word I won't tell Pamela. Now, where are we going?"

"You'll see."

W.W. escorted Selena from the Golden Empire by a side door. In the street men stared after her as he assisted her into his carriage. As the horses pulled them away from downtown, he commented on the new buildings, on the results of the latest fire, saying not a word about their destination.

At last the coachman halted the horses in front of a large well-appointed house standing apart from its neighbors with an iron fence surrounding the grounds.

"Have you bought yourself a new home?" she asked.

"In a way." Rhynne helped her down and offered his arm. They walked slowly through the open gates and up a brick walkway to the entry porch. Rhynne pulled a cord and she heard bells tinkle inside the house.

A large man dressed like an English butler opened the door. Selena had to remind herself not to stare. This, in San Francisco?

"Good day, Mr. Rhynne," the man said. "Nice to see you, sir."

"Hello, Talbot. Would you tell Madam Tussey I've brought a guest? Perhaps she should receive us in her private quarters."

"Of course, sir. May I take your hat?"

Selena and W.W. followed Talbot along a short hall and through a door into a small sitting room.

"I'll tell Madame you're here," Talbot said, bowing. He left the room.

"My curiosity has reached the bursting point," Selena warned Rhynne.

Moments later a well-corseted middle-aged woman with impossibly red hair entered and smiled at Rhynne, then looked appraisingly at Selena. "A real beauty!" she exclaimed.

Rhynne frowned and shook his head.

The woman raised her eyebrows, then nodded. "Private property, right?"

"I'd like to show my friend around the premises," he told her.

"Whatever you say, W.W. The place, after all, is yours. Nice to meet you, Miss . . . ?"

"Jones," Rhynne said hastily. "Her name is Jones."

"Miss Jones. If you ever need work, just remember you're more than welcome here any time."

"Thank you," Selena said faintly as Rhynne took her elbow to lead her from the room. "Wasn't Madam Tussey wearing an extreme amount of rouge?" she whispered to him. "And her hair!"

"It's mandatory. Like aprons on maids."

"Oh."

They passed through a large room, somewhat like a parlor, with a rosewood piano at the far end. Selena caught her breath when she saw the nude depicted on the gilt-framed canvas above the fireplace mantel. Surely what the woman was doing was, well, too private to be the subject of a painting. Her face flamed.

She thought she heard W.W. chuckle but when she glanced sideways he was smoothing his mustache. He led her through an archway toward a wide curving staircase. Two women looked down from the upstairs hall and as they began to climb the steps, Selena saw both of them had on transparent robes with nothing underneath.

"It's Mr. Rhynne," one said.

"Yeah, but who's she?" the other responded.

"Alice," Rhynne said, approaching them. "And Theresa, isn't it? I'm showing Miss Jones through. She'd like to see one of the rooms. One of the unoccupied rooms."

Both the women looked her up and down. Selena tried desperately not to stare at their bodies, which were so suggestively revealed. Alice turned away and threw open a door at the top of the steps. Selena stopped in the doorway.

Inside was an ornate brass bed covered with crimson velvet. On the wall hung another oil, this one of a man and woman and Selena looked away immediately. She'd had no idea such paintings existed. The ceiling above the bed reflected the room and she realized with astonishment a mirror had somehow been mounted there. She looked in confusion and with dawning realization at W.W.

"I believe Miss Jones has seen enough. Thank you, girls." Rhynne nodded politely and steered Selena down the stairs.

She held her words until they were back in the carriage.

"That was a—a house of ill repute, wasn't it?"

"A whorehouse, yes," he said bluntly. "I own it."

She stared at him.

"Oh, come, Selena, you've heard my name connected with such places before. It turns a decent profit and I make sure the girls are well taken care of and that they all *want* to be where they are. I'm no white slaver."

"But why did you bring me there?"

"Because that's where you'll wind up if you start singing at the Golden Empire. Not only my 'pretty waitress girls' are expected to satisfy the customers—the entertainers are too. It's part of an unspoken contract. The customers expect it and won't patronize you if you don't provide it. In Hangtown, things were different. There you could sing and the men were satisfied to dream about you. Not in San Francisco. Here they expect to be able to have you. Is that what you want, Selena? For any man who's taken with you to think he has the right to have you?"

She shuddered. "No! You know I'd never permit such a thing!"

"Pamela has made a great deal of money. You'll qualify for what passes for society in this town. You'll be desired by every man who sees you in whatever circles you move in, but at least you'll have the right to pick and choose. One or none, as the fancy takes you.

"I'm sorry you had to be exposed to Madam Tussey's, but I felt you had to be shocked into accepting the fact that you can't possibly sing in a public place in San Francisco."

Selena swallowed. "She—Madam Tussey offered me work!"

Rhynne grinned at her. "Well, why not? To her way of thinking it was a compliment to your attractiveness. All her girls are pretty."

She stared at him, then reluctantly began to smile, finally laughing out loud. "Oh, W.W.," she said. "There isn't another man like you in the whole world."

When Pamela sneezed, Selena jerked out of her reverie. She turned from the mirror to look at her mother. "You aren't getting another cold?"

"No, it's nothing."

"Mother, are you still friendly with King Sutton?"

"Friendly? I see him occasionally—why do you ask?"

"Oh, I don't know. I thought once maybe you and W.W. would marry."

"We're friends, Selena."

"Yes, of course."

"Don't be late tonight; you need your beauty sleep. We've yet to find *you* a husband who suits your fancy." Pamela yawned. "I'm retiring early, I have an appointment with Robert Gowdy tomorrow, plus some other business errands to see to."

"If you wish me to continue to act as your agent, I shall, of course, do so," Robert Gowdy said.

Pamela thought he sounded more like a great sulky boy than anything else. All because she had made this unlikely sum of money without taking his advice. She still had trouble believing how wealthy she actually was.

The hidden reason for Robert's dissatisfaction was that he suspected she listened to W.W.'s advice and not his. Which she did. But Robert would never be able to understand that she herself had a good head for business. In that way he was like her late husband. On the other hand, W.W. gave credit where credit was due.

Why then did she continue to see King Sutton? She no longer really loved him, indeed no longer respected him. Perhaps because he had no one else. Pamela sighed and gave her attention once more to Robert Gowdy who, whatever he felt about her, was an excellent agent and well worth the percentage she paid him.

"I've warned you before about your association with a known criminal, Lady Pamela," he said. "I should hate to think you'd give the Committee any reason to investigate you."

"Are you threatening me, Robert?"

"I'm not the threat, as you well know. I have it on good authority that they've imported a man to run Mr. Wordsworth Rhynne out of town. A former army captain, a man we both know—Barry Fitzpatrick."

Pamela smiled calmly, despite the sudden lurch of her heart. "And you expect me to be afraid of him? Come, Robert, you'll have to produce a more fearsome adversary than Barry."

"He's fought in a war, Lady Pamela. And he's been a Texas Ranger. He's not a man you can twist around your finger."

She shrugged. "We'll see. Meanwhile, you may

tell Mr. Horton that his offer on the lot on Fremont Street is so low as to be an insult. And thank you again for your efforts on my behalf." She rose and reached out her hand to him, smiling.

"You believe yourself unappreciated, but you're wrong," she told him.

Robert Gowdy held her hand a moment longer than necessary. He hated to let her go. Although he'd finally married and although he did love his wife, there would never be another woman like Lady Pamela.

Outside once again, Pamela raised her umbrella against the rain and turned toward the bay. She could have kept her carriage waiting, but then her driver would have known her destination and she preferred he didn't. Charlie Sung's place was only a few blocks from the shipping offices. She always took care to wear a widow's black when she ventured there, and, although this part of San Francisco had become more and more shabby these last two years, she had yet to be accosted.

Still, she glanced from the corners of her eyes at some of the passing rowdies and thought she'd not like to be on these streets after dark.

"Oh!" The exclamation jerked from her as a hand fastened on her arm. She whirled.

"Pamela, what a surprise to find you headed in my direction," W.W. said.

"You gave me a start."

"I meant to."

"Were you deliberately following me?"

"It's becoming more and more inconvenient to do so, to tell you the truth."

"What in heaven's name are you talking about?"

W.W. frowned at her. "Pamela, Ned has died. I was arranging for the funeral services when the boy brought me word you were with Gowdy and had sent away your carriage. I had to drop everything and hurry over here to see you were safe."

"Ned?" Tears filled Pamela's eyes. "Oh, W.W., I didn't even know he was sick."

"Cholera's a quick killer. Pamela, I want you to promise me you won't come to the docks alone again. Either Mac or Abe or Ned or myself has had to trail you every time you visited Charlie's. It's damned inconvenient. I've no more time to cater to your so-called sensibilities. Don't you think your coachman is well aware of your visits here? Whom do you think you're fooling?"

"No one has ever molested me."

"Now you know why. Don't think this scum doesn't know it's dangerous to tangle with W.W. Rhynne."

"You make me feel I've been very stupid."

"Exactly my intention. Here we are."

He nodded to the building Charlie Sung had altered so that the corners of the roof curled upward in temple fashion. Bright red Chinese characters decorated the door. Inside were glimmering multicolored Chinese shawls, bolts of silk, carved teakwood tables, boxes of choice teas, fans and sticks of incense. The fragrance of sandlewood permeated the store.

"We'd like to see Charlie," W.W. said to the old Chinese who tended the counter.

The man bowed and touched a small brass gong with a wooden mallet. Almost instantly a

Chinese girl in a cheongsam glided through the beaded curtains that concealed an inner doorway. The elderly man whispered to her and she disappeared again behind the curtain.

In a few moments Charlie's bland face appeared from the same inner doorway. Although he, too, wore a queue and dressed very like the old man, Charlie managed to convey an entirely different image. A Celestial, of course, but above and beyond that, a businessman.

He bowed and smiled at Pamela and W.W., folded his arms and waited.

"Always good to see you, Charlie," W.W. said. "Today I have a favor to ask." He stepped closer to Charlie and said something to him in such a low tone Pamela couldn't make out the words.

Charlie's face didn't change.

W.W. spoke again, still so softly she didn't know what was said.

Charlie nodded then. "For you, Mr. Rhynne, though with reluctance." Charlie's voice never failed to fascinate Pamela. He spoke with a cultured English accent. Pamela would have thought he was an Oxford graduate had she heard the voice without seeing him. But when she had ventured to ask him once, Charlie had assured her he'd never had the pleasure of voyaging to England.

Now Charlie touched the gong and the same girl appeared. He spoke to her in Chinese, then turned back to W.W. and Pamela.

"If you will please follow Plum Blossom."

Pamela stared at W.W. He motioned toward the girl with his head. Pamela had not been beyond the beaded curtain at any time before when she'd come for her laudanum. In fact, of late the old man simply handed her the bottles with a bow when she gave him the money and she didn't even see Charlie. What was Rhynne up to?

"Come along, Pamela," he said curtly.

To mask her confusion she spoke to Charlie. "Is Plum Blossom actually her name?" she asked. The girl was as fragile and lovely as a flower.

"The exact English translation is Early-Flowering-of-the-Plum-Tree," Charlie told her.

Pamela and W.W. walked behind Plum Blossom through the beaded curtain, along an ill-lit corridor and through a wooden door that she unlocked. Another corridor with many doors. The girl stopped before the last door, unlocked it and motioned them to precede her. She then relocked the door behind the three of them.

Pamela gasped. From a small platform she gazed down into a squalid smoky room where men lounged against dingy grey pallets. Round braziers stood near each pallet and although some of the men seemed asleep, others puffed on long exotic pipes. None of them paid any attention to the intruders. Pamela stared, uncomprehending.

"These, my dear, are opium smokers. There you see them dreaming their lives away."

She whirled to look at W.W. Although his tone had been mocking, his dark eyes were sad.

"As you can see, not all of them are Celestials, and not all are men." He inclined his head.

To Pamela's horror, she now noticed the person almost directly under them was a woman, a white woman.

"Oh, W.W., how could she?"

"The same as you could, Pamela. Only she's unluckier. And poorer."

Pamela bit her lip. This was unfair of W.W. It wasn't the same, not the same at all.

"The difference is only in degree," he said as though reading her mind. "You still keep yourself active. How long will you be able to?"

She didn't reply. Couldn't reply. Only she knew how hard it was to climb out of bed sometimes, to leave the warm fascination of her dreams behind and force herself to accept the responsibilities of the day. Wasn't it becoming more difficult? Would the day come when she didn't make the effort? But on the other hand the agony when she tried to give up laudanum was indescribable.

Pamela took a deep breath and straightened her shoulders. "Thank you for your concern," she said, her voice frosty. "You've made your point, misguided though it might be."

W.W. shook his head, but said nothing. He motioned to the girl that they were ready to leave.

Outside Charlie's, though the cold wind from the bay cleared her lungs of the sweet smell of opium, Pamela fancied she could still taste it. "How could you?" she said in a low intense voice to W.W. when he offered his arm. "How could you do this to me?"

"Because I love you," he said, looking directly at her.

Her eyes dropped; she had no answer.

Maria knocked on the door of Pamela's bedroom. When Pamela answered, she stuck her head in to announce there was a man at the door.

"He ask to see Lady Pamela," Maria said in her heavy accent. "He say Captain Fitzpatrick."

Pamela rose slowly from the chaise longue. She hadn't even heard the knocker. "I'll be down in a few minutes," she told Maria. "Show him into the parlor."

Rapidly she tidied her hair and smoothed her skirt. How foolish of her to have fallen asleep without changing into a dressing robe. Should she put on something more becoming than the black gown? It lacked even a crinoline. Meeting her eyes in the mirror she made a face. She was definitely not looking her best.

Quickly she undid the buttons and stepped out of the dress. What should she put on—the rose taffeta? With a modest crinoline, so she didn't appear overdressed. Yes, that was an improvement. These days black seemed to drain all the color from her face. She arranged her hair in a more elaborate chignon than she usually bothered with and descended the stairs, all too conscious of the rapid beating of her heart.

How would he look? Did he remember what there had been between them those last weeks on the trail? Pamela took several deep breaths as she approached the parlor door. When she entered she was smiling and composed.

"How nice of you to visit, Barry," she said. "I'd heard you were in San Francisco." She gave him her hand, looking into his bright blue eyes, the eyes she remembered so well.

"Hello, Lady Pamela," he said, holding her hand only for a brief moment.

"Why, Barry, you're so formal. Surely you can call me Pamela."

He nodded. "Pamela, then."

He was even more handsome than she remembered. The extra years had honed him. His bone structure was more prominent, the eagerness of his youth replaced by the assurance of a man who knew all there was to know about himself. An exciting man.

"Would you care for spirits? I can offer you some excellent French brandy. Or there's . . ."

"Thank you, no. Not now."

She raised her eyebrows. They stood facing one another but he made no move toward or away from her.

"Have you come on official business, then?" she asked, her voice mocking him. "Have you come to arrest me, perhaps?"

Barry tried not to stare at her. He'd been appalled when the man he had trailing Rhynne sent word that Rhynne had taken Pamela to Sung's opium den.

"I peered in through the window," the man had told him, "and they went into the back. So they weren't buying any tea, I'll vouch for that."

And now Pamela's eyes were strange, her pupils unnaturally small in this dim room with no lamps lit although it was nearly dusk.

"I apologize for my late visit," he said abruptly.

Pamela blinked, then looked about, suddenly aware of the rapidly darkening room. She laughed. "Maria isn't the best of servants," she said. "It's not easy to find capable help here." She turned to pull a cord to summon the maid.

Barry caught her arm. "No," he said. "Maybe it's best to talk with the lamps not lit."

She looked up coquettishly. "That depends on what you intend to say."

He released her arm. Pamela was still an attractive woman, yet she seemed somehow faded. With her eyes giving him the almost sure knowledge she used opium, he found the idea of holding her in his arms distasteful.

"I want you to stay away from Wordsworth Rhynne," he said gruffly.

Pamela drew back. "And what do you think gives you the right to order me about?"

"He's a rogue. You must know that."

"And you've been hired to dispose of him. Do you intend to dispose of me as well?"

"If I must," he said curtly.

"I don't believe you."

"I came here as a friend. I don't want to become your enemy. But W.W. Rhynne will be removed from San Francisco one way or another. It's in your best interests—and the interests of your daughter's reputation—to dissociate yourself from him completely."

"I believe you are already my enemy," she said slowly.

"You misunderstand. I told Selena . . ."

"You've talked to Selena?"

In the dark room she couldn't be sure she saw his face redden. Selena hadn't told her. Something twisted inside Pamela. Yes, he'd seen Selena and now she, Pamela, was suddenly old in his eyes. *That's* what was wrong with him.

I won't be jealous of my own daughter, she told herself. But her eyes filled with tears. She swallowed and forced herself to laugh, a sound that was brittle in her ears.

"I do believe our interview is at an end, Captain Fitzpatrick. I'll ask Maria to show you out, if you'll excuse me."

"Pamela . . ."

She turned back to him.

"I—I'm sorry."

"La, captain, and for what?" She left him then, knowing that if she stayed she'd disgrace herself by crying.

22

Rhynne strode into Pierre's on Dupont Street with a folded newspaper in his hand. He waved the maitre d' aside. Spotting King Sutton eating alone on the far side of the room, he crossed the restaurant, oblivious both of the waiters scurrying out of his way and the stares of the diners.

Sutton started to rise with his hand outstretched. Ignoring him, Rhynne threw the paper onto the table so hard the silverware rattled.

"What's the meaning of this?" he demanded.

"Now, W.W., how can you expect me to know? I haven't seen today's *Californian* yet." Sutton ran his hand through his grey hair.

Rhynne pointed to the editorial on the front page. "TIME FOR ACTION," the headline read. "Local Gambler Implicated In Mining Scheme" was the subhead. "The citizens of San Francisco have stood idly by for too long!" the story began.

When Sutton finished reading, he shook his head. "I have no idea how such a story came to be in Curie's sheet," he said. "You know he's been itching for a fight with someone to boost his circulation."

"This is your doing, Sutton. It's not the first time you've spread lies about me and the Golconda Mining Company."

Sutton started to get up. "Are you calling me a liar, sir?" he asked.

Rhynne grasped the front of Sutton's frock coat and shoved the bigger man back into his chair. "Take it any way you damn well please. I'll have no more. We're quits."

King Sutton glanced around the suddenly hushed dining room. "W.W.," he said placatingly, "not here. We'll go down the street to my place and discuss the matter over a drink."

"We'll go to the *Californian* office where you'll tell Fred Curie the truth."

"Let's go to my rooms at the Fremont. I can explain what you see there."

"I've heard enough of your explanations. They're a mix of lies and half-truths."

Sutton stood up, toppling his chair behind him. "I've killed men for less than that," he shouted.

"Are you challenging me to a duel like you did young O'Lee? Think long and hard before you do. I'm not a lad who's never fired a pistol in his life before."

"Gentlemen!" Pierre DuBois stepped between them. "I beseech you. My two friends, two of my best customers, two of the most esteemed of my clientele. Please."

"I apologize, Pierre," Sutton said. "This was none of my doing."

"Monsieur Sutton, Monsieur Rhynne," Pierre said. "How many time have I seen you eating here together, drinking the wines of France, laughing one with the other? And now this unfortunate contretemps. I, Pierre DuBois, cannot permit it. Not for myself, not for Pierre, not for the serenity of my other guests, but for yourselves. I cannot allow brother to turn against brother."

"You're right, Pierre," Rhynne said. "This should be of no concern of yours. We'll settle our differences elsewhere." He looked at Sutton. "But settle them we will. King?" He started for the door.

King Sutton sighed, threw his napkin to the table and followed. "Add the dinner to my account, Pierre," he said. "With my usual tip."

Pierre seemed about to object but shrugged instead. "As you wish, monsieur," he said.

Rhynne and Sutton walked in silence to the Fremont Hotel where they climbed the stairs to Sutton's second floor suite.

"Whisky?" Sutton asked when they were in the parlor.

Rhynne shook his head.

"I'll have one." Sutton poured whisky and drank, putting the glass on a table marred with the rings left by many other glasses. "Sit down, W.W.," he said.

"I prefer to stand."

Sutton walked about the room turning up the oil lamps. He shuffled through the papers on a desk then threw them down again. Opening a door at the rear of the room, he called, "Jed! Jed!"

There was no answer. "Where the hell's that black bastard gone now?" he asked no one in particular.

Rhynne tapped the folded newspaper against the side of his leg as he watched the other man. Finally Sutton slumped into an overstuffed armchair. The only sounds in the room were the ticking of the wall clock and the night noises of the city coming through the window.

Sutton reached for his glass and drank the rest of his whisky. "You were right to take me to task," he said. "The fault's mine and mine alone."

"Then you *were* responsible for the story?"

"A couple of nights ago I was bucking the tiger and having a few drinks and one thing led to another the way it does. I must have spun a tale or two about Hangtown and the Golconda. How was I to know I was talking to Curie's brother?"

"Some tale! A gross libel."

"You did lend me the money to start the venture. And the idea did come from your coup with the lottery. You have to admit that, W.W."

"I lent you the money to buy mining properties. How did I know you intended to sell shares, give the first buyers handsome profits with the money from new investors, salt the mines, sell more shares, get in over your head, turn belly up and lose everything? I have a question for you. Something that's bothered me for some time. King, how in the name of hell did you ever manage to run a cotton plantation?"

"Don't forget our slaves. We provide for them but there's no wages to pay. They're valuable property."

"You've lost Joshua now. And I shouldn't think you're planning to sell Jed."

"Joshua was a damn fool. And, no, of course I won't sell Jed. As for the cotton, we never much more than kept our heads above water, Beckworth and I. When I tried to raise money on the plantation last year I came up dry."

"I need some of the money I lent you, King."

"You need money? Wordsworth Rhynne?"

"Coleman's pushing me hard, shutting off my sources of credit to try to force me out. I'm a mite over-extended. The Golden Empire didn't come cheap." Rhynne saw no reason to mention that he could perhaps borrow more from Danny O'Lee. Danny was already in with so much he'd had to give him a quarter interest in the hotel.

Sutton looked away from him. "There's always Pamela," he said. "That land she bought over the years with the profits from the Hangtown Empire fetched her a pretty penny."

"I wouldn't ask Pamela for a cent, King. I wouldn't accept money from her if she offered it."

"Because she's a woman? She didn't hesitate to go to you in the beginning. Everything she has came from her partnership with you in Hangtown or Placerville or whatever they call the place now."

"Money pollutes just as badly as an open sewer. I've never felt about a woman the way I feel about Pamela. I'd do nothing to put our friendship in jeopardy."

"W.W., I still have assets. Don't raise your eyebrows. Give me a day to see if I can help you. Will you do that? Will you give me twenty-four hours?"

"Do I have a choice?"

"Not much of a one. You could always kill me,

I suppose. Sometimes I think I'd be better off dead. Not only me. Everyone else would be better off as well."

"You're talking like a fool."

"I'm tired. I've been drinking too much, gambling too much, losing too often, taking chances I never would take if I were in my right mind. I used to see life as sport, a contest where I won my share of the time and more. I don't seem to win any more."

Rhynne nodded slowly. "I think I will have a drink before I go," he said.

Sutton got up and poured a shot for Rhynne and another for himself.

"To the glories of the past," Sutton said.

"No, to the future."

They drank in silence.

"I shouldn't have bearded you in Pierre's," Rhynne told him. "If I have any excuse at all, which I don't, it's Ned dying as suddenly as he did."

"Cholera, I understand. There's talk of three more cholera deaths since yesterday."

"The *Californian* denies there's an epidemic. Claims cholera isn't contagious."

King Sutton almost smiled. "You can't believe what you read in that sheet," he said.

"We can agree on that." Rhynne put on his hat. "I'm not one for giving advice, King," he said, "but I think your string's run out here in San Francisco. It's time for you to ask for a new deal by leaving."

"Even though the next card might be the one I've been waiting for?" Sutton's voice held none of the hope of his words.

"I'll stop by tomorrow evening," Rhynne said. "For the money. Or as much of it as you can raise."

"I swear to God I'll have it for you."

King Sutton paced from the parlor to the dining room and back after Rhynne had gone. He looked at the clock and sighed. Still another hour. He opened the door at the rear of the room and called Jed's name. Again there was no answer. He went to the sideboard and poured himself another drink and sat sipping it, staring morosely into the whisky.

When he held his right hand in front of him, the opal in his ring caught the light from the lamp on the table and the gem glowed a fiery red. Jed and the ring, he thought. They were his only assets. He had nothing else except debts. He laughed. The black slave and the fire opal. Somehow the combination seemed incongruous to him. Jed and the opal, he said to himself. Jed and the opal.

An hour later, Pamela unlocked the door and entered the hotel room. She laid her shawl over the back of a chair, unpinned her hat and put it on the chair seat.

"You're late," King Sutton told her.

She said nothing.

He took her in his arms and kissed her.

"You've been drinking," she said.

"One or two, no more. Rhynne was here with me until an hour ago." She waited, expecting him to go on. Instead he asked, "Would you like a drink?"

She shook her head and walked across the room to the other door. When he followed her, she turned and said, "No, King. Wait here."

"Is something the matter, Pam? I've never seen you in this mood before."

"I'd just rather you waited."

"Ten minutes?"

"I'll be ready by then."

She shut the door behind her and went into the dining room. There were two doors facing her, the one beside the dumbwaiter leading to the rear hall and back stairs and the one to the bedroom. Pamela went into the bedroom. The large bed looked even more massive than usual in the shadowed light coming through the drapes on the windows overlooking Fremont Street.

She unhooked her shoes and placed them side by side on the floor. Unbuttoning her black taffeta, she stepped out of the dress and laid it on the back of a rocker. She took off her crinoline and removed her underclothing. Naked, she went to one of the windows where she slid the drape aside. Standing out of sight, she looked down into the street.

Two torches flared in front of the gambling hall across from her. In front of the hotel at the end of the block a man in colonial costume pealed a bell to lure passersby. She saw only men on the street, miners from the gold fields, mostly, but also Chinese with their hair in long queues, frockcoated gamblers, seamen, Mexicans, an occasional Indian or Californio.

Pamela's hands came up along her body to cup her breasts. King had been right. She felt so strange tonight. So alone, almost bereft. So emptied of feeling. She folded her arms under her breasts and shivered.

She left the window, pulled back the covers of the bed and slid between the sheets, drawing the blanket up until it was below her breasts. She laced her hands behind her head and waited.

King opened the door and stood at the foot of the bed looking down at her, his body glimmering whitely in the light from the window. He was naked. He drew in his breath when he saw her exposed breasts. After all this time, she thought with satisfaction, she could still excite him. He knelt beside the bed, kissing her breasts, his tongue circling her nipples. She did not move.

He took the covers and flung them off the bed onto the floor. Spreading her legs with his hands, he thrust at her roughly. She gasped, but she was ready for him and rose to meet him, her arms and legs enfolding him, expecting the throbbing rise to ecstasy. Nothing happened. What was the matter with him? She caressed him, her hands stroking his hair and back. What was wrong?

"Turn over," King told her.

She shifted in the bed until she was on her stomach, then raised herself to her knees. She felt his arms go around her waist, his fingers searching for her, his sex trying to enter her from behind. She moaned as the fingers of one of his hands caressed her; she trembled beneath him. His other hand sought her breast and she rose on her elbows so he could caress it with his hand.

Still nothing happened. All at once he rolled away and lay at the edge of the bed.

"King, I'm sorry," she said.

"It's not your fault. It's mine."

"Later?"

"No, I can't. I don't know what's wrong."

She got out of bed and began dressing.

Later, King began to complain.

"You haven't said two consecutive sentences to me all night," he told her. "Come to think of it, we haven't had much to say to one another at all lately."

"I don't feel like talking tonight."

He watched her. "When did it start to go bad between us, Pam?" he asked. "Was it because of Joshua? I don't understand exactly why but nothing was quite right after that."

"You promised them, King. You told both Jed and Joshua you'd free them."

"Yes, I did promise. When we made the money we came to California for. Only then, Pam."

"They thought you were going to free them after a year."

"A year? Never. I might have mentioned a year, I don't deny that. I never dreamed it would take longer. How could I have foreseen the bad luck we've had? I kept thinking maybe tomorrow, maybe next week, maybe next month."

"Joshua waited almost two years."

"I always expected Jed to be the one," King said, "not his brother. If either of them was to run off, I thought it would be Jed. He's young, he's strong, he's cheeky. But Joshua never said a word, never complained. And then one day he was gone."

"You could have let him go. Not tracked him down."

"We've discussed this a hundred times. If I had

let him go, Jed would have been next. I couldn't have that."

"Joshua's no good to you dead."

"He didn't have to try to swim that god-damned flooded river. He never was much of a swimmer. Jed loved the voyage around the Horn. He made a good sailor. But Joshua was always afraid we'd run aground. Why didn't he give himself up? Did I ever mistreat him? Did I flog him? Joshua was a fool."

"He wanted to be free."

"You're not a southerner. I wouldn't expect you to understand. Besides, you're a woman."

Pamela said nothing. She scratched her ankle.

"Rhynne's after me again for money," Sutton said.

"You'll get no more from me, King. I told you that after the last time."

"I know. Once a man's down, everyone turns his back on him. After they're through kicking him."

"Oh my God! King Sutton, I will not listen to that. You know what the matter is, what's truly wrong between us. You know it's not only Joshua. Certainly not the money. I could live with those things, much as I'd rather not have to. The real trouble's your broken promises. Your lies."

"I love you, Pam. That's no lie. And I need you."

"Oh, King, don't. You've killed whatever feeling there was between us just as surely as you killed Joshua. You love me? You love no one but yourself. King Sutton can love no one except King Sutton. He never could and he never will. Why not admit it?"

"What you really mean is I didn't marry you."

"You know I wanted to marry you. I never believed I would want to, not after the first time. But when I met you it was different. How long have you been promising to marry me? I'll never forget your asking me after the quarrel we had when Joshua drowned. A year ago, at least."

"I wanted to marry you, Pam. I still do."

"King, you'll never marry. You're not a marrying man. I thought you were at first. I realized you were down on your luck and needed help, needed someone to talk to, someone to encourage you and stand behind you. Yes, someone to love you. And I did love you. I wanted you. And later I wanted to be your wife. We were so good together that first year in Hangtown. I wanted to be your wife more than I've ever wanted anything in my life. You didn't seem to understand that."

"I understood, Pam."

"Then why didn't you do something about it?"

"I couldn't marry you then. I can't marry you now. I'm already married."

She stood still for a long moment staring at him.

"I should have told you in the beginning. After I didn't, every day made it harder until it became impossible. How could I tell you without losing you?"

"You're married." A statement, not a question.

"My wife is in Georgia."

"All this time, these two years and more, you've been married and you've never told me. What kind of man are you?"

"She's not well."

"Your wife's ill and you left her alone in Georgia to come to California?"

"She has melancholia. Involutional melancholia, the doctors call it. They say it has to do with her time of life. She sits for days on end staring at the wall and crying. That's all she ever does. I had her to every doctor in the state. They can't do anything for her. They give her medicine and it does no good, none at all."

"What's her name, King?"

"Betsy."

She went to him and knelt beside the bed, taking his head in her arms. "I don't know what to say, King," she told him.

"I loved her so much. I remember the first time I ever saw her, she was so . . ." He broke off, sobbing, and she rocked him in her arms. After a long time he quieted.

"Lie back on the pillow," she said. When he did, she drew the blankets up around him.

"Go to sleep now," she said.

"Will you kiss me goodnight?"

She leaned down and their lips met. When he put his arm around her shoulders and held her to him, she gently removed it and stood up.

"Not goodnight, King," she said. "Goodbye."

She walked through the parlor, picking up her hat and shawl, locked the room behind her and slipped the key under the door. In the street, she looked up at his window. She thought she saw King watching her but couldn't be sure. She walked to the corner where her carriage waited. She didn't look back again.

23

"And what do you have to report?" William Coleman asked.

"Not much as yet," Barry said. "On the surface, Wordsworth Rhynne is operating within the law."

"You talked to Sutton? You saw the story in the *Californian,* didn't you?"

"Yes is the answer to both questions. King Sutton was evasive and the investors I've questioned about the Golconda would just as soon forget the whole business. Sutton or Rhynne or whoever bilked them made them look like proper fools. As for Curie at the *Californian,* he has hearsay to back up his story, nothing more."

"I'm disappointed."

"As far as the mining scheme goes, all things considered, I think Rhynne was more a victim than anything else."

"If only gambling were illegal in California. It wasn't under the Mexicans and even now that we're a state we haven't been able to outlaw it. But we will, we will."

"When I have more definite results," Barry said, "I'll let you know."

"If Rhynne makes one slip . . ."

"We'll have him," Barry finished the sentence.

W.W. Rhynne hummed to himself, tapping his gold-headed cane on the boardwalk in time to the tune. He liked his new German tailor. Strauss had delivered the first order of miners' shirts and trousers for the Hangtown store a week ahead of the promised date. Good quality cloth, too. The tailor had told him he'd brought the denim west to sell as tenting, only the find the miners hadn't wanted tents as much as they'd wanted good durable pants.

Rhynne nodded to the clerk behind the desk in the lobby of the Fremont. What excuse would Sutton offer for not having the money for him tonight? Or would he have it? He might have pawned or sold his opal ring. Or gone to Pamela again. I'll never understand women, Rhynne thought. Still he smiled, thinking of her. That best portion of a woman's life, he paraphrased Wordsworth, her little, nameless, unremembered acts of kindness and of love.

He was at the top of the stairs when he heard the shot. He stopped, listening, expecting another. He heard nothing. The sound had come from the hall ahead of him. From Sutton's rooms?

The thought of Sutton killing himself leaped unbidden into Rhynne's mind. He rejected it. King Sutton? Never.

He strode along the hall and knocked on Sutton's door. There was no answer. He tried the knob, found the door unlocked and pushed it open. He sniffed. Gunpowder. A single lamp glowed on a table on the far side of the parlor. Sutton lay face down on the floor beside the table.

Rhynne quickly crossed the room, knelt, and turned Sutton over. He was breathing quick, shallow breaths. There was a wound in his upper left chest; the hole in his white shirt was rimmed with red.

Hearing a sound from the rear of the suite, Rhynne stood up. He threw open the door to the dining room and hurried through that room to the rear hall, shifting the cane to his left hand and taking a derringer from his pocket with his right. He went to the top of the stairs. He saw a fleeing figure in the shadows at the bottom of the stairwell. Rhynne fired, deliberately aiming too low to kill.

"Stop," he shouted.

The door at the bottom of the stairs slammed shut. Rhynne pounded down the steps, opened the door and ran out into the night. The alleyway was dark. He saw no one, heard no one, so he turned and climbed the stairs to Sutton's rooms.

He found a man kneeling beside Sutton and recognized the clerk he had seen a few minutes before in the lobby. McGregor? Yes, the man's name was McGregor.

"I couldn't catch him," Rhynne said.

McGregor stared at him. Belatedly, Rhynne realized he still held the derringer. He put the gun back into his pocket.

"I'll send for a doctor," McGregor said, slowly backing to the open door. Once out of Rhynne's sight, he ran along the corridor.

Rhynne went to Sutton and felt his pulse. It was weak but steady. The opal ring, he saw, was missing from Sutton's right hand. Rhynne looked around the room; nothing seemed to have been disturbed.

How did I manage to get into this? he wondered as he stood up. He recalled the angry confrontation with King Sutton the night before at Pierre's over the editorial in the newspaper. And tonight. He'd even fired his gun. Who'd believe his story that he'd surprised an assailant—a thief—and shot at him?

Certainly McGregor didn't, not by the looks of him when he fled the room. Nor would Coleman or Fitzpatrick. Even those who knew him might raise an eyebrow. He realized he would himself if asked to believe such an unlikely tale.

Rhynne walked swiftly to the rear hall and down to the alley where he turned away from the clamor of Fremont Street. He'd need money; he'd need time. He headed toward the Golden Empire.

He heard the summons of the Monumental Engine Company's bell, ignoring it until the ringing failed to stop after a few minutes. The Vigilantes' signal to assemble at Battery Street. Rhynne stopped. Not to the Empire, then; that would be the first place they'd look. To Rincon Hill and Pamela? No, the obvious hiding places would be the most dangerous.

Where then? Who would dare help him? It must be someone so unlikely the Committee would never suspect.

Wisps of fog drifted toward him. A man approached, glanced at him, and passed on. Rhynne fought down the urge to run, forcing himself to remain where he was. Don't panic, he told himself. Decide, then do whatever's necessary. He pulled his coat closer to ward off the chill of the fog.

Of course. Why hadn't he thought of him before? A long shot, but this was the time for long shots. Sometimes when you were losing you could recoup with one daring play. Not often, perhaps once out of ten times. If he had any luck left this would be that time.

Rhynne set off along the street with his cane thrust jauntily beneath his arm.

"Are you sure?" Barry Fitzpatrick asked.

"It's the God's truth. At the Fremont. McGregor saw the whole thing. Sutton and Rhynne had at each other and then Rhynne pulls a gun and shoots him."

"Is Sutton dead?"

"No, they say the doctor's with him now. He's hurt bad, though."

"How long ago did it happen?"

"Fifteen or twenty minutes."

Barry tossed the boy a coin. "You made good time," he told him.

"Any message for me to take back to Mr. Coleman?"

"Tell him I'll be by later tonight." The boy nodded and ran off.

As Barry strode along the street, the fog closed in around him. When he licked his lips he tasted the tang of salt. In the distance, the fire bell suddenly stopped.

These first few hours, Barry knew, were crucial. This was the time most mistakes were made and most opportunities lost. He must act and act decisively. He'd overestimated Rhynne, seen him as a devious, clever man, not one to shoot an enemy with a witness present. Barry shrugged. He'd been wrong before and probably would be again. The danger now was in thinking Rhynne too easy an adversary.

When he pushed his way into the Golden Empire, the gambling saloon was as crowded and noisy as he remembered it. Word of the shooting must not have reached here yet, he thought.

Barry looked for McSweeney as he made his way past the bar but the big man wasn't in sight. He opened the door leading to Rhynne's private quarters and went up the stairs. The hallway at the top was deserted; the door to Rhynne's office was locked.

Barry threw his weight against the door and heard wood splinter inside. Again he slammed his shoulder against it. The bolt tore from the inside wall and the door flew open. Barry stood just outside the doorway for a moment, listening until he was satisfied the dark room was empty, then went in, closing the door behind him. Groping along the top of the nearest table, he found a lamp, lit it and looked around.

The room seemed unchanged. He leafed through the papers on Rhynne's desk. Nothing there. He opened the top drawer and found a ledger for the Hangtown hotel and another for the store. He put them on top of the desk.

"So it's a robber you are now." McSweeney stood in the doorway with a Walker Colt in his hand.

"Rhynne shot King Sutton," Barry said.

McSweeney's blank stare told Barry he hadn't heard the news.

"Even if true, which I doubt, that gives you no license to steal."

"I'm looking for Rhynne."

"He's usually not to be found in his desk."

Barry said nothing.

"By whose authority?"

"The Committee of Vigilance."

McSweeney grunted. "That's no authority at all," he said. For a long minute he made no move, as though weighing his options.

"Rhynne's a hunted man," Barry said.

"We'll see what the sheriff has to say to all this." McSweeney motioned Barry to leave the room ahead of him.

Barry walked from behind the desk.

"Keep a comfortable distance," the big man told him.

Barry veered away from him toward the table. He swung his arm at the lamp, sending it hurtling to one side, at the same time throwing himself to the floor in the opposite direction. The lamp crashed but stayed lit; McSweeney's gun cracked, the shot going wild.

Before he could fire again, Barry hurled himself at McSweeney, twisted his wrist and sent the pistol spinning away to thud on the carpet. McSweeney leaped back, tripping on a cuspidor. Recovering, he lunged for Barry. Barry hit him in the eyes, kneed him in the groin, and the big man grunted with pain.

Seeing the pistol from the corner of his eye, Barry leaped to one side and grabbed it. McSweeney came at him, stopping abruptly when he came face to face with the muzzle of the Walker Colt.

"I wouldn't," Barry said when he saw McSweeney poise to charge him again. He clicked the hammer back, his finger tightening on the trigger.

McSweeney relaxed. "Another day," he said.

"Perhaps." Holding the gun on the big man, Barry went to the desk and picked up the two ledgers. He crossed the room, pausing at the door.

"I'm going out into that hall," he said. "And I'm going to wait there, maybe for one minute and maybe for five. If you come out while I'm still there, I'll kill you. Do you understand?"

"Like a guessing game," McSweeney said.

"Except it's a game you can only lose." Barry nodded to the clock on the bookshelves behind Rhynne's desk. "After five minutes," he said, "you can be sure I'll be gone."

Barry backed into the hall and along the corridor to the top of the stairs. There was no sign of McSweeney. Barry went down the stairs, thrusting the pistol in his belt. With the ledgers under his arm, he walked through the gambling hall and out into the fog.

"How did you know I'd help you?"

"I didn't," Rhynne said. "I took a chance. Isn't life one gamble after another?"

"Ja," Strauss said. "When I come to this country from Bavaria, to my brothers in New York City, that was a chance." He spoke with a heavy German accent, his speech so guttural that at times Rhynne had to listen intently to understand him. "When I sail for California with my denim," Strauss said, "that was a chance."

"You didn't like New York?"

"My brothers have carts. Wagons. Are peddlers. I'm not a peddler. I'm a merchant. Someday I'll be more than a merchant. Today there is only Strauss, the poor tailor. Soon I hire another man to sew with me and then another and another. One day Strauss will have a floor of a building with rows of men and women sewing. And not by hand; no, by machines. Imagine, machines for sewing."

"A sewing machine? Are there such things?"

"I saw one with my own eyes in New York." Strauss shook his head. "Too slow. Too clumsy. The work is not good. In five years, ten years, who knows?"

"You dream dreams, my friend."

"Can a man live with no dream?"

"My dream at the moment is to get from San Francisco to Hangtown."

"Ach, for the moment I forget. When a man dreams he forgets. Hangtown! Such a name. There you will be safe?"

"The Vigilantes have no power outside San Francisco."

"One might hide, perhaps, in a wagon?"

"I could. That's slow, especially with the rains and the mud coming. And dangerous. As a last resort, maybe."

"If only I made barrels to ship—or coffins. It would be easy to put you on a riverboat inside, with not a question from any man."

"How do you send your clothing to the mines?"

"In bales." Strauss threw out his hands to show their size. "Too small to hide a man. You couldn't breathe. Five years from now, who knows, I may hire ships to send my goods."

"Your trousers have been a great success."

"Because they are *gut*. Well made. The work of a German craftsman. I have only one complaint."

"And that is?"

"How would you like men to call their trousers by your first name?"

"Wordsworths? I don't think I'd mind if they bought them from me. Your name sounds much better than mine for trousers, though. I mean no offense, but I much prefer Levis to Wordsworths."

"Again we talk of Levi Strauss, not Wordsworth Rhynne. We must transport you to Hangtown."

"I have an idea, Levi. Perhaps in some way we could use your skill as a tailor."

"*Ja. Gut, gut.* I make you look like another person. No more Wordsworth Rhynne."

"I'll shave my mustache."

"And wear a dress. I could make you a dress with . . . How to say it? Like a *frau*."

"I'll wear a poke bonnet to cover my head and hide my face. Wear a veil, perhaps."

"Wordsworth Rhynne will be a tall woman. I, Strauss, would be a better one."

"Yet what a shame to shave your fine growth of beard. I'll walk with a stoop. I'll be an old woman with a cane traveling upriver to see my son in Sacramento."

"Your only son?"

"No, I have four sons." Rhynne smiled. "Two live in New York, one in Sacramento. You, Levi, are my fourth son and you shall see me off."

"Is Sutton dead?" Barry Fitzpatrick asked.

"No," Coleman said. "Curie was at the Fremont only a few minutes ago. King Sutton has at least three doctors treating him. They're afraid to move him from his room."

"Has he named his assailant?"

"No, he's still unconscious. I didn't see you as a man who picked nits, captain. There's no question Rhynne's the guilty one."

"I like to be sure, though I agree everything points to Rhynne. And there's been no word of his whereabouts?"

William Coleman looked at the other Committee members gathered in the Battery Street room. "Johnson?" he said, nodding to a tall, lean man.

"He's not at the Empire," Johnson said. "Never showed his face there after the shooting. Nor at the Buttle-Jones' on Rincon Hill. We've been to all his favorite haunts and come up with nothing. It's as though Rhynne's vanished into the fog."

"You have men blockading the roads and watching the docks?" Barry asked.

"We have," Coleman said. "All vehicles proceeding south on the peninsula are being stopped.

No ship leaves the harbor without being searched. We have boats patrolling the bay in case he tries to slip away in a small boat."

"I misjudged Rhynne once," Barry said, "and I may again. But I see him trying to outsmart us, using a devious method of escape. Perhaps one that's too devious for his own good. A direct, simple plan is usually the best."

"What else can we do?" Coleman asked. "Captain, do you have any suggestions? That, after all, is why we brought you here."

"Only one." Barry laid the two ledgers from Rhynne's office on Coleman's desk. "These show Rhynne's suppliers, the men he does business with. Men who are, in most cases, obligated to him. I suggest you identify them, list them and circulate the list, then watch their places of business. And watch them."

Coleman nodded. "A good idea," he said. "Consider it done."

The couple stood on the dock the next morning waiting for the riverboat's gangplank to be lowered. The man was short and erect and wore a black plug hat; the woman, who walked with a cane, was older and stooped, though still taller than the man. Her face was concealed by a mourning veil.

"My son," she murmured in a low voice only he could hear. "You have been very good to me."

"We Jews," Strauss said, "know what it is to be hunted. We know the fear of the words written on the outside of the shop, the fear of the knock on the door in the night. In Europe. Even in America. Where there is oppression, where there are vigilantes, there you will find Jews fighting them. You must know this. Why else did you come to me?"

"Aren't you afraid to help me?"

"What can they do to me, a poor immigrant tailor? So I make a few dollars less."

As the gangplank was lowered from the boat, a hansom clattered along the dock and stopped behind the waiting passengers. Two men got out.

"Mutter," Levi said. "Are you ill?"

"I know those men. One's Fitzpatrick, the other's Curie from the newspaper. They're both with the Committee."

Levi offered his arm. "A dutiful son helps his *Mutter* up the gangplank," he said. "Safety is meters away."

Barry Fitzpatrick watched the passengers climbing aboard the riverboat as Curie signaled to a man lounging nearby.

"This is Wilson," he told Barry when the man joined them.

"Is there anyone on your list with a shipment for upriver?" Barry asked him.

"Only one. Levi Strauss. We checked his consignment. There's nothing out of the ordinary. That's Strauss there in the top hat boarding the ship with the old woman."

"He's going to Sacramento?" Barry asked.

"No, his mother is."

"That's his mother with him?"

Wilson nodded. "Strauss made quite a point of it, matter of fact."

"Arrest her," Barry said.

Wilson and Curie stared at him.

"Damn it," Barry told them, "do what I say before the ship's halfway to Sacramento."

Wilson motioned to another man and they pushed their way up the gangplank. A few minutes later they were back with a bonnetless Rhynne between them, a prisoner.

"How did you know?" Curie asked. There was more than a little awe in his voice.

"Never in my life," Barry said, "do I remember seeing a woman who was taller than her son. Do you?"

24

Dr. Warner Phillips was the first physician to arrive at the Fremont Hotel after King Sutton was shot. A roly-poly man, Dr. Phillips bullied laymen though he was self-effacing with other doctors.

He had reason to be, for he had never attended medical college. Twenty years before, in Ashtabula, Ohio, when wearied of farming, Warner Phillips began teaching himself the healing arts by reading medical texts, since he'd always had a gift of healing farm animals. Finally he moved to Pennsylvania, where he nailed a shingle to his door and used his busy practice to continue his education.

"Experience is the best teacher," became his motto.

Dr. Phillips found King Sutton sprawled on the floor, bleeding profusely and unconscious. He tore away the clothing from the wound and saw that the bullet had entered Sutton's chest just above the first rib.

The doctor felt for a pulse. There seemed to be none in Sutton's left wrist, only a feeble one in his right. The patient's hands and feet were cold. Dr. Phillips put his finger into the wound and explored it. The bullet had slanted upward to emerge under Sutton's armpit.

Dr. Austin Dee arrived as Phillips completed his examination and immediately began his own. "There's an artery severed," he said when he was through.

"I beg to disagree, doctor," Phillips said. "Look, the hemorrhaging has stopped. I doubt if the artery's involved at all."

"The artery may be clotted for the moment but the least movement will tear it open again." Dee's tone was positive.

Phillips began applying mustard plaster to Sutton's hands and feet to try to restore his circulation. King moaned.

"Who's responsible for the fee if he dies?" Dr. Dee asked.

"The Committee of Vigilance, I understand."

"Good," Dr. Dee said. "We'll have to put in a sponge to plug that artery."

Dr. Phillips hesitated. Probably Dee was right, he thought. Wasn't the man a licentiate of the Royal College of Surgeons of Ireland? At least he claimed to be.

"I'm inclined to agree, doctor," Phillips said. "At least putting in a sponge will give us time to put our heads together."

Dr. Dee took a piece of white sponge the size

of a large hen's egg, moistened it with water, and shoved the sponge up into the wound. King Sutton moaned once and was quiet. Dee felt his pulse, then applied wet compresses and bandaged the wound.

"Now we'll let nature take its course," Dr. Dee said.

When a third physician, Dr. Chauncey Speer, arrived at the hotel an hour later he had to push his way through a throng milling outside waiting for news. In Sutton's rooms, he found the two doctors arguing in a parlor clouded with tobacco smoke.

"There's no question," Dr. Dee was saying, "but that cholera's caused by a morbid condition of the air. Miasma."

"Not at all," Dr. Phillips said. "My experience shows it comes from intemperance. I've seen three cases this past week and debauchery, drunkenness and bad food were involved in all three. Not to mention filth."

After inquiring what had been done for the patient, Dr. Speer went into the bedroom where he found the unconscious Sutton lying on his massive bed. Dr. Speer examined him and rejoined his colleagues.

"We can't wait any longer," he told them. "This artery question has to be settled now. If the artery's severed, we have to operate at once and suture it."

"Closing the artery's a risky business," Dr. Dee said. "I thought at first the artery was involved but now I'm not sure. The hemorrhaging has stopped."

"The risk must be taken. We can't leave that

sponge in there. As a temporary solution, I suppose it was better than nothing. As a permanent answer, it can only lead to putrefaction. At least that's my opinion."

"Well, I may have some crude opinions of my own," Dr. Dee said. "And one of them is that we wait. Leave the sponge in for the time being. We'll only kill the man if we try to take it out now. What do you say, Phillips?"

"And what in the name of heaven does Phillips know about it?" Speer asked.

"He is my patient, after all," Phillips said, his voice rising. "I was on the scene first, so the decision's mine." He had never liked Speer's overbearing ways and now the man was telling him how to treat his patient. Phillips had been wavering about whether to remove the sponge; now he made up his mind.

"I vote to leave the sponge in," he said. He glanced at Dr. Dee, who nodded.

Dr. Speer swung about, picking up his black satchel. "I can assume no further responsibility in this case," he said as he slammed the door behind him.

They left the sponge in. By the next morning King Sutton's left arm was paralyzed, his chest cold, blue, and swollen. The exit wound under his arm was draining fluid. He hadn't regained consciousness.

Dr. Phillips took Dr. Dee aside after they completed their examination. "Shouldn't we reconsider, doctor?" he asked. "Perhaps we should operate after all."

"Then why in the name of hell didn't you say so last night? Speer asked for your opinion then and you said leave the sponge in. Now you say take it out and, I suppose, you want to suture the artery. Why can't you make up your mind?"

"But doctor . . ." Phillips began.

"We can't operate. Didn't you see the extent of the swelling in the left breast? It must be congestion induced by the sponge."

"Isn't that a good reason to open him up? To let that fluid drain?"

"We've waited too long," Dee said. "It's too dangerous now. His condition's become too precarious."

"I think we should have another opinion."

"Speer again?"

"Good God, not that pompous ass. What about that army surgeon, Griffen? I'm told he's had experience with wounds in the Mexican War."

"Most army surgeons," Dr. Dee said, "aren't worth the powder to blow them up with. As you know. Why would they stay in the army if they can make a living practicing on the outside?"

"Still we should have another opinion. Especially after the fuss Speer's likely to make." Dr. Phillips walked to the window and looked down at the crowd waiting for news. "The Committee of Vigilance is involved. They jailed that gambler Rhynne; they'll put him on trial before the week's out. Whatever happens, whether Sutton lives or dies, there's bound to be an inquiry. The newspapers are into it, of course. I saw Curie in the corridor when I came here this morning."

"I acknowledge the merit of your position, doctor. Yes, I totally agree that another opinion is indicated. And this Griffen is probably as good as anyone else."

Dr. Griffen arrived at dusk. A stooped, arthritic man, he briskly examined the patient while mumbling to himself and dolefully shaking his head. When the three men came out of the bedroom, he glared at Phillips and Dee.

"Who put in that damned sponge?" he asked.

The two doctors looked at one another. "I did," Dee admitted. "After consulting with Dr. Phillips."

Griffen sighed.

"A temporary measure only, doctor," Dee said. "We had to do something to stop the hemorrhaging, and we did succeed in doing that."

"What do you recommend?" Dr. Phillips asked.

"It's too late to operate," Griffen said. "He'd die on the table. And it's too late to remove the sponge. I suggest we relieve the congestion with an incision under the armpit."

"Anything else?"

"We might all try praying."

When Dr. Griffen made the incision under the exit wound, great quantities of pus drained from the opening. King Sutton did not, however, rally. He remained stuporous. Dr. Phillips suggested they take turns at his bedside. Dr. Dee agreed but Dr. Griffen grunted and muttered something about a suspected case of cholera at the Presidio. He bid them goodnight and let himself out.

"I'll talk to the crowd out there," Dee said. He went into the parlor. "Kingman Sutton is still alive but moribund," he announced. "We're doing all we can, but we hold out little hope, as the wound appears mortal. We've been fortunate to be able to prevent the patient's suffering; we are struggling against odds to save him."

The message was passed from man to man along the corridor outside the room and was called from the window. "Dying, Sutton's dying." The word seemed to echo up from the street. "Dying, dying, dying."

"I'm given to understand, doctor," Curie said, "that there is considerable dispute among the attending physicians. Regarding the most appropriate treatment."

"Not at all. You can ask Drs. Phillips and Griffen if you like. We all freely aired our opinions, of course, since medicine is still far from an exact science. But we were unanimous in the treatment decided upon. Unfortunately the patient is not responding. And that, gentlemen, is God's will."

Danny O'Lee watched the armed Vigilantes escort Wordsworth Rhynne along the waterfront street toward the jail.

"They caught him boarding the Sacramento packet disguised as a woman," a man near Danny said. "He says he didn't shoot Sutton. Can you believe that?"

After the capture, Danny knew, they had taken Rhynne to the Committee's offices where the charge—attempted murder—was read to him. He was then marched through the city to the *Argonaut,* an old coastal freighter that had been converted into a jail.

Rhynne looked composed, almost nonchalant, as he walked up the ramp to the deck of the ship with his hands tied behind him. The *Argonaut* had been beached the month before and propped upright with four-by-four timbers. Eventually the land around and under the ship would be filled with dirt and rocks but now it perched high off the ground.

When Rhynne reached the top of the ramp he paused and looked to his right and left. Danny waved to him, trying to catch his eyes to give him some sign of encouragement. Rhynne, though, didn't appear to see him before he was pushed into the ship's cabin.

"They'll try him as soon as Sutton gives up the ghost and hang him the day after," someone said.

"*If* Sutton dies."

"I heard he's failing. They don't expect him to live out the day."

Only getting his just deserts, Danny thought. Had Rhynne shot him? Somehow Danny couldn't believe he had. Why would Rhynne kill Sutton when he had so much to lose and nothing to gain? In the heat of passion perhaps? Danny couldn't imagine Rhynne becoming so enraged he'd commit murder.

Danny crossed Portsmouth Street on his way to the Golden Empire. Although McSweeney and Abe Greene were running the gambling hall in Rhynne's absence, Danny was worried. After all, most of his money was invested there.

Where had the rest of his money gone? To Selena, for the most part. She had had an endless passion for clothes and jewelry, or so it seemed to Danny. As fast as the Luck O' the Irish Mine produced gold dust, Selena spent it. The lode and Selena's passion for him had both run out at the same time.

Strange, though. He had no regrets. Selena had been worth all he had spent on her.

Danny stopped short, staring at the two men walking ahead of him—both Vigilantes coming uptown from the *Argonaut*. One looked familiar, a big man with a neatly trimmed beard and a bit of a paunch. Who was he?

Danny increased his pace until he was only a few feet from the men as they paused on a street corner. One of them, not the man Danny thought he recognized, said, "The trial's tomorrow at nine, Duke, if Sutton dies."

Duke. Of course, Duke Olmsted. A leaner, better dressed Duke, but the same man who had killed Danny's father three years before.

Duke said something to his companion and they parted with a handshake, Duke walking on up California Street. Danny followed, his hand touching the butt of the Colt thrust under his belt. Since the duel with Sutton he'd practiced long hours with the Colt and had developed into a fair shot.

Danny lagged behind, watching as Duke nodded to men passing on the street. He must have been right here in San Francisco all this time and Danny hadn't been able to find him. Because he'd looked in all the wrong places. Duke no longer seemed a man who frequented waterfront hellholes.

I'll wait until he's alone, Danny told himself, and then I'll kill him. With no more warning, no more chance to defend himself than he gave my dad. I'll shoot him down and that will be the end of it.

A half mile from the docks, Duke Olmsted climbed the porch steps of a modest house and went inside. Danny found a barrel in an alley across the street, turned it on end, and boosted himself to the top. He settled down to wait.

Almost an hour went by before Olmsted came out of the house accompanied by a sallow-faced woman. She wore a grey dress and her hair was drawn into a bun at the back of her head. She looked up at Duke; he leaned over and kissed her lightly on the lips. When he set off for the city, the woman stood on the porch watching him until he was out of sight.

Danny pushed himself from the barrel and followed. They were almost to the Square when the city bell began to clang. The Vigilantes again? Danny wondered. Had Sutton died? No, the bell rang three times, was silent, then rang twice more. The signal was repeated, three and two, three and two.

Fire!

With the first ringing of the bell, Duke started to run. He turned up a side street with Danny a hundred feet behind. Danny saw smoke billow into the sky ahead of them. Men were running beside him; he heard the crackle of flames. He turned a corner and saw a storage shed burning in the middle of the block.

Flames shot skyward from the shed's roof and licked up the side of a house in front. A bucket brigade had already formed to throw water on the nearby buildings. The shed and house were doomed. With a great clatter a fire engine arrived, eight men pulling the four-wheeled vehicle.

"Knickerbocker Five," one of the firemen shouted as they stopped on the street in front of the burning buildings. "First again!" The volun-

teer firemen unrolled their hoses while two men
leaped to man the pumper.

Duke Olmsted ran to the uniformed fire captain, who clapped him on the shoulder and
pointed at the burning house. Duke ran to the
porch and disappeared inside. Danny followed,
dodging past restraining hands. Inside, he saw
Duke at the top of the stairs. The other man
paused, looking right and left, and Danny recalled
Rhynne doing the same a few hours earlier at the
top of the ramp leading to the *Argonaut*.

Danny looked around him. Smoke seeped into
the hallway from one of the doors leading to the
rear of the house, but the air was still compara-
tively clear. He raced from room to room, opening doors, calling out, looking to see if anyone
was left in the building. He found no one.

When he came back to the front hall, Duke was
just coming to the top of the stairs holding a handkerchief to his mouth. Danny positioned himself
at the bottom of the staircase, took out his Colt
and pointed it at Duke's chest. The other man
stopped and stared down at him.

"Lay that gun aside," he said. "Are you mad?"
Olmsted took a step toward him.

Danny fired to Duke's left, the bullet splintering
the stair rail. Olmsted drew back.

"You killed my father," Danny told him. "And
so I'm going to kill you."

"I never killed a man in my life."

"Three years ago we fought in a saloon on the
waterfront, you and I. Then you waited for us
outside. You and your cronies killed my father.
You never gave him a chance."

Duke looked at him, puzzled. A kind of comprehension cleared his face, but it was not the same understanding that Danny desired.

"I might have roistered a bit in my time," Duke said. "I may have been in a brawl or two before I married. I don't think I've ever seen you in my life. I know I never killed a man. Why do you think I joined the Vigilantes? I want an end to all that."

Danny cocked the pistol. He would shoot Olmsted and leave his body here in the burning house. No one would ever know he hadn't perished in the fire.

The moment stretched endlessly. Olmsted stood on the stairs, his eyes never leaving the Colt in Danny's hands, while the smoke drifted around them, the flames crackled in the rear of the house, and the men shouted in the street outside.

Danny remembered that fog-shrouded night when he and his father were set upon outside the saloon, remembered the duel with Sutton, the gun spinning from his hand, the fearful moment when he thought he'd been hit, Rhynne kneeling beside him, and now today, Rhynne, a prisoner of the Vigilantes, climbing the ramp to the *Argonaut*.

If he shot Olmsted, he'd be doing exactly what the Vigilantes intended to do to Rhynne. He'd be killing him out of hand, without proof, without a fair hearing. Without a hearing at all.

Danny eased the hammer of the pistol forward and tucked the gun into his belt.

"Perhaps I made a mistake," he said. "I'm not sure you're the man I'm looking for after all. If you are, may the death of my father be on your head for the rest of your days."

Olmsted drew a deep breath, coughing when he breathed in the smoke fumes. "We'd best be leaving here," he said. "There was no one upstairs."

"Nor down," Danny said.

They walked out of the burning house together.

Later, Danny downed a whisky at the bar of the Golden Empire. He put down his glass, nodded to McSweeney, and they climbed the stairs to Rhynne's office.

"We have two days, maybe three to free Rhynne," Danny said. "No more, perhaps less."

"Who's to lead us in the attempt?" McSweeney asked.

Danny went around the desk and sat in Rhynne's chair. "I am," he said.

"You think you're the lad for the job?"

"No," Danny said quickly. "I'm not the lad for the job. I'm the *man*."

He never saw Duke Olmsted again. Yet he knew that it was Duke and the way he had been able to handle the situation with Duke that let him call himself a man.

25

Pamela put the handkerchief containing the lump of camphor up to her nose and inhaled before approaching the next pallet. What had the coroner's jury called the first case? Death by visitation of God? Even now, with the overcrowded hospitals turning away cholera victims, the *Californian* persisted in claiming that the fear of cholera was as bad as the disease, itself able to kill, and that thinking cholera contagious was ridiculous.

Back home, Dr. Graves had claimed just the opposite; Asiatic cholera was definitely contagious, he said. And Dr. Graves was one of England's most prominent physicians. Perhaps the camphor wasn't as much of a protection against miasma as Dr. Gunn had suggested in his *Home*

Book of Health, but the aromatic fumes were preferable to the stench around her.

Pamela bent over the sufferer, a bearded man with eyes sunk so deep she was reminded of the holes in a skull. His skin was cold, his lips blue. He desperately needed to be cleaned; she could smell that without looking under the blanket. But she shook her head and left him.

No use, she told herself. I've only so much strength and he's as good as dead. I must save myself and the medicine for the ones who have a chance.

The next patient was a boy in his teens who stared fearfully up at her. "How do you feel?" she asked. "Can you swallow?"

He nodded weakly. Carefully she measured a teaspoonful of laudanum and inserted the medicine between the boy's cracked lips. She'd had to pay Charlie Sung a fortune for the last shipment. Although she'd tried to stop taking the opiate herself, she found she couldn't. Not if she wanted to be capable of anything beyond turning and tossing miserably in bed.

"Water," the boy whispered.

Pamela went to the pail in the center of the room, stepping around patients. Almost every foot of the floor was crowded with sick and dying. Using the tin dipper, she poured water into the cup she carried in her canvas bag. She'd learned not to look too carefully at the water nor to object to the green scum often visible in the pail. At least someone still bothered to bring water regularly.

The next patient was past all human help. Pamela closed the young woman's eyes and pulled the blanket over her face. She took a square of yellow calico from her bag and laid it on top of the blanket so that the undertaker's assistant would spot the dead body quickly. Inhaling the camphor fumes, she moved on.

When she could take no more, Pamela went outside to let cold wind from the bay dissipate the lingering odors of sickness. The sky was overcast but the rain held off.

Last night she had dreamed of the Orient, warm sun, brilliant colors, soft silken cushions. She had been in the harem of a sultan who found her the most desirable of all women. Even the eunuch guard had gazed on her with dark lustful eyes. It had been a wonderful dream at first; she'd often had such erotic dreams since she'd started using laudanum.

But then, when she'd been summoned to the sultan and went to his glittering, jewel-studded chamber, the dream went awry. For as she approached the curtained bed, one very much like the Louis XIV bed W.W. Rhynne had given Selena, her anticipation turned to dread, knowing what she'd see when she drew aside the cloth-of-gold curtains.

She saw the same sight every hour of every day.

Cholera. The sultan obscenely dead in his own wastes. And the horror of it was that the sultan was no stranger. He was W.W.

Pamela bit her lip, remembering. No use to try not to think about W.W.; he appeared in her dreams anyway. He wasn't dead of cholera, of course. He didn't even have the disease, but he was as good as dead and she could do nothing.

Damn Barry Fitzpatrick for interfering!

Not that Rhynne wasn't capable of shooting a

man. At first she'd thought he probably had shot King. Then, when she'd learned the opal ring was missing, she dismissed the idea. W.W. was a gambler, yes, he took other men's money by his skill and luck. But he wasn't a common thief. Tears filled her eyes. W.W. wasn't common in any sense of the word. She'd done her mourning for King even before she knew of his wounding. In a way King would be better off dead. But not W.W.

If only there was some way to save him. She was so tired, so exhausted from caring for cholera victims. And if she didn't come to the hospital every day there would be no one to take her place.

"Oh, W.W.," she said aloud, "what can I do?"

A drop of rain struck her upturned face, then another, and she fled back into the hospital to escape the downpour, nearly colliding with a young man in the entry. He was holding a sick child.

At first she paid attention only to the child, taking her from the man's arms and carrying her to the cot that had held the dead woman.

"Can you help her?" the man asked hoarsely.

Pamela glanced up. "I'll try," she said. She blinked, peering intently at him. He had a familiar look but she couldn't place him.

"Ain't there a doctor here?" he asked. "I know it must be the cholera for I had it myself and like to have died."

"One of the doctors comes in every few hours," Pamela said, trying to look unobtrusively at him. He was a giant bear of a man though gaunt-faced

from illness. And she'd known him somewhere,
she was certain.

He didn't seem to recognize her, though. But
she must look quite different from Lady Pamela
in her plain brown cotton without any crinoline.
And she had a brown cotton cloth tied over her
hair, too. No, he wouldn't be likely to connect
her with Lady Buttle-Jones.

Turning her attention back to the child, Pamela saw the little girl was desperately ill. She
sprawled on the cot like a rag doll, her eyes
closed. When Pamela put the teaspoon containing a few drops of laudanum to her lips she
whimpered but didn't move.

"She's very bad," Pamela said.

The young man clenched his fists. "She's only
been sick a few hours," he said. "God in His
mercy spared me, but I fear for her." He lowered
his head.

All at once Pamela remembered. The wagon
train. So long ago. Howard Tedder. Then she
shook her head. This man was too young to be
Howard. Nazareth, of course, now the image of
his father. Her eyes widened in shock. If this was
Nazareth . . .

She dropped to her knees beside the cot, gently
pushing the girl's dark hair back from her forehead. She leaned close to the small face. "Lydia,"
she murmured so low Nazareth couldn't hear.
"Lydia May."

The girl opened sunken blue eyes, then closed
them as if the effort had been too great.

Pamela scrambled to her feet. "I'll heat some
bricks," she said. "She needs to be kept warm."

Nazareth Tedder. A boy when Selena had lain with him in a wagon and conceived Lydia May. And now, the little girl, the little girl was . . . Pamela choked back her sobs.

Despite the warm bricks at her feet, despite massage with cayenne pepper dissolved in brandy, despite the laudanum and Pamela's desperate attention, Lydia May grew steadily worse. Pamela saw no hope for her; it was just a matter of time, and there was precious little left.

Pamela looked up at Nazareth with tear-filled eyes. "I tried," she said brokenly. "I did all I could."

"I saw you did," he said. "I'm grateful, ma'am. Everywhere else I went no one would help. Poor little thing didn't have nobody but me. She always was sort of puny but I—" He broke off and covered his eyes with his hand. "I loved Lydia May. I don't know what to do now; I just don't."

"I'm sorry, Nazareth." Pamela laid her hand on his arm.

He blinked tears away, his expression changing. "How come you know me?"

"Because I—I'm Lydia May's grandmother, God help me," Pamela said.

Nazareth stepped back from her, scowling. "You are that," he muttered. "I see that now."

"I'm sorry," she repeated.

After a moment he took a deep shuddering breath. "I expect you couldn't help it," he said. "But that daughter of yours will burn for all eternity. If Lydia May had had a proper mother to take care of her, she wouldn't have come to this." He lurched past Pamela to pick up the child's body.

"Where are you going? We—we have men here who . . ." Pamela began.

Nazareth brushed past her with Lydia May in his arms. "No!" he said. "I won't let her die here. I won't let Selena come and pretend to weep over her corpse. That's all your daughter ever did— pretend! The Tedders care for their own. I'll see to her burial myself. God damn you all!" With the dying child in his arms, he burst into sobs and ran from the hospital.

Selena hummed as she pirouetted in front of the pier glass in her bedroom, examining the new peach gown from all angles. A shirred bodice bound at the scooped neck with satin binding showed off just enough of her breasts to be intriguing. The vee of the bodice where it joined the skirt made her small waist look even tinier. And the cage crinoline thrust the skirts out excitingly.

"Sounds like a mighty sad song you're humming," Veronie said. "Ain't you happy?"

Selena glanced back at her maid. "All Irish airs are plaintive," she confided to Veronie. "The Irish like to make themselves cry."

The girl shook her head doubtfully. Selena already knew Veronie wasn't especially bright but she was a wizard with curls and could mend a seam so not a thread showed. What more did one expect from a personal maid?

Selena sang the words:

*"The harp that once through Tara's halls
Its soul of music shed*

Now hangs as mute on Tara's walls
As though that soul were fled."

"Don't make no kind of sense," Veronie said. "But you sure got a pretty voice. All the gentlemen say so too."

Selena smiled at her. The peach gown was definitely provocative. That new dressmaker on California Street showed a true French flair. If only she could persuade Pamela to have a few gowns made. Her mother's clothes were all so drab. But Pamela insisted fashion wasn't important to the sick.

Selena grimaced. How could her mother go into those ghastly charnel houses they called hospitals? "Someone has to look after the cholera patients," Pamela kept saying. "I can't understand how people can pass by the sick and suffering without even a second glance."

I can understand very well, Selena thought. I can't bear sickness.

"You sure got a lot of gentlemen after you," Veronie said.

Selena's mouth twisted wryly. "Like a bitch in heat," Barry Fitzpatrick had growled at her. "All the pack gathering 'round." Jealous, that was his trouble. Barry intrigued her, but since he'd trapped W.W. she'd refused to see him and would continue to do so. She loved W.W. almost like a father.

The front door opened and closed and she heard Pamela's light step on the stairs. Waving her hand at Veronie in dismissal, Selena waited for her mother to come along the hall. Seeing the peach gown ought to be enough to persuade her . . .

Selena's thoughts broke off abruptly as Pamela appeared in the doorway.

"Mother! What's the matter? Are you ill?" Selena hurried toward her, reaching out her hand.

"I'm not sick," Pamela said, clasping her daughter's hand. "No, I'm quite all right."

Selena examined her mother's tired face with concern. "But something *is* wrong, isn't it?"

Pamela pulled away and lowered her face into her hands. "Oh, Selena, my dear child. I don't know how to tell you."

"Is it W.W.? Oh my God, have they lynched him?"

"No, no, he's safe enough in jail for the time being at least."

"The cholera then. Who is it, who's sick? Barry? Danny O'Lee?"

Pamela shook her head. "They're fine as far as I know. But it is the cholera and it's killed her, your—my—"

Tears rolled down Pamela's cheeks. "So young to die, her life hardly begun. When I found out who she was, for a moment I wished I'd been taken instead."

"Mother, what *are* you talking about? Who's dead?"

"Lydia May."

Selena stood for a moment without speaking. A muscle twitched in her face. Pamela held out her arms but her daughter ignored them. Swiftly, she told Selena of Nazareth's coming to the hospital, of the child too far gone to save.

"I told you long ago it was too late," Selena said. She turned away to sit at a vanity table where she picked up a powder puff.

Pamela watched her unbelievingly as she continued her toilette. "You can't be thinking of going out this evening," she cried. "Not now!"

"Of course I'm going out. Lee will be picking me up in less than an hour."

Pamela held the black umbrella over her head, staring down at the muddy burying hole. The wind-blown drizzle lashed her face and she could feel moisture seeping into her shoes. Nazareth Tedder stood on the opposite side of the grave, still gaunt-faced from his own bout with cholera. He did not look at her. He had not informed her personally of Lydia May's death. But she had read the burial notice in the newspaper and had come to mourn her grandchild, despite him.

"My fellow mourners," the minister began, "though we weep today, we must teach our hearts to rejoice that an unsullied soul is safe in the bosom of Jesus."

Pamela shut her ears to the minister's voice and tried to ignore the chill wet of the day and Nazareth's icy unfriendliness. Water trickled into the newly dug hole. She thought of the small body in the miniature coffin soon to be lowered into it. The poor child. She glanced from under her lashes at Nazareth. To her surprise he was staring past her, his eyes dry of tears and narrowed with hatred. She turned. She was astonished, yet unbelievably relieved at what she saw.

Muffled in a black cloak, Selena climbed the

path toward them. She had no umbrella and the wind had blown her hair loose so that it swirled wildly about her black bonnet. With her face pale with grief, human grief, a mother's grief, she might have been an angel coming to gather up her child's soul.

She did not stand next to Pamela but stayed back, apart from them all. Pamela eyed her nervously, dividing her attention between the minister and Selena.

There was a stir on Nazareth's side of the grave, of people, his few friends, whispering to one another. If only W.W. could be here, Pamela thought. He'd knew how to handle any unpleasantness before it started.

Now the men were lowering the coffin. The white blossoms Nazareth had placed on it spilled into the muck as the box tilted, their sweet smell rising from the grave. Nazareth's face twisted. He glared across at Selena. He seemed, to Pamela, almost joyful, but it was the maddened joy of contemplated revenge.

"Whore!" he hissed. Hands pulled at him, led him away.

Pamela started toward Selena. Before she could reach her, Selena crumpled face down into the mud.

"I'm not sure you should be up," Pamela said.

"I haven't time to waste in bed if I'm to be of any help." Nevertheless Selena huddled in one of the overstuffed chairs looking pinched and miserable.

"You may still have a fever."

"Oh, mother, I'm not planning to die young."

"I know what W.W. would say," Pamela told her. "He would quote Shelley: 'The good die first, and they whose hearts are dry as summer dust burn to the socket.' "

Selena sighed. "I'm afraid King Sutton puts the lie to that one. He wasn't a good man."

Pamela paid her no attention. "Well, at least it wasn't the cholera you had. Thank God the epidemic seems to be diminishing. There've been no new cases."

Selena looked at her. "You haven't mentioned King since Danny O'Lee sent us word of his death this afternoon. And mother, I know you and King were . . ."

"We won't speak of him, if you don't mind, Selena. He was dead to me long before that bullet ever was fired."

The knocker banged against the front door. "That must be Danny now," Pamela said.

Maria appeared in the archway. "Mr. O'Lee," she said in her accented English. "And a . . ." She paused, casting a quick glance behind her. In her confusion she lapsed into Spanish. "Señor Jed."

Pamela blinked, then moved forward, smiling to greet the men.

"Ah, you're still as lovely as the dawn," Danny told her.

"Sunset is more appropriate these days," Pamela said wryly. "I am getting on, you know." She smiled at Danny. "How have you been? When we received your note we decided we would do everything we could to help free W.W."

"Selena," Danny said, nodding at her politely.

Selena waved her hand languidly. "Mr. O'Lee." She smiled softly them. "Hello, Dan," she said.

He grinned at her.

"How have *you* been, Jed?" Pamela asked. "Are you getting along all right? I didn't think when King—Mr. Sutton—was shot I should have . . ."

"Thank you all the same, missus." The big black man bowed his head and then nodded toward Danny. "Mr. O'Lee's been taking care of me since then," he said.

"Jed's going to help us free Rhynne," Danny said. "Now that King Sutton's dead they'll hang him sure if we can't spirit him away."

The knocker banged again.

"I asked Mac, Mr. McSweeney, to join us to-night," Danny said. "If that's all right with you."

"Anything that will help free W.W. is fine with me," Pamela said.

McSweeney seemed even less at ease in the parlor than Jed. He sat gingerly on the very edge of a wing-backed chair, turning his hat in his hands.

"What can we do?" Pamela asked.

"That we don't know as yet," Danny said. "First we want to see the lay of the land. Perhaps with your aid, Pamela. No one looks quite so respectable and innocent as when escorting a lady."

"Anything I can do, I shall."

"When the time comes, Mac and Jed will provide the muscle. I'll be in charge of distractions, as will you, Pamela."

"You haven't told me what my part will be," Selena complained.

"Ah, well, Selena, you will have to eliminate the greatest danger of all."

"And what might that be?"

"Not what. Who. Captain Barry Fitzpatrick."

26

The trial of Wordsworth Rhynne was held at the office of the Committee of Vigilance on Battery Street a few mornings after King Sutton had died.

Raymond Curie, brother of the owner of the *Californian*, described meeting Sutton at Bidwell's Saloon several days before the shooting. Sutton, Curie said, claimed he had lost a considerable sum of money in Rhynne's Golconda mining scheme.

Jacques Chavalier, a waiter at Pierre's, told of the angry exchange between the two men the evening before the shooting. Wordsworth Rhynne, he said, threatened Sutton in a loud and abusive manner.

Floyd McGregor testified that he was at the desk in the lobby of the Fremont when he heard what sounded like a shot. Going upstairs, he found King Sutton on the floor of his room, mortally wounded. A few minutes later the defendant, Rhynne, appeared from the next room with a derringer in his hand. Rhynne had fled by the time McGregor returned to Sutton's rooms after sending for a physician.

Dr. Warner Phillips stated that he was the first physician to treat King Sutton. "The wound appeared to have severed an artery below the clavicle," he said. "The patient lingered almost four days before succumbing."

"Did Kingman Sutton recover consciousness?" William Coleman asked.

"Only once to my knowledge and then he was but semi-conscious."

"Did he speak?"

"Yes, he did. He repeated a name several times."

Coleman seemed surprised. "And that name was?"

"Betsy," Dr. Phillips said. "From a later examination of his effects it was determined that Betsy Summers Sutton of Athens, Georgia, was his wife."

Coleman nodded. "Death was a direct result of the bullet wound in Sutton's chest?"

"Yes."

Captain Barry Fitzpatrick described attempts to find Rhynne after the shooting. "His quarters were searched, the Golden Empire, all the places he was known to frequent. He wasn't to be found."

"And where was he apprehended?"

"On the Long Wharf boarding a riverboat for Sacramento."

"How was Mr. Rhynne dressed?"

"As a woman. He wore a black dress, a large hat, and a black veil." Barry did not mention Levi Strauss, who had been warned by the Committee and released.

"Not exactly what you would describe as the attire of an innocent man going about his business, was it, captain?"

"No, sir."

"Was a derringer found on the suspect?"

"Yes, sir."

"Had the gun been fired recently?"

"Yes. In my opinion sometime in the two days prior to Mr. Rhynne's apprehension."

Wordsworth Rhynne testified in his own behalf. He admitted he had quarreled with Sutton, denied a role in the mining scheme other than as an investor, and described finding King on the floor of his parlor at the Fremont.

"I pursued someone to the alley at the rear of the hotel," Rhynne said. "I fired at him but he escaped."

"A man?"

"I couldn't be sure although, yes, I believe it was a man."

"When you first came upon Mr. Sutton, had anything on his person or in the room been disturbed?"

"His opal ring was missing."

"That ring has not been recovered," Coleman told the fifteen men who had been chosen to sit as the jury. "I suggest," he said, turning to Rhynne, "that you took the ring to make the crime appear to be a robbery. That's the truth of the matter, isn't it?"

"No." Rhynne rose from his chair and faced the jury. "I did not kill King Sutton," he said, emphasizing each word. "I had no reason to kill him, no profit to gain by his death. Do you kill a man who owes you money? Of course not. The reverse is more likely to be the case. If you hang me, and I know you fully intend to, an innocent man's blood will be on your hands." He looked at each juror in turn. "On all your hands."

He sat down amidst silence.

At eleven o'clock the jury began its deliberations and reached a verdict at eleven-twenty.

"We find Wordsworth Rhynne guilty of murder," the chairman said.

The men gathered in the Committee rooms cheered.

"The punishment?"

"He's to be hanged tomorrow at sunrise."

Shortly after one o'clock, Danny O'Lee and Pamela joined the throng gathered in front of the *Argonaut*. It was an orderly crowd, men for the most part. They stared at the beached ship with avid curiosity, little different from the crowds that gather at the scene of a particularly brutal murder or to view the charred remains of a fire. They talked quietly, recounting details of the shooting of King Sutton and the trial and naming the Vigilantes who came and went past the guard at the foot of the ramp leading to the ship.

"There's Fitzpatrick," Danny said, nodding toward the *Argonaut*'s rail. When Pamela saw Barry look in their direction, she quickly turned her head away. After Barry had once more disappeared inside the ship's cabin, Danny and Pamela walked to the far side of the dirt street where they could talk without being overheard.

"If we had a cannon," Danny said grimly, "we could blow a great hole in the side of that ship. Then we could rush in and free Rhynne."

"We might kill him; we have no idea where he is. Besides, Danny, we have no way to get a cannon."

"I'm just supposing," Danny said. "The mind needs exercise to work properly. If we could only storm the jail, like the French stormed the Bastille."

"I'm afraid in this instance the mob's on the jailors' side, not ours."

"Ah, if only we knew how many jailors there were on that ship. With the comings and goings at times I think four or five, and then again I think there may be as many as ten or more. Perhaps it's by stealth we'll enter the ship, disguising ourselves first."

"W.W.'s disguise certainly didn't succeed. What are we to dress up as? Red Indians? They did that once in Boston. Proper San Francisco businessmen?"

Danny shook his head. "A strange place, surely, for a jail. A ship . . ."

"Well, they're using other ships as hotels and stores. Why not a jail? Better, I suppose, than leaving them to rot."

They stared at the *Argonaut*. The ship, built with a V-shaped keel for speed, loomed some twenty feet above the ground. Eight timbers had been placed on each side of the hull to prop the *Argonaut* upright until the land around her could be fllled.

"Perhaps," Pamela said, "something could be done when W.W.'s taken from the ship in the morning to be . . ." She hesitated. There was a catch in her voiec when she went on. "To be hanged."

"No, they intend to do their dirty work aboard the vessel, or so goes the tale in the city."

As a man, somewhat the worse for drink, passed them, he lashed out with his cane as though beheading imaginary flowers. On a sudden thought, Danny was surprised it wasn't a guillotine they'd be using on the morrow. How the mob would relish the sight of blood! A hanging's tame sport unless the trap's poorly sprung and the poor bastard dangles at the end of the rope.

"Danny," Pamela said, "we have to do something *soon*."

"There's one wild notion I have, Pamela, and who's to say it won't work?" He took a gold watch from his pocket and glanced at it. "Two o'clock. Let's find the others. We have only sixteen hours left."

"Selena said she'd wait at the Golden Empire," Pamela told him. "What's your plan?"

"Mac will be there too, and Jed. We'll go to the Empire and I'll tell all of you there."

At seven that evening, Selena, wearing her new peach gown with a cage crinoline flaring it out and carrying a peach-colored parasol, walked to the ramp leading to the *Argonaut*. The guard barred her way.

"I must see Captain Fitzpatrick at once," she said imperiously. "I've been looking for him all afternoon and finally discovered quite by chance he was here of all places. I'd begun to believe he was hiding from me."

"The captain is busy, miss." The guard leered at the low cut of Selena's gown.

Selena stamped her foot. "Barry Fitzpatrick is never too busy to see me. Never. Now please tell him I'm here."

"I'm sorry, miss. I have orders not to trouble him."

She laughed. "Do I look like I intend to trouble him? Actually I'm only a messenger. Leland particularly stressed that I deliver his note to Barry with my own hand." She held out her hand, gloved in pearl grey. "Lee said to me, 'Who can I trust in these parlous times?' and I told him he could always count on me, that I would find Barry Fitzpatrick if it took a year and a day and personally deliver his message. And so here I am." She smiled up at the guard.

Involuntarily he smiled back before going to a rope strung behind the ramp rail. When he pulled it Selena heard a bell ring on the ship and in a few minutes Barry appeared at the top of the ramp.

"Selena," he said, coming toward her. "What in hell are you doing here?"

"She said she had a message," the guard told him.

Selena started up the ramp but Barry took her by the arm and led her back down. Glancing at the guard, he drew Selena some distance away. She heard water lapping against the piling nearby as she drew off her gloves.

"All right, Selena," Barry said. "Do you really have a message?"

"No," she admitted. "I'm here to beg you to release W.W. He's not guilty, you know he's not, and still you're going to let them hang him."

"There's nothing I could do even if I wanted to. It's out of my hands. Now come, Selena, let me take you home."

She started to cry. "Barry," she sobbed, "how can you be so cruel, so heartless?"

He let her rest her head on his shoulder. When she finally raised her face to his, he smelled mignonette and something else besides. "Selena," he asked, "have you been drinking?"

"I may have had a sip or two of brandy," she said. She stood on tiptoe and kissed him on the lips.

"Oh, Barry," she said, clinging to him, "I couldn't help myself."

He disentangled himself from her arms.

"Are you trying to bribe me?" he asked. "Are you offering yourself in exchange for Rhynne?"

She flew at him, scratching and clawing his face. Barry tried to elude her but one of her hands found and raked his cheek. He finally grasped her arms and held her away. Selena wrenched loose and ran. Feeling her shoes sink into the rain-softened earth she tried to stop but fell into the mud and water at the edge of the bay.

When she looked up she saw Barry standing over her, his tall figure outlined against the lights of the city.

"Do you really think I'm a loose woman?" she asked in a small voice.

"No, you're an impetuous young girl involved in something she doesn't understand. Now let me help you up."

She gave him her hand and he pulled her to her feet. "My dress," she wailed, "my bag, my parasol. They're all ruined."

"Come over here." He took her to where, in the light from the flares in the road, she could see her torn and mud-spattered gown. She did her best to clean it off, but felt it was hopeless.

"Oh, Barry," she said, close to tears, "this was the first time I've worn it. What a sight I must be."

"You'd look lovely to me no matter what you wore."

"Captain Fitzpatrick. Always the gallant."

She let him lead her back toward the ship. "Now may I escort you home?" he asked.

"Only if I can freshen up first. I took hours getting ready, you know. Literally hours. And all for you." She stopped walking and looked up at his strong, impassive face.

"Barry," she said, "I told you how we girls used to feel about you when we were on the trail. I still feel the same way and have ever since that first day when I met you again in our new house. You think I'm a girl who teases and flirts and acts foolishly. Probably I'm not the kind of girl you really like. I can almost picture the kind you do, the sort of girl a man like you would want to marry, someone quietly pretty. Demure. Good at sewing and running a house. I'm not like that; I never will be. Still that doesn't change the way I feel about you."

"Selena," he said, "I—" He looked away, seeming confused. "Come along," he said gruffly, propelling her up the ramp to the ship. "We'll have you cleaned up in no time."

"Aren't you afraid to allow me on board? I might spirit Mr. Rhynne away."

"He's safely locked up 'tween decks where you'll never even see him."

The men on deck clustered around them, each, Selena saw, with a pistol in his belt. They raised their eyebrows when they saw the scratches on Barry's cheeks but made no comment.

"The young lady fell," Barry told them. "I'm going to let her use the necessary for a few minutes."

The men stood aside, amused at the captain's evident discomfiture.

Barry indicated a door on the far side of the cabin. When Selena emerged five minutes later her face was washed, her hair brushed, and she had restored some semblance of order to her clothes.

"I feel so much better now," she said, taking Barry's arm. They walked down the ramp to the street where Barry helped her into his rig. He clucked to the horse and they set off through the city toward Rincon Hill.

"Selena," he said as they rode along Portsmouth Street. "Did you actually believe you could persuade me to release Rhynne? Or entice me to?"

She sighed. "I suppose not, but I had to do something. This afternoon I said to myself, 'Selena, if you don't try to help that poor unfortunate man imprisoned aboard that ship, you'll never be able to look at yourself in the mirror again.' So I tried. Was there more I could have done?"

"No. You did all you could."

"I should have known you'd be clever enough to see through my little strategems. That's why I had the glass of brandy before I came, to fire up my courage. I'm afraid all it did was make me dizzy."

When they left Market Street to climb Rincon, Selena turned from Barry and looked back at the city. As she did she put her hand over the side of the carriage, letting a folded piece of paper fall to the ground.

After the rig was out of sight, Danny O'Lee stepped from the shadows and retrieved the paper. He held the penciled note beside his lantern. "Rhynne 'tween decks," he read. "One guard ashore, five on ship. All armed."

For a moment he stared up the hill, thinking of Selena, remembering holding her in his arms. "Damn you, Fitzpatrick," he said.

He turned and, as he made his way toward the docks, tore the note into shreds, scattering the pieces along the way.

"Your house is dark," Barry said as he helped Selena from the rig.

"Pamela must still be at the church."

"The church? She's one of the last I'd have expected to get religious."

"She didn't," Selena said, unlocking the door. "She's trying to make arrangements with Reverend Courtney to have him see Mr. Rhynne in the morning. At five o'clock. There was some question as to whether the Reverend would consent to go or not."

"I can understand why." Barry went around the parlor lighting the lamps. "From what I heard this Rhynne's rather an unsavory type."

"Barry, you don't understand him. I know he's owned brothels and gambling saloons, does own them. And he can be ruthless. On the other hand, he's one of the kindest and most thoughtful men I know. He likes children, loves to quote poetry. I always think of him as a terribly lonely man. He needs someone, Barry. Someone like Pamela."

"Pamela? Pamela and Rhynne? Are you out of your mind? Lady Buttle-Jones and a common gambler?"

"Why not? Two years ago I would have scoffed too. Even last year. Now I'm not sure. My mother's changed since she's been here in California. We all have." Selena lowered her face into her hands. "I keep forgetting Rhynne will hang in the morning."

Barry put his arms around her. "I can't free Rhynne. If there's anything else I can do, I will."

"Hold me, Barry, that's all I want. Just hold me."

He kissed the top of her hair. She could feel excitement grow in him. "Where is everyone?" Barry asked. "The servants?"

"This is Thursday, their night off. There's no one here." She nestled against him. "I'm frightened, Barry. I hate being alone. Ever since I was a child, I've always been afraid that one day I'd have no one. That I'd be old and alone. I couldn't stand that. I think I'd kill myself first."

"You'll never be alone."

She shook her head, shivering.

"You're cold." He held her away from him. "You should change that dress. It's still wet, I can feel it. You must be soaked through."

"You will stay, won't you, Barry? At least until Pamela comes home?"

"Of course I will. Now go along and change your clothes. There's enough illness about as it is."

He means the cholera, Selena thought. She turned her head to hide the tears which had come unbidden to her eyes. Lydia May. The coffin garlanded with white flowers being lowered into the grave. I've been so selfish, Selena thought. I'll change, she promised herself. I'll become a different person.

"Are you all right?" Barry asked.

She nodded. Holding her skirts, she ran up the stairs.

In the dark of her bedroom she took off her wet shoes, then unbuttoned and stepped out of her dress. She glanced out the window at the city, the yellow glow of the lamps, the myriad lights shining through the canvas of the tents. She looked carefully along the waterfront where the brightness of the docks met the dark of the bay.

Seeing nothing unusual, she sighed. Could Danny bring off his plan? She shook her head doubtfully. Such a wild scheme, just like him. Wistfully she recalled nursing him after the duel. He was such a boy then. But he'd changed too these last few years; Dan O'Lee had become a man.

Selena removed the rest of her clothes, found a towel, and rubbed herself briskly. Going to her wardrobe she took out her white silk robe and held it in front of the window. Through the diaphanous cloth she could clearly see the lights of San Francisco.

Smiling, she slipped into the robe and tied the sash. When she turned to leave the room to go down to the parlor, she stopped with a gasp.

Barry Fitzpatrick stood watching her from the doorway.

Danny walked up to the bar of Paddy's Saloon.

"I'll be wanting something to warm the lads standing guard across the street," he told the barman.

"A hot toddy it is, then."

Danny watched him mix the drink. When he was done, the barman plunged a glowing red poker into the pitcher to heat it.

Danny threw a gold coin on the bar, took the pitcher and walked across the road humming to himself. Only four or five stragglers still huddled together staring at the jail. Danny supposed more would be arriving as the hour for the hanging neared.

The guard stepped from the shadows with a lantern in one hand, a pistol in the other.

"Sure and I'm bringing you a toddy," Danny said. "Compliments of Paddy himself."

"It's cold as a witch's tit tonight," the guard said. "Put the pitcher there like a good lad." He nodded to the top of a packing case.

Danny hurled the toddy in the guard's face.

Taking a truncheon from under his coat, he struck the man on the back of the head. The guard pitched to the ground. Danny snatched up the pistol and thrust it under his belt. He shielded the guard's lantern, then gagged and bound him.

When the guard was thoroughly trussed, he dragged him into the shadows a short distance away. Then, returning to the ramp, he looked up at the ship. No one was about. Unshielding the lantern, he held it aloft, lowered it, then held it aloft once more. He saw an answering light a hundred yards away along the road.

Smiling grimly, Danny took up his post next to the ramp. In a few minutes, he knew, all hell would break loose.

27.

"Barry," she whispered. She backed toward the window.

Barry took a step toward her. He said nothing and in the darkness she couldn't see his face.

A prickle of excitement ran along her arms even though she told herself she must get him out of the bedroom. It was too early, too soon. Selena drew her robe together and started for the door just as Barry came into the room toward her. She moved quickly to one side. Only when she saw it looming beside her did she realize she'd stepped toward the Louis XIV bed.

Barry reached for her but she held him off, putting her hands against his chest.

"Good heavens, Captain Fitzpatrick," she said. "I thought you had scruples about entering a lady's bedroom." The huskiness in her voice belied the light note she'd intended.

He grasped her wrists and brought her hands down to her sides. For a moment he stood facing her, not moving, with his chest lightly touching her breasts, and then his lips brushed her lips. Even though she turned her head away, his lips found hers. She hesitated, then kissed him. As the kiss lengthened, a tingling coursed through her body. She knew she was seducing him and she knew why she was doing it. But the knowledge of her ulterior motive didn't interfere with her enraptured response.

She kissed him hungrily and heard him draw in his breath. His hands came up along her sides to her breasts. His mouth nuzzled her throat as he nipped her flesh with his teeth. When the tip of his tongue explored the convolutions of her ear, Selena gasped with surprise and pleasure.

"Barry!" she whispered urgently.

He tried to cover her lips with his.

"No, wait. Stop. I heard a sound. Like a carriage in the street."

She stood frozen in his arms, listening.

"I hear nothing," he said.

"I'm sure *I* did. It must be Pamela back from the church. And you left your rig outside."

Reluctantly, he released her. "I'll see," he said. He stopped at the door and came back, kissing her quickly. She clung to him. Again he turned from her and she heard his footsteps on the stairs.

She looked from the window. Still nothing. How much longer would Danny wait? She sighed, the taste of Barry's kisses still on her lips, the excitement still smoldering within her. How much longer could she delay him?

When Barry returned to the house, he lit a candle in the parlor, holding it in front of him as he climbed the stairs. He pushed open the door to Selena's bedroom. Where was she? Seeing the drawn curtains on the Louis XIV bed, he smiled to himself. He found the rope next to the wall and pulled its tasseled end.

The curtains parted to reveal an empty bed.

"Damn," he said.

Shielding the candle flame wtih one hand, he walked into the hallway. Outside he heard the hoot of an owl; a board creaked somewhere below him. He descended the stairs, pausing at the bottom when he saw a light in the rear of the house.

When he came to the open kitchen door he stopped and stared. Selena sat at the table with her back to him. "What in the name of hell are you doing?" he asked her.

She looked over her shoulder at him. "I was hungry, Barry. I haven't had a morsel of food since morning. This is cold oatmeal; I love cold oatmeal." She raised a spoonful to her mouth. "Would you like a dish?"

"Don't you want to know if that was Pamela coming back?"

"I can see it wasn't. It must have been the Marrows next door. Would you like something else if you don't want any oatmeal? Tea? Perhaps a brandy?"

He shook his head as he watched her eat another spoonful of the oatmeal. "It's very good," she said. "Maria made it this morning."

He came around the table and his stare made her look down at her French robe, which had gaped open. She pulled the thin silk together at her throat.

When she had eaten the last of the oatmeal, Selena walked to the larder in the pantry. "I'm still hungry," she said.

Barry came up behind her and before she realized what he intended scooped her into his arms. "So am I," he said. "But not for food." He carried her through the house and up the stairs.

"Your rig," she said.

"I put the rig where no one will see it."

He kicked open the door to her bedroom.

"Pamela's late now. She'll be home any moment."

"We'll lock your door. She'll never know I'm here."

"You think of everything, don't you?" she purred, smiling to herself. Not quite everything, Captain Fitzpatrick, she thought.

He dropped her on the bed, tugging at the sash around her waist, freeing it, parting the negligee and exposing her breasts. Peeling the silk robe from her arms, he yanked it away. He gathered her naked body into his arms and she felt his clothing on her body, tantalizingly harsh. She writhed against him, pulling him close while she fumbled at his clothes.

When at last he was naked, he knelt above her, poised, waiting. She raised her mouth to his, only their lips meeting. Then his arms drew her upwards to him.

She felt him against her, his seeking hands, hot

against her legs. She moaned, the trembling beginning deep inside her, gathering force. Gently he lowered her back to the bed and, kissing her with ever increasing hunger, got onto the bed with her. She cried out. He groaned with the pleasure of it. And then . . .

One side of the bed collapsed, tumbling them in a heap against the wall.

Selena giggled. The giggle grew, turned into a laugh and she laughed until tears ran down her face.

Barry scrambled out of the bed, went to the dresser and lit a candle. When he returned, Selena, quiet now, was lying in the crevice between bed and wall with her fingers laced behind her head.

"Oh, Barry," she said.

"I'll see if I can repair the damage." He put the candle holder on the floor and peered under the bed.

Selena sat up. "No, Barry, you don't have to." Alarm crept into her voice.

"What in God's name is this under here?" he demanded.

Danny heard the crackle of flames, a series of loud pops, and then a thunderous roar. He watched a rocket streak into the sky to burst in a star-like explosion over the bay.

My God, he thought, we'll have the whole city here. I didn't know there would be rockets.

"What's that?" The voice came from the deck above him.

"Fire," he called back. He put as much alarm into his voice as he could. "Fire! Down along the docks!"

He heard more questioning voices from the *Argonaut*. This was a critical moment, he knew, the first of many. Would the five guards leave their posts on board the ship? He had assumed they had been ordered not to. There was no way he could be sure.

"It's the Chinaman's warehouse," one of the guards said. "He must have fireworks stored in there."

Another explosion rocked the dock area. Good old Charlie Sung, Danny thought. And Pamela, since the money, after all, was hers. He saw that the curiosity seekers on the street had left to hurry to the fire. When Danny glanced covertly up at the ship, all five guards were ranged along the rail.

All right, Mac, he thought, it's up to you.

At the sound of the first explosion three men had slipped out of the shadows of a warehouse adjacent to the ship's starboard side. Abe Greene led the way, a spade over his shoulder; McSweeney came next, a sledgehammer gripped in both hands; Jed followed. All three carried coils of rope looped to their belts.

When Abe came to the first of the pine supports propping up the ship on the bay side, he dug furiously in the loose earth next to it. Each of the four-by-fours, he discovered, was buried a foot or more in the soggy ground and toed against a stake. After a few minutes Abe had bared the base of the timber and moved on to the next.

Positioning himself, McSweeney swung the sledgehammer and struck the first post near its base. The timber shifted an inch at the most. He swung again. Another few inches. McSweeney raised the hammer a third time, swung in a great arc, the sledge thudding against the wood and sending the timber bursting from the ground. Mud spattered him. He ignored it.

As McSweeney moved on, Jed grasped the loosened post in both of his huge hands. He shifted from side to side. The timber was still spiked to the ship's side. Grunting, he swung it back and forth like a pendulum, twisting it in his hands. The timber came free; Jed let it fall to the ground.

Before he went on, Jed glanced up at the dark deck of the ship. He saw no one. Through the rigging the sky glowed a dull orange and from a distance came the pop-pop-pop of fireworks. A rocket rose in a red arc and erupted over the city.

Abe and Mac worked their way along until they had dislodged all eight of the timbers. Jed wrenched each from the side of the ship save the two in the center. These he purposely left spiked on.

"Get back," McSweeney warned. The three men trotted away from the ship. When they reached the warehouse, McSweeney took a pistol and fired three times into the air. They waited. Would the guards hear the shots above the sound of exploding fireworks?

A light appeared on deck. Good, McSweeney thought. When he fired again, they heard shouts and saw men rushing to the railing on their side. The three men held their breath.

"She's not going to topple," Abe muttered.

"Jed," McSweeney said, thrusting the pistol

back into his belt, "it's up to us." The two men ran toward the ship, grasped the ends of the two middle timbers and lifted them to their shoulders.

A shot came from the deck of the *Argonaut*.

"Now!" McSweeney shouted. The two men strained forward. They felt a give. Were the spikes pulling free? No. With a shuddering wrench the ship slowly began to fall toward them.

"Here she comes!" McSweeney shouted.

They dropped the timbers and, amid cries and curses from the ship, ran. The dark form of the *Argonaut* plunged at them as they scrambled back against the side of the warehouse. With a great crash the ship hit the ground.

"Now remember," McSweeney said, "there's five of them."

They charged ahead, guided by the curses and shouts of the guards. They found four of them at once, either stunned or lying injured so that they gave no more than token resistance. With their ropes, they tied and gagged all four. But the fifth man was nowhere to be found.

By the time they were done, Danny was beside them dragging a ladder. They propped it against the side of the ship. Danny, carrying a lantern, climbed up to the deck, McSweeney right behind him. Abe and Jed stayed on the ground.

"We only found four men," McSweeney said as they moved swiftly towards a hatch near the stern. "Are you sure there were five?"

"Yes, I saw five."

"He could have been thrown under the ship. He might have gotten away. I wish I knew."

Reaching the hatch, Danny unbolted and lifted

its cover. Lowering the lantern into the dark hold, he saw a face peering up at him.

"Danny O'Lee himself," a surprised Rhynne said. "Well, I'll be damned. Give me a hand, boy, and I'll be right with you."

Danny reached down, took Rhynne's hand, and helped him up the narrow hatchway. Rhynne winced as he tried to stand. "It's nothing," he said. "I bruised my leg when the ship keeled over. No bones broken, thank God."

"Are there any others down there?" Danny asked.

"I'm the one and only prisoner. And all of the guards were on deck."

"Let's go," Danny said to McSweeney.

They ran back to the ladder and climbed down toward Jed and Abe. As they neared the ground, a mud-bespattered man stepped out of the shadow of the warehouse brandishing a pistol. Jed swung around to face him.

"Go no farther," the guard said to him. He waved his gun at the three men still on the ladder. "You there," he said, "put your hands up as high as they'll go and grab a rung. Right-o. The first man that moves is dead."

Jed advanced slowly on the guard with his hands outreaching, like a giant cat about to pounce. The guard edged back, shaking his head.

"Not another step," he warned.

"Jed," Rhynne called down to him. "For Christ's sake, don't."

Jed moved on toward the guard as though he hadn't heard. The guard pulled the trigger.

* * *

Barry held up a handful of yellow dust and pebbles.

Selena peered over the edge of the mattress. "It looks like gold," she said solemnly.

He weighed the ore in his hand. "You're damned right it's gold." He looked under the bed again. "I'm surprised your floor didn't give way long before this," he said. "There must be hundreds of pounds of ore here."

He looked up at her. "How did this gold come to be here, Selena? And don't tell me you don't know."

"I put it there. Leland says the banks are safe but I don't trust them. Not after what I've read about the Panic of '37."

Barry stood up. Seeing the suspicion in his eyes, she pulled the sheet up to her chin.

"That's not what I meant," he said. "How did you get this gold, Selena? What did you have to do for it?"

"I sang for it," she said defiantly.

"You sang?"

"Yes, you must have heard about my singing in Hangtown at the start of the gold rush. I sang at the Empire and afterwards the miners would throw gold on the stage. Nuggets of gold, pouches of gold dust, hundreds of dollars worth of gold. God knows, they had plenty of it. Abe Greene used to go around with a broom and sweep it up for me. I never spent any. I told you how afraid I am of being alone when I'm old. To be alone and poor at the same time would be too much to bear."

"Selena, are you telling me the truth? All this gold came from your singing at Hangtown?"

"Barry, have I ever lied to you?"

She watched a variety of expressions cross his face. Doubt, incredulity, a desire to believe her. What was he thinking?

"Barry," she said, "I'm truly sorry if you can't bring yourself to believe me. Tell me, how do *you* think I came to have all this gold?"

He hesitated.

"Tell me, Barry. Tell me the truth."

"I think you earned the gold by your singing, Selena."

"You truly believe me then?"

"Yes, I do."

"Barry, do you know something?"

"What?"

"You make a strange and wonderful picture kneeling on the floor looking under my bed. And you with not a stitch of clothing on."

He looked down at himself. "I'd forgotten," he said.

"Come here, Barry. Come to me."

He approached the bed. "Snuff out the candle, Barry," she told him. He leaned down and pinched the flame between his fingers.

"Do you want me to pull the mattress down onto the floor?" he asked.

"Not yet. Come closer." She put her hands on his thighs. "Closer, Barry, closer." She felt his hands on the top of her head. "Barry," she whispered and then she didn't speak for a long while.

The pistol misfired, the hammer clicking but the charge failing to ignite. Jed swatted the gun from the guard's hand and pinioned the man's arms to his sides. McSweeney leaped from the ladder. Quickly, they overpowered, tied and gagged him.

Danny led Rhynne and the others through the mud away from the *Argonaut* along the bay side of the warehouses. They heard the water lapping on the shore below them.

"Where are we bound?" Rhynne asked.

"To the *Golden Arrow*. She leaves for the Islands on the morning tide."

"The Sandwich Islands? Hawaii? That's going to take a bit of getting used to."

"There's no alternative. This city will be an armed camp in the morning. The Committee's likely to shoot you first and question you later. I doubt you'll be safe anywhere in California for a time."

"I fear you're right."

"Here's the rowboat," Danny said.

Jed shoved the boat into the water and stood holding its prow. "Jed and I will row you out to the ship," Danny told Rhynne.

Rhynne extended his hand to McSweeney. They shook hands, then Rhynne clasped the big man to him. He did the same with Abe. "I'm leaving Mr. O'Lee in charge at the Empire," he told them. "Though I'll be back, never fear."

He clambered into the boat. Danny and Jed followed, Jed taking his place at the oars.

"The *Golden Arrow* has signed Jed on as a seaman," Danny said once they were underway.

Rhynne nodded. "He's a free man with Sutton dead and no one to claim him."

"A free man," Jed's voice boomed out. They

both looked at him in surprise. "A free man," the black said again.

"The *Arrow* goes on to the islands of the far Pacific," Danny said. "Jed expects to settle there."

Rhynne said wryly, "Maybe I should too. Except that I've come to think of San Francisco as my home. The next time I see her she'll be bigger and noisier and more crowded than ever, I expect."

"With the gold and all, no doubt you're right."

"No, Danny, not because of the gold. There'll be a time soon when the miners will wonder why they're going through all the toil and trouble. They'll pack up and go home."

"Just leaving the gold in the ground?" Danny was dubious.

"There'll be less and less gold to be found and it will be more and more difficult and expensive to get it out. Gold has already made California a state, a free state; she'll grow and prosper. And change. I see her as a beautiful and wealthy woman with San Francisco the glittering diadem on her brow."

"You sound like a poet yourself sometimes," Danny told him. "I'll look after things until it's right for you here again. But I don't know if I want to stay here all the rest of my life."

"Yes, the lure of the unknown calls to youth. And speaking of the unknown, about Pamela . . ."

"It was her money paid Charlie Sung for the fireworks display. And for your passage."

"I thought as much. When you speak to her, tell her that when last you saw W.W. Rhynne he was a man of 'cheerful yesterdays and confident tomorrows.' "

"That I will."

The bow of the *Golden Arrow* loomed over them. To the east they saw the first light of dawn streaking the sky the color of gold.

"One additional message for Pamela, Danny. Tell her I'll always love her."

The morning light woke Barry Fitzpatrick. He blinked, raised himself on one elbow and looked down at the still sleeping Selena. Her golden hair spilled across the blanket; she smiled in her sleep. Barry shook his head. He just couldn't seem to get his fill of looking at her.

Slowly Selena opened her eyes. She sat up with a sheet around her breasts and stretched.

"You're beautiful, Selena," Barry said.

"Even now? Even with my hair like this?"

He pushed stray strands away from her face. "More than ever," he said.

She smiled at him, almost shyly.

"A strange thing," Barry said. "When we were together last night, you and I, I thought I saw rockets shooting across the sky and bombs exploding in the air." He watched her. "You know," he added drily, "it's never been that way for me before? What do you make of it?"

"Oh, my God, I forgot." She knelt on the mattress so she could look from the window.

"What do you see?"

"The *Golden Arrow*," Selena said, "sailing out of the bay."

"I'm surprised you're well enough acquainted with ships to be able to tell one from another."

"I know the lines of the *Golden Arrow*."

"Because she's taking your friend Mr. Rhynne to the Islands?"

She swung around and stared at him. He was grinning. "You knew?"

"Let's say I suspected," Barry said. "I heard the bell tolling this morning, early. The Vigilantes' bell. I imagine that means Rhynne made good his escape."

"And you did nothing to stop him?"

Barry shrugged. "I *think* he killed Sutton. I'm not sure. To me, a surmise isn't enough to justify hanging a man."

"Then all last night you were toying with me."

Barry laughed. "You have it backwards. I wanted you, Selena, still do. You were the one toying with me. What will I mean to you now that you know Rhynne's safe? Nothing."

"That's not true, Barry, not true at all." She reached out her arms. "Come to me. I'll prove it."

He did. And she did.

28

Dan O'Lee nodded casually to the maitre d' as the man bowed him out of the dining room. Who'd ever thought it? A respected businessman and him not yet twenty-five.

"Oh, Dan." The girl on his arm, a dark-haired beauty named Arabella, smiled up at him. "It's been a lovely evening."

"That it has, and no end in sight."

He'd bed her tonight in his private suite at the Golden Empire. There was no doubt of it in his mind. He could tell by the way she swayed against him, by the look in her eyes. And she wouldn't expect marriage either. He'd learned to avoid the ones who did.

Marriage was a long way off, if ever. He was having too good a time coming into his own. He felt himself growing into a feeling of independence. Nobody really needed him, and he needed nobody. It was a wonderful feeling. He could look around and see what he wanted to do with the rest of his life. Why, even if Selena should suddenly reappear in his life, he'd not be ready to marry her. It just wasn't what he wanted.

Danny put his arm around Arabella, but he sighed. Marry Selena, no. But for all their airs and graces not a one of these lovely ladies ever made him feel as Selena had.

Barry Fitzpatrick pulled the tasseled cord, the curtains of the Louis XIV bed parted, and he greeted the morning sunlight with a frown. He wasn't used to sleeping late.

Selena stirred beside him, opened her eyes, yawned, and sat up. "What time is it?" she asked.

"Must be getting on for seven."

"Do you always get up so early? And go to bed so early?"

"On the trail you get used to living by the sun. It's a mighty good habit and one I don't want to lose."

Selena yawned again. "In the city," she said, "we hardly ever see the sun. At least I don't."

"It won't take you long to get used to the change," he told her.

Selena looked at him from the corners of her eyes but remained silent.

Barry put a pillow behind his back and sat up. I'll tell her how I'm thinking of settling down, he thought. Thinking of staying here in San Francisco, of buying a house. Selena fluffed a pillow and also sat up. I'll wait until he leaves, she thought, pull the curtains and go back to sleep.

"The Committee of Vigilance has had second thoughts," Barry said.

"About Rhynne's escape?"

'I was referring more to my part in that affair. They hired me to rid the city of W.W. Rhynne and, of course, I did it in less than a week's time. With some assistance from circumstance, I'll admit; I don't mean to take all the credit. I think Coleman's just as glad they never hanged the man, guilty though he probably was. They're beginning to realize the case against him wasn't as airtight as they thought."

"The city's all abuzz about the escape from the *Argonaut*," Selena said. "Everyone says Danny O'Lee was at the bottom of it, though no one knows for sure."

"So with Coleman satisfied," Barry went on, "and some of the more cautious members of the Committee happy there was no hanging to explain away, and with all the unhappiness with the state of law and order in San Francisco, a delegation of citizens approached me yesterday with a proposition."

"They say Danny led ten men aboard the *Argonaut*," Selena said. "They were like pirates, brandishing pistols and cutlasses. They captured the guards after overturning the ship with gunpowder they stole before they set Charlie Sung's warehouse afire. In the melee, Danny and his men freed W.W. and smuggled him aboard the *Golden Arrow*."

"What the delegation suggested," Barry said, "was that I run for sheriff. The election's next month and they think with my record in the war, my experience as a Texas Ranger, and the fact I haven't made anyone in San Francisco too unhappy, I'd win easily. They're willing to finance the campaign, as a matter of fact."

"Every night," Selena said, "he's seen with a different woman in Bidwell's or the Bella Union or Pierre's. He's a good-looking man, Danny is. Not as good-looking as you, of course."

"I think this is what I've been seeking all this time," Barry said. "There'd be excitement and more than enough work to keep me busy. I've always liked taking a confused mess and ordering it. As I did on the trail and in the army. As sheriff I'd be doing that and, more important, I'd be helping make this city a better place to live. I like San Francisco. I intend to settle down here."

"He seems a completely different person from the man I knew in Hangtown."

Barry looked at her. "Who are you talking about, Selena?" he asked.

"Dan O'Lee."

"Is O'Lee all you can think about? I'll wager you haven't heard a word I've said."

"Yes, I have, Barry. You've been telling me you're about to run for sheriff. I think it's a wonderful idea. I believe in doing what you really want to do." Her hand crept under the covers until she touched his leg.

"Selena? Now?"

Her hand caressed him.

"Now," she said.

Wordsworth Rhynne looked at his face in the mirror nailed to the cabin wall. He was getting used to seeing himself without his mustache; perhaps he'd stay clean-shaven for a time. He wondered, though, if he'd ever get used to the pitching and tossing of the *Golden Arrow*.

A movement caught Rhynne's eye. Looking up into the mirror he saw a woman watching him from the doorway. He stared in amazement, then spun around and stood up.

She smiled uncertainly and he remembered the first time he had seen her, years before in the Parker House when he had come to her room, surprising her as she had now surprised him. So much had changed since that day, and so little.

"Who are you?" he demanded, as she had demanded then.

Startled, she took a step back. Then, remembering their first meeting, her smile broadened.

"Pamela Buttle-Jones," she said, her eyes challenging him. "At your service."

"A lady doesn't enter a gentleman's room," he said, "even aboard a ship."

"Some of the leading citizens of San Francisco might scoff if they heard me called a lady. As for your being a gentleman, I'll accept your own evaluation."

"I was hoping to see you," he said. "I have a confidential matter to discuss."

"Go on."

"I believe in being direct, Pamela. I propose to borrow five thousand dollars from you to begin a venture in Hawaii."

"And your collateral?"

"My wits. Nothing more."

"I agree."

"You agree?"

"If you meet my conditions."

"And they are?"

"I've disposed of all my laudanum, W.W. You're to see I get no more. I may beg you and cajole you and threaten you. No matter what I may do or say, you're not to give me any."

"I accept the condition. Are there others? Interest perhaps?"

She crossed the small cabin, put her hands on his shoulders and kissed him. Rhynne held her to him, kissing her lingeringly, tenderly.

Pamela drew back. "You may consider the interest paid," she said.

The ship plowed into a swell, making the timbers shudder and groan. His arms tightened about her. "It's a long voyage," Rhynne said, "and we don't know what lies ahead. The dice are probably loaded and the cards stacked against us. Luck may have turned her back on me for good and all."

"Your luck turned once, it can turn again and for the better this time."

"I think perhaps it has, Pamela. When O'Lee pulled off that hatch cover, that was the start. And now you being here. Pamela, when I first looked in that mirror I was surprised by joy. I thought I beheld a phantom. And that's what you are, a phantom of delight."

"Even at the age of . . . ahem, thirty-five?"

He smiled. "I'll think so even if, perchance, you should one day turn thirty-six."

"Ah, W.W., am I to have no secrets from you? I never intend to be thirty-six. I've decided to be thirty-five for the rest of my life."

"You will be, Pamela; to me you will be."

"And to think when I'm finally aboard a ship I'm off in the opposite direction from England, sailing on the wrong ocean." She shook her head. "Do you know, W.W., I don't even care? It's not only that I wouldn't fit in any more but that England no longer fits me. Good heavens, W.W., I believe I've become an American!"

He sketched a bow. "The pleasure is ours, Lady Pamela."

The smile faded from her face. "I have one other condition I've not mentioned yet."

"And that is?"

"You must answer one question. Did you kill King Sutton? Answer me straight."

"I swear to God I didn't."

"Do you know who did?"

He shook his head. "I suspect we'll never know."

Two months later the *Golden Arrow* sailed south and west from the Islands before a following wind on her port quarter. There had been a storm the day before and the seas still ran high.

Jed stood in lee of the fo'c'sle. He respected the sea, its immensity, its great brooding loneliness. Here he was free, as free as a man ever becomes.

Reaching inside the top of his shirt he removed the small buckskin pouch tied around his neck, undid the thong and turned the pouch over. He took the ring that fell into his palm and slipped it onto the little finger of his right hand.

Holding his hand in front of him, he stared into the red depths of the fire opal.